STRAY PEARLS

MEMOIRS OF MARGARET DE RIBAUMONT, VISCOUNTESS OF BELLAISE

By

CHARLOTTE YONGE

Double 9
BOOKS

Stray Pearls

Memoirs Of Margaret De Ribaumont, Viscountess Of Bellaise

by Charlotte Yonge

ISBN: 978-93-58591-84-2

Published by

DOUBLE 9 BOOKS

2/13-B, Ansari Road, Daryaganj
New Delhi – 110002
info@double9books.com
www.double9books.com
Tel. 011-40042856

ABOUT THE AUTHOR

Charlotte M. Yonge was an English novelist and historian, born on August 11, 1823, in Otterbourne, Hampshire, England. She is best known for her prolific writing career, which spanned over 60 years and produced more than 160 works, including novels, children's books, and historical studies. Yonge's writing was strongly influenced by her deep religious beliefs and her interest in history and education. Many of her novels, such as "The Heir of Redclyffe" and "Heartsease," explore moral and religious themes and are known for their wholesome and uplifting tone. She also wrote numerous works for children, including the popular "Book of Golden Deeds," which features stories of heroism and selflessness. In addition to her writing, Yonge was a prominent figure in the Church of England and was involved in various philanthropic and educational endeavors. She founded a school for girls in her hometown and was a supporter of the National Society for Promoting Religious Education. Yonge died on May 24, 1901, in Otterbourne, Hampshire, England. Her legacy as a writer and educator continues to be celebrated, and her works remain popular with readers today.

CONTENTS

PREFACE

No one can be more aware than the author that the construction of this tale is defective. The state of French society, and the strange scenes of the Fronde, beguiled me into a tale which has become rather a family record than a novel.

Formerly the Muse of the historical romance was an independent and arbitrary personage, who could compress time, resuscitate the dead, give mighty deeds to imaginary heroes, exchange substitutes for popular martyrs on the scaffold, and make the most stubborn facts subservient to her purpose. Indeed, her most favoured son boldly asserted her right to bend time and place to her purpose, and to make the interest and effectiveness of her work the paramount object. But critics have lashed her out of these erratic ways, and she is now become the meek hand maid of Clio, creeping obediently in the track of the greater Muse, and never venturing on more than colouring and working up the grand outlines that her mistress has left undefined. Thus, in the present tale, though it would have been far more convenient not to have spread the story over such a length of time, and to have made the catastrophe depend upon the heroes and heroines, instead of keeping them mere ineffective spectators, or only engaged in imaginary adventures for which a precedent can be found, it has been necessary to stretch out their narrative, so as to be at least consistent with the real history, at the entire sacrifice of the plot. And it may be feared that thus the story may partake of the confusion that really reigned over the tangled thread of events. There is no portion of history better illustrated by memoirs of the actors therein than is the Fronde; but, perhaps, for that very reason none so confusing.

Perhaps it may be an assistance to the reader to lay out the bare historical outline like a map, showing to what incidents the memoirs of the Sisters of Ribaumont have to conform themselves.

When Henry IV. succeeded in obtaining the throne of France, he found the feudal nobility depressed by the long civil war, and his exchequer exhausted. He and his minister Sully returned to the policy of Louis XI., by which the nobles were to be kept down and prevented from threatening the royal power. This was seldom done by violence, but by giving them employment in the Army and Court, attaching them to the person of the King, and giving them offices with pensions attached to them.

The whole cost of these pensions and all the other expenses of Government fell on the townspeople and peasantry, since the clergy and the nobles to all generations were exempt from taxation. The trade and all the resources of the country were taking such a spring of recovery since the country had been at peace, and the persecution of the Huguenots had ceased, that at first the taxation provoked few murmurs. The resources of the Crown were further augmented by permitting almost all magistrates and persons who held public offices to secure the succession to their sons on the payment of a tariff called LA PAULETTE, from the magistrate who invented it.

In the next reign, however, an effort was made to secure greater equality of burthens. On the meeting of the States-General—the only popular assembly possessed by France—Louis XIII., however, after hearing the complaints, and promising to consider them, shut the doors against the deputies, made no further answer, and dismissed them to their houses without the slightest redress. The Assembly was never to meet again till the day of reckoning for all, a hundred and seventy years later.

Under the mighty hand of Cardinal Richelieu the nobles were still more effectually crushed, and the great course of foreign war begun, which lasted, with short intervals, for a century. The great man died, and so did his feeble master; and his policy, both at home and abroad, was inherited by his pupil Giulio Mazarini, while the regency for the child, Louis XIV., devolved on his mother, Anne of Austria—a pious and well-meaning, but proud and ignorant, Spanish Princess—who pinned her faith upon Mazarin with helpless and exclusive devotion, believing him the only pilot who could steer her vessel through troublous waters.

But what France had ill brooked from the high-handed son of her ancient nobility was intolerable from a low-born Italian, of graceful but insinuating manners. Moreover, the war increased the burthens of the country, and, in the minority of the King, a stand was made at last.

The last semblance of popular institutions existed in the Parliaments of this was the old feudal Council of the Counts of Paris, consisting of the temporal and spiritual peers of the original county, who had the right to advise with their chief, and to try the causes concerning themselves. The immediate vassals of the King had a right to sit there, and were called Paris De France, in distinction from the other nobles who only had seats in the

Parliament in whose province their lands might lie. To these St. Louis, in his anxiety to repress lawlessness, had added a certain number of trained lawyers and magistrates; and these were the working members of these Parliaments, which were in general merely courts of justice for civil and criminal causes. The nobles only attended on occasions of unusual interest. Moreover, a law or edict of the King became valid on being registered by a Parliament. It was a moot question whether the Parliament had the power to baffle the King by refusing to register an edict, and Henry IV. had avoided a refusal from the Parliament of Paris, by getting his edict of toleration for the Huguenots registered at Nantes.

The peculiarly oppressive house-tax, with four more imposts proposed in 1648, gave the Parliament of Paris the opportunity of trying to make an effectual resistance by refusing the registration. They were backed by the municipal government of the city at the Hotel de Ville, and encouraged by the Coadjutor of the infirm old Archbishop of Paris, namely, his nephew, Paul de Gondi, titular Bishop of Corinth in partibus infidelium, a younger son of the Duke of Retz, an Italian family introduced by Catherince de Medici. There seemed to be a hope that the nobility, angered at their own systematic depression, and by Mazarin's ascendency, might make common cause with the Parliament and establish some effectual check to the advances of the Crown. This was the origin of the party called the Fronde, because the speakers launched their speeches at one another as boys fling stones from a sling (fronde) in the streets.

The Queen-Regent was enraged through all her despotic Spanish haughtiness at such resistance. She tried to step in by the arrest of the foremost members of the Opposition, but failed, and only provoked violent tumults. The young Prince of Conde, coming home from Germany flushed with victory, hated Mazarin extremely, but his pride as a Prince of the Blood, and his private animosities impelled him to take up the cause of the Queen. She conveyed her son secretly from Paris, and the city was in a state of siege for several months. However, the execution of Charles I. in England alarmed the Queen on the one hand, and the Parliament on the other as to the consequences of a rebellion, provisions began to run short, and a vague hollow peace was made in the March of 1649.

Conde now became intolerably overbearing, insulted every one, and so much offended the Queen and Mazarin that they caused him, his brother, and the Duke of Bouillon, to be arrested and imprisoned at Vincennes. His wife, though a cruelly-neglected woman whom he had never loved, did her utmost to deliver him, repaired to Bordeaux, and gained over the

Parliament there, so that she held out four months against the Queen. Turenne, brother to Bouillon, and as great a general as Conde, obtained the aid of Spaniards, and the Coadjutor prevailed on the King's uncle, Gaston, Duke of Orleans, to represent that the Queen must give way, release the Princes, part with Mazarin, and even promise to convoke the States-General. Anne still, however, corresponded with the Cardinal, and was directed by him in everything. Distrust and dissension soon broke out, Conde and the Coadjutor quarrelled violently, and the royal promises made to both Princes and Parliament were eluded by the King, at fourteen, being declared to have attained his majority, and thus that all engagements made in his name became void.

Conde went of to Guienne and raised an army; Mazirin returned to the Queen; Paris shut its gates and declared Mazarin an outlaw. The Coadjutor (now become Cardinal de Retz) vainly tried to stir up the Duke of Orleans to take a manly part and mediate between the parties; but being much afraid of his own appanage, the city of Orleans, being occupied by either army, Gaston sent his daughter to take the charge of it, as she effectually did—but she was far from neutrality, being deluded by a hope that Conde would divorce his poor faithful wife to marry her. Turenne, on his brother's release, had made his peace with the Court, and commanded the royal army. War and havoc raged outside Paris; within the partisans of the Princes stirred the populace to endeavour to intimidate the Parliament and municipality into taking their part. Their chief leader throughout was the Duke of Beaufort, a younger son of the Duke of Vendome, the child of Gabrille d'Estrees. He inherited his grandmother's beauty and his grandfather's charm of manner; he was the darling of the populace of Paris, and led them, in an aimless sort of way, whether there was mischief to be done; and the violence and tumult of this latter Fronde was far worse than those of the first.

A terrible battle in the Faubourg St. Antoine broke Conde's force, and the remnant was only saved by Mademoiselle's insisting on their being allowed to pass through Paris. After one ungrateful attempt to terrify the magistrates into espousing his cause and standing a siege on his behalf, Conde quitted Paris, and soon after fell ill of a violent fever.

His party melted away. Mazarin saw that tranquillity might be restored if he quitted France for a time. The King proclaimed an amnesty, but with considerable exceptions and no relaxation of his power; and these terms the Parliament, weary of anarchy, and finding the nobles had cared merely for their personal hatreds, not for the public good, were forced to accept.

Conde, on his recovery, left France, and for a time fought against his country in the ranks of the Spaniards. Beaufort died bravely fighting against the Turks at Cyprus. Cardinal de Retz was imprisoned, and Mademoiselle had to retire from Court, while other less distinguished persons had to undergo the punishment for their resistance, though, to the credit of the Court party be it spoken, there were no executions, only imprisonments; and in after years the Fronde was treated as a brief frenzy, and forgotten.

Perhaps it may be well to explain that Mademoiselle was Anne Genevieve de Bourbon, daughter of Gaston, Duke of Orleans, by his first wife, the heiress of the old Bourbon branch of Montpensier. She was the greatest heiress in France, and an exceedingly vain and eccentric person, aged twenty-three at the beginning of the Fronde.

It only remains to say that I have no definite authority for introducing such a character as that of Clement Darpent, but it is well known that there was a strong under-current of upright, honest, and highly-cultivated men among the bourgeoisie and magistrates, and that it seemed to me quite possible that in the first Fronde, when the Parliament were endeavouring to make a stand for a just right, and hoping to obtain further hopes and schemes, and, acting on higher and purer principles than those around him, be universally misunderstood and suspected.

C. M. YONGE.

CHAPTER I. — WHITEHALL BEFORE THE COBWEBS.

I have long promised you, my dear grandchildren, to arrange my recollections of the eventful years that even your father can hardly remember. I shall be glad thus to draw closer the bonds between ourselves and the English kindred, whom I love so heartily, though I may never hope to see them in this world, far less the dear old home where I grew up.

For, as perhaps you have forgotten, I am an English woman by birth, having first seen the light at Walwyn House, in Dorsetshire. One brother had preceded me — my dear Eustace — and another brother, Berenger, and my little sister, Annora, followed me.

Our family had property both in England and in Picardy, and it was while attending to some business connected with the French estate that my father had fallen in love with a beautiful young widow, Madame la Baronne de Solivet (nee Cheverny), and had brought her home, in spite of the opposition of her relations. I cannot tell whether she were warmly welcomed at Walwyn Court by any one but the dear beautiful grandmother, a Frenchwoman herself, who was delighted again to hear her mother tongue, although she had suffered much among the Huguenots in her youth, when her husband was left for dead on the S. Barthelemi.

He, my grandfather, had long been dead, but I perfectly remember her. She used to give me a sugar-cake when I said 'Bon soir, bonne maman,' with the right accent, and no one made sugar-cake like hers. She always wore at her girdle a string of little yellow shells, which she desired to have buried with her. We children were never weary of hearing how they had been the only traces of her or of her daughter that her husband could find, when he came to the ruined city.

I could fill this book with her stories, but I must not linger over them; and indeed I heard no more after I was eight years old. Until that time my brother and I were left under her charge in the country, while my father and mother were at court. My mother was one of the Ladies of the Bedchamber of Queen Henrietta Maria, who had been enchanted to find in her a countrywoman, and of the same faith. I was likewise bred up in their Church, my mother having obtained the consent of my father, during a dangerous illness that followed my birth, but the other children were all brought up as Protestants. Indeed, no difference was made between Eustace and me when we were at Walwyn. Our grandmother taught us both alike to make the sign of the cross, and likewise to say our prayers and the catechism; and oh! we loved her very much.

Eustace once gave two black eyes to our rude cousin, Harry Merricourt, for laughing when he said no one was as beautiful as the Grandmother, and though I am an old woman myself, I think he was right. She was like a little fairy, upright and trim, with dark flashing eyes, that never forgot how to laugh, and snowy curls on her brow.

I believe that the dear old lady made herself ill by nursing us two children day and night when we had the smallpox. She had a stroke, and died before my father could be fetched from London; but I knew nothing of all that; I only grieved, and wondered that she did not come to me, till at last the maid who was nursing me told me flatly that the old lady was dead. I think that afterwards we were sent down to a farmer's house by the sea, to be bathed and made rid of infection; and that the pleasure of being set free from our sick chambers and of playing on the shore drove from our minds for the time our grief for the good grandma, though indeed I dream of her often still, and of the old rooms and gardens at Walwyn, though I have never seen them since.

When we were quite well and tolerably free from pock-marks, my father took us to London with him, and there Eustace was sent to school at Westminster; while I, with little Berry, had a tutor to teach us Latin and French, and my mother's waiting-maid instructed me in sewing and embroidery. As I grew older I had masters in dancing and the spinnet, and my mother herself was most careful of my deportment. Likewise she taught me such practices of our religion as I had not learnt from my grandmother, and then it was found that I was to be brought up differently from Eustace and the others. I cried at first, and declared I would do like Eustace and my father. I did not think much about it; I was too childish and thoughtless to be really devout; and when my mother took me in secret to the queen's little chapel, full of charming objects of devotion, while the others had to sit still during sermons two hours long, I began to think that I was the best off.

Since that time I have thought much more, and talked the subject over both with my dear eldest brother and with good priests, both English and French, and I have come to the conclusion, as you know, my children, that the English doctrine is no heresy, and that the Church is a true Church and Catholic, though, as my home and my duties lie here, I remain where I was brought up by my mother, in the communion of my husband and children.

I know that this would seem almost heresy to our good Pere Chavand, but I wish to leave my sentiments on record for you, my children.

But how I have anticipated my history! I must return, to tell you that when I was just sixteen I was told that I was to go to my first ball at Whitehall. My hair was curled over my forehead, and I was dressed in white satin, with the famous pearls of Ribaumont round my neck, though of course they were not to be mine eventually.

I knew the palace well, having often had the honour of playing with the Lady Mary, who was some years younger than I, so that I was much less alarmed than many young gentlewomen there making their first appearance. But, as my dear brother Eustace led me into the outer hall, close behind my father and mother, I heard a strange whistle, and, looking up, I saw over the balustrade of the gallery a droll monkey face looking out of a mass of black curls, and making significant grimaces at me.

I knew well enough that it was no other than the Prince of Wales. He was terribly ugly and fond of teasing, but in a good-natured way, always leaving off when he saw he was giving real pain, and I liked him much better than his brother, the Duke of York, who was proud and sullen. Yet one could always trust the Duke, and that could not be said for the Prince.

By the time we had slowly advanced up the grand staircase into the banqueting-hall, and had made our reverences to the king and queen—ah, how stately and beautiful they looked together!—the Prince had stepped in some other way, and stood beside me.

'Well, Meg,' he said, in an undertone—'I beg pardon, Mrs. Margaret—decked out in all her splendour, a virgin for the sacrifice!'

'What sacrifice, sir?' I asked, startled.

'Eh!' he said. 'You do not know that le futur is arrived!'

'She knows nothing, your Highness,' said Eustace.

'What, oh, what is there to know?' I implored the Prince and my brother in turn to inform me, for I saw that there was some earnest in the Prince's jests, and I knew that the queen and my mother were looking out for a good match for me in France.

'Let me show him to you,' presently whispered the Prince, who had been called off by his father to receive the civilities of an ambassador. Then he pointed out a little wizened dried-up old man, who was hobbling up to kiss Her Majesty's hand, and whose courtly smile seemed to me to sit most unnaturally on his wrinkled countenance. I nearly screamed. I was forced to bite my lips to keep back my tears, and I wished myself child enough to be able to scream and run away, when my mother presently beckoned me forward. I hardly had strength to curtsey when I was actually presented to the old man. Nothing but terror prevented my sinking on the floor, and I heard as through falling waters something about M. le Marquis de Nidemerle and Mrs. Margaret Ribmont, for so we were called in England.

By and by I found that I was dancing, I scarcely knew how or with whom, and I durst not look up the whole time, nor did my partner address a single word to me, though I knew he was near me; I was only too thankful that he did not try to address me.

To my joy, when we had made our final reverences, he never came near me again all the evening. I found myself among some young maidens who were friends of mine, and in our eager talk together I began to forget what had passed, or to hope it was only some teasing pastime of the Prince and Eustace.

When we were seated in the coach on the way to our house my father began to laugh and marvel which had been the most shy, the gallant or the lady, telling my mother she need never reproach the English with bashfulness again after this French specimen.

'How will he and little Meg ever survive to-morrow's meeting!' he said.

Then I saw it was too true, and cried out in despair to beg them to let me stay at home, and not send me from them; but my mother bade me not be a silly wench. I had always known that I was to be married in France and the queen and my half-brother, M. de Solivet, had found an excellent parti for me. I was not to embarrass matters by any folly, but I must do her credit, and not make her regret that she had not sent me to a convent to be educated.

Then I clung to my father. I could hold him tight in the dark, and the flambeaux only cast in a fitful flickering light. 'Oh, sir,' said I, 'you cannot wish to part with your little Meg!'

'You are your mother's child, Meg,' he said sadly. 'I gave you up to her to dispose of at her will.'

'And you will thank me one of these days for your secure home,' said my mother. 'If these rogues continue disaffected, who knows what they may leave us in England!'

'At least we should be together,' I cried, and I remember how I fondled my father's hand in the dark, and how he returned it. We should never have thought of such a thing in the light; he would have been ashamed to allow such an impertinence, and I to attempt it.

Perhaps it emboldened me to say timidly: 'If he were not so old —'

But my mother declared that she could not believe her ears that a child of hers should venture on making such objections — so unmaidenly, so undutiful to a parti selected by the queen and approved by her parents.

As the coach stopped at our own door I perceived that certain strange noises that I had heard proceeded from Eustace laughing and chuckling to himself all the way. I must say I thought it very unkind and cruel when we had always loved each other so well. I would hardly bid him good-night, but ran up to the room I shared with nurse and Annora, and wept bitterly through half the night, little comforted by nurse's assurance that old men were wont to let their wives have their way far more easily than young ones did.

CHAPTER II. — A LITTLE MUTUAL AVERSION.

I had cried half the night, and when in the morning little Nan wanted to hear about my ball, I only answered that I hated the thought of it. I was going to be married to a hideous old man, and be carried to France, and should never see any of them again. I made Nan cry too, and we both came down to breakfast with such mournful faces that my mother chid me sharply for making myself such a fright.

Then she took me away to the still-room, and set me for an hour to make orange cakes, while she gave orders for the great dinner that we were to give that day, I knew only too well for whose sake; and if I had only known which orange cake was for my betrothed, would not it have been a bitter one! By and by my mother carried me off to be dressed. She never trusted the tiring-woman to put the finishing touches with those clumsy English fingers; and, besides, she bathed my swollen eyelids with essences, and made me rub my pale cheeks with a scarlet ribbon, speaking to me so sharply that I should not have dared to shed another tear.

When I was ready, all in white, and she, most stately in blue velvet and gold, I followed her down the stairs to the grand parlour, where stood my father, with my brothers and one or two persons in black, who I found were a notary and his clerk, and there was a table before them with papers, parchment, a standish, and pens. I believe if it had been a block, and I had had to lay my head on it, like poor Lady Jane Grey, I could not have been much more frightened.

There was a sound of wheels, and presently the gentleman usher came forward, announcing the Most Noble the Marquis de Nidemerle, and the Lord Viscount of Bellaise. My father and brothers went half-way down the stairs to meet them, my mother advanced across the room, holding me in one hand and Annora in the other. We all curtsied low, and as the gentlemen advanced, bowing low, and almost sweeping the ground with the plumes in their hats, we each had to offer them a cheek to salute after the English fashion. The old marquis was talking French so fast that I could not understand him in the least, but somehow a mist suddenly seemed to clear away from before me, and I found that I was standing before that alarming table, not with him, but with something much younger—not much older, indeed, than Eustace.

I began to hear what the notary was reading out, and behold it was—'Contract of marriage on the part of Philippe Marie Francois de Bellaise, Marquis de Nidermerle, and Eustace de Ribaumont, Baron Walwyn of Walwyn, in Dorset, and Baron de Ribaumont in Picardy, on behoof of Gaspard Henri Philippe, Viscount de Bellaise, nephew of the Marquis de Nidemerle, and Margaret Henrietta Maria de Ribaumont, daughter of the Baron de Ribaumont.'

Then I knew that I had been taken in by the Prince's wicked trick, and that my husband was to be the young viscount, not the old uncle! I do not think that this was much comfort to me at the moment, for, all the same, I was going into a strange country, away from every one I had ever known.

But I did take courage to look up under my eye-lashes at the form I was to see with very different eyes. M. de Ballaise was only nineteen, but although not so tall as my father or brother, he had already that grand military bearing which is only acquired in the French service, and no wonder, or he had been three years in the Regiment de Condé, and had already seen two battles and three sieges in Savoy, and now had only leave of absence for the winter before rejoining his regiment in the Low Countries.

Yet he looked as bashful as a maiden. It was true that, as my father said, his bashfulness was as great as an Englishman's. Indeed, he had been bred up at his great uncle's chateau in Anjou, under a strict abbe who had gone with him to the war, and from whom he was only now to be set free upon his marriage. He had scarcely ever spoken to any lady but his old aunt—his parents had long been dead—and he had only two or three times seen his little sister through the grating of her convent. So, as he afterwards confessed, nothing but his military drill and training bore him through the affair. He stood upright as a dart, bowed at the right place, and in due time signed his name to the contract, and I had to do the same. Then there ensued a great state dinner, where he and I sat together, but neither of us spoke to the other; and when, as I was trying to see the viscount under my eyelashes, I caught his eyes trying to do the same by me, I remember my cheeks flaming all over, and I think his must have done the same, for my father burst suddenly out into a laugh without apparent cause, though he tried to check himself when he saw my mother's vexation.

When all was over, she highly lauded the young gentleman, declaring that he was an example of the decorum with which such matters were

CHAPTER III. — CELADON AND CHLOE

My tears were soon checked by dreadful sea-sickness. We were no sooner out of Dover than the cruel wind turned round upon us, and we had to go beating about with all our sails reefed for a whole day and night before it was safe to put into Calais.

All that time I was in untold misery, and poor nurse Tryphena was worse than I was, and only now and then was heard groaning out that she was a dead woman, and begging me to tell some one to throw her over board.

But it was that voyage which gave me my husband. He was not exactly at his ease, but he kept his feet better than any of the other gentlemen, and he set himself to supply the place of valet to his uncle, and of maid to me, going to and fro between our cabins as best he could, for he fell and rolled whenever he tried to more; sharp shriek or howl, or a message through the steward, summoned him back to M. le Marquis, who had utterly forgotten all his politeness and formality towards the ladies.

However, our sufferings were over at last. My husband, who was by this time bruised from head to foot by his falls, though he made no complaints, came to say we should in a few moments be in port. He helped me to dress, for Tryphena thought she was dead, and would not move; and he dragged me on deck, where the air revived me, and where one by one the whole party appeared, spectacles of misery.

M. le Marquis did not recover himself till he was on shore, and caused himself to be assisted to the quay between his nephew and the valet, leaving me to myself; but the dear viscount returned for me, and after he had set me ashore, as he saw I was anxious about Tryphena, he went back and fetched her, as carefully as if she had been a lady, in spite of the grumblings of his uncle and of her own refractoriness, for she was horribly frightened, and could not understand a word he said to her.

Nevertheless, as soon as we had all of us come to ourselves, it turned out that he had gained her heart. Indeed, otherwise I should have had to send her home, for she pined sadly for some time, and nothing but her love for me and her enthusiastic loyalty to him kept her up during the first months.

As to my husband and me, that voyage had made us as fond of one another's company on one side of the Channel as we had been afraid of it before on the other, but there was no more riding together for us. I had to travel in the great coach with M. le Marquis, the three ladies, and all our women, where I was so dull and weary that I should have felt ready to die, but for watching for my husband's plume, or now and then getting a glance and a nod from him as he rode among the other gentlemen, braving all their laughter at his devotion; for, bashful as he was, he knew how to hold his own.

I knew that the ladies looked on me as an ugly little rustic foreigner, full of English mauvaise honte. If they tried to be kind to me, it was as a mere child; and they went on with their chatter, which I could hardly follow, for it was about things and people of which I knew nothing, so that I could not understand their laughter. Or when they rejoiced in their return from what they called their exile, and found fault with all they had left in England, my cheeks burned with indignation.

My happy hours were when we halted for refreshments. My husband handed me to my place at table and sat beside me; or he would walk with me about the villages where we rested. The ladies were shocked, and my husband was censured for letting me 'faire l'Anglaise,' but we were young and full of spirits, and the being thus thrown on each other had put an end to his timidity towards me. He did indeed blush up to his curls, and hold himself as upright as a ramrod, when satire was directed to us as Celadon and Chloe; but he never took any other notice of it, nor altered his behaviour in consequence. Indeed, we felt like children escaping from school when we crept down the stairs in early morning, and hand-in-hand repaired to the church in time for the very earliest mass among the peasants, who left their scythes at the door, and the women with their hottes, or their swaddled babies at their backs. We would get a cup of milk and piece of barley-bread at some cottage, and wander among the orchards, fields, or vineyards before Mesdames had begun their toiles; and when we appeared at the dejeuner, the gentlemen would compliment me on my rouge au naturel, and the ladies would ironically envy my English appetite.

Sometimes we rested in large hostels in cities, and then our walk began with some old cathedral, which could not but be admired, Gothic though it were, and continued in the market-place, where the piles of fruit, vegetables, and flowers were a continual wonder and delight to me. My husband would buy bouquets of pinks and roses for me; but in the coach the ladies always said they incommoded them by their scent, and obliged me to throw them away. The first day I could not help shedding a few tears, for I feared he would think I did not value them; and then I perceived that they thought the little Englishwoman a child crying for her flowers. I longed to ask them whether they had ever loved their husbands; but I knew how my mother would have looked at me, and forbore.

Once or twice we were received in state at some chateau, where our mails had to be opened that we might sup in full toilet; but this was seldom, for most of the equals of M. le Marquis lived at Paris. Sometimes our halt was at an abbey, where we ladies were quartered in a guest-chamber without; and twice we slept at large old convents, where nobody had lived since the Huguenot times, except a lay brother put in by M. l'Abbe to look after the estate and make the house a kind of inn for travelers. There were fine walled gardens run into wild confusion, and little neglected and dismantled shrines, and crosses here and there, with long wreaths of rose and honeysuckle trailing over them, and birds' nests in curious places. My Viscount laughed with a new pleasure when I showed him the wren's bright eye peeping out from her nest, and he could not think how I knew the egg of a hedge-sparrow from that of a red-breast. Even he had never been allowed to be out of sight of his tutor, and he knew none of these pleasures so freely enjoyed by my brothers; while as to his sister Cecile, she had been carried from her nurse to a convent, and had thence been taken at fourteen to be wedded to the grandson and heir of the Count d'Aubepine, who kept the young couple under their own eye at their castle in the Bocage.

My husband had absolutely only seen her twice, and then through the grating, and the marriage had taken place while he was in Savoy last autumn. He knew his brother-in-law a little better, having been his neighbour at Nid de Merle; but he shrugged his shoulders as he spoke of 'le chevalier,' and said he was very young, adored by his grandparents, and rather headstrong.

As to growing up together in the unity that had always existed between an absolute surprise to him to find that my dear brother was grieved at parting with me. He said he had lain and heard our shouts in the passages with wonder as we played those old games of ours.

'As though you were in a den of roaring wild beasts,' I said; for I ventured on anything with him by that time, voices, I teased him about his feelings at having to carry off one of these same savage beasts with him; and then he told me how surprised he had been when, on the last evening he spent in his chamber in our house, Eustace had come and implored him to be good to me, telling him—ah, I can see my dear brother's boyish way!—all my best qualities, ranging from my always speaking truth to my being able to teach the little dog to play tricks, and warning him of what vexed or pained me, even exacting a promise that he would take care of me when I was away from them all. I believe that promise was foremost in my husband's mind when he waited on me at sea. Nay, he said when remembered the tears in my brother's eyes, and saw how mine arose at the thought, his heart smote him when he remembered that his sister's marriage had scarcely cost him a thought or care, and that she was an utter stranger to him; and then we agreed that if ever we had children, we would bring them up to know and love one another, and have precious recollections in common. Ah! l'homme propose, mais Dieu dispose.

It was only on that day that it broke upon me that we were to be separated immediately after our arrival in Paris. M. de Bellaise was to go to his regiment, which was at garrison at Nancy, and I was to be left under the charge of old Madame la Marquise de Nidemerle at Paris. I heard of it first from the Marquise himself in the coach, as he thanked one of the ladies who invited me—with him—to her salon in Paris, where there was to be a great entertainment in the summer. When I replied that M. de Bellaise would have rejoined his regiment, they began explaining that I should go into society under Madame de Nidemerle, who would exert herself for my sake.

I said no more. I knew it was of no use there; but when next I could speak with my husband—it was under an arbour of vines in the garden of the inn where we dine—I asked him whether it was true. He opened large eyes, and said he knew I could not wish to withdraw him from his duty to his king and country, even if he could do so with honour.

'Ah! no,' I said; 'I never thought of that.' But surely the place of a wife was with her husband, and I had expected to go with him to his garrison at Nancy, and there wait when he took the field. He threw himself at my feet, and pressed my hands with transport at what he called this unheard-of proof of affection; and then I vexed him by laughing, for I could not help thinking what my brothers would have said, could they have seen us thus.

Still he declared that, in spite of his wishes, it was hardly possible. His great-uncle and aunt would never consent. I said they had no right to interfere between husband and wife, and he replied that they had brought him up, and taken the place of parents to him; to which I rejoined that I was far nearer to him. He said I was a mutinous Englishwoman; and I rejoined that he should never find me mutinous to him.

Nay, I made up my mind that if he would not insist on taking me, I would find means to escape and join him. What! Was I to be carried about in the coach of Madame de Nidemerle to all the hateful salons of Paris, while my husband, the only person in France whom I could endure, might be meeting wounds and death in the Low Countries while I might be dancing!

So again I declined when the ladies in the coach invited me to their houses in Paris. Should I go to a convent? they asked; and one began to recommend the Carmelites, another the Visitation, another Port Royal, till I was almost distracted; and M. le Marquis began to say it was a pious and commendable wish, but that devotion had its proper times and seasons, and that judgment must be exercised as to the duration of a retreat, etc.

'No, Monsieur,' said I, 'I am not going into a convent. A wife's duty is with her husband; I am going into garrison at Nancy.'

Oh, how they cried out! There was such a noise that the gentlemen turned their horses' heads to see whether any one was taken ill. When they heard what was the matter, persecution began for us both.

We used to compare our experiences; the ladies trying to persuade me now that it was improper, now that I should be terrified to death now that I should become too ugly to be presentable; while the gentlemen made game of M. de Bellaise as a foolish young lover, who was so absurd as to encumber himself with a wife of whom he would soon weary, and whose presence would interfere with his enjoyment of the freedom and diversions of military life. He who was only just free from his governor, would he saddle himself with a wife? Bah!

He who had been so shy defended himself with spirit; and on my side I declared that nothing but his commands, and those of my father, should induce me to leave him. At Amiens we met a courier on his way to England, and by him we dispatched letters to my father.

M. de Nidemerle treated all like absurd childish nonsense, complimenting me ironically all the while; but I thought he wavered a little before the journey was over, wishing perhaps that he had never given his nephew a strange, headstrong, English wife, but thinking that, as the deed was done, the farther off from himself she was the better.

At least, he no longer blamed his nephew and threatened him with his aunt; but declared that Madame de Rambouillet would soon put all such folly out of our minds.

I asked my husband what Madame de Rambouillet could have to do with our affairs; and he shrugged his shoulders and answered that the divine Arthenice was the supreme judge of decorum, whose decisions no one could gainsay.

CHAPTER IV. — THE SALON BLEU

We arrived at Paris late in the day, entering the city through a great fortified gateway, and then rolling slowly through the rough and narrow streets. You know them too well, my children, to be able to conceive how strange and new they seemed to me, accustomed as I was to our smooth broad Thames and the large gardens of the houses in the Strand lying on its banks.

Our carriage turned in under the porte cochere of this Hotel de Nidemerle of ours, and entered the courtyard. My husband, his uncle, and I know not how many more, were already on the steps. M. de Nidemerle solemnly embraced me and bade me welcome, presenting me at the same time to a gentlemen, in crimson velvet and silver, as my brother. My foolish heart bounded for a moment as if it could have been Eustace; but it was altogether the face of a stranger, except for a certain fine smile like my mother's. It was, of course, my half-brother, M. le Baron de Solivet, who saluted me, and politely declared himself glad to make the acquaintance of his sister.

The Marquis then led me up the broad stairs, lined with lackeys, to our own suite of apartments, where I was to arrange my dress before being presented to Madame de Nidemerle, who begged me to excuse her not being present to greet me, as she had caught cold, and had a frightful megrim.

I made my toilet, and they brought me a cup of eau sucree and a few small cakes, not half enough for my hungry English appetite.

My husband looked me over more anxiously than ever he had done before; and I wished, for his sake, that I had been prettier and fitter to make a figure among all these grand French ladies.

My height was a great trouble to me in those unformed days. I had so much more length to dispose of than my neighbours, and I knew they remarked me the more for it; and then my hair never would remain in curl for half an hour together. My mother could put it up safely, but since I had left her it was always coming down, like flax from a distaff; and though I had in general a tolerably fresh and rosy complexion, heat outside and agitation within made my whole face, nose and all, instantly become the colour of a clove gillyflower. It had so become every afternoon on the journey, and I knew I was growing redder and redder every moment, and that I should put him, my own dear Viscount, to shame before his aunt.

'Oh! my friend,' I sighed, 'pardon me, I cannot help it.'

'Why should I pardon thee?' he answered tenderly. 'Because thou hast so great and loving a heart?'

'Ah! but what will thine aunt think of me?'

'Let her think,' he said. 'Thou art mine, not Madame's.'

I know not whether those words made me less red, but they gave me such joyous courage that I could have confronted all the dragoons, had I been of the colour of a boiled lobster, and when he himself sprinkled me for the last time with essences, I felt ready to defy the censure of all the marchionesses in France.

My husband took me by the hand and led me to the great chamber, where in an alcove stood the state bed, with green damask hangings fringed with gold, and in the midst of pillows trimmed with point-lace sat up Madam la Marquis, her little sallow face, like a bit of old parchment, in the midst of the snowy linen, and not—to my eyes—wearing a very friendly aspect.

She had perhaps been hearing of my wilfulness and insubordination, for she was very grand and formal with me, solemnly calling me Madame la Vicomtesse, and never her niece, and I thought all the time that I detected a sneer. If I had wished for my husband's sake to accompany him, I wished it ten thousand times more when I fully beheld the alternative.

Ah! I am writing treason. Had I been a well-trained French young girl I should have accepted my lot naturally, and no doubt all the family infinitely regretted that their choice has fallen on one so impracticable.

I was happier as the supper-table, to which we were soon summoned, for I had become accustomed to M. de Nidemerle, who was always kind to me. Poor old man, I think he had hoped to have something young and lively in his house; but I never thought of that, and of course my husband was my only idea.

M. de Solivet set by me, and asked many questions about my mother and the rest of the family, treating me more as a woman than anyone else had done. Nor was it long before I caught slight resemblances both to my mother and to my brother Berenger, which made me feel as home with him. He was a widower, and his two daughters were being educated in a convent, where he promised to take me to visit them, that I might describe them to their grandmother.

Poor little things! I thought them very stiff and formal, and pitied them when I saw them; but I believed they were really full of fun and folic among their companions.

M. de Solivet was consulted on this wild scheme of mine, and the Marchioness desired him to show me its absurdity. He began by arguing that it was never when to act in the face of custom, and that he had only known of two ladies who had followed their husbands to the wars, and both them only belonged to the petite noblesse, and were no precedent for me! One of them had actually joined her husband when wounded and made prisoner, and it was said that her care had saved his life!

Such a confession on his part rendered me the more determined, and we reminded M. de Nidemerle of his promise to consult Madame de Rambouillet, though I would not engage even then to abide by any decision except my father's, which I daily expected. I overheard people saying how much M. de Bellaise was improved by his marriage, and how much more manly and less embarrassed he had become, and I felt that my resolution made him happy, so that I became the more determined.

Children, you who have laughed at Les Precieuses can have little idea what the Hotel de Rambouillet was when, three nights after arrival, I went thither with my husband and his uncle and aunt.

The large salon, hung and draped with blue velvet, divided by lines of gold, was full of people ranged in a circle, listening eagerly to the recital of poem by the author, an Abbe, who stood in the midst, declaiming each couplet with emphasis, and keeping time with his foot, while he made gestures with his uplifted hand. Indeed, I thought at first he was in a furious passion and was going to knock someone down, till I saw calmly everyone sat; and then again I fancied we had come to a theatre by mistake; but happily I did not speak, and, without interrupting the declamation, chairs were given us, and exchanging a mute salutation with a lady of a noble cast of beauty, who guided us to seats, we quietly took our places. She was Julie d'Argennes, the daughter of Madame de Rambouillet. A gentlemen followed her closely, the Duke of Montausier, who adored her, but whom she could not yet decide on accepting.

I found it difficult to fit from laughing as the gestures of the Abbe, especially when I thought of my brother and how they would mock them; but I knew that this would be unpardonable bad taste, and as I had come in too late to have the clue to the discourse, I amused myself with looking about me.

Perhaps the most striking figure was that of the hostess, with her stately figure, and face, not only full of intellect, but of something that went far beyond it, and came out of some other higher world, to which she was trying to raise this one.

Next I observed a lady, no longer in her first youth, but still wonderfully fair and graceful. She was enthroned in a large arm-chair, and on a stool beside her sat her daughter, a girl of my own age, the most lovely creature I had ever seen, with a profusion of light flaxen hair, and deep blue eyes, and one moment full of grave thought, at another of merry mischief. A young sat by, whose cast of features reminded me of the Prince of Wales, but his nose was more aquiline, his dark blue eyes far more intensely bright and flashing, and whereas Prince Charles would have made fun of all the flourishes of our poet, they seemed to inspire in this youth an ardour he could barely restrain, and when there was something vehement about Mon epee et ma patrie he laid his hand on his sword, and his eyes lit up, so that he reminded me of a young eagle.

This was the Princess of Conde, who in the pride of her youthful beauty had been the last flame of Henri IV., who had almost begun a war on her account; this was her lovely daughter, Mademoiselle de Bourbon, and her sons, the brave Duke of Enghien, with his deformed brother, the Prince of Conti.

When the recital was over, there was a general outburst of applause, in which M. de Nidemerle joined heartily. Madame de Rambouillet gave her meed of approbation, but her daughter, Mademoiselle d' Argennes, took exception at the use of the word chevaucher, for to ride, both as being obsolete, and being formed from the name of a single animal, instead of regularly derived from a Latin verb.

The Abbe defended his word, and for fully twenty minutes there was an eager argument, people citing passages and derivations, and defining shades of meaning with immense animation and brilliant wit, as I now understand, though then it seemed to me a wearisome imbroglio about a trifle. I did not know what real benefit was done by these discussions in purifying the language from much that was coarse and unrefined. Yes, and far more than the language, for Madame de Rambouillet, using her great gifts as a holy trust for the good of her neighbour, conferred no small benefit on her generation, nor is that good even yet entirely vanished. Ah! If there were more women like her, France and society would be very different.

When the discussion was subsiding, Mademoiselle d' Argennes came to take me by the hand, and to present us to the queen of the salon.

'Here, my mother, are our Odoardo and Gildippe,' she said.

You remember, my children, that Odoardo and Gildippe are the names bestowed by Tasso on the English married pair who went together on the first crusade, and Gildippe continued to be my name in that circle, my nom de Parnasse, as it was called — nay, Madame de Montausieur still gives it to me.

The allusion was a fortunate one; it established a precedent, and, besides, English people have always been supposed to be eccentric. I am, however, doing the noble lady injustice. Arthenice, as she was called by an anagram of her baptismal name of Catherine, was no blind slave to the conventional. She had originality enough to have been able to purify the whole sphere in which she moved, and to raise the commonplace into the ideal. 'Excuse me,' she said to her friends, and she led my husband apart into a deep window, and there, as he told me, seemed to look him through and through. And verily he was one who needed not to fear such an inspection, any more than the clearest crystal.

Then, in like manner, she called for me, and made me understand that I was condemning myself to a life of much isolation, and that I must be most circumspect in my conduct, whole, after all, I might see very little of my husband; I must take good care that my presence was a help and refreshment, not a burden and perplexity to him, or he would neglect me and repent my coming. 'It may seem strange,' she said, 'but I think my young friend will understand me, that I have always found that, next of course to those supplied by our holy religion, the best mode of rendering our life and its inconveniences endurable is to give them a colouring of romance.' I did not understand her then, but I have often since thought of her words, when the recollection of the poetical aspect of the situation has aided my courage and my good temper. Madame de Rambouillet looked into my eyes as she spoke, then said: 'Pardon an old woman, my dear;' and kissed my brow, saying: 'You will not do what I have only dreamt of.'

Finally she led us forward to our great-uncle, saying: 'Madame le Marquis, I have conversed with these children. They love one another, and so long as that love lasts they will be better guardians to one another than ten governors or twenty dames de compagnie.'

In England we should certainly not have done all this in public, and my husband and I were terribly put to the blush; indeed, I felt my whole head and neck burning, and caught a glimpse of myself in a dreadful mirror, my white bridal dress and flaxen hair making my fiery face look, my brothers would have said, 'as if I had been skinned.'

And then, to make it all worse, a comical little crooked lady, with a keen lively face, came hopping up with hands outspread, crying: 'Ah, let me see her! Where is the fair Gildippe, the true heroine, who is about to confront the arrows of the Lydians for the sake of the lord of her heart?'

'My niece,' said the Marquis, evidently gratified by the sensation I had created, 'Mademoiselle de Scudery does you the honour of requesting to be presented to you.'

I made a low reverence, terribly abashed, and I fear it would have reduced my mother to despair, but it was an honour that I appreciated; for now that I was a married woman, I was permitted to read romances, and I had just begun on the first volume of the Grand Curus. My husband read it to me as I worked at my embroidery, and you may guess how we enjoyed it.

But I had no power of make compliments—nay, my English heart recoiled in anger at their making such an outcry, whether of blame or praise, at what seemed to me the simplest thing in the world. The courtesy and consideration were perfect; as soon as these people saw that I was really abashed and distressed, they turned their attention from me. My husband was in the meantime called to be presented to the Duke of Enghien, and I remained for a little while unmolested, so that I could recover myself a little. Presently a soft voice close to me said 'Madame,' and I looked up into the beautiful countenance of Anne Genevieve de Bourbon, her blue eyes shining on me with the sweetest expression. 'Madame,' she said, 'permit me to tell you how glad I am for you.'

I thanked her most heartily. I felt this was the real tender sympathy of a being of my own age and like myself, and there were something so pathetic in her expression that I felt sorry for her.

'You are good! You will keep good,' she said.

'I hope so, Mademoiselle,' I said.

'Ah! yes, you will. They will not make you lose your soul against your will!' and she clenched her delicate white hand.

'Nobody can do that, Mademoiselle.'

'What! Not when they drag you to balls and fete away from the cloister, where alone you can be safe?'

'I hope not there alone,' I said.

'For me it is the only place,' she repeated. 'What is the use of wearing haircloth when the fire of the Bourbons is in one's blood, and one has a face that all the world runs after?'

'Mais, Mademoiselle,' I said; 'temptation is only to prove our strength.'

'You are strong. You have conquered,' she said, and clasped my hand. 'But then you loved him.'

I suppose I smiled a little with my conscious bliss, for this strange young princess hastily asked: 'Did you love him? I mean, before you were married.'

'Oh no,' I said, glad to disavow what was so shocking in my new country.

'But he is lovable? Ah! that is it. While you are praying to Heaven, and devoting yourself to a husband whom you love, remember that if I ruin my soul, it is because they would have it so!'

At that moment there was a pause. A gentleman, the Marquis de Feuquieres, had come in, bringing with him a very young lad, in the plian black gown and white collar of a theological student; and it was made known that the Marquis had been boasting of the wonderful facility of a youth was studying at the College of Navarre, and had declared that he could extemporise with eloquence upon any subject. Some one had begged that the youth might be fetched and set to preach on a text proposed to him at the moment, and here he was.

Madame de Rambouillet hesitated a little at the irreverence, but the Duke of Enghien requested that the sermon might take place, and she consented, only looking at her watch and saying it was near midnight, so that the time was short. M. Voiture, the poet, carried round a velvet bag, and each was to write a text on a slip of paper to be drawn out at haphazard.

We two showed each other what we wrote. My husband's was—'Love is strong as death;' mine—'Let the wife cleave unto her husband.' But neither of them was drawn out. I saw by the start that Mademoiselle de Bourbon gave that it was hers, when the first paper was taken out—'Vanity of vanities, all is vanity!' a few minutes were offered to the young Abbe to collect his thoughts, but he declined them, and he was led to a sort of a dais at the end of the salon, while the chairs were placed in a half-circle. Some of the ladies tittered a little, though Madame de Rambouillet looked grave; but they composed themselves. We all stood and repeated the Ave, and then seated ourselves; while the youth, in a voice already full and sweet, began solemnly: 'What is life? what is man?'

I can never convey to you how this world and all its fleeting follies seemed to melt away before us, and how each of us felt our soul alone in the presence of our Maker, as though nothing mattered, or ever would matter, but how we stood with Him. One hardly dared to draw one's breath. Mademoiselle de Bourbon was almost stifled with the sobs she tried to restrain lest her mother should make her retire. My husband held my hand, and pressed it unseen. He was a deeper, more thoughtful man ever after he heard that voice, which seemed to come, as it were, from the Angel at Bochim who warned the Israelites; and that night we dedicated ourselves to the God who had not let us be put asunder.

I wished we could have gone away at once and heard no more, and so must, I think, the young preacher have felt; but he was surrounded with compliments. M. Voiture said he had never heard 'so early nor so late a sermon;' while others thronged up with their compliments.

Madame de Rambouillet herself murmured: 'He might be Daniel hearing the compliments of Belshazzar on his deciphering the handwriting,' so impassively did he listen to the suffrages of the assembly, only replying by a bow.

The Duke of Enghien, boldest of course, pressed up to him and, taking his hand, begged to know his name.

'Bossuet, Monseigneur,' he answered.

There were one or two who had the bad taste to smile, for Bossuet (I must tell my English kindred) means a draught-ox; but once more the lovely sister of the young Duke grasped my hand and said: 'Oh, that I could hide myself at once! Why will they not let me give myself to my God? Vanity of vanities! why am I doomed?'

I was somewhat frightened, and was glad that a summons of 'my daughter' from the Princess of Conde interrupted these strange communications. I understood them better when we were called upon to ell the old Marchioness the names of every one whom we had met at the Hotel de Rambouillet, and on hearing of the presence of Mademoiselle de Bourbon she said: 'Ah! yes, a marriage is arranged for the young lady with the Duke of Longueville.'

'But!' exclaimed my husband, 'the Duke is an old man, whose daughter is older than I.'

'What has that to do with it?' said his aunt. 'There is not much blood in France with which a Montmorency Bourbon can match. Moreover, they say the child is devote, and entetee on Madam de Port Royal, who is more than suspected of being outree in her devotion; so the sooner she is married the better!'

Poor beautiful girl, how I pitied her then! Her lovely, wistful, blue eyes haunted me all night, in the midst of my own gladness; for a courier had come that evening bringing my father's reply. He said my mother deplored my unusual course, but that for his part he liked his little girl the better for her courage, and that he preferred that I should make my husband's home happy to my making it at court. All he asked of me was to remember that I had to guard the honour of my husband's name and of my country, and he desired that I should take Tryphena with me wherever I went.

CHAPTER V. — IN GARRISON.

I am almost afraid to dwell on those happiest days of my life that I spent in garrison. My eyes, old as they are, fill with tears when I am about to write of them, and yet they passed without my knowing how happy they were; for much of my time was spent in solitude, much in waiting, much in anxiety; but ah! there then always was a possibility that never, never can return!

Nancy seems to me a paradise when I look back to it, with its broad clean streets and open squares, and the low houses with balconies, and yet there I often thought myself miserable, for I began to learn what it was to be a soldier's wife. Madame de Rambouillet had kindly written to some of her friends in the duchy of Lorraine respecting me, and they assisted us in obtaining a lodging and servants. This might otherwise have been difficult, for the Duke was I the Spanish army, while we held his territories, and naturally we were not in very good odour with the people.

My husband had to leave me, immediately after he had placed me in my little house at Nancy, to join the army in Germany under Marshal Guebrian. I lived through that time by the help of the morning mass, of needlework, and of the Grand Cyrus, which I read through and then began again. My dear husband never failed to send me a courier once a week with letters that were life to me, and sometimes I heard from England; but my mother's letters were becoming full of anxiety, affairs were looking so ill for the king.

After a gallant victory over the Swedes my Viscount returned to me without a wound, and with distinguished praise from the Marshal. That was an important winter, for it saw the deaths of the great Cardinal and of King Louis XIII., moreover of the old Marchioness. My husband's loving heart sorrowed for her and for his uncle; but that same week brought thee to my arms, my dear son, my beloved Gaspard! Oh! what a fight Tryphena and I had to prevent his being stifled in swaddling clothes! And how all the women predicted that his little limbs would be broken and never be straight.

That winter was only clouded by the knowledge that spring would take my husband away again. How good he was to me! How much pleasure and amusement he gave up for my sake! He had outgrown his bashfulness and embarrassment in this campaign, and could take his place in company, but re remained at home with me. Had neither the grace nor the vivacity that would have enabled me to collect a society around me, and I seldom saw his brother officers except my brother M. de Solivet, and his great friend M. de Chamillard, who was quite fatherly to me.

The Duke of Enghien took the command of the army of Picardy, and asked for our regiment. I entreated not to be sent back to Paris, and prevailed to be allowed to take up my abode at Mezieres, where I was not so far from the camp but that my dear M. de Bellaise could sometimes ride over and see me. He told me of the murmur of the elder men of the army that the fiery young inexperienced prince was disregarding all the checks that the old Marshal de l'Hopital put in his way; but he himself was delighted, and made sure of success. The last time he came he told me he heard that Rocroy was invested by the enemy. I was made to promise that in case of any advance on the enemy's part I would instantly set off for Paris. He said it was the only way to make him fight with a free heart, if a battle there were, and not repent of having permitted me to follow him, and that I must think of my child as well as myself; but he did not expect any such good fortune as a battle, the old marshal was so set against it!

But I knew that he did expect a battle, by the way he came back and back again to embrace me and his child.

I have waited and watched many times since that day, but never as I then waited. With what agony I watched and prayed! how I lived either before the altar, or at the window! how I seemed to be all eyes and ears! How reports came that there was fighting, then that we had the day, then that all was lost! Then came a calm, and it was said that Marshal de l'Hospital had refused to fight, and was in full retreat, with the Duke of Enghien cursing and swearing and tearing his hair. My landlord had a visit from the mayor to say that he must prepare to have some men billeted on him, and I sent out to inquire for horses, but decided that, as it was only our own troops retreating, there would be plenty of time. Then one of the maids of the house rushed in declaring that firing was plainly to be heard. Half the people were out in the streets, many more had gone outside the city to listen. Tryphena sat crying with fright, and rocking the baby in her lap, and wishing she had never come to this dreadful country. Alas! poor Tryphena she would have been no better off in her own at that moment! I ran from window to door, unable to rest a moment, listening to the cries in the streets, asking the landlady what she heard, and then running back to my own room to kneel in prayer, but starting up at the next sound in the streets.

At last, just before sunset, on that long, long 19th of May, all the bells began to ring, clashing as if mad with joy, and a great roaring shout burst out all over the city: 'Victory! Victory! Vive le Roi! Vive le Duc d'Enghien!'

I was at the window just in time to see a party of splendid horsemen, carrying the striped and castellated colours of Spain, galloping through the town, followed by universal shouts and acclamations. My man-servant, Nicole, frantic with joy, came in to tell me that they had only halted at the inn long enough to obtain fresh horses, on their way to the Queen-Regent with the news of the great victory of Rocroy. More standards taken, more cannon gained, more of the enemy killed and captive than could be counted, and all owing to the surpassing valour of the Duke of Enghien!

'And my husband!' I cried, and asked everybody, as if, poor little fool that I was, any one was likely to know how it fared with one single captain of the dragoons of Conde on such a day as that.

The good landlady and Tryphena both tried to reassure me that if there were ill news it would have been sent to me at once; but though they persuaded me at last to go to bed, I could not sleep, tossing about and listening till morning light, when I dropped into a sound sleep, which lasted for hours. I had longed for the first morning mass to go and pray there, but after all I only heard the bells through my slumber, feeling as if I could not rouse myself, and then—as it seemed to me, in another moment—I heard something that made me turn round on my pillow and open my eyes, and there he stood—my husband himself. His regiment had surpassed itself; he had received the thanks of his colonel; he had but snatched a few hours' sleep, and had ridden off to assure his Gildippe of his safety by her own eyes, and to rejoice over our splendid victory.

And yet he could not but shudder as he spoke. When they had asked a Spanish prisoner how many there had been in the army, 'Count the dead,' he proudly answered. Nor could my husband abstain from tears as he told me how the old Spanish guards were all lying as they stood, slain all together, with their colonel, the Count of Fontanes, at their head, sitting in the armchair in which he had been carried to the field, for he was more than eighty years old, and could not stand or ride on account of the gout.

The Duke of Enghien had said that if he had not been victorious, the next best thing would be to have died like that.

But his charges, his fire, his coolness, his skill, the vehemence which had triumphed over the caution of the old marshal, and the resolution which had retrieved the day when his colleague was wounded; of all this M. de Bellaise spoke with passionate ardour and enthusiasm, and I—oh! I think that was the happiest and most glorious day of all my life!

When we went together to mass, how everybody looked at him! and when we returned there was quite a little crowd—M. le Gouverneur and his officials eager to make their compliments to M. de Bellaise, and to ask questions about the Duke and about the battle, and whether he thought the Duke would march this way, in which case a triumphal entry should be prepared. They wanted to have regaled M. de Bellaise with a banquet, and were sadly disappointed when he said he had only stolen a few hours to set his wife's heart at rest, and must return immediately to the camp.

There was little after that to make me anxious, for our army merely went through a course of triumphs, taking one city after another in rapid succession. I remained at Mezieres, and M. de Bellaise sometimes was able to spend a few days with me, much, I fear, to the derision of his fellow-soldiers, who could not understand a man's choosing such a form of recreation. We had been walking under the fine trees in the PLACE on a beautiful summer evening, and were mounting the stairs on our return home, when we heard a voice demanding of the hostess whether this were the lodging of Captain de Bellaise.

I feared that it was a summons from the camp, but as the stranger came forward I saw that he was a very young man in the dress of a groom, booted, spurred, and covered with dust and dried splashes of mud, though his voice and pronunciation were those of a gentleman.

'Do you bring tidings from M. le Marquis?' inquired my husband, who had recognized our livery.

'Ah! I have deceived you likewise, and no wonder, for I should not have known you, Philippe,' cried the new comer.

'Armand d'Aubepine! Impossible! I thought your child was a girl,' exclaimed my husband.

'And am I to waste my life and grow old ingloriously on that account?' demanded the youth, who had by this time come up to our rooms.

'Welcome, then, my brother,' said my husband a little gravely, as I thought. 'My love,' he added, turning to me, 'let me present to you my brother-in-law, the Chevalier d'Aubepine.'

With infinite grace the Chevalier put a knee to the ground, and kissed my hand.

'Madame will be good enough to excuse my present appearance,' he said, 'in consideration of its being the only means by which I could put myself on the path of honour.'

'It is then an evasion?' said my husband gravely.

'My dear Viscount, do not give yourself the airs of a patriarch. They do not suit with your one-and-twenty years, even though you are the model of husbands. Tell me, where is your hero?'

'The Duke? He is before Thionville.'

'I shall be at his feet in another day. Tell me how goes the war. What cities are falling before our arms?'

He asked of victories; M. de Bellaise asked of his sister. 'Oh! well, well, what do I know?' he answered lightly, as if the matter were beneath his consideration; and when I inquired about his child, he actually made a grimace, and indeed he had barely seen her, for she had been sent out to be nursed at a farmhouse, and he did not even recollect her name. I shall never forget how he stared, when at the sound of a little cry my husband opened the door and appeared with our little Gaspard, now five months old, laughing and springing in his arms, and feeling for the gold on his uniform. The count had much the same expression with which I have seen a lady regard me when I took a caterpillar in my hand.

'Ah! ah!' cried our Chevalier; 'with all his legs and arms too! That is what comes of marrying an Englishwoman.' [he did not know I was within hearing, for I had gone in to give Tryphena orders about the room he would occupy.] 'Beside, it is a son.'

'I hope one day to have a daughter whom I shall love the more, the more she resembles her mother,' said my husband, to tease him.

'Bah! You will not have to detest her keeping you back from glory! Tell me, Philippe, could a lettre de cachet reach me here?'

'We are on French soil. What have you been doing, Armand?'

'Only flying from inglorious dullness, my friend. Do not be scandalized, but let me know how soon I can reach the hero of France, and enroll myself as a volunteer.'

'The Duke is at Binche. I must return thither tomorrow. You had better eat and sleep here tonight, and then we can decide what is to be done.'

'I may do that,' the youth said, considering. 'My grandfather could hardly obtain an order instantaneously, and I have a fair start.'

So M. de Bellaise lent him some clothes, and he appeared at supper as a handsome lively-looking youth, hardly come to his full height, for he was only seventeen, with a haughty bearing, and large, almost fierce dark eyes, under eyebrows that nearly met.

At supper he told us his story. He was, as you know the only scion of the old house of Aubepine, his father having been killed in a duel, and his mother dying at his birth. His grandparents bred him up with the most assiduous care, but (as my husband told me) it was the care of pride rather than of love. When still a mere boy, they married him to poor little Cecile de Bellaise, younger still, and fresh from her convent, promising, on his vehement entreaty, that so soon as the succession should be secured by the birth of a son, he should join the army.

Imagine then his indignation and despair when a little daughter—a miserable little girl, as he said—made her appearance, to prolong his captivity. For some centuries, he said—weeks he meant—he endured, but then came the tidings of Rocroy to drive him wild with impatience, and the report that there were negotiations for peace completed the work. He made his wife give him her jewels and assist his escape from the window of her chamber; bribed a courier—who was being sent from M. de Nidemerle to my husband—to give him his livery and passport and dispatches, and to keep out of sight; and thus passed successfully through Paris, and had, through a course of adventures which he narrated with great spirit, safely reached us. Even if the rogue of a courier, as he justly called his accomplice, had betrayed him, there was no fear but that he would have time to put himself on the roll of the army, whence a promising young noble volunteer was not likely to be rejected.

My husband insisted that he should write to ask the pardon of his grandfather, and on that condition engaged to introduce him to the Duke and to the lieutenant-colonel of his regiment. M. de Bellaise then inquired anxiously after the health of our uncle, who, on the death of his wife, had retired to his own estate at Nid de Merle, close to the Chateau d'Aubepine. Of this the young gentleman could tell little or nothing.

'Bah!' he said, adding what he thought was a brilliant new military affirmation, unaware that it was as old as the days of the League. 'What know I? He is, as all old men are, full of complaints.'

Handsome, graceful, courteous, spirited as was this young Chevalier, I could not like him, and I afterwards told my husband that I wondered at his assisting him.

'My love,' he said, 'the Chateau d'Aubepine is dull enough to die of. The poor fellow was eating out his own heart. He has followed his instinct, and it is the only thing that can save him from worse corruption.'

'His instinct of selfishness,' I said. 'His talk was all of glory, but it was of his own glory, not his duty nor the good of his country. He seems to me to have absolutely no heart!'

'Do not be hard on him; remember how he has been brought up.'

'You were brought up in like manner by two old people.'

'Ah! but they loved me. Besides, my tutor and his were as different as light and darkness.'

'And your poor little sister,' I said.

'She must have won his gratitude by her assistance. He will have learnt to love her when he returns. Come, ma mie, you must forgive him. If you knew what his captivity was, you could not help it. He was the play-fellow of my boyhood, and if I can help him to the more noble path, my aid must not be wanting, either for his sake or that of my sister.'

How wise and how noble these two years had made my dear husband; how unlike the raw lad I had met at Whitehall! It was the training in self-discipline that he had given himself for my sake—yes, and for that of his country and his God.

CHAPTER VI. — VICTORY
DEARLY BOUGHT

No difficulty was made about enrolling the Chevalier d'Aubepine as a volunteer in the regiment of Conde, and as the lettre de cachet, as my brother De Solivet said, the Cardinal understood his game too well to send one to bring back a youth who had rushed to place himself beneath the banners of his country in the hands of a prince of the blood.

Indeed, we soon learned that there was no one to pursue him. His grandfather had a stroke of apoplexy in his rage on hearing of the arrest, and did not survive it a week, so that he had become Count of Aubepine. The same courier brought to my husband a letter from his sister, which I thought very stiff and formal, all except the conclusion: 'Oh, my brother, I implore you on my knees to watch over him and bring him back to me!'

Yet, as far as we knew and believed, the young man had never written at all to his poor little wife. My husband had insisted on his producing a letter to his grandfather; but as to his wife, he shrugged his shoulders, said that she could see that he was safe, and that was enough for her.

He was, in fact, like one intoxicated with the delights of liberty and companionship. He enjoyed a certain eclat from the manner of his coming, and was soon a universal favourite among the officers. Unfortunately, the influence and example there were not such as to lead him to think more of his wife. The Duke of Enghien had been married against his will to a poor little childish creature, niece to Cardinal de Richelieu, and he made it the fashion to parade, not only neglect, but contempt, of one's wife. He was the especial hero of our young Count's adoration, and therefore it was the less wonder that, when in the course of the winter, the chaplain wrote that the young Madame le Comtesse was in the most imminent danger, after having given birth to the long desired son and heir, he treated the news with supreme carelessness. We should never have known whether she lived or died, had not the courier, by whom M. de Bellaise wrote to her as well as to his uncle, brought back one of her formal little letters, ill-spelt and unmeaning, thanking Monsieur son frere and Madame sa femme for their goodness, and saying she was nearly recovered.

'It cuts me to the heart to receive such letters,' said my husband, 'and to feel how little I can be to her. Some day I hope I may know her better, and make her feel what a brother means.'

All this happened while we were in garrison for the winter at Nancy. Again we offered M. d'Aubepine a room in our house; but though he was, in his way, fond of my husband, and was polite to me, he thought a residence with us would interfere with his liberty, and, alas! his liberty consisted in plunging deeper and deeper into dissipation, gambling, and all those other sports which those about him made him think the privileges of manhood. We could do nothing; he laughed at M. de Bellaise, and so indeed did these chosen friends of his. I believe plenty of wit was expended on us and our happy domestic life; but what was that to us? The courage of M. de Bellaise was well known, and he had so much good-temper and kindness that no one durst insult him.

He was doubly tender to me that winter and spring because the accounts from England were so sad. My dear brother Berenger had been killed at the battle of Alresford, and affairs looked very ill for the royal cause. I wept for my brother; but, ah! those tears were as nothing compared with what I was soon to shed.

The Duke of Enghien arrived. He was not to take the command of the army of the Low Countries, but of that of Germany. He came on the very day we had heard of the loss of Freiburg in Brisgau, and all was at once activity. I saw the inspection of the army just outside the city, and a glorious sight it was; bodies of infantry moving like one great machine, squadrons of cavalry looking invincible, all glittering with gold, and their plumes waving, the blue and gold banners above their heads; and the dear regiment of Conde, whence salutes from eye and hand came to me and my little Gaspard as they rode past.

I did not tremble as in the last campaign. Ah! perhaps I did not pray so much. I heard of the crossing of the Rhine at Brisach, and then came rumours of a tremendous battle at Freiburg. The bells had only just begun to ring, when Pierre, our groom, galloped into the town, and sent up at once his packet. His master, he said, was wounded, but not badly, and had covered himself with glory. I tore open the packet. There were a few lines by his own dear hand;—

'My heart—I shall be with thee soon to rest in thy care—D.G. Kiss your son. Thy B.'

The rest of the packet was from my half-brother De Solivet, and told how, in the frightful attack on the vineyard at Freiburg, seven times renewed, my dear, dear Philippe had received a shot in the knee, just as he was grasping a Bavarian standard, which he carried off with him. He would have returned to the charge, but faintness overpowered him, and he was supported on horseback from the field to the tent. The wound had been dressed, and the surgeon saw no occasion for alarm. M. de Solivet, who had a slight wound himself, and M. d'Aubepine, who was quite uninjured, though he had done prodigies of valour, would tend him with all their hearts. I had better send the carriage and horses at once to bring him back, as the number of wounded was frightful, and means of transport were wanting. Then followed a message of express command from my husband that I was not to think of coming with the carriage. He would not have me at Freiburg on any account.

I submitted; indeed I saw no cause for fear, and even rejoiced that for a long time I should have my husband to myself. I made all ready for him, and taught my little Gaspard now he would say: 'Soyez le bienvenu, mon papa.'

So passed a week. Then one day there was a clanking of spurs on the stairs; I flew to the door and there stood M. d'Aubepine.

'Is he near?' I cried, and then I saw he was white and trembling.

'Ah! no,' he cried; 'he is at Brisach! We could bring him no farther. Can you come with me, Madame? He asked incessantly for you, and it might—it might be that your coming may revive him.'

And then this wild headstrong youth actually sank into a chair, hid his face on the table, and sobbed as if his heart would break.

I had no time for weeping then. I sent for the first physician in Nancy, and offered him any sum in the world to accompany me; I had to make almost wild efforts to procure a horse, and at last had to force one from the governor by my importunities. I collected wine and cordials, and whatever could be of service, and after his first outburst my young brother-in-law helped me in a way I can never forget. No doubt the pestiferous air caused by the horrible carnage of Freiburg had poisoned the wound. As soon as possible my husband was removed; but the mischief had been already done; the wound was in a bad state, fever had set in, and though he struggled on stage after stage, declaring that he should be well when he saw me, the agony had been such on the last day that they barely got him to Brisach, and he there became delirious, so that M. de Solivet decided on remaining with him, while the Count came on to fetch me. He had ridden ever since four o'clock in the morning, and yet was ready to set out again as soon as my preparations were complete. Oh, I can never overlook what he was to me on that journey!

Hope kept us up through that dismal country—the path of war, where instead of harvest on the August day we saw down-trodden, half-burned wheat fields, where a few wretched creatures were trying to glean a few ears of wheat. Each village we passed showed only blackened walls, save where at intervals a farmhouse had been repaired to serve as an estafette for couriers from the French army. The desolation of the scene seemed to impress itself on my soul, and destroy the hopes with which I had set forth; but on and on we went, till the walls of Brisach rose before us.

He was in the governor's quarters, and only at the door, I perceived the M. d'Aubepine had much doubted whether we should find him alive. However, that one consolation was mine. He knew me; he smiled again on me; he called me by all his fondest names; he said that now he could rest. For twenty-four hours we really thought that joy was working a cure. Alas! then he grew worse again, and when the pain left him, mortification had set in, and we could only send for a priest to administer the last Sacraments.

I am an old woman now, and what was then the cruelest anguish touches me with pleasure when I think how he called me his guardian angel, and thanked me for having been his shield from temptation, placing his son in my sole charge, and commending his sister and his old uncle to me—his poor little sister whose lot seemed to grieve him so much. He talked to the Count, who wept, tore his hair, and made promises, which he really then intended to execute, and which at least comforted my Philippe.

The good priest who attended him said, he had never seen anything more edifying or beautiful, and that he had never heard the confession of a military man showing a purer heart, more full of holy love, trust, and penitence. There was a great peace upon us all, as his life ebbed away, and even the Count stood silent and awestruck. They took me away at last. I remember nothing but the priest telling me that my husband was in Paradise.

I felt as if it were all a dream, and when presently my brother came and took my hand, I cried out: 'Oh, wake me! Wake me!' And when he burst into tears I asked what he meant.

Looking back now I can see how very kind he was to me, though I made little return, being altogether bewildered by the sudden strangeness of my first grief. Poor M. de Solivet! he must have had a heavy charge for Armand d'Aubepine was altogether frantic with grief, and did nothing to help him, while I could not weep, and sat like a statue, hardly knowing what they said to me. Nay, when the tidings came that my father had been killed in the battle of Marston Moor three weeks before, I was too dull and dead to grieve. Eustace had written to my husband in order that he might prepare me; I opened the letter, and all that I can remember feeling was that I had no one to shield me.

I had but one wish and sense of duty at that moment, namely, to carry home those dear remains to the resting-place of his father in Anjou, where I hope myself to rest. It was of no use to tell me that all places would be alike to my Philippe when we should awake on the Resurrection day. I was past reason, and was possessed with a feeling that I would be sacrilege to leave him among the countless unnamed graves of the wounded who, like him, had struggled as far as Brisach to die. I fancied I should not be able to find him, and, besides, it was an enemy's country! I believe opposition made me talk wildly and terrify my brother; at any rate, he swore to me that the thing should be done, if only I would return to Nancy and to my child. I fancied, most unjustly, that this was meant to deceive me, and get me out of the way while they buried him whom I loved so much, and I refused to stir without the coffin.

How my brother contrived it, I do not know, but the thing was done, and though I was but a cart that carried the coffin to Nancy, I was pacified.

At Nancy he arranged matters more suitably. Here M. d'Aubepine, in floods of tears, took leave of me to return to the army, and M. de Solivet, whose wound disabled him from active service, undertook to escort me and my precious to Anjou.

It was a long tedious journey, and my heart beats with gratitude to him when I think what he undertook for me, and how dreary it must have been for him, while I was too dead and dull to thank him, though I hope my love and confidence evinced my gratitude in after life.

My dearest went first in a hearse drawn by mules, as was also my large carriage, — that which we had so joyously bought together, saying it would be like a kind of tent on our travels. I traveled in it with my child and my women, and M. de Solivet rode with our men-servants. Our pace was too slow for the fatigue to be too much for him, and he always preceded me to every place where we halted to eat, or where we lodged for the night, and had everything ready without a thought or a word being needful from me. He always stood ready to give me his arm to take me to hear mass before we set out each day. The perfect calm, and the quiet moving on, began to do me good. I felt as if the journey had always been going on, and only wished it were endless, for when it was over I should feel my desolation, and have no more to do for my Philippe. But I began to respond to my poor boy's caresses and playfulness a little more; I was not so short and maussade with my women or with my good brother, and I tried to pray at mass. My brother has since told me that he never felt more relieved in his life than once when he made little Gaspard bring me some blue corn-flowers and wheat, which reminded me of my English home, so that I began to weep so profusely, that he carried away the poor frightened child, and left me to Tryphena.

One afternoon at a little village there was a look of festival; the bells were ringing, everybody was hurrying to the church, and when we stopped at the door of the inn my brother came to the carriage-window and said he was afraid that we should not find it easy to proceed at once, for a mission priest was holding a station, and no one seemed able to attend to anything else.

'He is a true saint! he is just about to preach,' said the landlady, who had come out with her gayest apron, her whitest cap, and all her gold chains. 'Ah! the poor lady, it would do her heart good to hear him preach; and by that time the roast would be ready—an admirable piece of venison, sent for the occasion. There he is, the blessed man!'

And as I had just alighted from the carriage, for our mules had made a double stage and could not go farther, I saw coming from the prebytere three or four priests, with the sexton and the serving boys. One of them, a spare thin man, with a little bronze crucifix in his hand, paused as he saw the hearse drawn up, clasped his hands in prayer, and then lifted them in benediction of him who lay within. I saw his face, and there was in it an indescribable heavenly sweetness and pity which made me say to my brother: 'I must go and hear him.'

My brother was so glad to hear me express any wish, that I believe, if I had asked to go and dance on the village green, he would almost have permitted it; and leaving my little one to play in the garden under Tryphena's care, he gave me his arm, and we went into the church, crowded—crowded so that we could hardly find room; but my deep mourning made the good people respectfully make place for us and give us chairs.

Ah! that sermon! I cannot tell you it in detail; I only know that it gave the strongest sense of healing balm to my sore heart, and seemed in a wonderful way to lift me up into the atmosphere where my Philippe was gone, making me feel that what kept me so far—far from him was not death, nor his coffin, but my own thick husk of sin and worldliness. Much more there was, which seems now to have grown into my very soul; and by the time it was over I was weeping tears no longer bitter, and feeling nothing so much as the need to speak to that priest.

M. de Solivet promised that I should, but we had long to wait, for the saintly Abbe de Paul would not postpone the poor to the rich; nor could my grief claim the precedence, for I was not the only broken-hearted young widow in France, nor even in that little village.

I cannot be grateful enough to my brother that he put up with all the inconveniences of sleeping at this little village, that I might carry out what he though a mere woman's enthusiastic fancy: but in truth it was everything to me. After vespers the holy man was able to give me an hour in the church, and verily it was the opening of new life to me. Since my light had been taken from me, all had been utter desolate darkness before me. He put a fresh light before me, which now, after fifty years, I know to have been the dawn of better sunshine than even that which had brightened my youth— and I thank my good God, who has never let me entirely lose sight of it.

Very faint, almost disappointing, it seemed to me then. I came away from my interview feeling as if it had been vain to think there could be any balm for a crushed heart, and yet when I awoke the next morning, and dressed myself to hear mass before resuming my journey, it was with the sense that there I should meet a friend and comforter. And when I looked at my little son, it was not only with dreary passionate pity for the unconscious orphan, but with a growing purpose to bring him up as his father's special charge,—nay, as that from even a greater and nearer than my Philippe.

While, as we journeyed on, I gradually dwelt less on how piteous my arrival would be for myself, and thought more and more of its sadness for the poor old Marquis who had loved his nephew so much, till, instead of merely fearing to reach Nid de Merle, I began to look forward to it, and consider how to comfort the poor old man; for had not my husband begged me to be the staff of his old age, and to fill a daughter's place to him?

CHAPTER VII. — WIDOW AND WIFE

We had avoided Paris, coming through Troyes and Orleans, and thus our sad strange journey lasted a full month. Poor old M. de Nidemerle had, of course, been prepared for our coming, and he came out in his coach to meet us at the cross-roads. My brother saw the mourning liveries approaching, and gave me notice. I descended from my carriage, intending to go to him in his, but he anticipated me; and there, in the middle of the road, the poor old man embraced me, weeping floods of passionate tears of grief. He was a small man, shrunk with age, and I found him clinging to me so like a child that I felt an almost motherly sense of protection and tenderness towards his forlorn old age; but my English shyness was at the moment distressed at the sense of all the servants staring at such a meeting, and I cried out: 'Oh, sir! you should not have come thus.' 'What can I do, but show all honour to the heroic wife of my dear child?' sobbed he; and, indeed, I found afterwards that my persistence in bringing home my dearest to the tombs of his forefathers had won for me boundless gratitude and honour. They took the hearse to the church of the convent at Bellaise, where its precious burthen was to rest. The obsequies, requiem, and funeral mass were to take place the next day, and in the meantime I accompanied the Marquis to the chateau, and we spent the evening and great part of the night in talking of him whom we had both loved so dearly, and in weeping together.

Then came the solemn and mournful day of the funeral. I was taken early to the convent, where, among the nuns behind the grille, I might assist at these last rites.

Thickly veiled, I looked at no one except that I curtsied my thanks to the Abbess before kneeling down by the grating looking into the choir. My grief had always been too deep for tears, and on that day I was blessed in a certain exaltation of thoughts which bore me onward amid the sweet chants to follow my Philippe, my brave, pure-hearted, loving warrior, onto his rest in Paradise, and to think of the worship that he was sharing there.

So I knelt quite still, but by and by I was sensible of a terrible paroxysm of weeping from some one close to me. I could scarcely see more than a black form when I glanced round, but it seemed to me that it was sinking; I put out my arm in support, and I found a head on my shoulder. I knew who it must be—my husband's poor little sister, Madame d'Aubepine, and I held my arm round her with an impulse of affection, as something that was his; but before all was over, I was sure that she was becoming faint, and at last I only moved just in time to receive her in my lap and arms, as she sank down nearly, if not quite, unconscious.

I tore back the heavy veil that was suffocating her, and saw a tiny thin white face, not half so large as my little Gaspard's round rosy one. Numbers of black forms hovered about with water and essences; and one tall figure bent to lift the poor child from me, apologizing with a tone of reproof, and declaring that Madame la Comtesse was ashamed to inconvenience Madame.

'No,' I said; 'one sister could not inconvenience another,' and I felt the feeble hand stealing round my waist, and saw a sort of smile on the thin little lips, which brought back one look of my Philippe's. I threw off my own veil, and raised her in my arms so as to kiss her, and in that embrace I did indeed gain a sister.

I did not heed the scolding and the murmuring; I lifted her; she was very small, and light as a feather; and I was not merely tall, but very strong, so I carried her easily to a chamber, which one of the nuns opened for us, and laid her on the bed. She clung to me, and when some one brought wine, I made her drink it, and prayed that they would leave us to ourselves a little while.

I know now that nothing but the privileges of my position on that day would have prevailed to get that grim and terrible dame de compagnie out of the room. However, we were left alone, and the first thing the poor young thing did when she could speak or move, was to throw herself into my arms and cry:

'Tell me of him!'

'He sent his love. He commended you to me,' I began.

'Did he? Oh, my dear hero! And how is he looking?'

So it was of her husband, not her brother, that she was thinking. I gave me a pang, and yet I could not wonder; and alas, d'Aubepine had not given me any message at all for her. However, I told her what I thought would please her—of his handsome looks, and his favour with the Duke of Enghien, and her great dark eyes began to shine under their tear-swollen lids; but before long, that terrible woman knocked at the door again to say that Madame la Comtesse's carriage was ready, and that M. le Marquis awaited Madame la Vicomtesse.

We arranged our disordered dress, and went down hand-in-hand. The Marquis and the Abbess both embraced the poor little Countess, and I assured her that we would meet again, and be much together.

'Madame la Comtesse will do herself the honour of paying her respects to Madame la Vicomtesse,' said the dame de compagnie with the elder M. d'Aubepine, and had regulated her household of late years.

'I congratulate myself on not belonging to that respectable household,' said my brother.

M. de Nidemerle laughed, and said the good lady had brought with her a fair share of Calvinist severity. In fact, it was reported that her conversion had been stimulated by the hope that she should be endowed with her family property, and bestowed in marriage on the young d'Aubepine, the father of the present youth, and that disappointment in both these expectations had embittered her life. I was filled with pity for my poor little sister-in-law, who evidently was under her yoke; and all the more when, a day or two later, the tow ladies came in great state to pay me a visit of ceremony, and I saw how pale and thin was the little Countess, and how cowed she seemed by the tall and severe duenna.

Little Gaspard was trotting about. The Marquis was delighted with the child, and already loved him passionately; and the little fellow was very good, and could amuse himself without troubling any one.

He took refuge with me from Mademoiselle de Gringrimeau; but as I held him to kiss his aunt, her eyes filled with tears; and when I asked whether her little girl could walk as well as he did, she faltered so that I was startled, fearing that the child might have died and I not have heard of it.

'She is out at nurse,' at last she murmured.

'Children are best at farms,' said Mademoiselle de Gringrimeau; 'Madame la Comtesse Douariere is not to be incommoded.' The old man held out his arms to my little boy, and said something of his being a pleasure instead of an inconvenience; but though the lady answered politely, she looked so severe that my poor child hid his face on my bosom and began to cry, by way of justifying her.

However, when she was gone, both the gentlemen agreed that the little fellow was quite right, and showed his sense, and that if they had been only two years old, they would have cried too.

That was all in my favour when I entreated M. de Nidemerle to let me have a visit from my sister-in-law,—not a mere call of ceremony, but a stay at the chateau long enough for me to get acquainted with her. Not only was she the only sister of my dear Philippe, but the Marquis, her uncle, was her guardian and only near relative, so that he had a right to insist, more especially as the old Countess was imbecile and bedridden.

I think he felt towards me much as he would have done if he had been shut up in a room with Gaspard, ready to give me anything I begged for, provided I would not cry. He was very good to me, and I could not but be sorry for the poor, bereaved, broken old man, and try to be a daughter to him; and thus our relations were very different from what they had been on our journey to Paris together in the coach. At any rate, he promised me that I should be gratified, and the day after my brother left us, he actually went over to Chateau d'Aubepine, and brought off his niece in the carriage with him, presenting her to me in the hall like the spoils of war. She was frightened, formal, and ceremonious all super time, but I thought she was beginning to thaw, and was more afraid of the Marquis than of me. We played at cards all the evening, the Cure being sent for to make up the set, and now and then I caught her great eyes looking at me wistfully; indeed, I was obliged to avoid them lest they should make me weep; for it was almost the look that my Philippe used to cast on me in those early days when we had not begun to know one another.

At last we went up to bed. The rooms were all en suite, and I had given her one opening into mine, telling her we would never shut the door save when she wished it. I saw her gazing earnestly at her brother's portrait and all the precious little objects consecrated to his memory, which I had arranged by my benitier and crucifix, but I did not expect her firs exclamation, when our woman had left us: 'Ah! Madame, how happy you are!'

'I was once!' I sighed.

'Ah! but you ARE happy. You have your child, and your husband loved you.'

'But your husband lives, and your children are well.'

'That may be. I never see them. I have only seen my daughter twice, and my son once, since they were born. They will not let them come to the chateau, and they say there is no road to the farms.'

'We will see to that,' I said, and I made her tell me where they were; but she knew no more of distances than I did, never going anywhere save in the great family coach. Poor child! When I called her Cecile, she burst into tears, and said no one had called her by that name since she had left her friend Amelie in the convent, and as to calling me Marguerite, Mademoiselle de Gringrimeau would be sure to say it was bourgeois and ill-bred to use familiar names, but then we need never let her hear us.

I took the poor little forlorn creature to sleep with me, and then, and in the course of the next day or two, the whole sad state of things came before me.

The little Cecile de Bellaise had been carried to a convent at Angers from the farm that she could just remember. Here she had spent all the happy days of her life. The nuns ere not strict, and they must have been very ignorant, for they had taught her nothing but her prayers, a little reading, some writing, very bad orthography, embroidery, and heraldry; but they were very good-natured, and had a number of pensionnaires who seemed to have all run wild together in the corridors and gardens, and played all sorts of tricks on the nuns. Sometimes Cecile told me some of these, and very unedifying they were, — acting ghosts in the passages, fastening up the cell doors, ringing the bells at unearthly hours, putting brushes or shoes in the beds, and the like practical jokes.

Suddenly, from the midst of these wild sports, while still a mere child under fourteen, Cecile was summoned to be married to Armand d'Aubepine, who was two years older, and was taken at once to Chateau d'Aubepine.

There was no more play for her; she had to sit upright embroidering under the eyes of Madame la Comtesse and of Mademoiselle de Gringrimeau; nor did she ever go out of doors except for a turn on the terrace with the ladies, or a drive in the great coach. Of course they were disappointed in having such a little unformed being on their hands, but they must have forgotten that they had ever been young themselves, when they forced her to conform rigidly to the life that suited them, and which they thought the only decorous thing for a lady of any age.

There was nothing else that was young near her except her husband, and he thought her an ugly little thing, and avoided her as much as possible. He had expected to be freed from his tutor on his marriage, and when he was disappointed, he was extremely displeased, and manifested his wrath by neglect of her. His governor must have been a very different one from my dear husband's beloved abbe, fro I know that if I had been five times as ugly and stupid as I was, my Philippe would have tried to love me, because it was his duty — and have been kind to me, because he could not be unkind to any one. But the Chevalier d'Aubepine had never learnt to care for any one's pleasure but his own; he was angry at, and ashamed of, the wife who had been imposed on him; he chafed and raged at not being permitted to join the army and see the world; and in the meantime he, with the connivance of his governor, from time to time escaped at night to Saumur, and joined in the orgies of the young officers in garrison there.

Nevertheless, through all his neglect, Cecile loved him with a passionate, faithful adoration, surpassing all words, just as I have seen a poor dog follow faithfully a savage master who gives him nothing but blows. She never said a word of complaint to me of him. All I gathered of this was from her simple self-betrayals, or from others, or indeed what I knew of himself; but the whole sustenance of that young heart had been his few civil words at times when he could make her useful to him. I am persuaded, too, that Mademoiselle de Gringrimeau exercised her spite in keeping the two young creatures from any childish or innocent enjoyments that might have drawn them together. If etiquette were the idol of that lady, I am sure that spite flavoured the incense she burned to it.

I think, if I had been in Cecile's position, I should either have gone mad, or have died under the restraint and dreariness; but she lived on in the dull dream of half-comprehended wretchedness, and gave birth to her daughter, but without being in the least cheered, for a peasant woman was in waiting, who carried the child off while she was still too much exhausted to have even kissed it. All she obtained was universal murmuring at the sex of the poor little thing. It seemed the climax of all her crimes, which might be involuntary, but for which she was made to suffer as much as if they had been her fault.

Her husband was more displeased than any one else; above all when he heard the news of Rocroy; and then it was that he devised the scheme of running away, and in discussing it with her became more friendly than ever before. Of course it was dreadful to her that he should go to the war, but the gratification of helping him, keeping his secret, plotting with him, getting a few careless thanks and promises, carried the day, and bore her through the parting. 'He really did embrace me of his own accord,' said the poor young creature; and it was on that embrace that she had ever since lived, in hope that when they should meet again he might find it possible to give her a few shreds of affection.

Of course, when she was found to have been cognizant of his departure, she was in the utmost disgrace. Rage at his evasion brought on the fit of apoplexy which cost the old count his life; and the blame was so laid upon her, not only by Mademoiselle de Gringrimeau, but by Madame and by her confessor, that she almost believed herself a sort of parricide; and she had not yet completed the course of penitential exercises that have been imposed on her.

By the time—more than half a year later—her son was born, the old countess had become too childish to be gratified for more than a moment. Indeed, poor Cecile herself was so ill that she survived only by a wonder, since no one cared whether she lived or died, except her own maid, who watched over her tenderly, and gave her, when she could read it, a letter from her husband upon the joyful news. She wore that letter, such as it was, next her heart, and never told her how my husband had absolutely stood over him while he wrote it.

So she recovered, if it can be called recovery—for her health had been shattered by all this want of the most care and consideration; she was very weak and nervous, and suffered constantly from headache, and her looks were enough to break one's heart. I suppose nothing could have made her beautiful, but she had a strange, worn, blighted, haggard, stunted look, quite dreadful for one not yet eighteen; she was very short, and fearfully thin and pale, but out of the sad little face there looked my Philippe's eyes, and now and then his smile.

After talking till late I fell asleep, and when I woke to dress for morning mass, I found that she had not slept at all, and had a frightful headache. I bade her lie still till I came back, and she seemed hardly able to believe in such luxury. Mademoiselle said nothing but resolution was wanting to shake off a headache.

'Have you found it so?' I asked.

'At any rate, it is better than the doses Mademoiselle gives me,' she said.

'You shall try my remedy this time,' I said; and I set out for the little village church, which stood at the garden-gate, with a fixed determination that this state of things—slow torture and murder, as it seemed to me—should not go on. If one work bequeathed to me by my dear Philippe was to take care of his uncle, another surely was to save and protect his sister.

CHAPTER VIII. — MARGUERITE TO THE RESCUE.

It was in my favour that M. de Nidemerle had conceived a very high opinion of me, far above my deserts. My dear husband's letters had been full of enthusiasm for me. I found them all among the Marquis's papers; and his tenderness and gratitude, together with the circumstances of my return, had invested me with a kind of halo, which made me a sort of heroine in his eyes.

Besides, I did my best to make the old man's life more cheerful. I read him the Gazette that came once a week, I played at cards with him all the evening, and I sometimes even wrote or copied his letters on business; and, when I sat at my embroidery, he liked to come and sit near me, sometimes talking, playing with Gaspard, or dozing. He was passionately fond of Gaspard, and let the child domineer over him in a way that sometimes shocked me.

Thus he was ready to believe what I told him of his niece, and assured me I might keep her with me as long as I wished, if the Countess, her mother-in-law, would consent. The first thing we did together was that I took her to see her children. The boy was at a farm not very far off; he was seven months old, and a fine healthy infant, though not as clean as I could have wished; but then Tryphena and I had been looked on as barbarians, who would certainly be the death of Gaspard, because we washed him all over every evening, and let him use his legs and arms. Cecile was enchanted; she saw an extraordinary resemblance between her son and his father; and hugged the little form like one who had been famished.

Our search for the little Armantine was less prosperous. Cecile could not ride, nor could even walk a quarter of a mile without nearly dying of fatigue; nay, the jolting of the coach as we drove along the road would have been insupportable to her but for her longing to see her little one. We drove till it was impossible to get the coach any farther, and still the farm was only just in sight.

I jumped out and said I would bring the child to her, and I went up between the hedges with two lackeys behind me, till I came to a farmyard, where three or four children, muddy up to the very eyes, were quarrelling and playing with the water of a stagnant pool. I made my way through animals, dogs, and children, to the farm kitchen, where an old grandmother and a beggar sat on two chairs opposite to one another, on each side of the fire, and a young woman was busy over some raw joints of an animal. They stared at me with open mouths, and when I said that Madame la Comtesse d'Aubepine was come to see her child, and was waiting in the carriage, they looked as if such a thing had never been heard of before. The young woman began to cry — the old woman to grumble. I think if they had dared, they would have flown into a passion, and I was really alarmed lest the child might be sick or even dead. I told them impressively who I was, and demanded that they would instantly show me the little one.

The young woman, muttering something, stepped out and brought in her arms the very dirtiest child of the whole group I had left in the gutter, with the whole tribe behind her. My first impulse was to snatch it up and carry it away to its mother, taking it home at once to Nid de Merle; but it squalled and kicked so violently when I held out my arms to it, that it gave me time to think that to carry it thus away without authority might only bring Cecile into trouble with those who had the mastery over her, and that to see it in such a condition could only give her pain. I should not have objected to the mere surface dirt of grubbing in the farmyard (shocking as it may sound to you, Mademoiselle mes Petites Filles). Eustace and I had done such things at Walwyn and been never the worse for it; but this poor little creature had a wretched, unwholesome, neglected air about her that made me miserable, and the making her fit to be seen would evidently be a long business, such as could hardly be undertaken in the midst of the salting of a pig, which was going on.

I therefore promised the woman a crown if she would make the child tidy and bring her to Nid de Merle on the Sunday. Something was muttered about Mademoiselle having said the child was not to be constantly brought to the house to incommonde Madame la Comtesse; but I made her understand that I meant Nid de Merle, and trusted that the hope of the money would be a bait.

Cecile was sorely disappointed when I returned without the child, and conjured me at once to tell her the worst, if it were indeed dead; but she let herself be pacified by the hope of seeing it on Sunday, and indeed she was half dead with fatigue from the roughness of the road.

The child was duly brought by the foster-mother who was in the full costume of a prosperous peasant, with great gold cross and gay apron; but I was not better satisfied about the little on, though she had a cleaner face, cap, and frock. Unused to the sight of black, she would let neither of us touch her, and we could only look at her, when she sat on her nurse's knee with a cake in her hand. I was sure she was unhealthy and uncared for, her complexion and everything about her showed it, and my Gaspard was twice her size. It was well for the peace of the young mother that she knew so little what a child ought to be like, and that her worst grief was that the little Armantine would not go to her.

'And oh! they will send her straight into a convent as soon as she is weaned, and I shall never have her with me!' sighed Cecile.

'ON' ON had done many harsh things towards my poor little sister-in-law, and I began now to consider of whom ON now consisted. It seemed to me to be only Mademoiselle de Gringrimeau acting in the name of the doting Countess and the absent husband, and that one resolute effort might emancipate the poor young thing.

I was still considering the matter, and rallying my forces, when a message came from the Chateau l'Aube that Madame la Douariere was dying, and Madame la Comtesse must return instantly. I went with her; I could not let her return alone to Mademoiselle's tender mercies, and the Marquis approved and went with us. In fact, the two chateaux were not two miles apart, through the lanes and woods, though the way by the road was much longer.

The old Countess lingered another day and then expired. Before the funeral ceremonies were over, I had seen how Mademoiselle de Gringrimeau tyrannise over this young sister-in-law, who was still a mere gentle child, and was absolutely cowed by the woman. When I tried to take her home with me, Mademoiselle had the effrontery to say that the Count himself, as well as the late dowager, had given her authority over Madame as dame de compagnie, and that she did not consider it etiquette to visit after so recent a bereavement, thus decidedly hitting at me.

However, I had made up my mind. I entreated my poor weeping Cecile to hold out yet a little longer in hope; and then I returned home to lay the whole situation before the Marquis, and to beg him to assert his authority as uncle, and formally request that she might reside under his protection while her husband was with the army—a demand which could hardly fail to be granted.

I wrote also to M. d'Aubepine, over whom I thought I had some influence, and added likewise a letter to my half-brother De Solivet, explaining the situation, and entreating him to get the young gentleman into his lodgings, and not let him out till he had written his letters, signed and sealed them!

The plan answered. In due time our courier returned, and with all we wanted in the way of letters, with one great exception, alas! any true sign of tenderness for the young wife. There was a formal letter for her, telling her to put herself and her children under the charge of her uncle and her brother's widow, leaving the charge of the chateau and the servants to the intendant and to Mademoiselle de Gringrimeau. The poor child had to imbibe what her yearning heart could extract from the conventional opening and close. I have my share of the budget still, and her it is:—

'MADAME—You still love to play your part of beneficent angel, and wish to take on your shoulder my impedimenta. Well, be it so then; though I have no hope that you will make thereof (en) anything like yourself. Kissing your hands.

'LE COMTE D'AUBEPINE.'

His whole family was thus disposed of in two letters of the alphabet (en).

M. de Nidemerle received a polite request to undertake the charge of his niece, and Mademoiselle had likewise her orders, and I heard from my brother how he had smiled at my commands, but had found them necessary, for Armand d'Aubepine had been exactly like a naughty boy forced to do a task. Not that he had the smallest objection to his wife and children being with me—in fact, he rather preferred it; he only hated being troubled about the matter, wanted to go to a match at tennis, and thought it good taste to imitate the Duke of Enghien in contempt for the whole subject. Would he ever improve? My brother did not give much present hope of it, saying that on returning to winter quarters he had found the lad plunged all the deeper in dissipation for want of the check that my dear husband had been able to impose on him; but neither M. de Solivet nor the Marquis took it seriously, thinking it only what every youth in the army went through, unless he were such a wonderful exception as my dear Philippe had been.

Cecile could hardly believe that such peace and comfort were in store for her, and her tyrant looked as gloomy as Erebus at losing her slave, but we did not care for that; we brought her home in triumph, and a fortnight's notice was given to the foster-mother in which to wean Mademoiselle d'Aubepine and bring her to Nid de Merle.

That fortnight was spent by our guest in bed. As if to justify Mademoiselle de Gringrimeau, she was no sooner under my care than she had a sharp illness; but Tryphena, who had been so instructed by my grandmother, Lady Walwyn, as to be more skilful than any doctor, declared that it was in consequence of the long disregard of health and strain of spirits, and so managed her that, though never strong, she improved much in health, and therewith in looks. Beautiful she could hardly be, as the world counts beauty, but to me her sweet, tender, wistful expression made her countenance most lovable, and so did her gentle unmurmuring humility. She sincerely believed that all the cruel slights she underwent were the result of her own ugliness, stupidity, and ignorance, and instead of blaming her husband, she merely pitied him for being tied to her. As to grating that her brother had been a better man than her husband, she would have thought that high treason—the difference was only that her dear Marguerite was so pretty, so clever, amiable, and well taught, that she had won his heart.

In truth, I had outgrown the ungainliness of my girlhood, and, now that it did not matter to any one, had become rather a handsome woman, and it was of no use to tell her that I had been worse than she, because there was so much more of me, when my dear young husband gave me the whole of his honest heart.

To make herself, at least, less dull was her next desire. One reason why she had so seldom written was that she knew she could not spell, and Mademoiselle insisted on looking over her letters that they might not be a disgrace. I doubted whether M. le Comte would have discovered the errors, but when the Marquis praised some letters that I had written to amuse him from Nancy and Mezieres, she was fired with ambition to write such clever letters as might bewitch her husband. Besides, if she could teach her daughter, the child need not be banished to a convent.

I began to give her a few lessons in the morning, and to read to her. And just then there came to Nid de Merle, to see me, the good Abbe Bonchamp, the excellent tutor to whom my dear Philippe always said he owed so much. The good man had since had another employment, and on quitting it, could not help gratifying his desire to me and see the wife and child of his dear pupil, as indeed I had begged him to do, if ever it were in his power, when I fulfilled my husband's wishes by writing his last greeting and final thanks to the good man.

I remember the dear quaint form riding up on a little hired mule, which he almost concealed with his cassock. Above, his big hat looked so strange that Gaspard, who was wonderfully forward for his age, ran up to me crying: 'A droll beast, mamma! it had four legs and a great hat!' while little Armantine fled crying from the monster.

All the servants were, however, coming out eagerly to receive the blessing of the good man, who had mad himself much beloved in the household. The Marquis embraced him with tears, and presented him to me, when he fell on his knee, took my hand, pressed it to his lips and bathed it with his tears, and then held Gaspard to his breast with fervent love.

It was necessary to be cheerful before M. de Nidemerle. He had truly loved his nephew, and mourned for him, but the aged do not like a recurrence to sorrow, so the abbe amused him with the news brought from Saumur, and our party at cards was a complete one that evening.

But the next day, the Abbe, who had loved his pupil like a son, could talk of him to me, and it was a comfort I cannot express to my aching heart to converse with him. Everything had settled into an ordinary course. People fancied me consoled; I had attended to other things, and I could not obtrude my grief on the Marquis or on Cecile; but on! My sick yearning for my Philippe only grew the more because I might not mention him or hear his name. However, the Abbe only longed to listen to all I could tell him of the last three years, and in return to tell me much that I should never otherwise have known of the boyhood and youth of my dear one.

I felt as if the good man must never leave us, and I entreated M. de Nidemerle to retain him at once as governor to little Gaspard. The Marquis laughed at securing a tutor for a child not yet three years old; but he allowed that the boy could not be in better hands, and, moreover, he was used to the Abbe, and liked to take his arm and to have him to make up the party at cards, which he played better than the cure.

So the Abbe remained as chaplain and as tutor, and, until Gaspard should be old enough to profit by his instructions, Cecile and I entreated him to accept us as pupils. I had begun to feel the need of some hard and engrossing work to take off my thoughts alike from my great sorrow and my pressing anxieties about my English home, so that I wished to return to my Latin studies again, and the Abbe helped me to read Cicero de Officiis again, and likewise some of the writings of St. Gregory the Great. He also read to both of us the Gospels and Mezeray's HISTORY OF FRANCE, which I did not know as an adopted Frenchwoman ought to know it, and Cecile knew not at all; nay, the nuns had scarcely taught her anything, even about religion, nor the foundations of the faith.

No, I can never explain what we, both of us, owe to the Abbe Bonchamp. You, my eldest grandchild, can just recollect the good old man as he sat in his chair and blessed us ere he passed to his rest and the reward of his labours.

CHAPTER IX. — THE FIREBRAND
OF THE BOCAGE.

Yes, the life at Nid de Merle was very peaceful. Just as exquisitely happy it was in spite of alarms, anxieties, perplexities, and discomforts, so when I contemplate my three years in Anjou I see that they were full of peace, though the sunshine of my life was over and Cecile had never come.

We had our children about us, for we took little Maurice d'Aubepine home as soon as possible; we followed the course of devotion and study traced for us by the Abbe; we attended to the wants of the poor, and taught their children the Catechism; we worked and lived like sisters, and I thought all that was life to me was over. I forgot that at twenty-two there is much life yet to come, and that one may go through many a vicissitude of feeling even though one's heart be in a grave.

The old Marquis did not long remain with us. He caught a severe cold in the winter, and had no strength to rally. Tryphena would have it that he sank from taking nothing but tisanes made of herbs; and that if she might only have given him a good hot sack posset, he would have recovered; but he shuddered at the thought, and when a doctor came from Saumur, he bled the poor old gentleman, faintings came on, and he died the next day. I was glad Tryphena's opinion was only expressed in English.

The poor old man had been very kind to me, and had made me love him better than I should have supposed to be possible when we crossed from Dover. The very last thing he had done was to write to my mother, placing his hotel at Paris at her disposal in case she and her son should find it expedient to leave England; and when his will was opened it proved that he had left me personal guardian and manager of the estates of his heir, my little Gaspard, now M. de Nidemerle, joining no one with me in the charge but my half-brother the Baron de Solivet.

I had helped him, read letters to him, and written them for him, and overlooked his accounts enough for the work not to be altogether new and strange to me, and I took it up eagerly. I had never forgotten the sermon by the holy Father Vincent, whom the Church has since acknowledged as a saint, and our excellent Abbe had heightened the impression that a good work lay prepared for me; but he warned me to be prudent, and I am afraid I was hot-headed and eager.

Much had grieved me in the six months I had spent in the country, in the state of the peasantry. I believe that in the Bocage they are better off than in many parts of France, but even there they seemed to me much oppressed and weighed down. Their huts were wretched—they had no chimneys, no glass in the windows, no garden, not even anything comfortable for the old to sit in; and when I wanted to give a poor rheumatic old man a warm cushion, I found it was carefully hidden away lest M. l'Intendant should suppose the family too well off.

Those seigniorial rights then seemed to me terrible. The poor people stood in continual fear either of the intendant of the king or of the Marquis, or of the collector of the dues of the Church. At harvest time, a bough was seen sticking in half the sheaves. In every ten, one sheaf is marked for the tithe, tow for the seigneur, two for the king; and the officer of each takes the best, so that only the worst are left for the peasant.

Nay, the only wonder seemed to me that there were any to be had at all, for our intendant thought it his duty to call off the men from their own fields for the days due from them whenever he wanted anything to be done to our land (or his own, or his son's-in-law), without the slightest regard to the damage their crops suffered from neglect.

I was sure these things ought not to be. I thought infinitely more good might be done by helping the peasants to make the most of what they had, and by preventing them from being robbed in my son's name, than by dealing out gallons of soup and piles of bread at the castle gates to relieve the misery we had brought on them, or by dressing the horrible sores that were caused by dirt and bad food. I told the Abbe, and he said it was a noble inspiration in itself, but that he feared that one lady, and she a foreigner, could not change the customs of centuries, and that innovations were dangerous. I also tried to fire with the same zeal for reformation the Abbess of Bellaise, who was a young and spirited woman, open to conviction; but she was cloistered, and could not go to investigate matters as I did, with the Abbe for my escort, and often with my son. He was enchanted to present any little gift, and it was delightful that the peasants should learn to connect all benefits with Monsieur le Marquis, as they already called the little fellow.

I think they loved me the better when they found that I was the grandchild of the Madame Eustace who had been hidden in their cottages. I found two or three old people who still remembered her wanderings when she kept the cows and knitted like a peasant girl among them. I was even shown the ruinous chamber where my aunt Thistlewood was born, and the people were enchanted to hear how much the dear old lady had told me of them, and of their ways, and their kindness to her.

I encouraged the people to make their cottages clean and not to be afraid of comforts, promising that our intendant at least should not interfere with them. I likewise let him know that I would not have men forced to leave their fields when it would ruin their crops, and that it was better that ours should suffer than theirs. He was obsequious in manner and then disobeyed me, till one day I sent three labourers back again to secure their own hay before they touched ours. And when the harvest was gathered in the Abbe and I went round the fields of the poor, and I pointed out the sheaves that might be marked, and they were not the best.

I taught the girls to knit as they watched their cows, and promised to buy some of their stockings, so that they might obtain sabots for themselves with the price. They distrusted me at first, but before long, they began to perceive that I was their friend, and I began to experience a nice kind of happiness.

Alas! even this was too sweet to last, or perhaps, as the good Abbe warned me, I was pleasing myself too much with success, and with going my own way. The first murmur of the storm came thus: I had been out all the afternoon with the Abbe, Armantine's bonne, and the two children, looking at the vineyards, which always interested me much because we have none like them in England. In one, where they were already treading the grapes, the good woman begged that M. le Marquis and Mademoiselle would for once tread the grapes to bring good luck. They were frantic with joy; we took off their little shoes and silk stockings, rolled them up in thick cloths, and let them get into the trough and dance on the grapes with their little white feet. That wine was always called 'the Vintage of le Marquis.' We could hardly get them away, they were so joyous, and each carried a great bunch of grapes as a present to the little boy at home and his mother.

We thought we saw a coachman's head and the top of a carriage passing through the lanes, and when we came home I was surprised to find my sister-in-law in tears, thoroughly shaken and agitated.

Mademoiselle de Gringrimeau had been to see her, she said, and had told her the Count was in Paris, but had not sent for her; and I thought that enough to account for her state; but when the children began to tell their eager story, and hold up their grapes to her, she burst again into tears, and cried: 'Oh, my dear sister, if you would be warned. It is making a scandal, indeed it is! They call you a plebeian.'

I grew hot and angry, and demanded what could be making a scandal, and what business Mademoiselle de Gringrimeau had to meddle with me or my affairs.

'Ah! but she will write to my husband, and he will take me from you, and that would be dreadful. Give it up. Oh, Marguerite, give it up for MY sake!'

What was I to give up? I demanded. Running about the country, it appeared, like a farmer's wife rather than a lady of quality, and stirring up the poor against their lords. It was well known that all the English were seditious. See what they had done to their king; and here was I, beginning the same work. Had not the Count's intendant at Chateau d'Aubepine thrown in his teeth what Madame de Bellaise did and permitted? He was going to write to Monseigneur, ay, and the king's own intendant would hear of it, so I had better take care, and Mademoiselle had come out of pure benevolence to advise Madame la Comtesse to come and take refuse at her husband's own castle before the thunderbolt should fall upon me, and involve her in my ruin.

I laughed. I was sure that I was neither doing nor intending any harm; I thought the whole a mere ebullition of spite on the duenna's part to torment and frighten her emancipated victim, and I treated all as a joke to reassure Cecile, and even laughed at the Abbe for treating the matter more seriously, and saying it was always perilous to go out of a beaten track.

'I thought the beaten track and wide road were the dangerous ones,' I said, with more lightness, perhaps, than suited the subject.

'Ah, Madame,' he returned gravely, 'you have there the truth; but there may be danger in this world in the narrow path.'

The most effectual consolation that I could invent for Cecile was that if her husband thought me bad company for her, he could not but fetch her to her proper home with him, as soon as peace was made. Did I really think so? The little thing grew radiant with the hope.

Days went on, we heard nothing, and I was persuaded that the whole had been, as I told Cecile, a mere figment of Mademoiselle de Gringrimeau's.

I had written to beg my mother, with my brother and sister, to come and join us, and I as already beginning to arrange a suite of rooms for them, my heart bounding as it only can do at the thought of meeting those nearest and dearest of one's own blood.

I remember that I was busy giving orders that the linen should be aired, and overlooking the store of sheets, when Gaspard and Armantine from the window called out: 'Horses, horses, mamma! fine cavaliers!'

I rushed to the window and recognized the Solivet colours. No doubt the baron had come to announce the arrival of my mother and the rest, and I hastened down to meet him at the door, full of delight, with my son holding my hand.

My first exclamation after the greeting was to ask where they were, and how soon they would arrive, and I was terribly disappointed when I found that he had come alone, and that my mother, with Eustace and Annora, were at the Hotel de Nidemerle, at Paris, without any intention of leaving it. He himself had come down on business, as indeed was only natural since he was joined with me in the guardianship of my little Marquis, and he would likewise be in time to enjoy the chase over the estates.

He said no more of his purpose then, so I was not alarmed; and he seemed much struck with the growth and improvement of Gaspard. I had much to hear of the three who were left to me of my own family. M. de Solivet had never seen them before, and could hardly remember his mother, so he could not compare them with what they were before their troubles; but I gathered that my mother was well in health, and little the worse for her troubles, and that my little Nan was as tall as myself, a true White Ribaumont, with an exquisite complexion, who would be all the rage if she were not so extremely English, more English even than I had been when I had arrived.

'And my brother, my Eustace. Oh, why did he not come with you?' I asked.

And M. de Solivet gravely answered that our brother was detained by a suit with the Poligny family respecting the estate of Ribaumont, and, besides, that the rapidity of the journey would not have agreed with his state of health. I only then fully understood the matter, for our letter had been few, and had to be carefully written and made short; and though I knew that, at the battle of Naseby, Eustace had been wounded and made prisoner, he had written to me that his hurt was not severe, and that he had been kindly treated, through the intervention of our cousin Harry Merrycourt, who, to our great regret, was among the rebels, but who had become surety for Eustace and procured his release.

I now heard that my brother had been kept with the other prisoners in a miserable damp barn, letting in the weather on al sides, and with no bedding or other comforts, so that when Harry Merrycourt sought him out, he had taken a violent chill, and had nearly died, not from the wound, but from pleurisy. He had never entirely recovered, though my mother thought him much stronger and better since he had been in France, out of sight of all that was so sad and grievous to a loyal cavalier in England.

'They must come to me,' I cried. 'He will soon be well in this beautiful air; I will feed him with goat's mild and whey, and Tryphena shall nurse him well.'

M. de Solivet made no answer to this, but told me how delighted the Queen of England had to welcome my mother, whom she had at once appointed as one of her ladies of the bedchamber; and then we spoke of King Charles, who was at Hampton Court, trying to make terms with the Parliament, and my brother spoke with regret and alarm of the like spirit of resistance in our own Parliament of Paris, backed by the mob. I remember it was on that evening that I first heard the name Frondeurs, or Slingers, applied to the speechifiers on either side who started forward, made their hit, and retreated, like the little street boys with their slings. I was to hear a great deal more of that name.

It was not till after supper that I heard the cause of M. de Solivet's visit. Cecile, who always retired early, went away sooner than usual to leave us together, so did the Abbe, and then the baron turned to me and said: 'Sister, how soon can you be prepared to come with me to Paris?'

I was astounded, thinking at first that Eustace's illness must be more serious than he had led me to suppose, but he smiled and said notre frere de Volvent, which was the nearest he could get to Walwyn, had nothing do with it; it was by express command of the Queen Regent, and that I might thank my mother and the Queen of England that it was no worse. 'This is better than a letter de catche,' he added, producing a magnificent looking envelope with a huge seal of the royal French arms, that made me laugh rather nervously to brave my dismay, and asked what he called THAT. He responded gravely that it was no laughing matter, and I opened it. It was an official order that Gaspard Philippe Beranger de Bellaise, Marquis de Nidemerle, should be brought to the Louvre to be presented to the King.

'Well,' I said, 'I must go to Paris. Ought I to have brought my boy before? I did not know that he ought to pay his homage till he was older. Was it really such a breach of respect?'

'You are a child yourself, my sister,' he said, much injuring my dignity. 'What have you not been doing here?'

Then it came on me. The intendant of the King had actually written complaints of me to the Government. I was sewing disaffection among the peasants by the favours I granted my own, teaching them for rebellion like that which raged in England, and bringing up my son in the same sentiments. Nay, I was called the Firebrand of the Bocage! If these had been the days of the great Cardinal de Richelieu, my brother assured me, I should probably have been by this time in the Bastille, and my son would have been taken from me for ever!'

However, my half-brother heard of it in time, and my mother had flown to Queen Henrietta, who took her to the Queen-Regent, and together they had made such representations of my youth, folly, and inexperience that the Queen-Mother, who had a fellow-feeling for a young widow and her son, and at last consented to do nothing worse than summon me and my child to Paris, where my mother and her Queen answered for me that I should live quietly, and give no more umbrage to the authorities; and my brother De Solivet had been sent off to fetch me!

I am afraid I was much more angry than grateful, and I said such hot things about tyranny, cruelty, and oppression that Solivet looked about in alarm, lest walls should have ears, and told me he feared he had done wrong in answering for me. He was really a good man, but he could not in the least understand why I should weep hot tears for my poor people whom I was just hoping to benefit. He could not enter into feeling for Jacques Bonhomme so much as for his horse or his dog; and I might have argued for years without making him see anything but childish folly in my wishing for any mode of relief better than doles of soup, dressing wounds, and dowries for maidens.

However, there was no choice; I was helpless, and resistance would have done my people no good, but rather harm, and would only have led to my son being separated from me. Indeed, I cherished a hope that when the good Queen Anne heard the facts she might understand better than my half-brother did, and that I might become an example and public benefactor. My brother must have smiled at me in secret, but he did not contradict me.

My poor mother and the rest would not have been flattered by my reluctance to come to Paris; but in truth the thought of them was my drop of comfort, and if Eustace could not come to me I must have gone to him. And Cecile—what was to become of Cecile?

To come with me of course. Here at least Solivet agreed with me, for he had as great a horror of Mademoiselle de Gringrimeau as I had, and knew, moreover, that she wrote spiteful letters to the Count d'Aubepine about his poor little wife, which happily were treated with the young gentleman's usual insouciance. Solivet was of my opinion that the old demoiselle had instigated this attack. He thought so all the more when he heard that she was actually condescending to wed the intendant of Chateau d'Aubepine. But he said he had no doubt that my proceedings would have been stopped sooner or later, and that it was well that it should be done before I committed myself unpardonably.

Madame d'Aubepine had been placed in my charge by her husband, so that I was justified in taking her with me. Her husband had spent the last winter at Paris, but was now with the army in the Low Countries, and the compliments Solivet paid me on my dear friend's improvement in appearance and manner inspired us with strong hopes that she might not attract her husband; for though still small, pale, and timid, she was very unlike the frightened sickly child he had left.

I believe she was the one truly happy person when we left the Chateau de Nid de Merle. She was all radiant with hope and joy, and my brother could not but confess she was almost beautiful, and a creature whom any man with a heart must love.

CHAPTER X. — OLD THREADS TAKEN UP.

I think M. de Solivet realised a little better what the sacrifice was to me, or rather how cruel the parting was to my poor people, when we set forth on our journey. We had tried to keep the time of our departure a secret, but it had not been possible to do so, and the whole court was filled with people weeping and crying out to their young lord and their good lady, as they called me, not to abandon them, kissing our dresses as we walked along, and crowding so that we could hardly pass.

Indeed, a lame man, whom I had taught to make mats, threw himself before the horses of our carriage, crying out that we might as well drive over him and kill him at once; and an old woman stood up almost like a witch or prophetess, crying out: 'Ah! that is the way with you all. You are like all the rest! You gave us hope once, and now you are gone to your pleasure which you squeeze out of our heart's blood.'

'Ah, good mother,' I said; 'believe me, it is not by my own will that I leave you; I will never forget you.'

'I trust,' muttered Solivet, 'that no one is here to report all this to that intendant de Roi,' and he hurried me into the carriage; but there were tears running down his cheeks, and I believe he emptied his purse among them, though not without being told by some of the poor warm-hearted creatures that no money could repay them for the loss of Madame la Comtesse.

'I did not know how sweet it is to be beloved,' he said to me. 'It is almost enough to tempt one to play the role de bon seigneur.'

'Ah! brother, if you would. You are no foreigner, you are wiser and would not make yourself suspected like me.'

He only laughed and shrugged his shoulders; but he was as good to our poor as it is possible to be as we live here in France, where we are often absolutely complelled to live at court, and our expenses there force us to press heavily on our already hard-driven peasants. I sometimes wonder whether a better time will come, when out good Duke of Burgundy tries to carry out the maxims of Monseigneur the Archbishop of Cambray; but I shall not live to see that day. [Footnote: No wonder Madame de Bellaise's descendants dust not publish these writings while the ancien regime continued!]

In due time we arrived in Paris. It was pouring with rain, so no one came to meet us, though I looked out at every turn, feeling that Eustace must indeed be unwell, or no weather would have kept him from flying to meet his Meg. Or had he in these six long years ceased to care for me, and should I find him a politician and a soldier, with his heart given to somebody else and no room for me?

My heart beat so fast that I could hardly attend to the cries of wonder and questions of the two children, and indeed of Cecile, to whom everything was as new and wonderful as to them, though in the wet, with our windows splashed all over, the first view of Paris was not too promising. However, at last we drove beneath our own porte cochere, and upon the steps there were all the servants. And Eustace, my own dear brother, was at the coach-door to meet us and hand me out.

I passed from his arms to those of my mother, and then to my sister's. Whatever might come and go, I could not but feel that there was an indefinable bliss and bien-etre in their very presence! It was home—coming home—more true content and rest than I had felt since that fatal day at Nancy.

My mother was enchanted with her grandson, and knew how to welcome Madame d'Aubepine as one of the family, since she was of course to reside with us. The Abbe also was most welcome to my mother.

How we all looked at one another, to find the old beings we had loved, and to learn the new ones we had become! My mother was of course the least altered; indeed, to my surprise, she was more embonpoint than before, instead of having the haggard worn air that I had expected, and though she wept at first, she was soon again smiling.

Eustace, Baron Walwyn and Ribaumont, as he now unfortunately had become, sat by me. He was much taller than when we had parted, for had not then reached his full height, and he looked the taller from being very thin. His moustache and pointed beard had likewise changed him, but there was clear bright colour on his cheek, and his dear brown eyes shone upon me with their old sweetness; so that it was not till we had been together some little time that I found that the gay merry lad whom I had left had become not only a man, but a very grave and thoughtful man.

Annora was a fine creature, well grown, and with the clearest, freshest complexion, of the most perfect health, yet so pure and delicate, that one looked at her like a beautiful flower; but it somehow struck me that she had a discontented and almost defiant expression. She seemed to look at me with a sort of distrust, and to be with difficulty polite to Madame d'Aubepine, while she was almost rude to the Abbe. She scarcely uttered a word of French, and made a little cry and gesture of disgust, when Gaspard replied to her in his native tongue, poor child.

She was the chief disappointment to me. I had expected to find, not indeed my little playfellow, but my own loving sister Nan; and this young lady was like a stranger. I thought, too, my mother would have been less lively, she seemed to me to have forgotten everything in the satisfaction of being at Paris. At first I feared she was looking at me with displeasure, but presently I observed that she had discarded her widow's veil, and looked annoyed that I still wore mine. Otherwise she was agreeable surprised in me, and turned to M. de Solivet, saying:

'Yes, my son, you are right, she is belle, assez belle; and when she is dressed and has no more that provincial air, she will do very well.'

It was Eustace, my brother, who gave me unmixed delight that evening, unmixed save for his look of delicate health, for that he should be graver was only suitable to my feelings, and we knew that we were in perfect sympathy with one another whenever our eyes met, as of old, while we had hardly exchanged a word. And then, how gracious and gentle he was with poor little Madame d'Aubepine, who looked up to him like a little violet at the food of a poplar tree!

Supper passed in inquires after kinsfolk and old friends. Alas! of how many the answer was—slain, missing since such a battle. In prison, ruined, and brought to poverty, seemed to be the best I could hear of any one I inquired after. That Walwyn was not yet utterly lost seemed to be owing to Harry Merrycourt.

'He on the wrong side!' I exclaimed.

'He looks on the question as a lawyer,' said my brother; 'holding the duty of the nation to be rather to the law than to the sovereign.'

'Base! Unworthy of a gentleman!' cried my mother. 'Who would believe him the kinsman of the gallant Duc de Mericour?'

'He would be ashamed to count kindred with tat effeminate petit maitre!' cried Annora.

'I think,' said Eustace, 'that the wrong and persecution that his Huguenot grandfather suffered at the hands of his French family have had much power in inspiring him with that which he declares is as much loyalty as what I call by that honoured name.'

'You can speak of him with patience!' cried my mother.

'In common gratitude he is bound to do so,' said Annora.

For not only had Colonel Merrycourt preserved our brother's life after Naseby, but he had found a plea of service to the King which availed at the trial that followed at Westminster. Harry had managed to secure part of the estate, as he had likewise done for our other kindred the Thistlewoods, by getting appointed their guardian when their father was killed Chalgrove. But soldiers had been quartered on both families; there had been a skirmish at Walwyn with Sir Ralph Hopton, much damage had been done to the house and grounds, and there was no means of repairing it; all the plate had been melted up, there was nothing to show for it but a little oval token, with the King's head on one side, and the Queen's on the other; and as to the chaplet of pearls—

There was a moment's silence as I inquired for them. Annora said:

'Gone, of course; more hatefully than all the rest.'

My brother added, with a smile that evidently cost him an effort:

'You are the only pearl of Ribaumont left, Meg, except this one,' showing me his ring of thin silver with one pearl set in it; 'I kept back this one in memory of my grandmother. So Nan will have to go to her first ball without them.'

And had little Nan never been to a ball? No; she had never danced except that Christmas when a troop of cavaliers had been quartered at Walwyn—a merry young captain and his lieutenant, who had sent for the fiddles, and made them have a dance in the hall, Berenger, and Nan, and all. And not a week after, the young captain, ay, and our dear Berry, were lying in their blood at Alresford. Had Nan's heart been left there? I wondered, when I saw how little she brightened at the mention of the Court ball where she was to appear next week, and to which it seemed my mother trusted that I should be invited in token of my being forgiven.

I tried to say that I had never meant to return to the world, and that I still kept to my mourning; but my mother said with authority that I had better be grateful for any token of favour that was vouchsafed to me. She took me into her apartment after supper, and talked to me very seriously; telling me that I must be very careful, for that I had been so imprudent, that I should certainly have been deprived of the custody of my son, if not imprisoned, unless my good godmother, Queen Henrietta, and herself had made themselves responsible for me.

I told my mother that I had done nothing, absolutely nothing, but attend to the wants of my son's people, just as I had been used to see my grandmother, and my aunt Thistlewood, or any English lady, do at home.

'And to what had that brought England?' cried my mother. 'No, child, those creatures have no gratitude nor proper feeling. There is nothing to do but to keep them down. See how they are hampering and impeding the Queen and the Cardinal here, refusing the registry of the taxes forsooth, as if it were not honour enough to maintain the King's wars and the splendour of his Court, and enable the nobility to shine!'

'Surely it is our duty to do something for them in return,' I said; but I was silenced with assurances that if I wished to preserve the wardship of my child, I must conform in everything; nay, that my own liberty was in danger.

Solivet had hinted as much, and the protection of my child was a powerful engine; but — shall I confess it? — it galled and chafed me terribly to feel myself taken once more into leading-strings. I, who had for three years governed my house as a happy honoured wife, and for three more had been a chatelaine, complimented by the old uncle, and after his death, the sole ruler of my son's domain; I was not at all inclined to return into tutelage, and I could not look on my mother after these six years, as quite the same conclusive authority as I thought her when I left her. The spirit of self-assertion and self-justification was strong within me, and though I hope I did not reply with ingratitude or disrespect, I would make no absolute promise till I had heard what my brother Walwyn said of my position in its secular aspect, and the Abbe Bonchamps in its religious point of view. So I bade my mother good-night, and went to see how Cecile fared in her new quarters, which, to her grief, were in a wing separated from mine by a long corridor.

My mother had arranged everything, ruling naturally as if she were the mistress of the house. Thus she installed me in the great room where I had seen the old Marquis, though I would rather she had retained it, and given me that which I had occupied when I was there with my husband. However, I made no objection, for I felt so much vexed that I was extremely afraid of saying something to show that I thought she ought to remember that this was my house, and that she was my guest. I would not for the world have uttered anything so ungenerous and unfilial; and all I could do that night was to pray that she might not drive me to lose my self-command, and that I might both do right and keep my child.

I was too restless and unhappy to sleep much, for I knew my feelings were wrong, and yet I was sure I was in the right in my wish to do good to the poor; and the sense of being bridled, and put into leading-strings, poisoned the pleasure I had at first felt in my return to my own family. I cannot describe the weary tumult of thought and doubt that tossed me, till, after a brief sleep, I heard the church-bells. I rose and dressed for early mass, taking my boy, who always awoke betimes, leaving the house quietly, and only calling my trusty lackey Nicolas to take me to the nearest Church, which was not many steps off. I do not think I found peace there: there was too much SELF in me to reach that as yet; but at any rate I found the resolution to try to bend my will in what might be indifferent, and to own it to be wholesome for me to learn submission once more.

As I was about to enter our court, I heard a little cough, and looking round I saw a gentleman and lady coming towards the house. They were my brother and sister, who had been to the daily prayers at the house of Sir Richard Browne, the English ambassador. I was struck at my first glance with the lightsome free look of Annora's face but it clouded ad grew constrained in an instant when I spoke to her.

They said my mother would not be awake nor admit us for an hour or two, and in the meantime Eustace was ready to come to my apartments, for indeed we had hardly seen one another. Annora anxiously reminded him that he must take his chocolate, and orders were given that this should be served in my cabinet for us both.

There is no describing what that interview was to us. We, who had been one throughout our childhood, but had been parted all through the change to man and woman, now found ourselves united again, understanding one another as no other being could do, and almost without words, entering into full sympathy with one another. Yes, without words, for I was as certain as if he had told me that Eustace had undergone some sorrow deeper than even loss of health, home, and country. I felt it in the chastened and sobered tone in which he talked to me of my cares, as if he likewise had crossed the stream of tears that divides us from the sunshine of our lives.

He did not think what I had attempted in Anjou foolish and chimerical—he could look at the matter with the eyes of an English lord of the manor, accustomed not to view the peasant as a sponge to be squeezed for the benefit of the master, but to regard the landlord as accountable for the welfare, bodily and spiritual, of his people. He thought I had done right, though it might be ignorantly and imprudently in the present state of things; but his heart had likewise burned within him at the oppression of the peasantry, and, loyal cavalier as he was, he declared that he should have doubted on which side to draw his sword had things thus in England. He had striven to make my mother and Queen Henrietta understand the meaning of what I had been doing, and he said the complaints sent up had evidently been much exaggerated, and envenomed by spite and distrust of me as a foreigner. He could well enter into my grief at the desertion of my poor people, for how was it with those at Walwyn, deprived of the family to whom they had been used to look, with many widows and orphans made by the war, and the Church invaded by a loud-voiced empty-headed fanatic, who had swept away all that had been carefully preserved and honoured! Should he ever see the old home more?

However, he took thought for my predicament. I had no choice, he said, but to give way. To resist would only make me be treated as a suspected person, and be relegated to a convent, out of reach of influencing my son, whom I might bring up to be a real power for good.

Then my dear brother smiled his sweetest smile, the sweeter for the sadness that had come into it, and kissed my fingers chivalrously, as he said that after all he could not but be grateful to the edict that had brought back to him the greatest delight that was left to him. 'Ah,' I said, 'if it had only been in Anjou!'

'If it had only been in Dorset, let us say at once,' he answered.

Then came the other question whether I might not stay at home with the children, and give myself to devotion and good works, instead of throwing off my mourning and following my mother to all the gaieties of the court.

'My poor mother!' said Eustace. 'You would not wish to make your example a standing condemnation of her?'

'I cannot understand how she can find pleasure in these things,' I cried.

'There is much in her that we find it hard to understand,' Eustace said; 'but you must remember that this is her own country, and that though she gave it up for my father's sake, England has always been a land of exile to her, and we cannot wonder at her being glad to return to the society of her old friends.'

'She has Annora to be with her. Is not that enough?'

'Ah, Meg, I trusted to you to soothe poor Annora and make her more comfortable.'

'She seems to have no intention of putting herself under my influence,' I said, rather hurt.

'She soon will, when she finds out your English heart,' said Eustace. 'The poor child is a most unwilling exile, and is acting like our old friends the urchins, opposing the prickles to all. But if my mother has Annora to watch over, you also have a charge. A boy of this little man's rank,' he said, stroking the glossy curls of Gaspard, who was leaning on my lap, staring up in wonder at the unknown tongue spoken by his uncle, 'and so near the age of the king, will certainly be summoned to attend at court, and if you shut yourself up, you will be unable to follow him and guide him by your counsel.'

That was the chief of what my dear brother said to me on that morning. I wrote it down at the moment because, though I trusted his wisdom and goodness with all my heart, I thought his being a Protestant might bias his view in some degree, and I wanted to know whether the Abbe thought me bound by my plans of devotion, which happily had not been vows.

And he fully thought my brother in the right, and that it was my duty to remain in the world, so long as my son needed me there; while, as to any galling from coming under authority again, that was probably exactly what my character wanted, and it would lessen the danger of dissipation. Perhaps I might have been in more real danger in queening it at Nid de Merle than in submitting at Paris.

CHAPTER XI. — THE TWO QUEENS.

After all, I was put to shame by finding that I had done my poor mother an injustice in supposing that she intended to assume the government of the house, for no sooner was I admitted to her room than she gave me up the keys, and indeed I believe she was not sorry to resign them, for she had not loved housewifery in her prosperous days, and there had been a hard struggle with absolute poverty during the last years in England.

She was delighted likewise that I was quite ready to accompany her to thank Queen Henrietta for her intercession, and to take her advice for the future, nor did she object for that day to my mourning costume, as I was to appear in the character of a suppliant. When I caught Annora's almost contemptuous eyes, I was ready to have gone in diamonds and feathers.

However, forth we set, attended by both my brothers. Lord Walwyn indeed held some appointment at the little court, and in due time we were ushered into the room where Queen Henrietta was seated with a pretty little girl playing at her feet with a dog, and a youth of about seventeen leaning over the elbow of her couch telling her something with great animation, while a few ladies were at work, with gentlemen scattered among them. How sociable and friendly it looked, and how strangely yet pleasantly the English tones fell on my ear! And I was received most kindly too. 'Madame has brought her—our little—nay, our great conspirator, the Firebrand of the Bocage. Come, little Firebrand,' exclaimed the Queen, and as I knelt to kiss her hand she threw her arms round me in an affectionate embrace, and the Prince of Wales claimed me as an old acquaintance, saluted me, and laughed, as he welcomed me to their court of waifs and strays, cast up one by one by the tide.

His little sister, brought by the faithful Lady Morton in the disguise of a beggar boy, had been the last thus to arrive. A very lovely child she was, and Prince Charles made every one laugh by taking her on his knee and calling her Piers the beggar boy, when she pointed to her white frock, called herself 'Pincess, pincess, not beggar boy,' and when he persisted, went into a little rage and pulled his black curls.

My poor Queen, whom I had left in the pride and mature bloom of beauty, was sadly changed; she looked thin and worn, and was altogether the brown old French-woman; but she was still as lively and vivacious, and full of arch kindness as ever, a true daughter of the Grand Monarque, whose spirits no disasters could break. When the little one became too noisy, she playfully ordered off both the children, as she called them, and bade me sit down on the footstool before her couch, and tell her what I had been doing to put intendants, cardinals and Queens themselves into commotion. The little Lady Henrietta was carried off by one of the attendants, but the Prince would not go; he resumed his former position, saying that he was quite sure that Madame de Bellaise was in need of an English counsel to plead her cause. He had grown up from a mischievous imp of a boy to a graceful elegant-looking youth. His figure, air, and address were charming, I never saw them equaled; but his face was as ugly as ever, though with a droll ugliness that was more winning than most men's beauty, lighted up as it was by the most brilliant of black eyes and the most engaging of smiles. You remember that I am speaking of him as he was when he had lately arrived from Jersey, before his expedition to Scotland. He became a very different person after his return, but he was now a simple-hearted, innocent lad, and I met him again as an old friend and playfellow, whose sympathy was a great satisfaction in the story I had to tell, though I was given in a half-mocking way. My mother began by saying:

'The poor child, it is as I told your Majesty; she has only been a little too charitable.'

'Permit me, Madame,' I said, 'I did not give half so much as most charitable ladies.'

Then the explanation came, and the Queen shook her head and told me such things would not do here, that my inexperience might be pardonable, but that the only way to treat such creatures was to feed them and clothe them for the sake of our own souls.

Here the Prince made his eyes first flash and then wink at me.

'But as to teach them or elevating them, my dear, it is as bad for them as for ourselves. You must renounce all such chimeras, and if you had a passion for charity there is good Father Vincent to teach you safe methods.'

I brightened up when I heard of Father Vincent, and my mother engaged for me that I should do all that was right, and appealed to my brother De Solivet to assure the Queen that there had been much malignant exaggeration about the presumption of my measures and the discontent of other people's peasants.

Queen Henrietta was quite satisfied, and declared that she would at once conduct me to her sister-in-law, the Queen-Regent, at the Tuileries, since she had of course the 'petites entrees,' take her by storm as it were, and it was exactly the right hour when the Queen would be resting after holding council.

She called for a looking-glass, and made one of her women touch up her dress and bring her a fan, asking whether I had ever been presented. No, my first stay in Paris had been too short; besides, my rank did not make it needful, as my husband was only Viscount by favour of his uncle, who let him hold the estate.

'Then,' said the Prince, 'you little know what court is!'

'Can you make a curtsey?' asked the Queen anxiously.

I repeated the one I had lately made to her Majesty, and they all cried out:

'Oh, oh! that was all very well at home.'

'Or here before I married,' added Queen Henrietta. 'Since Spanish etiquette has come in, we have all been on our good behaviour.'

'Having come from a barbarous isle,' added the Prince.

The Queen therewith made the reverence which you all know, my grand-daughters, but which seemed to me unnatural, and the Prince's face twinkled at the incredulity he saw in mine; but at the moment a private door was opening to give admission to a figure, not in itself very tall, but looking twice its height from its upright, haughty bearing. There was the Bourbon face fully marked, with a good deal of fair hair in curls round it, and a wonderful air of complete self-complacency.

This was la grande Mademoiselle, daughter of Gaston Duke of Orleans, and heiress through her mother of the great old Montpensier family, who lived at the Palais Royal with her father, but was often at the Louvre. She stood aghast, as well she might, thinking how little dignity her aunt, the Queen of England, had to be acting as mistress of deportment to a little homely widow. The Prince turned at once.

'There is my cousin,' said he, 'standing amazed to see how we have caught a barbarous islander of our own, and are trying to train her to civilization. Here—let her represent the Queen-Regent. Now, Meg— Madame de Bellaise, I mean—imitate me while my mother presents me,' he ran on in English, making such a grotesque reverence that nobody except Mademoiselle could help laughing, and his mother made a feint of laying her fan about his ears, while she pronounced him a madcap and begged her niece to excuse him.

'For profaning the outskirts of the majesty of the Most Christian King,' muttered the Prince, while his mother explained the matter to her niece, adding that her son could not help availing himself of the opportunity of paying her his homage.

Mademoiselle was pacified, and was graciously pleased to permit me to be presented to her, also to criticize the curtsey which I had now to perform, my good Queen being so kind in training me that I almost lost the sense of the incongruity of such a lesson at my age and in my weeds. In fact, with my mother and my godmother commanding me, and Eustace and the Prince of Wales looking on, it was like a return to one's childhood. At last I satisfied my royal instructress, and as she agreed with my mother that my mourning befitted the occasion off we set en grande tenue to cross the court to the Tuileries in a little procession, the Queen, attended by my mother and Lady Morton as her ladies, and by Lord Jermyn and Eustace as her gentlemen-in-waiting.

Mademoiselle also came, out of a sort of good-natured curiosity, but the Prince of Wales shook his head.

'I have no mind to show Madame the value of a tabouret,' he said. 'Believe me, Meg, I may sit on such an eminence in the august presence of my mother and my regent aunt, but if my small cousin, the Most Christian King, should enter, I must be dethroned, and a succession of bows must ensue before we can either of us be seated. I always fear that I shall some day break out with the speech of King Lear's fool: 'Cry you mercy, I took you for a joint stool.''

This passed while I, who came in the rear of the procession, was waiting to move on, and I believe Queen Henrietta was descanting to her niece on the blessing that her son's high spirits never failed him through all their misfortunes.

However, in due time we reached the apartments of the Queen-Regent, the way lined with guards, servants, and splendid gentlemen, who all either presented arms or bowed as our English Queen passed along, with an easy, frank majesty about her that bespoke her a daughter of the place, and at home there. But what gave me the most courage was that as the door of her bedroom was opened to admit Queen Henrietta, Mademoiselle, my mother, and myself, I saw a black cassock, and a face I knew again as that of the Holy Father Vincent de Paul, who had so much impressed me, and had first given me comfort.

It was a magnificent room, and more magnificent bed, and sitting up among her lace and cambric pillows and coverlets was Queen Anne of

Austria, in a rich white lace cap and bedgown that set off her smooth, fair, plump beauty, and exquisite hands and arms. Ladies stood round the bed. I did not then see who any of them were, for this was the crisis of my fate, and my heart beat and my eyes swam with anxiety. Queen Henrietta made her low reverence, as of course we did, and some words of sisterly greeting ensued, after which the English queen said:

'My sister, I have made you this early visit to bring you my little suppliant. Allow me to present to your Majesty, Madame la Vicomtesse de Bellaise, who is sincerely sorry to have offended you.'

(That was true; I was sincerely sorry that what I had done could offend.)

My kind godmother went on to that I had offended only out of ignorance of the rights of seigneurs, and from my charitable impulses, of which she knew that her Majesty would approve, glancing significantly towards Father Vincent as she did so. She was sure, she added, that Her Majesty's tenderness of heart must sympathise with a young widow, whose husband had fallen in the service of the King, and who had an only son to bring up. I felt the Regent's beautiful blue eyes scanning me, but it was not unkindly, though she said:

'How is this, Madame? I hear that you have taught the peasants to complain of the seigniorial rights, and to expect to have the corvee and all other dues remitted.'

I made answer that in truth all I had done was to remit those claims here and there which had seemed to me to press hard upon the tenants of our own estate; and I think the Regent was moved by a look from Father Vincent to demand an example, so I mentioned that I would not have the poor forced to carry our crops on the only fine day in a wet season.

'Ah, bah!' said Queen Anne; 'that was an over-refinement, Madame. It does not hurt those creatures to get wet.'

She really had not the least notion that a wetting ruined their crops; and when I would have answered, my godmother and mother made me a sign to hold my tongue, while Queen Henrietta spoke:

'Your Majesty sees how it is; my godchild has the enthusiasm of charity, and you, my sister, with your surroundings, will not blame her if she has carried it a little into excess.'

'Your Majesty will pardon me for asking if there can be excess?' said Father Vincent. 'I think I recognize this lady. Did I not meet Madame at the little village of St. Felix?'

'Oh yes, my father,' I replied. 'I have ever since blessed the day, when you comforted me and gave me the key of life.'

'There, father,' said the Regent, 'it is your doing; it is you that have made her a firebrand. You must henceforth take the responsibility.'

'I ask no better of your Majesty,' said the holy man.

'Ah! your Majesty, I can ask no better,' I said fervently; and I knelt to kiss the beautiful hand which Anne of Austria extended to me in token of pardon.

'It is understood, then,' said she, in a gracious though languid way, as if weary of the subject, 'that your Majesty undertakes that Madame becomes more prudent in the future, and puts her benevolence under the rule of our good father, who will never let her go beyond what is wise in the bounds of a young woman's discretion.'

It might be hard to believe that I had been indiscreet, but the grand stately self-possession of that Spanish lady, and the evident gratification of my mother and Queen Henrietta, quite overpowered me into feeling like a criminal received to mercy, and I returned thanks with all the genuine humility they could desire; after which the regent overpowered my mother with wonder at her graciousness by inquiring a day for him to kiss the King's hand in the Tuileries gardens.

By this time her breakfast was being brought in (it was about one o'clock), and Queen Henrietta carried us off without waiting for the ceremony of the breakfast, or of the toilet, which began with the little King presenting his mother with her chemise, with a tender kiss. Mademoiselle remained, and so did Father Vincent, whom the regent was wont to consult at her breakfast, both on matters of charity and of Church patronage.

My mother was delighted that I had come off so well; she only regretted my being put under Father Vincent, who would, she feared, render me too devout.

The next afternoon, which was Sunday, we went, all except my brother and sister, who had what my mother called Puritan notions as to Sunday, to see royalty walk in the Tuileries gardens. The Queen was there, slowly pacing along with one of her sons on each side, and beautiful boys they were, in their rich dresses of blue velvet and white satin, with rich lace garnishings, their long fair hair on their shoulders, and their plumed hats less often on their heads than in their hands, as they gracefully acknowledged the homage that met them at each step. Perhaps I thought my Gaspard quite as beautiful, but every widow's only son is THE king of her heart; and we had so trained the boy that he did his part to perfection kneeling and kissing the hand which King Louis extended to him. Yet it had—to me who was fresh to such scenes—something of the air of a little comedy, to see such gestures of respect between the two children so splendidly dressed, and neither of them yet nine years old.

The little King did his part well, presented M. le Marquis de Nidemerle to his brother the Duke of Anjou, asked graciously whether he could ride and what games he loved best, and expressed a courteous desire that they might often meet.

My sister-in-law was also presented to the Queen, who filled her with ecstasy by making her some compliment on the services of M. la Comte d'Aubepine, and thus began our career at court. We were in favour, and my mother breathed freely.

CHAPTER XII. — CAVALIERS IN EXILE.

My safety and freedom being thus secure, I was asked, as mistress of the house, whether I would continue the custom my mother had begun of receiving on a Monday, chiefly for the sake of our exiled countryfolk at Paris.

It had been left in doubt, till my fate and my wishes should be known, whether the reunion should take place on the Monday or not; but all lived so simply and within so short a distance that it was very easy to make it known that Lady Walwyn and Madame de Bellaise would receive as usual.

The rule in ordinary French society was then as now, to offer only eau-sucree, sherbets, and light cakes as refreshments, but my mother told me with some disgust that it was necessary to have something more substantial on the buffet for these great Englishmen.

'Yes,' said Annora, 'I do believe it is often the only meal worth the name that they get in a week, unless my brother invites them to supper.'

On learning this Tryphena and I resolved that though pies were the most substantial dish at present prepared, we would do our best another time to set before them such a round of salt beef as would rejoice their appetites; and oh! the trouble we had in accomplishing it.

Meantime I submitted to be dressed as my mother wished, much indeed as I am now, except that my hair was put into little curls, and I had no cap. The Queen-Regent wore none, so why should I? Moreover, my mother said that it would not be good taste to put on any jewels among the English.

Alas! I could see why, as the salon filled with gentlemen and ladies, far fewer of the last than the first, for some wives had been left at home with their children to keep possession of the estates, and send what supplies they could to their lords in exile. Some, like brave Lady Fanshawe, traveled backwards and forwards again and again on their husbands' affairs; and some who were at Paris could not afford a servant nor leave their little children, and others had no dress fit to appear in. And yet some of the dresses were shabby enough—frayed satin or faded stained brocade, the singes and the creases telling of hard service and rough usage. The gentlemen were not much better: some had their velvet coats worn woefully at the elbows, and the lace of their collars darned; indeed those were the best off, for there were some who had no ladies to take care of them, whose fine Flanders lace was in terrible holes.

Some gallants indeed there were to ruffle it as sprucely as ever, and there were a few who had taken service as musketeers or archers of the guard; but these were at that time few, for the King was still living, and they did not despair of an accommodation which would soon bring them home again. As my mother had predicted, the gentlemen with the ragged lace tried in vain to affect indifference to the good things on the buffet, till they had done their devoir by me as their hostess. Eustace and Nan were on the watch and soon were caring for them, and heaping their plates with food, and then it was that my sister's face began to light up, and I knew her for herself again, while there was a general sound of full gruff English voices all round, harsh and cracking my mother called it, but Nan said it was perfect music to her, and I think she began to forgive me when she found that to me likewise it had a sound of home.

But my mother was greatly gratified that evening, for there appeared in our salon the dark bright face of the Prince of Wales, closely followed by a tall handsome man in the prime of life, whom I had never seen before.

'Do not derange yourself,' said Prince Charles, bending his black head, bowing right and left, and signing with his hand to people to continue their occupations. 'I always escape to places where I can hear English tongues, and I wanted to congratulate Madame on her reception yesterday, also to present to her my cousin Prince Rupert, who arrived this afternoon.'

Prince Rupert and some of the wiser and more politic gentlemen, Eustace among them, drew apart in consultation, while the Prince of Wales stood by me.

'They are considering of a descent on the Isle of Wight to carry off my father from Carisbrooke,' he said.

'And will not your Highness be with them?' I asked.

'Oh yes, I shall be with them, of course, as soon as there is anything to be done; but as to the ways and means, they may arrange that as they choose. Are you to be at Madame de Choisy's ball?'

I was quite provoked with him for being able to think of such matters when his father's rescue was at stake; but he bade me ask his mother and mine whether it were not an important question, and then told me that he must make me understand the little comedy in which he was an actor.

Prince as he was, I could not help saying that I cared more for the tragedy in which we all might be actors; and he shrugged his shoulders, and said that life would be insupportable if all were to be taken in the grand serious way. However, Prince Rupert appealed to him, and he was soon absorbed intò the consultation.

My brother told us the next morning of the plan. It was that Prince Rupert, with the ships which he had in waiting at Harfleur, should take a trusty band of cavaliers from Paris, surprise Carisbrooke, and carry off His Sacred Majesty. Eustace was eager to go with them, and would listen to no representations from my mother of the danger his health would incur in such an expedition in the month of November. She wept and entreated in vain.

'What was his life good for,' he said, 'but to be given for the King's service?'

Then she appealed to me to persuade him, but he looked at me with his bright blue eyes and said:

'Meg learned better in Lorraine;' and I went up and kissed him with tears in my eyes, and said: 'Ah! Madame, we have all had to learn how loyalty must come before life, and what is better than life.'

And then Annora cried out: 'Well said, Margaret! I do believe that you are an honest Englishwoman still.'

My brother went his way to consult with some of the other volunteers, and my mother called for her sedan chair to go and see whether she could get an order from Queen Henrietta to stop him, while Annora exclaimed:

'Yes! I know how it is, and mother cannot see it. Eustace cares little for his life now, and the only chance of his ever overgetting it is the having something to do. How can he forget while he lives moping here in banishment, with nothing better to do than to stroke the Queen's spaniels?'

Then of course I asked what he had to get over. I knew he had had a boyish admiration for Millicent Wardour, a young lady in Lady Northumberland's household, but I had never dared inquire after her, having heard nothing about her since I left England. My sister, whose mistrust of me had quite given way, told me all she knew.

Eustace had prevailed on my father to make proposals of marriage for her though not willingly, for my father did not like the politics of her father, Sir James Wardour, and my mother did not think the young gentlewoman a sufficient match for the heir of Walwyn and Ribaumont. There was much haggling over the dowry and marriage portion, and in the midst, Sir James himself took, for his second wife, a stern and sour Puritan dame. My mother and she were so utterly alien to each other that they affronted one another on their first introduction, and Sir James entirely surrendered himself to his new wife; the match was broken off, and Millicent was carried away into the country, having returned the ring and all other tokens that Eustace had given her.

'I never esteemed her much, said Nan. 'She was a poor little white, spiritless thing, with a skin that they called ivory, and great brown eyes that looked at one like that young fawn with the broken leg. If I had been Eustace, I would have had some one with a little more will of her own, and then he would not have been served as he was.' For the next thing that was heard of her, and that by a mere chance, was that she was marred to Mynheer van Hunker, 'a rascallion of an old half-bred Dutchman,' as my hot-tongued sister called him, who had come over to fatten on our misfortunes by buying up the cavaliers' plate and jewels, and lending them money on their estates. He was of noble birth, too, if a Dutchman could be, and he had an English mother, so he pretended to be doing people a favour while he was filling his own coffers; and, worst of all, it was he who had bought the chaplet of pearls, the King's gift to the bravest of knights.

The tidings were heard in the midst of war and confusion, and so far as Nan knew, Eustace had made no moan; but some months later, when he was seeking a friend among the slain at Cropredy Bridge, he came upon Sir James Wardour mortally wounded, to whom he gave some drink, and all the succour that was possible. The dying man looked up and said: 'Mr. Rib'mont, I think. Ah! sir, you were scurvily used. My lady would have her way. My love to my poor wench; I wish she were in your keeping, but—' Then he gave some message for them both, and, with wandering senses, pained Eustace intensely by forgetting that he was not indeed Millicent's husband, and talking to him as such, giving the last greeting; and so he died in my brother's arms.

Eustace wrote all that needed to be said, and sent the letters, with the purse and tokens that Sir James had given him for them, with a flag of truce to the enemy's camp.

Then came still darker days—my father's death at Marston Moor, the year of losses, and Eustace's wound at Naseby, and his illness almost to death. When he was recovering, Harry Merrycourt, to whom he had given his parole, was bound to take him to London for his trial, riding by easy stages as he could endure it, whilst Harry took as much care of him as if he had been his brother. On the Saturday they were to halt over the Sunday at the castle of my Lord Hartwell, who had always been a notorious Roundhead, having been one of the first to take the Covenant.

Being very strong, and the neighbourhood being mostly of the Roundhead mind, his castle had been used as a place of security by many of the gentry of the Parliamentary party while the Royal forces were near, and they had not yet entirely dispersed, so that the place overflowed with guests; and when Harry and Eustace came down to supper, they found the hall full of company. Lord Walwyn was received as if he were simply a guest. While he was being presented to the hostess on coming down to supper, there was a low cry, then a confusion among the ladies, round some one who had fainted.

'The foolish moppet,' said my unmerciful sister, 'to expose herself and poor Walwyn in that way!'

I pitied her, and said that she could not help it.

'I would have run my finger through with my bodkin sooner than have made such a fool of myself,' returned Nan. 'And to make it worse, what should come rolling to my poor brother's feet but three or four of our pearls? The pearls of Ribaumont! That was the way she kept them when she had got them, letting the string break, so that they rolled about the floor anyhow!'

She had heard all this from Harry Merrycourt, and also that my brother had gathered up the pearls, and, with some other gentlemen, who had picked them up while the poor lady was carried from the room, had given them to my Lady Hartwell to be returned to Madame van Hunker, not of course escaping the remark from some of the stricter sort that it was a lesson against the being adorned with pearls and costly array.

Madame van Hunker's swoon had not surprised any one, for she was known to have been in very delicate health ever since a severe illness which she had gone through in London. She had been too weak to accompany her husband to Holland, and he had left her under the care of Lady Hartwell, who was a kinswoman of her own. Harry had only seen her again at supper time the next day, when he marveled at the suffering such a pale little insignificant faded being could cause Eustace, who, though silent and resolute, was, in the eyes of one who knew him well—evidently enduring a great trial with difficulty.

I heard the rest from my brother himself.

He was in no condition to attend the service the next day, not being able to walk to the Church, nor to sit and stand in the draughty building through the prayer and preaching that were not easily distinguished from on another. He was glad of such a dispensation without offence, for, children, though you suppose all Protestants to be alike, such members of the English Church as my family, stand as far apart from the sects that distracted England as we do from the Huguenots; and it was almost as much against my brother's conscience to join in their worship, as it would be against our own. The

English Church claims to be a branch of the true Catholic Church, and there are those among the Gallicans who are ready to admit her claim.

Harry Merrycourt, who was altogether a political, not a religious rebel, would gladly have kept Lord Walwyn company; but it was needful not to expose himself to the suspicion of his hosts, who would have bestowed numerous strange names on him had he absented himself.

And thus Eustace was left alone in the great hall, lord and lady, guests and soldiers, men and maids, all going off in procession across the fields; while he had his choice of the cushions in the sunny window, or of the large arm-chair by the wood fire on the hearth.

All alone there he had taken out his Prayer-book, a little black clasped book with my father's coat-of-arms and one blood-stain on it—he loved it as we love our Book of the Hours, and indeed, it is much the very same, for which reason it was then forbidden in England—and was kneeling in prayer, joining in spirit with the rest of his Church, when a soft step and a rustle of garments made him look up, and he beheld the white face and trembling figure of poor Millicent.

'Sir,' she said, as he rose, 'I ask your pardon. I should not have interrupted your devotions, but now is your time. My servant's riding-dress is in a closet by the buttery hatch, his horse is in the stable, there is no sentry in the way, for I have looked all about. No one will return to the house for at least two hours longer; you will have full time to escape.'

I can see the smile of sadness with which my brother looked into her face as he thanked her, and told her that he was on his parole of honour. At that answer she sank down into a chair, hiding her face and weeping— weeping with such an agony of self-abandonment and grief as rent my brother's very heart, while he stood in grievous perplexity, unable to leave her alone in her sorrow, yet loving her too well and truly to dare to console her. One or two broken words made him think she feared for his life, and he made haste to assure her that it was in no danger, since Mr. Merrycourt was assured of bearing him safely through. She only moaned in answer, and said presently something about living with such a sort of people as made her forget what a cavalier's truth and honour were.

He were sorely shaken, but he thought the best and kindest mode of helping her to recover herself would be to go on where he was in the morning prayer, and, being just in the midst of their Litany, he told her so, and read it aloud. She knelt with her head on the cushions and presently sobbed out a response, growing calmer as he went on.

When it was ended she had ceased weeping, though Eustace said it was piteous to see how changed she was, and the startled pleading look in the dark eyes that used to look at him with such confiding love.

She said she had not heard those prayers since one day in the spring, when she had stolen out to a house in town where there was a gathering round one of the persecuted minister, and alas! her stepdaughters had suspected her, and accused her to their father. He pursued her, caused the train-bands to break in on the congregation and the minister to be carried off to prison. It was this that had brought on the sickness of which she declared that she hoped to have died.

When Eustace would have argued against this wish, it brought out all that he would fain never have heard nor known.

The poor young thing wished him to understand that she had never been untrue to him in heart, as indeed was but too plain, and she had only withdrawn her helpless passive resistance to the marriage with Mr. van Hunker when Berenger's death had (perhaps willfully) been reported to her as that of Eustace de Ribaumont. She had not known him to be alive till she had seen him the day before. Deaths in her own family had made her an heiress sufficiently well endowed to excite Van Hunker's cupidity, but he had never affected much tenderness for her. He was greatly her elder, she was his second wife, and he had grown-up daughters who made no secret of their dislike and scorn. Her timid drooping ways and her Majesty sympathies offended her husband, shown up before him as they were by his daughters, and, in short, her life had been utterly miserable. Probably, as Annora said, she had been wanting in spirit to rise to her situation, but of course that was not as my brother saw it. He only beheld what he would have cherished torn from him only to be crushed and flung aside at his very feet, yet so that honour and duty forbade him to do anything for her.

What he said, or what comfort he gave her, I do not fully know, for when he confided to me what grief it was that lay so heavily on his heart and spirits, he dwelt more on her sad situation than on anything else. The belief in her weakness and inconstancy had evoked in him a spirit of defiance and resistance; but when she was proved guiltless and unhappy, the burden, though less bitter, was far heavier. I only gathered that he, as the only like-minded adviser she had seen for so long, had felt it his duty to force himself to seem almost hard, cold, and pitiless in the counsel he gave her.

I remember his very words as he writhed himself with the pain of remembrance: 'And then, Meg, I had to treat the poor child as if I were stone of adamant, and chide her when my very heart was breaking for her. One moment's softening, and where should we have been? And now I have added to her troubles that fancy that I was obdurate in my anger and implacability.' I assured him that she would honour and thank him in her heart for not having been weak, and he began to repent of what he had left to be inferred, and to assure me of his having neither said nor done anything that could be censured, with vehement laudation of her sweetness and modesty.

The interview had been broken up by the sight of the return from Church. Mrs. Van Hunker had had full time to retire to her room and Eustace to arrange himself, so that no one guessed at the visitor he had had. She came down to supper, and a few words and civilities had passed between them, but he had never either seen or heard of her since.

Harry Merrycourt, who had known of the early passages between them, had never guessed that there was more than the encounter in the hall to cause the melancholy which he kindly watched and bore with in my brother, who was seriously ill again after he reached their lodgings in London, and indeed I thought at the time when he was with me in Paris, that his decay of health chiefly proceeded from sorrow of heart.

CHAPTER XIII. — MADEMOISELLE'S TOILETTE.

We were to go to Madame de Choisy's assembly. She was the wife of the Chanceller of the Duke of Orleans, and gave a fete every year, to which all the court went; and, by way of disarming suspicion, all the cavaliers who were in the great world were to attend to order that their plans might not be suspected.

Our kind Queen Henrietta insisted on inspecting Nan and me before we went. She was delighted with the way in which my mother had dressed our hair, made her show how it was done, and declared it was exactly what was suited to her niece, Mademoiselle, none of whose women had the least notion of hair-dressing. She was going herself to the Luxembourg to put the finishing touches, and Nan and I must come with her. I privately thought my mother would have been more to the purpose, but the Queen wanted to show the effect of the handi-work. However, Nan disliked the notion very much, and showed it so plainly in her face that the Queen exclaimed: 'You are no courtier, Mademoiselle de Ribaumont. Why did you not marry her to her Roundhead cousin, and leave her in England, Madame? Come, my god-daughter, you at least have learnt the art of commanding your looks.'

Poor Annora must have had a sad time of it with my mother when we were gone. She was a good girl, but she had grown up in rough times, and had a proud independent nature that chafed and checked at trifles, and could not brood being treated like a hairdresser's block, even by Queens or Princesses. She was likewise very young, and she would have been angered instead of amused at the scene which followed, which makes me laugh whenever I think of it.

The Queen sent messages to know whether the Prince of Wales were ready, and presently he came down in a black velvet suits slashed with white and carnation ribbons, and a little enameled jewel on his gold chain, representing a goose of these three colours. His mother turned him all round, smoothed his hair, fresh buckled his plume, and admonished him with earnest entreaties to do himself credit.

'I will, Madame,' he said. 'I will do my very utmost to be worthy of my badge.'

'Now, Charles, if you play the fool and lose her, I will never forgive you.'

I understood it soon. The Queen was bent on winning for her son the hand of Mademoiselle, a granddaughter of France, and the greatest heiress there. If all were indeed lost in England, he would thus be far from a landless Prince, and her wealth might become a great assistance to the royal cause in England. But Mademoiselle was several years older than the Prince, and was besides stiff, haughty, conceited, and not much to his taste, so he answered rather sullenly that he could not speak French.

'So much the better,' said his mother; 'you would only be uttering follies. When I am not there, Rupert must speak for you.'

'Rupert is too High-Dutch to be much of a courtier,' said the Prince.

'Rupert is old enough to know what is for your good, and not sacrifice all to a jest,' returned his mother.

By this time the carriage had reached the Palais Royal. We were told that Mademoiselle was still at her toilette, and up we all went, through ranks of Swiss and lackeys, to her apartments, to a splendid dressing-room, where the Princess sat in a carnation dress, richly ornamented with black and white, all complete except the fastening the feather in her hair. The friseur was engaged in this critical operation, and whole ranks of ladies stood round, one of them reading aloud one of Plutarch's Lives. The Queen came forward, with the most perfect grace, crying: 'Oh, it is ravishing! What a coincidence!' and pointing to her son, as if the similarity in colours had been a mere chance instead of a contrivance of hers.

Then, with the most gracious deference in the world, so as not to hurt the hairdresser's feelings, she showed my head, and begged permission to touch up her niece's, kissing her as she did so. Then she signed to the Prince to hold her little hand-mirror, and he obeyed, kneeling on one knee before Mademoiselle; while the Queen, with hands that really were more dexterous than those of any one I ever saw, excepting my mother, dealt with her niece's hair, paying compliments in her son's name all the time, and keeping him in check with her eye. She contrived to work in some of her own jewels, rubies and diamonds, to match the scarlet, black and white. I have since found the scene mentioned in Mademoiselle's own memoirs, but she did not see a quarter of the humour of it. She was serene in the certainty that her aunt was paying court to her, and the assurance that her cousin was doing the same, though she explains that, having hopes of the Emperor, and thinking the Prince a mere landless exile, she only pitied him. Little did she guess how he laughed at her, his mother, and himself, most of all at her airs, while his mother, scolding him all the time, joined in the laugh, though she always maintained that Mademoiselle, in spite of her overweening conceit and vanity, would become an excellent and faithful wife, and make her husband's interests her own.

'Rather too much so,' said the Prince, shrugging his shoulders; 'we know what the Margaret of Anjou style of wife can do for a King of England.'

However, as he always did what any one teased him about, if it were not too unpleasant, and as he was passionately fond of his mother, and as amused by playing on the vanity of la grande Mademoiselle, he acted his part capitally. It was all in dumb show, for he really could not speak French at that time, though he could understand what was said to him. He, like a good many other Englishmen, held that the less they assimilated themselves to their French hosts, the more they showed their hopes of returning home, and it was not till after his expedition to Scotland that he set himself to learn the language.

Queen Henrietta's skill in the toilette was noted. She laughingly said that if everything else failed her she should go into business as a hairdresser, and she had hardly completed her work, before a message was brought from Queen Anne to desire to see Mademoiselle in her full dress.

I do not know what would have become of me, if my good-natured royal godmother, who never forgot anybody, had not packed me into a carriage with some of the ladies who were accompanying Mademoiselle. That lady had a suit of her own, and went about quite independently of her father and her stepmother, who, though a Princess of Lorraine, was greatly contemned and slighted by the proud heiress.

I was put au courant with all this by the chatter of the ladies in the coach. I did no know them, and in the dark they hardly knew who was there. Men with flambeaux ran by the side of the carriage, and now and then the glare fell across a smiling face, glanced on a satin dress, or gleamed back from some jewels; and then we had a long halt in the court of the Tuileries, while Mademoiselle went to the Queen-Regent to be inspected. We waited a long time, and I heard a great deal of gossip before we were again set in motion, and when once off we soon found ourselves in the court of the Hotel de Choisy, where we mounted the stairs in the rear of Mademoiselle, pausing on the way through the anteroom, in order to give a final adjustment to her head-dress before a large mirror, the Prince of Wales standing obediently beside her, waiting to hand her into the room, so that the two black, white, and carnation figures were reflected side by side, which was, I verily believe, the true reason of her stopping there, for Queen Henrietta's handiwork was too skilful to require retouching. Prince Rupert was close by, to act as interpreter, his tall, powerful figure towering above them both, and his dark eyes looking as if his thoughts were far off, yet keeping in control the young Prince's great inclination to grimace and otherwise make game of Mademoiselle's magnificent affectations and condescensions.

I was rather at a loss, for the grand salon was one sea of feathers, bright satins and velvets, and curled heads, and though I tried to come in with Mademoiselle's suite I did not properly belong to it, and my own party were entirely lost to me. I knew hardly any one, and was quite unaccustomed to the great world, so that, though the Prince's dame de compagnie was very kind, I seemed to belong to no one in that great room, where the ladies were sitting in long rows, and the gentlemen parading before them, paying their court to one after another, while the space in the middle was left free for some distinguished pair to dance the menuet de la cour.

The first person I saw, whom I knew, was the Duchess of Longueville, more beautiful than when I had met her before as Mademoiselle de Bourbon, perfectly dazzling, indeed, with her majestic bearing and exquisite complexion, but the face had entirely lost that innocent, wistful expression that had so much enchanted me before. Half a dozen gentlemen were buzzing round her, and though I once caught her eye she did not know me, and no wonder, for I was much more changed than she was. However, there I stood forlorn, in an access of English shyness, not daring to take a chair near any of the strangers, and looking in vain for my mother or one of my brothers.

'Will not Madame take a seat beside me?' said a kind voice. 'I think I have had the honour of making her acquaintance,' she added, as our eyes met; 'it is the Gildippe of happier times.'

Then I knew her for Mademoiselle d'Argennes, now duchess of Montausieur, the same who had been so kind to me at the Hotel de Rambouillet on my first arrival at Paris. Most gladly did I take my seat by her as an old friend, and I learned from her that her mother was not present, and she engaged me to go and see her at the Hotel de Rambouillet the next morning, telling me that M. de Solivet had spoken of me, and that Madame de Rambouillet much wished to see me. Then she kindly told me the names of many of the persons present, among whom were more gens de la robe than it was usual for us of the old nobility to meet. They were indeed ennobled, and thus had no imposts to pay, but that did not put them on a level with the children of crusaders. So said my mother and her friends, but I could not but be struck with the fine countenance and grave collected air of the President Matthieu de Mole, who was making his bow to the hostess.

Presently, in the violet robes of a Bishop, for which he looked much too young, there strolled up a keen-faced man with satirical eyes, whom Madame de Montausieur presented as 'Monseigneur le Coadjuteur.' This was the Archbishop of Corinth, Paul de Gondi, Coadjutor to his uncle, the Archbishop of Paris. I think he was the most amusing talker I ever heard, only there was a great spice of malice in all that he said — or did not say; and Madame de Montausier kept him in check, as she well knew how to do.

At last, to my great joy, I saw my brother walking with a young man in the black dress of an advocate. He came up to me and the Duchess bade me present him, declaring herself delighted to make the acquaintance of a brave English cavalier, and at the same time greeting his companion as Monsieur Darpent. Eustace presently said that my mother had sent him in quest of me, and he conducted me through the salon to another apartment, where the ladies, as before, sat with their backs to the wall, excepting those who were at card-tables, a party having been made up for Monsieur. On my way I was struck both with the good mien and good sense of the young lawyer, who still stood conversing with my brother after I had been restored to my mother. The cloud cleared up from Annora's face as she listened, making her look as lovely and as animated as when she was in English company. The conversation was not by any means equally pleasing to my mother, who, on the first opportunity, broke in with 'My son,' and sent my brother off in search of some distinguished person to whom she wished to speak, and she most expressingly frowned off his former companion, who would have continued the conversation with my sister and me, where upon Nan's face, which was always far too like a window, became once more gloomy.

When we went home, it appeared that my mother was will satisfied that I should be invited to the Hotel de Rambouillet. It was a distinguished thing to have the entree there, though for her part she thought it very wearisome to have to listen to declamations about she knew not what; and there was no proper distinction of ranks kept up, any more than at the Hotel de Choisy, where one expected it. And, after all, neither Monsieur nor Madame de Rambouillet were of the old noblesse. The Argennes, like the Rambouillets, only dated from the time of the League, when they had in private confirmed the sentence of death on the Duke of Guise, which had been carried out by his assassination. Strange to look at the beautiful and gentle Julie, and know her to be sprung from such a stem!

Then my mother censured Eustace for bad taste in talking over his case with his lawyer in public. He laughed, and assured her that he had never even thought of his suit, but had been discussing one of the pictures on the walls, a fine Veronese—appealing to me if it were not so; but she was not satisfied; she said he should not have encouraged the presumption of that little advocate by presenting him to his sisters.

Eustace never attempted argument with her, but went his own way; and when Annora broke out with something about Mr. Hyde and other lawyers, such as Harry Merrycourt, being company for any one in London, she was instantly silenced or presuming to argue with her elders.

I had a happy morning with Mesdames de Rambouillet and De Montausier, who showed the perfect union of mother and daughter.

In the little cabinet where Madame de Rambouillet read and studied so much in order to be able to fill her eminent position, she drew out from me all my story and all my perplexities, giving me advice as a wise woman of my own church alone could do, and showing me how much I might still do in my life at Paris. She advised me, as I had been put under Father Vincent's guidance, to seek him at the Church of St. Sulpice, where, on certain days of the week, he was accessible to ladies wishing to undertake pious works. For the rest, she said that a little resolution on my part would enable me to reserve the early part of the day for study and the education of my son; and she fully approved of my giving the evenings to society, and gave me at once the entree to her circle. She insisted that I should remain on that day and dine with her, and Madame de Montausier indited two charming billets, which were sent to invite our family to join us there in the evening.

'It will not be a full circle,' she said; 'but I think your brother treats as a friend a young man who is there to make his first essai.'

'M. Darpent?' I asked; and I was told that I was right, and that the young advocate had been writing a discourse upon Cicero which he was to read aloud to the fair critics and their friends. Madame de Montausier added that his father was a counselor in the Parliament, who had originally been a Huguenot, but had converted himself with all his family, and had since held several good appointments. She thought the young man, Clement Darpent, likely to become a man of mark, and she did not like him the less for having retained something of the Huguenot gravity.

The dinner was extremely pleasant; we followed it up by a walk in the beautifully laid out gardens; and after we had rested, the reception began, but only in the little green cabinet, as it was merely a select few who were to be admitted to hear the young aspirant. I watched anxiously for the appearance of my family, and presently in came Eustace and Annora. My mother had the migraine, and my brother had taken upon him, without asking leave, to carry off my sister!

I had never seen her look so well as she did, with that little spirit of mischief upon her, lighting her beautiful eyes and colouring her cheeks. Madame de Rambouillet whispered to me that she was a perfect nymph, with her look of health and freshness. Then M. Darpent came in, and his grave face blushed with satisfaction as he saw his friend, my Lord Walwyn, present.

His was a fine face, though too serious for so young a man. It was a complete oval, the hair growing back on the forehead, and the beard being dark and pointed, the complexion a clear pale brown, the eyes with something of Italian softness in them, rather than of French vivacity, the brows almost as if drawn with a pencil, the mouth very grave and thoughtful except when lighted by a smile of unusual sweetness. As a lawyer, his dress was of plain black with a little white collar fastened by two silken tassels (such as I remember my Lord Falkland used to wear). It became him better than the gay coats of some of our nobles.

The circle being complete by this time, the young orator was placed in the midst, and began to read aloud his manuscript, or rather to recite it, for after the fire of his subject began to animate him, he seldom looked at the paper.

It was altogether grand and eloquent discourse upon the loyalty and nobility of holding with unswerving faith to the old laws and constitutions of one's country against all fraud, oppression, and wrong, tracing how Cicero's weak and vain character grew stronger at the call of patriotism, and how eagerly and bravely the once timid man finally held out his throat for the knife. It might be taken as the very highest witness to the manner in which he had used his divine gift of rhetoric, that Fulvia's first thought was to show her bitter hatred by piercing his eloquent tongue! 'Yes, my friends,' he concluded, with his eyes glancing round, 'that insult to the dead was the tribute of tyranny to virtue!'

Annora's hands were clasped, her cheeks were flushed, her eyes glanced with the dew of admiration, and there were others who were carried along by the charm of the young orator's voice and enthusiasm; but there were also anxious glances passing, especially between the divine Arthenice and her son-in-law, M. de Montausier, and when there had been time for the compliments the discourse merited to be freely given, Madame de Rambouillet said: 'My dear friend, the tribute may be indeed the highest, but it can scarcely be the most appreciable either by the fortunate individual or his friends. I therefore entreat that the most eloquent discourse of our youthful Cicero of admires who have listened to it.'

Everybody bowed assent, but the young man himself began, with some impetuosity: 'Madame will believe me that I had not the slightest political intention. I spoke simply as a matter of history.'

'I am perfectly aware of it, Monsieur,' returned the Marquise; 'but all the world does not understand as well as I do how one may be carried away by the fervour of imagination to identify oneself and one's surroundings with those of which one speaks.'

'Madame is very severe on the absent,' said M. Darpent.

'Monsieur thinks I have inferred more treason than he has spoken,' said Madame de Rambouillet gaily. 'Well, be it so; I am an old woman, and you, my friend, have your career yet to come, and I would have you remember that though the great Cesar be dead, yet the bodkin was not in his time.'

'I understand, Madame, after the lion comes the fox. I thank you for your warning until the time—'

'Come, come, we do not intend to be all undone in the meantime,' exclaimed Madame de Rambouillet. 'Come, who will give us a vaudeville or something joyous to put out the grand serious, and send us home gay. My dear Countess,' and she turned to a bright-looking young lady, 'relate to us, I entreat of you, one of your charming fairy tales.'

And the Countess d'Aulnoy, at her request, seated herself in a large arm-chair, and told us with infinite grace the story I have so often told you, my grandchildren, of the White Cat and the three princes.

CHAPTER XIV. — COURT APPOINTMENT

The expected descent on the Isle of Wight did not take place, for though Prince Rupert was High Admiral, so large a portion of the fleet was disaffected that it was not possible to effect anything. Before long, he went back to the ships he had at Helvoetsluys, taking the Prince of Wales with him. My brother Walwyn yielded to an earnest entreaty that he would let us take care of him at Paris till there was some undertaking really in hand. Besides, he was awaiting the issue of his cause respecting the Ribaumont property in Picardy, to which the Count de Poligny set up a claim in right of a grant by King Henry III. in the time of the League. It must be confessed that the suit lingered a good deal, in spite of the zeal of the young advocate, M. Clement Darpent, — nay, my mother ad my brother De Solivet sometimes declared, because of his zeal; for the Darpent family were well known as inclined to the Fronde party.

They had been Huguenots, but had joined the Church some twenty years before, as it was said, because of the increased disabilities of Huguenots in the legal profession, and it was averred that much of the factious Calvinist leaven still hung about them. At this time I never saw the parents, but Eustace had contracted a warm friendship with the son, and often went to their house. My mother fretted over this friendship far more, as Annora used to declare, than if he had been intimate with the wildest of the roistering cavaliers, or the most dissipated of the petits maitres of Paris. But Eustace was a man now, made older than his twenty-five years by what he had undergone, and though always most respectful to my mother, he could not but follow his own judgment and form his own friendships. And my mother's dislike to having Clement Darpent at the Hotel de Nidemerle only led to Walwyn's frequenting the Maison Darpent more than he might have done if he could have seen his friend at home without vexing her.

I do not think that he much liked the old Counsellor, but he used to say that Madame Darpent was one of the most saintly beings he had ever seen. She had one married daughter, and two more, nuns at Port Royal, and she was with them in heart, the element of Augustinianism in the Jansenist teaching having found a responsive chord in her soul from her Calvinist education. She spent her whole time, even while living in the world, in prayers, pious exercises, and works of charity, and she would fain have induced her son to quit secular life and become one of those recluses who inhabited the environs of Port Royal, and gave themselves to labour of mind and of hand, producing works of devotion and sacred research, and likewise making a paradise of the dreary unwholesome swamp in which stood Port Royal des Champs. Clement Darpent had, however, no vocation for such a life, or rather he was not convinced in his own mind that it was expedient for him. He was eight or nine years old when the conversion of his family had taken place, and his mother had taught him carefully her original faith. Her conversation had been, no one could doubt, most hearty and sincere, and her children had gone with her in all simplicity; but the seeds she had previously sown in her son's mind sprang up as he grew older, and when Eustace became his friend, he was, though outwardly conforming, restless and dissatisfied, by no means disposed to return to Calvinism, and yet with too much of the old leaven in him to remain contented in the Church. He was in danger of throwing off all thought of faith and of Divine things in his perplexity, and I know many of our advisers would say this was best, provided he died at last in the bosom of the Catholic Church; but I can never think so, and, as things stood, Eustace's advice aided him in remaining at that time where he was, a member of the Church. My brother himself was, my mother ardently hoped, likely to join our communion. The Abbe Walter Montagu who had himself been a convert, strove hard to win him over, trying to prove to him that the English Church was extinct, stifled by her own rebellious heretic children, so soon as the grace that was left in her began to work so as to bring her back to Catholic doctrine and practice. His argument was effectual with many of our fugitives, but not with my brother. He continued still to declare that he believed that his Church was in the course of being purified, and would raised up again at last; and his heart was too loyal to desert her, any more than his King, because of her misfortunes. No one shall ever make me believe that he was wrong. As to Annora, I believe she would rather have been a Huguenot outright than one of us, and she only half trusted me for a long time.

We had begun to settle down into regular habits; indeed, except for the evenings, our days were almost more alike than when in the country. I had gone, as Madame de Rambouillet had advised me, to Father Vincent, and he introduced me to the excellent Madame Goussault, who had the sweetest old face I ever saw. She made me a member of the society for attending the poor in the Hotel Dieu, and my regular days were set apart, twice a week, for waiting on the sick. We all wore a uniform dress of dark stuff, with a white apron and tight white cap, and, unless we were very intimate, were not supposed to recognize one another.

There was good reason for this. At the next bed to that of my patient there was a lady most tenderly, if a little awkwardly, bathing a poor man's face with essences. Her plump form, beautiful hands, and slightly Spanish accent, could only belong to one person, I thought, but I could hardly believe it, and I turned my eyes away, and tried the more diligently to teach my poor ignorant patient the meaning of his Pater and Ave, when suddenly there was a burst of scolding and imprecation from the other bed. The essence had gone into the man's eye, and he, a great rough bucheron, was reviling the awkwardness and meddling of ladies in no measured terms, while his nurse stood helplessly wringing her white hands, imploring his pardon, but quite unaware of what was to be done. Happily, I had a sponge and some warm water near, and I ran up with it and washed the man's eyes, while the lady thanked me fervently, but the man growled out:

'That is better; if women will come fussing over us with what they don't understand—You are the right sort; but for her—'

'Do not stop him,' hastily said the lady, with her hand on my arm. 'I love it! I rejoice in it! Do not deprive me, for the love of Heaven!'

I knew who she was then, and Madame de Montausier told me I was right; but that I must keep the secret; and so I did, till after Queen Anne of Austria was dead. She would not let her rank deprive her of the privilege of waiting on the poor, unknown and unthanked; and many hours, when those who blamed her for indolence supposed her to be in bed, she was attending the hospital.

Cecile was never strong enough to give her attendance there, but she made clothes which were given to the patients when they came out. We spent our mornings much as of old; the two elder children generally went to mass with me at St. Germain l'Auxerrois, and if the day were fine, I would take them for a few turns in the Tuileries Gardens afterwards before I taught them their little lessons, and gave my orders to the servants.

Then all the family met a breakfast, after which Gaspard had half an hour more of study with the Abbe, for he was beginning Latin, and was a very promising scholar. He prepared his tasks with me before breakfast, and got on admirably.

Then, unless I had to be at the hospital, we sat together at our embroidery—Cecile, Annora, and I—while the Abbe read to us. It was very hard to poor Nan to sit still, work, and listen. She had been used to such an active unsettled life during the war, and had been put to so many shifts, having at times for months together to do servant's work, that she knew not how to be quiet. Embroidery seemed to her useless, when she had cooked and washed, and made broths, and scraped lint for the wounded, and she could not care for the history of the Romans, even when Eustace had given her his word they were not Roman Catholics.

She used to say she had the cramp, or that her foot was asleep, and rush off to play with the children, or to see if my mother wanted her. My mother did not care for the reading, but she did want Nan to learn to sit in her chair and embroider, like a demoiselle bien elevee, instead of a wild maiden of the civil wars. However, my mother spent most of her day in waiting on the Queen of England, who was very fond of her, and liked to have her at her levee, so that we really saw very little of her.

My brother, when not needed by his Queen, nor in consultation with the cavaliers, or with his lawyers, would often join in our morning's employment. He was not strong, and he liked to recline in a lager chair that I kept ready for him, and listen while the Abbe read, or sometimes discuss with him questions that arose in the reading, and this was a great relief to Nan, who seldom declared that her feet tingled when he was there.

After our dinner we either walked in the garden where the children played, or went out to make visits. In the evening there were receptions. We had one evening to which, as I said, came our poor exiled countrymen, and there were other assemblies, to some of which we went by invitation; but at the Hotel de Rambouillet, and one or two others we knew we were always welcome. There we heard M. Corneille read the Cid, on of his finest pieces, before it was put on the stage. I cannot describe how those noble verses thrilled in our ears and heart, how tears were shed and hands clasped, and how even Annora let herself be carried along by the tide. Clement Darpent was often there, and once or twice recited again, but Madame de Rambouillet always took care first to know what he was going to say. A poem upon St. Monica was the work of his that I liked bets, but it was not so much admired as verses more concerned with the present.

The Prince of Conde came back to Paris for a few weeks, and my poor Cecile was greatly disappointed that her husband remained in garrison and did not come with him. 'But then,' as she said to console herself, 'every month made the children prettier, and she was trying to be a little more nice and agreeable.'

Two appointments were made for which I was less grateful than was my mother. My little son was made one of the King's gentlemen of the bedchamber, and Mademoiselle requested me to be one of her ladies-in-waiting. She was very good-natured, provided she thought herself obeyed, and she promised that my turn should always come at the same time as my son's, so that I might be at home with him. I was a little laughed at, and my former name of Gildippe was made to alternate with that of Cornelia; but French mothers have always been devoted to their sons, and there was some sympathy with me among the ladies.

I owned that my presence was required at home, for Gaspard generally came back a much naughtier boy than he went, and with a collection of bad words that I had to proscribe. Before the Queen-Regent, the little King and the Duke of Anjou were the best boys in the world, and as stately and well-mannered as become the first gentlemen of France; but when once out of her sight they were the most riotous and mischievous children in the world, since nobody durst restrain, far less punish them. They made attacks on the departments of the stewards and cooks, kicking and biting any one who tried to stop them, and devouring fruit and sweetmeats till their fine clothes were all bedaubed, and they themselves indisposed, and then their poor valets suffered for it. The first time this happened my poor Gaspard was so much shocked that he actually told the King that it was dishonourable to let another suffer for his fault.

'I would have you to know, Monsieur le Marquis,' said Louis XIV., drawing himself up, 'that the King of France is never in fault.'

However, I will say for His Majesty that it was the Duke of Anjou who told the Queen that the little Nidemerle had been disrespectful, and thus caused the poor child to be sent home, severely beaten, and with a reprimand to me for not bringing him up better.

I leave you to guess how furious I was, and how I raged about the house till I frightened my mother, Annora backing me up with all her might. We were almost ready to take Gaspard in our hands and escape at once to England. Even in its present sad state I should at least be able to bring up my boy without having him punished for honourable sentiments and brave speeches. Of course it was the Abbe on the one hand, and Eustace on the other, who moderated me, and tried to show me, as well as my son, that though the little Louis might be a naughty boy, the kingly dignity was to be respected in him.

'Thou wouldst not blame thy mother even if she were in fault,' argued Eustace.

'But my mother never is in fault,' said Gaspard, throwing himself into my arms.

'Ah, there spoke thy loyal heart, and a Frenchman should have the same spirit towards his King.'

'Yes,' broke out Annora; 'that is what you are all trying to force on your children, setting up an idol to fall down and crush yourselves! For shame,

Walwyn, that you, an Englishman, should preach such a doctrine to the poor child!'

'Nay, you little Frondeuse, there is right and safety in making a child's tongue pay respect to dignities. He must separate the office from the man, or the child.'

All that could be done was that I should write a humble apology for my son. Otherwise they told me he would certainly be taken from so dangerous a person, and such a dread always made me submissive to the bondage in which we were all held.

Was it not strange that a Queen who would with her own hands minister to the suffered in the hospital should be so utterly ignorant of her duties in bringing up the heir of the great kingdom? Gaspard, who was much younger, could read well, write, and knew a little Latin and English, while the King and his brother were as untaught as peasants in the fields. They could make the sign of the cross and say their prayers, and their manners COULD be perfect, but that was all. They had no instruction, and their education was not begun. I have the less hesitation in recording this, as the King has evidently regretted it, and has given first his son, then his grandsons, the most admirable masters, besides having taken great pains with himself.

I suppose the Spanish dislike to instruction dominated the Queen, and made her slow to inflict on her sons what she so much disliked, and she was of course perfectly ignorant of their misbehaviour.

I am sorry to say that Gaspard soon ceased to be shocked. His aunt declared that he was becoming a loyal Frenchman who he showed off his Louvre manners by kicking the lackeys, pinching Armantine, and utterly refusing to learn his lessons for the Abbe, declaring that he was Monsieur le Marquis, and no one should interfere with him. Once when he came home a day or two before me, he made himself quite intolerable to the whole house, by insisting on making Armantine and her little brother defend a fortress on the top of the stairs, which he attacked with the hard balls of silk and wool out of our work-baskets. Annora tried to stop him, but only was kicked for her pains. It was his HOTEL he said, and he was master there, and so he went on, though he had given poor Armantine a black eye, and broken two panes of glass, till his uncle came home, and came upon him with a stern 'Gaspard.' The boy began again with his being the Marquis and the master, but Eustace put him down at once.

'Thou mayst be Marquis, but thou art not master of this house, nor of thyself. Thou art not even a gentleman while thou actest thus. Go to thy room. We will see what thy mother says to this.'

Gaspard durst not struggle with his uncle, and went off silent and sulky; but Eustace had subdued him into penitence before I came home. And I can hardly tell how, but from that time the principle of loyalty to the sovereign, without imitation of the person, seemed to have been instilled into the child, so that I feel, and I am sure he will agree with me, that I owe my son, and he owes himself, to the influence of my dear brother.

Had it not been for leaving him, my service to Mademoiselle would have been altogether amusing. True, she was marvelously egotistical and conceited, but she was very good-natured, and liked to make those about her happy. Even to her stepmother and little sisters, whom she did not love, she was never unkind, though she lived entirely apart, and kept her own little court separately at the Louvre, and very odd things we did there.

Sometimes we were all dressed up as the gods and goddesses, she being always Minerva—unless as Diana she conducted us as her nymphs to the chase in the park at Versailles. Sometimes we were Mademoiselle Scudery's heroines, and we wrote descriptions of each other by these feigned names, some of which appear in her memoirs. And all the time she was hoping to marry the Emperor, and despising the suit of Queen Henrietta for our Prince of Wales, who, for his part, never laughed so much in secret as when he attended this wonderful and classical Court.

CHAPTER XV. — A STRANGER THANKSGIVING DAY.

There was a curious scene in our salon the day after the news had come of the great victory of Lens. Clement Darpent had been brought in by my brother, who wished him to hear some English songs which my sister and I had been practicing. He had been trying to learn English, and perhaps understood it better than he could speak it, but he was somewhat perplexed by those two gallant lines—

'I could not love thee, dear, so much,

Loved I not honour more.'

Annora's eyes flashed with disappointed anger as she said, 'You enter not into the sentiment, Monsieur. I should have hoped that if any Frenchman could, it would be you!'

'For my part,' observed my mother, 'I am not surprised at the question not being appreciated by the gens de la robe.'

I saw Eustace look infinitely annoyed at this insult to his friend's profession, and to make it worse, Gaspard, who had come home that morning from the palace, exclaimed, having merely caught the word 'honour'—

'Yes, the gens de la robe hate our honour. That is why the King said, when news of our great victory came, 'Oh, how sorry the Parliament will be!'

'Did he?' exclaimed my mother. 'Is it true, my grandson?'

'True; yes indeed, Madame ma Grandmere,' replied Gaspard. 'And you should have seen how all the world applauded him.'

'I would not have applauded him,' said Eustace sadly. 'I would have tried to teach him that nothing can be of more sad omen for a king than to regard his Parliament as his enemy.'

'My son,' returned my mother, 'if you must utter such absurdities, let it not be before this child. Imagine the consequence of his repeating them!'

'Ah! sighed Darpent, 'it would be well if only, through child lips or any others, the King and his mother could learn that the Parliament can heartily rejoice in all that is for the true glory and honour in justice and in the well-being of her people, and that we love above all!'

'There,' said I, glad to turn the conversation from the dangerous political turn it was taking, 'I knew it was merely the language and not the sentiment of our song that Monsieur Darpent did not comprehend.'

And when it was translated and paraphrased, he exclaimed, 'Ah! truly Mademoiselle may trust me that such sentiments are the breath of life to those who are both French and of the robe. May ONE at least live to prove it to her!'

The times were threatening in France as well as in England, for if in the latter realm, the thunderbolt had fallen, in the former, the tempest seemed to be gathering. They say that it dispersed after a few showers, but there are others who say that it is only stored up to fall with greater fury in later times. Ah, well! if it be so, I pray that none of mine may be living to see it, for I cannot conceal from myself that there is much among us that may well call down the vengeance of Heaven. Yet, if our good Duke of Burgundy fulfil the promise of his youth, the evil may yet be averted.

The Parliament of Paris had made an attempt to check the reckless exactions of the Court by refusing to register the recent edicts for taxation, and it was this that made the Queen so angry with them. Eustace began to explain that it had been the unfortunate endeavour to raise money without the consent of Parliament that had been the immediate cause of the troubles in England for which they were still suffering. This implied censure of King Charles so displeased my mother that she declared that she would listen to such treason no longer, started up and quitted the room, calling Annora with her. Poor Annora gave one of her grim looks, but was obliged to obey; I did not feel bound to do the same, as indeed I stood in the position of hostess: so I remained, with Gaspard leaning on my lap, while my brother and M. Darpent continued their conversation, and the latter began to describe the actual matter in debate, the Paulette, namely, the right of magistrates to purchase the succession to their offices for their sons, provided a certain annual amount was paid to the Crown. The right had to be continually renewed by fresh edicts for a certain term. This term was now over, and the Crown refused to renew it except on condition that all that salaries should be forfeited for four years. To our English notions the whole system was a corruption, but the horrible ill faith of the Court, which ruined and cheated so many families, was nevertheless shocking to us. Clement Darpent, who had always looked on the Paulette as a useful guarantee, and expected to succeed to his father's office as naturally as Eustace had done to the baronies of Walwyn and Ribaumont, could not then see it in the same light, and expatiated on the speeches made by the Councillors Broussel, Blancmesnil, and others, on the injustice of such a measure.

Gaspard caught the name of Blancmesnil, and looking up, he said 'Blancmesnil! It is he that the King says is a scoundrel to resist his will; but he will soon be shut up. They are going to arrest him.'

'Pray how long have they taken little imps like thee into their counsels?' demanded Eustace, as we all sat petrified at this announcement.

'It was the Duke of Anjou who told me,' said Gaspard. 'He was sitting at the foot of the Queen's bed when she settled it all with M. le Cardinal. They will send to have coup de main made of all those rogues as soon as the Te Deum is over tomorrow at Notre Dame, and then there will be no more refusing of money for M. le Prince to beat the Spaniards with.'

'The Duke should choose his confidants better,' said Eustace. 'Look here, my nephew. Remember from henceforth that whatever passes in secret council is sacred, and even if told to thee inadvertently should never be repeated. Now leave us; your mother needs you no longer.'

My little boy made his graceful bow at the door, looking much perplexed, and departed. I rose likewise, saying I would forbid him to repeat his dangerous communication, and I trusted that it would do him no harm.

'Madame,' said M. Darpent, 'I will not conceal from you that I shall take advantage of what I have heard to warn these friends of my father.'

'You cannot be expected to do otherwise,' said Eustace; 'and truly the design is so arbitrary and unjust that, Cavalier as I am, I cannot but rejoice that it should be baffled.'

'And,' added Darpent, before I could speak, 'Madame may be secure that no word shall pass my lips respecting the manner in which I received the warning.'

I answered that I could trust him for that. I could not expect any more from him, and indeed none of us were bound in honour. The fault was with the Duke of Anjou, who, as we all know, was an incorrigible chatter-box all his life, and never was trusted with any State secrets at all; but his mother must have supposed him not old enough to understand what she was talking about, when she let him overhear such a conversation.

Gaspard had, however, a private lecture from both of us on the need of holding his tongue, both on this matter and all other palace gossip. He was no longer in waiting, and I trusted that all would be forgotten before his turn came again; but he was to join in the state procession on the following day, a Sunday, when the King and Queen-Regent were return thanks at Notre Dame for the victory at Lens.

Ah, children! we had victories then. Our Te Deums were not sung with doubting hearts, to make the populace believe a defeat a victory — a delusion to which this French nation of ours is only too prone. My countryman, Marlborough, and the little truant Abbe, Eugene of Savoy, were not then the leaders of the opposite armies; but at the head of our own, we had M. le Prince and the Vicomte de Turenne in the flower of their age, and our triumphs were such that they might well intoxicate the King, who was, so to speak, brought up upon them. It was a magnificent sight, which we all saw from different quarters — my mother in the suite of the Queen of England, Gaspard among the little noblemen who attended the King, I among the ladies who followed Mademoiselle, while my brother and sister, though they might have gone among their own Queen's train, chose to shift for themselves. They said they should see more than if, like us, they formed part of the pageant; but I believe the real reason was, that if they had one early to Queen Henrietta's apartments in full dress, they must have missed their English prayers at the Ambassador's, which they never chose to do on a Sunday.

The choir part of the nave was filled with tribunes for the royal family and their suites; and as the most exalted in rank went the last, Mademoiselle, and we ladies behind her, came to our places early enough to see a great deal of the rest of the procession. The whole choir was already a field of clergy and choristers, the white robes of the latter giving relief to the richly-embroidered purple and lace-covered robes of the Bishops, who wore their gold and jeweled mitres, while their richly-gilded pastoral staves and crosses were borne before them. The Coadjutor of Paris, who was to be the Celebrant, was already by the Altar, his robes absolutely encrusted with gold; and just after we had taken our places there passed up the Cardinal, with his pillars borne before him, in his scarlet hat and his robes.

Every lady was, according to the Spanish fashion, which Queen Anne had introduced, in black or in white — the demoiselles in white, the married in black — and all with the black lace veil on their heads. The French ladies had murmured much at this, but there is no denying that the general effect was much better for the long lines of black above and white below, and as there was no restriction upon their jewellery, emeralds, rubies, and diamonds flashed wherever the light fell on them.

Beyond, a lane was preserved all down the length of the nave by the tall, towering forms of the Scottish archers, in their rich accoutrements, many of them gallant gentlemen, who had served under the Marquess of Montrose; and in the aisles behind them surged the whole multitude—gentlemen, ladies, bourgeois, fishwives, artisans, all sorts of people, mixed up together, and treating one another with a civility and forbearance of which my brother and sister confessed and English crowd would have been incapable, though they showed absolutely no reverence to the sacred place; and I must own the ladies showed as little, for every one was talking, laughing, bowing to acquaintance, or pointing out notorieties, and low whispers were going about of some great and secret undertaking of the Queen-Regent. Low, did I say! Nay, I heard the words 'Blancmesnil and Broussel' quite loud enough to satisfy me that if the attempt had been disclosed, it would not be possible to fix the blame of betraying it on my little son more than on twenty others. Indeed the Queen of England observed to her niece, loud enough for me to hear her, that it was only too like what she remembered only seven years ago in England, when her dear King had gone down to arrest those five rogues of members, and all had failed because of that vile gossip Lady Carlisle.

'And who told my Lady Carlisle?' demanded Mademoiselle with some archness; whereupon Queen Henrietta became very curious to know whether the handsome Duke of Beaufort were, after his foolish fashion, in the crowd, making himself agreeable to the ladies of the market-place.

Trumpets, however, sounded, and all rose from their seats, as up the nave swept Queen Anne, her black mantilla descending over her fair hair from a little diamond crown, her dress—white satin—with a huge long blue velvet train worked with gold fleurs-de-lys, supported by four pair of little pages in white satin. Most regal did she look, leading by the hand the little Duke of Anjou; while the young King, who was now old enough to form the climax of the procession, marched next after in blue and gold, holding his plumed hat in his hand, and bowing right and left with all his royal courtesy and grace, his beautiful fair hair on his shoulders, shining with the sun. And there was my little Marquis among the boys, who immediately followed him in all his bright beauty and grace.

Most glorious was the High Mass that followed. Officer after officer marched up and laid standard after standard before the Altar, heavy with German blazonry, or with the red and gold stripes of Aragon, the embattled castles of Castille, till they amounted to seventy-three. It must have been strange to the Spanish Queen to rejoice over these as they lay piled in a gorgeous heap before the high Altar, here and there one dim with weather or stained with blood. The peals of the Te Deum from a thousand voices were unspeakably magnificent, and yet through them all it seemed to me that I heard the wail not only of the multitudes of widowed wives and sonless parents, but of the poor peasants of all the nation, crying aloud to Heaven for the bread which they were forbidden to eat, when they had toiled for it in the sweat of their brow. Yes, and which I was not permitted to let them enjoy!

Ah! which did the Almighty listen to? To the praise, or to the mourning, lamentation, and woe? You have often wondered, my children, that I absented myself from the Te Deums of victory while we had them. Now you know the reason.

And then I knew that all this display was only an excuse under which the Queen hid her real design of crushing all opposition to her will. She wanted to commit an injustice, and silence all appeals against it, so that the poor might be more and more ground down! How strange in the woman whom I had seen bearing patiently, nay, joyfully, with the murmurs of the faggot-seller in the hospital! Truly she knew not what she did!

As she left the Cathedral, and passed M. de Comminges, a lieutenant of her Guards, she said: 'Go, and Heaven be with you.'

I was soon at home safely with my boys, to carry an account of our doings to my dear little M. d'Aubepine, who, unable to bear the fatigue and the crush of Notre Dame, had taken her little children to a Mass of thanksgiving celebrated by our good Abbe at the nearest Church.

We waited long and long for the others to come. I was not uneasy for my mother, who was with the Queen; but the servants brought reports that the canaille had risen, and that the streets were in wild confusion. We could see nothing, and only heard wild shouts from time to time. What could have become of Eustace and Annora? My mother would have been afraid that with their wild English notions they had rushed into something most unsuitable to a French demoiselle, and I was afraid for Eustace, if they were involved in any crowd or confusion, for his strength was far from being equal to his spirit. We watched, sure that we heard cries and shouts in the distance, the roar of the populace, such as I remembered on that wedding day, but sharper and shriller, as French voices are in a different key from the English roar and growl.

It passed, however, and there was long silence. Gaspard and Armantine stood at the window, and at last, as evening twilight fell, cried out that a carriage was coming in at the porte cochere. Presently Annora ran into the room, all in a glow, and Eustace followed more slowly.

'Have you been frightened?' she cried. 'Oh, we have had such an adventure! If they had not screamed and shrieked like peacocks, or furies, I could have thought myself in England.'

'Alack! that a tumult should seem like home to you, sister,' said Eustace gravely.

Then they told how at the ambassador's chapel they had heard that good Lady Fanshawe, whom they had known in England, had arrived sick and sad, after the loss of a young child. They determined, therefore, to steal away from Notre Dame before the ceremony was over, and go to see whether anything could be done for her. They could not, however, get out so quickly as they expected, and they were in the Rue de Marmousets when they saw surging towards them a tremendous crowd, shouting, screeching, shrieking, roaring, trying to stop a carriage which was being urged on with six horses, with the royal guards trying to force their way. Eustace, afraid of his sister being swept from him, looked for some escape, but the mob went faster than they could do; and they might soon have been involved in it and trampled down. There seemed no opening in the tall houses, when suddenly a little door opened close to them, and there was a cry of surprise; a hand was put out.

'You here! Nay, pardon me, Mademoiselle; take my arm.'

Clement Darpent was there. A few steps more, and taking out a small key, he fitted it into the same little door, and led them into a dark passage, then up a stair, into a large room, simply furnished, and one end almost like an oratory. Here, looking anxiously from the window, was an old lady in a plain black dress and black silk hood, with a white apron and keys at her girdle.

'My mother,' said Clement, 'this gentleman and lady, M. le Baron de Ribaumont and Mademoiselle sa soeur, have become involved in this crowd. They will do us the favour of taking shelter here till the uproar is over.'

Madame Darpent welcomed them kindly, but with anxious inquiries. Her son only threw her a word in answer, prayed to be excused, and dashed off again.

'Ah! there he is. May he be saved, the good old man,' cried Madame Darpent.

And they could see a carriage with four horses containing the Lieutenant Comminges holding a white-haired old man, in a very shabby dressing-gown; while soldiers, men, women, boys, all struggled, fought, and shrieked round it, like the furies let loose. The carriage passed on, but the noise and struggle continued, and Madame Darpent was soon intensely anxious about her son.

It seemed that Clement had carried his warnings, and that four or five of the councillors had taken care to be beyond the walls of Paris;

among them his own father, the Councillor Darpent, who was a prudent man, and thought it best to be on the right side. The President Broussel, a good-humoured, simple, hearty old man, was not quite well, and though he thanked his young friend, he would not believe any such harm was intended against him as to make him derange his course of medicine.

Thus, when Comminges marched into the house to arrest him, he was sitting at dinner, eating his bouillon, in dressing-gown and slippers. His daughter cried out that he was not fit to leave the house. At the same time, an old maid-servant put her head out at a window, screaming that her master was going to be carried off.

He was much beloved, and a host of people ran together, trying to break the carriage and cut the traces. Comminges, seeing that no time was to be lost, forced the poor old lawyer down to the carriage just as he was, in his dressing-gown and slippers, and drove off. But the mob thickened every moment, in spite of the guards, and a very few yards beyond where they had taken refuge at Madame Darpent's, a large wooden bench had been thrown across the street, and the uproar redoubled round it—the yells, shrieks, and cries ringing all down the road. However, the carriage passed that, and dashed on, throwing down and crushing people right and left; so that Madame Darpent was first in terror for her son, and then would fain have rushed out to help the limping, crying sufferers.

They heard another horrible outcry, but could see no more, except the fluctuating heads of the throng below them, and loud yells, howls, and maledictions came to their ears. By and by, however, Clement returned, having lost his hat in the crowd; with blood on his collar, and with one of his lace cuffs torn, though he said he was not hurt.

'They have him!' he said bitterly; 'the tyranny has succeeded!'

'Oh, hush, my son! Take care!' cried his mother.

'M. le Baron and I understand one another, Madame,' he said, smiling.

He went on to tell that the carriage had been overturned on the Quai des Orfevres, just opposite the hotel of the First President. Comminges sprang out, sword in hand, drove back the crowd, who would have helped out Broussel, and shouted for the soldiers, some of whom kept back those who would have succoured the prisoner with their drawn swords. Clement himself had been slightly touched, but was forced back in the scuffle; while the good old man called out to him not to let any one be hurt on his behalf.

Other soldiers were meantime seizing a passing carriage, and taking out a poor lady who occupied it. Before it could be brought near, the raging crowd had brought axes and hacked it to pieces. Comminges and his soldiers, well-armed, still dragged their victim along till a troop of the Queen's guards came up with another carriage, in which the poor old President was finally carried off.

'And this is what we have to submit to from a Spaniard and an Italian!' cried Clement Darpent.

He had come back to reassure his mother and his guests, but the tumult was raging higher than ever. The crowd had surrounded the Tuileries, filling the air with shouts of 'Broussel! Broussel!' and threatening to tear down the doors and break in, overwhelming the guards. Eustace and his host went out again, and presently reported that the Marshal de Meileraye had been half killed, but had been rescued by the Coadjutor, who was giving the people all manner of promises. This was verified by shouts of 'Vive le Roi!' and by and by the crowd came past once more, surrounding the carriage, on the top of which was seated the Coadjutor, in his violet robes, but with his skull cap away, and his cheek bleeding from the blow of a stone. He was haranguing, gesticulating, blessing, doing all in his power to pacify the crowd, and with the hope of the release of the councilors all was quieting down; and Clement, after reconnoitering, thought it safe to order the carriage to take home his guests.

'No one can describe,' said my sister, 'how good and sweet Madame was, though she looked so like a Puritan dame. Her face was so wonderfully calm and noble, like some grand old saint in a picture; and it lighted up so whenever her son came near her, I wanted to ask her blessing! And I think she gave it inwardly. She curtsied, and would have kissed my hand, as being only bourgeois, while I was noble; but I told her I would have no such folly, and I made her give me a good motherly embrace!'

'I hope she gave you something to eat,' I said, laughing.

'Oh, yes; we had an excellent meal. She made us eat before sending us home, soup, and ragout, and chocolate—excellent chocolate. She had it brought as soon as possible, because Eustace looked so pale and tired. Oh, Meg! She is the very best creature I have seen in France. Your Rambouillets are nothing to her! I hope I may see her often again!'

And while Eustace marveled if this were a passing tumult or the beginning of a civil war, my most immediate wonder was what my mother would say to this adventure.

CHAPTER XVI. — THE BARRICADES

My mother did not come home till the evening, when the streets had become tolerably quiet. She had a strange account to give, for she had been at the palace all the time in attendance on Queen Henrietta, who tried in vain to impress her sister-in-law with a sense that the matter was serious. Queen Anne of Austria was too proud to believe that a parliament and a mob could do any damage to the throne of France, whatever they might effect in England.

There she sat in her grand cabinet, and with her were the Cardinal, the Duke of Longueville, and many other gentlemen, especially Messieurs de Nogent and de Beautru, who were the wits, if not the buffoons of the Court, and who turned all the reports they heard into ridicule. The Queen-Regent smiled in her haughty way, but the Queen of England laid her hand sadly on my mother's arm and said, 'Alas, my dear friend, was it not thus that once we laughed?'

Presently in came Marshal de la Meilleraye and the Coadjutor, and their faces and gestures showed plainly that they were seriously alarmed; but M. de Beautru, nothing daunted, turned to the Regent, saying, 'How ill Her Majesty must be, since M. le Coadjutor is come to bring her extreme unction,' whereupon there was another great burst of applause and laughter.

The Coadjutor pretended not to hear, and addressing the Queen told her that he had come to offer his services to her at a moment of pressing danger. Anne of Austria only vouchsafed a little nod with her head, by way at once of thanks, and showing how officious and superfluous she thought him, while Nogent and Beautru continued to mimic the dismay of poor Broussel, seized in his dressing-gown and slippers, and the shrieks of his old housekeeper from the window. 'Did no one silence them for being so unmanly?' cried Annora, as she heard this.

'Child, thou art foolish!' said my mother with dignity. 'Why should the resistance of canaille like that be observed at all, save to make sport?'

For my poor mother, since she had been dipped again into the Court atmosphere, had learned to look on whatever was not noble, as not of the same nature with herself. However, she said that Marshal de la Meilleraye, a thorough soldier, broke in by assuring the Queen that the populace were in arms, howling for Broussel, and the Coadjutor began to describe the fierce tumult through which he had made his way, but the Cardinal only gave his dainty provoking Italian smile, and the Queen-Regent proudly affirmed that there neither was nor could be a revolt.

'We know,' added Mazarin, in his blandest tone of irony, 'that M. le Coadjuteur is so devoted to the Court, and so solicitous for his flock, that a little over-anxiety must be pardoned to him!'

This was while shouts of 'BROUSSEL! BROUSSEL!' were echoing through the palace, and in a few moments came the Lieutenant-Colonel of the Guards to say that the populace were threatening to overpower the soldiers at the gates; and next came the Chancellor, nearly frightened out of his wits, saying that he had seen the people howling like a pack of wolves, carrying all sorts of strange weapons, and ready to force their way in. Then old Monsieur Guitauet, the Colonel of the Guards, declared 'that the old rogue Broussel must be surrendered, dead or alive.'

'The former step would not be accordant with the Queen's piety nor her justice,' broke in the Coadjutor; 'the second might stop the tumult.'

'I understand you, M. le Coadjuteur,' broke out the Queen. 'You want me to set Broussel at liberty. I would rather strangle him with my own hands, and those who—'

And she held those plump white hands of hers almost close to the Archbishop's face, as if she were ready to do it, but Cardinal Mazarin whispered something in her ear which made her less violent, and the next moment the lieutenant of police came in, with such a terrific account of the fury of the mob and their numbers, that there was no more incredulity; it was plain that there was really a most frightful uproar, and both the Regent and the Cardinal entreated the Coadjutor to go down and pacify the people by promises. He tried to obtain from the Queen some written promise.

'He was right,' said Eustace.

'Right!' cried my mother. 'What! to seek to bind Her Majesty down by written words, like a base mechanical bourgeois? I am ashamed of you, my son! No, indeed, we all cried out upon him, Archbishop though he were, and told him that Her Majesty's word was worth ten thousand bonds.'

'May it be so proved!' muttered Eustace, while my mother went on to describe how the Coadjutor was pressed, pushed, and almost dragged down the great stair-case to speak to the infuriated people who were yelling and shrieking outside the court. Monsieur de Meilleraye went before him, backed by all the light horse drawn up in the court, and mounting his horse, drew his sword crying, 'Vive le Roi! Liberty for Broussel!' he was met by a cry of 'To arms, to arms!' and there was a rush against him, some trying to pull him off his horse, and one attacking him with a rusty old sword. The Marshal fired at him and he fell, severely wounded, just as the Coadjutor came down, and seeing him lying in the gutter like one dead, knelt down by him, heard his confession, and absolved him.

(It was afterwards said that the man was a pick-lock, but we always suspected that the Coadjutor had made the worst of him by way of enhancing a good story.)

Just as the absolution was finished, some more of the mob came up, and one threw a stone which hit the Archbishop on the cheek, and another pointed a musket at him. 'Unhappy man,' he cried, 'if your father saw you!' This seemed to touch the man; he cried: 'Vive le Coadjuteur!' And so easily were the people swayed, that they all began to applaud him to the skies, and he led them off to the market-place.

'We thought ourselves rid of them,' said my mother, 'we began to breathe again, and I was coming home, but, bah! No such thing! They are all coming back, thirty or forty thousand of them, only without their weapons. At least the gentlemen said so, but I am sure they had them hidden. Up comes M. Le Coadjuteur again, the Marshal de Meileraye leading him by the hand up the Queen, and saying: 'Here, Madame, is one to whom I owe my life, but to whom your Majesty owes the safety of the State, nay, perhaps of the palace.''

The Queen smiled, seeing through it all, said my mother, and the Coadjutor broke in: 'The matter is not myself, Madame, it is Paris, now disarmed and submissive, at your Majesty's feet.'

'It is very guilty, and far from submissive,' said the Queen angrily; 'pray, if it were so furious, how can it have been so rapidly tamed?' And then M. de Meilleraye must needs break in furiously: 'Madame, an honest man cannot dissemble the state of things. If Broussel is not set at liberty, tomorrow there will not be one stone upon another at Paris.'

But the Queen was firm, and put them both down, only saying: 'Go and rest, Monsieur, you have worked hard.'

'Was that all the thanks he had?' exclaimed Annora.

'Of course it was, child. The Queen and Cardinal knew very well that the tumult was his work; or at least immensely exaggerated by him, just to terrify her into releasing that factious old mischief-maker! Why, he went off I know not where, haranguing them from the top of his carriage!'

'Ah! that was where we saw him,' said Nan. 'Madame, indeed there was nothing exaggerated in the tumult. It was frightful. They made ten times the noise our honest folk do in England, and did ten times less. If they had been English, M. Broussel would be safe at home now!'

'No the tumult was not over-painted, that I can testify,' said my brother.

But when my mother came to hear how he and Annora had witnessed the scene from the windows of M. Darpent's house, her indignation knew no bounds. I never saw her so angry with Eustace as she now was, that he should have taken his sister into the house of one of these councillors; a bourgeois house was bad enough, but that it should have been actually one of the disaffected, and that the Darpent carriage should have been seen at our door, filled her with horror. It was enough to ruin us all for ever with the Court.

'What have we to do with the Court?' cried my sister, and this, of course, only added fuel to the flame, till at last my mother came to declaring that she should never trust her daughter with my brother again, for he was not fit to take care of her.

But we were all surprised by Eustace, when he bade my mother goodnight, quietly bending his dark curled head, ad saying: 'My mother, I ask your pardon, I am sorry I offended you.'

'My son, my dear son,' she cried, embracing him. 'Never think of it more, only if we never go home, I cannot have your sister made a mere bourgeoise.'

'How could you, brother!' cried Annora, waiting outside the door. 'Now you have owned yourself in the wrong!'

'I have not said so, Nan,' he answered. 'I have simply said I was sorry to have offended my mother, and that is true; I could not sleep under her displeasure.'

'But you do not care about ruining yourself with this perfidious foreign Court.'

'Not a rush, so long as I do not bring Meg and her son into danger.'

Things were quiet that night, but every one knew that it was only a lull in the storm.

I set off to morning mass with my son and little Armantine as usual, thinking all would be quiet so early in our part of the city, but before the service was over there was the dull roar of the populace in a fury to be heard in the distance, and Nicole met me at the church door entreating me to get home as quickly as possible.

To my dismay there was a large heavy chain across the end of the street, not such as to stop foot passengers, but barring the way against carriages, and the street was fast filling with shopkeepers, apprentices, market-women, and all sorts of people. The children clung to my hands, half frightened and half eager. Suddenly we saw a carriage stopped by the chain, and the people crowding round it. Out of it sprang two gentlemen and a lady, and began hurrying forward like people hunted. I drew the children back into the church porch, and was shocked to see that those who were then fleeing in haste and terror were the Chancellor, M. Seguier, with his brother, the Bishop of Meaux, and his daughter the beautiful young Duchess de Sully. I tried to attract their attention and draw them into the church as a place of safety, but they were in too much haste and terror to perceive me, and a man began shouting after them:

'To arms, friends, to arms! There's the enemy. Kill him! and we shall have vengeance for all we suffer!'

The mob rushed after, shouting horribly. Armantine began to cry, and I took her in my arms, while Nicole held my son.

The whole crowd rushed past us, never heeding us, as we stood above them, and as we were only thirty yards from home I hoped soon to reach it, though I hesitated, as the screeches, yells, and howls were still to be heard lower down the street, and fresh parties of men, women, and children kept rushing down to join the throng. If it should surge back again before we could get home, what would become of us?

Suddenly Gaspard cried out: 'My uncle!' And there was indeed my brother. 'Good heavens!' he cried, 'you there, sister! They told me you were gone to church, but I could hardly believe it! Come home before the mob comes back.'

I asked anxiously for the Chancellor, and heard he had escaped into the Hotel de Luynes, which was three doors beyond ours. He had set out at six in the morning for the palace, it was believed to take orders for breaking up the Parliament. His daughter, thinking there might be danger, chose to go with him, and so did his brother the Bishop; but the instant he was known to be entangled in the streets, the mob rose on him, the chains were put up, he had to leave his carriage and flee on foot to the Hotel de Luynes, where his brother-in-law lived. There the door was open, but no one was up but an old servant, and, in the utmost terror, the unhappy Chancellor rushed into a little wainscoted closet, where he shut himself up, confessing his sins to the Bishop, believing his last moments were come. In fact, the mob did search all over the hotel, some meaning to make him a hostage for Broussel, and others shouting that they would cut him to pieces to show what fate awaited the instruments of tyranny. They did actually beat against the wainscot of his secret chamber, but hearing nothing, they left the spot, but continued to keep guard round the house, shouting out execrations against him.

Meantime Eustace had brought us safely home, where the first thing we did was to hurry up to the balcony, where Annora was already watching anxiously.

Presently, Marshal de Meilleraye and his light horse came galloping and clattering down the street, while the mob fled headlong, hither and thither, before them. A carriage was brought out, and the Chancellor with his brother and daughter was put into it, but as they were driving off the mob rallied again and began to pursue them. A shot was fired, and a poor woman, under a heavy basket, fell. There was another outburst of curses, screams, howls, yells, shots; and carriage, guards, people, all rushed past us, the coach going at the full speed of its six horses, amid a shower of stones, and even bullets, the guards galloping after, sometimes firing or cutting with their swords, the people keeping up with them at a headlong pace, pelting them with stones and dirt, and often firing at them, for, indeed, the poor young Duchess received a wound before they could reach the palace. Meanwhile others of the mob began ransacking the Hotel de Luynes in their rage at the Chancellor's escape, and they made dreadful havoc of the furniture, although they did not pillage it.

My mother wept bitterly, declaring that the evil days she had seen in England were pursuing her to France; and we could not persuade her that we were in no danger, until the populace, having done their worst at the Hotel de Luynes, drifted away from our street. Eustace could not of course bear to stay shut up and knowing nothing, and he and the Abbe both went out different ways, leaving us to devour our anxiety as best we could, knowing nothing but that there was a chain across each end of our street, with a double row of stakes on either side, banked up with earth, stones, straw, all sorts of things, and guarded by men with all manner of queer old weapons that had come down from the wars of the League. Eustace even came upon one of the old-fashioned arquebuses standing on three legs to be fired; and, what was worse, there was a gorget with the portrait of the murderer of Henri III. enameled on it, and the inscription 'S. Jacques Clement,' but the Coadjutor had the horrible thing broken up publicly. My brother said things did indeed remind him of the rusty old weapons that were taken down at the beginning of the Rebellion. He had been to M. Darpent's, and found him exceedingly busy, and had learned from him that the Coadjutor was at the bottom of all this day's disturbance. Yes, Archbishop de Gondi himself. He had been bitterly offended at the mocking, mistrustful way in which his services had been treated, and besides, reports came to him that Cardinal talked of sending him of Quimper Corentin, and Broussel to Havre, and the Chancellor to dismiss the Parliament! He had taken counsel with his friends, and determined to put himself and the head of the popular movement and be revenged upon the Court, and one of his familiar associates, M. d'Argenteuil, had disguised himself as a mason, and led the attack with a rule in his hand, while a lady, Madame Martineau, had beaten the drum and collected the throng to guard the gates and attack the Chancellor. There were, it was computed, no less than 1260 barricades all over Paris, and the Parliament was perfectly amazed at the excitement produced by the capture of Broussel. Finding that they had such supporters, the Parliament was more than ever determined to make a stand for its rights—whatever they might be.

The Queen had sent to command the Coadjutor to appease the sedition, but he had answered that he had made himself so odious by his exertions of the previous day that he could not undertake what was desired of him.

The next thing we heard was that the First President, Mathieu Mole, one of the very best men then living, had gone at the head of sixty-six Counsellors of Parliament, two and two, to seek an audience of the Queen. They were followed by a huge multitude, who supposed Broussel to be still at the Palais Royal.

The Counsellors were admitted, but the Queen was as obdurate as ever. She told them that they, their wives and children, should answer for this day's work, and that a hundred thousand armed men should not force her to give up her will. Then she got up from her chair, went out of the room, and slammed the door! It is even said that she talked of hanging a few of the Counsellors from the windows to intimidate the mob; but Mademoiselle assured me that this was not true; though M. de Meilleraye actually proposed cutting off Broussel's head and throwing it out into the street.

The Counsellors were kept waiting two hours in the Great Gallery, while the mob roared outside, and the Cardinal, the Dukes of Orleans and Longueville, and other great nobles, argued the matter with the Queen. The Cardinal was, it seems, in a terrible fright. The Queen, full of Spanish pride and high courage, would really have rather perished than yielded to the populace; but Mazarin was more and more terrified, and at last she yielded, and consented to his going to the Counsellors to promise the release of the prisoners. He was trembling all over, and made quite an absurd appearance, and presently the Parliament men appeared again, carrying huge sealed letters; Broussel's was borne by his nephew in triumph. We could hear the Vivas! With which the people greeted them, as the promise of restoration was made known. At eleven at night there was a fresh outcry, but this was of joy, for M. Blancmesnil had actually come back from Vincennes; but the barricades were not taken down. There was to be no laying down of arms till Broussel appeared, and there were strange noises all night, preventing sleep.

At eight o'clock the next morning Broussel had not appeared; the people were walking about in a sullen rage, and this was made worse by a report that there were 10,000 soldiers in the Bois de Boulogne ready to chastise the people. We could see from our house-top the glancing or arms at every barricade where the sun could penetrate, and in the midst came one of the servants announcing Monsieur Clement Darpent.

He had a sword by his side, and pistols at his belt, and he said that he was come to assure the ladies that there would be no danger for them. If any one tried to meddle with the house, we might say we were friends of M. Darpent, and we should be secure. If the account of the soldiers outside were true, the people were determined not to yield to such perfidy; but he did not greatly credit it, only it was well to be prepared.

'Alas! my friend,' said Eustace, 'this has all too much the air of rebellion.'

'We stand on our rights and privileges,' said Darpent. 'We uphold them in the King's name against the treachery of a Spanish woman and an Italian priest.'

'You have been sorely tried,' said Eustace; 'but I doubt me whether anything justifies taking arms against the Crown.'

'Ah! I am talking to a Cavalier,' said Clement. 'But I must not argue the point. I must to my barricade.'

Nan here came forward, and desired him to carry her commendations and thanks to Madame sa mere, and he bowed, evidently much gratified. She durst not go the length of offering her good wishes, and she told me I ought to have been thankful to her for the forbearance, when, under a strong sense of duty, I reproved her. Technically he was only Maitre Darpent, and his mother only would have been called Mademoiselle. Monsieur and Madame were much more jealously limited to nobility than they are now becoming, and the Darpents would not purchase a patent of nobility to shelter themselves from taxation. For, as Eustace said, the bourgeoisie had its own chivalry of ideas.

There was no more fighting. By ten o'clock Broussel was in the city, the chains were torn down, the barricades leveled, and he made a triumphal progress. He was taken first to Notre Dame, and as he left the carriage his old dressing-gown was almost torn to pieces, every one crowding to kiss it, or his feet, calling him their father and protector, and anxiously inquiring for his health. A Te Deum was sung—if not so splendid, much more full of the ring of joy than the grand one two days before! Engravings of his portrait were sold about the streets, bearing the inscription 'Pierre Broussel, father of his country;' and the good-natured old man seemed quite bewildered at the honours that had befallen him.

There were a few more alarms that night and the next day, but at last they subsided, the barricades were taken down, and things returned to their usual state, at least to all outward appearance.

CHAPTER XVII. — A PATIENT GRISEL

Matters seemed to be getting worse all round us both in France and England. King Charles was in the hands of his enemies, and all the good news that we could hear from England was that the Duke of York had escaped in a girl's dress, and was on board the fleet at helvoetsluys, where his brother the Prince of Wales jointed him.

And my own dear brother, Lord Walwyn, declared that he could no longer remain inactive at Paris, so far from intelligence, but that he must be with the Princes, ready to assist in case anything should be attempted on the King's behalf. We much dreaded the effect of the Dutch climate on his health. And while tumultuous assemblies were constantly taking place in Parliament, and no one could guess what was coming next, we did not like parting with our protector; but he said that he was an alien, and could do nothing for us. The army was on its way home, and with it our brother de Solivet, and M. d'Aubepine; and his clear duty was to be ready to engage in the cause of his own King. We were in no danger at Paris, our sex was sufficient protection, and if we were really alarmed, there could be no reason against our fleeing to Nid de Merle. Nay, perhaps, if the Court were made to take home the lesson, we might be allowed to reside there, and be unmolested in making improvements. He had another motive, which he only whispered to me.

'I cannot, and will not, give up my friend Darpent; and it is not fitting to live in continual resistance to my mother. It does much harm to Annora, who is by no means inclined to submit, and if I am gone there can be no further question of intercourse.'

I thought this was hard upon us all. Had we not met M. Darpent at the Hotel Rambouillet, and was he not a fit companion for us?

'Most assuredly,' said Eustace; 'but certain sentiments may arise from companionship which in her case were better avoided.'

As you may imagine, my grandchildren, I cried out in horror at the idea that if M. Darpent were capable of such presumption, my sister, a descendant of the Ribaumonts, could stoop for a moment to favour a mere bourgeois; but Eustace, Englishman as he was, laughed at my indignation, and said Annora was more of the Ribmont than the de Ribaumont, and that he would not be accessory either to the breaking of hearts or to letting her become rebellious, and so that he should put temptation out of her way. I knew far too well what was becoming to allow myself to suppose for a moment that Eustace thought an inclination between the two already could exist. I forgot how things had been broken up in England.

As to Annora, she thought Eustace's right place was with the Prince, and she would not stretch out a finger to hold him back, only she longed earnestly that he would take us with him. Could he not persuade our mother that France was becoming dangerous, and that she would be safe in Holland? But of course he only laughed at that; and we all saw that unless the Queen of England chose to follow her sons, there was no chance of my mother leaving the Court.

'No, my sister,' said Eustace tenderly, 'there is nothing for you to do but to endure patiently. It is very hard for you to be both firm and resolute, and at the same time dutiful; but it is a noble part in its very difficulty, and my Nan will seek strength for it.'

Then the girl pressed up to him, and told him that one thing he must promise her, namely, that he would prevent my mother from disposing of her hand without his consent.

'As long as you are here I am safe,' said she; 'but when you are gone I do not know what she may attempt. And here is this Solivet son of hers coming too!'

'Solivet has no power over you,' said Eustace. 'You may make yourself easy, Nan. Nobody can marry you without my consent, for my father made me your guardian. And I doubt me if your portion, so long as I am living, be such as to tempt any man to wed such a little fury, even were we at home.'

'Thanks for the hint, brother,' said Annora. 'I will take care that any such suitor SHALL think me a fury.'

'Nay, child, in moderation! Violence is not strength. Nay, rather it exhausts the forces. Resolution and submission are our watchwords.'

How noble he looked as he said it, and how sad it was to part with him! my mother wept most bitterly, and said it was cruel to leave us to our fate, and that he would kill himself in the Dutch marshes; but when the actual pain of parting with him was over, I am not sure that she had not more hope of carrying out her wishes. She would have begun by forbidding Annora to go, attended only by the servants, to prayers at the England ambassador's: but Eustace had foreseen this, and made arrangements with a good old knight and his lady, Sir Francis Ommaney, always to call for my sister on their way to church, and she was always ready for them. My mother used to say that her devotion was all perverseness, and now and then, when more than usually provoked with her, would declare that it was quite plain that her poor child's religion was only a heresy, since it did not make her a better daughter.

That used to sting Annora beyond all measure. Sometimes she would reply by pouring out a catalogue of all the worst offences of our own Church, and Heaven knows she could find enough of them! Or at others she would appeal to the lives of all the best people she had ever heard of in England, and especially of Eustace, declaring that she knew she herself was far from good, but that was not the fault of her religion, but of herself; and she would really strive to be submissive and obliging for many days afterwards.

Meantime the Prince of Conde had returned, and had met the Court at Ruel. M. d'Aubepine and M. de Solivet both were coming with him, and my poor little Cecile wrote letter after letter to her husband, quite correct in grammar and orthography, asking whether she should have the Hotel d'Aubepine prepared, and hire servants to receive him; but she never received a line in reply. She was very anxious to know whether the concierge had received any orders, and yet she could not bear to betray her ignorance.

I had been startled by passing in the street a face which I was almost sure belonged to poor Cecile's former enemy, Mademoiselle Gringrimeau, now the wife of Croquelebois, the intendant of the estate; and setting old Nicole to work, I ascertained that this same agent and his wife were actually at the Hotel d'Aubepine, having come to meet their master, but that no apartments were made ready for him, as it was understood that being on the staff he would be lodge in the Hotel de Conde.

'His duty!' said Cecile; 'he must fulfil his duty, but at least I shall see him.'

But to hear of the intendant and his wife made me very uneasy.

The happier wives were going out in their carriages to meet their husbands on the road, but Cecile did not even know when he was coming, nor by what road.

'So much the better,' said our English Nan. 'If I had a husband, I would never make him look foolish in the middle of the road with a woman and a pack of children hanging on him!'

No one save myself understood her English bashfulness, shrinking from all display of sentiment, and I—ah! I had known such blissful meetings, when my Philippe had been full of joy to see me come out to meet him. Ah! will he meet me thus at the gates of Paradise? It cannot be far off now!

I knew I should weep all the way if I set out with my mother to meet her son; and Cecile was afraid both of the disappointment if she did not meet her husband, and of his being displeased if he should come. So she only took with her Annora and M. de Solivet's two daughters, Gabrielle and Petronille, who were fetched from the Convent of the Visitation. There they sat in the carriage, Nan told me, exactly alike in their pensionnaire's uniform, still and shy on the edge of the seat, not daring to look to the right or left, and answering under their breath, so that she longed to shake them. I found afterwards that the heretic Mademoiselle de Ribaumont was a fearful spectacle to them, and that they were expecting her all the time to break out in the praises of Luther, or of Henry VIII., or of some one whom they had been taught to execrate; and whenever she opened her lips they thought she was going to pervert them, and were quite surprised when she only made a remark, like other people, on the carriages and horsemen who passed them.

Meanwhile Cecile saw her little girl and boy dressed in their best, and again rehearsed the curtsey and the bow and the little speeches with which they were to meet their father. She was sure, she said, that whatever he might think of her, he must be enchanted with them; and truly they had beautiful eyes, and Armantine was a charming child, though Maurice was small and pale, and neither equaled my Gaspard, who might have been White Ribaumont for height and complexion, resembling much his uncle Walwyn, and yet in countenance like his father. Then Cecile and I, long before it was reasonable, took our station near a window overlooking the porte-cochere. I sat with my work, while the children watched on the window-seat, and she, at every exclamation of theirs, leaped up to look out, but only to see some woodcutter with his pile of faggots, or a washer-woman carrying home a dress displayed on its pole, or an ell of bread coming in from the baker's; and she resumed her interrupted conversation on her security that for the children's sake her husband would set up his household together with her at the Hotel d'Aubepine. She had been learning all she could, while she was with us, and if she could only be such that he need not be ashamed of her, and would love her only a little for his children's sake, how happy she should be!

I encouraged her, for her little dull provincial convent air was quite gone; she had acquired the air of society, my mother had taught her something of the art of dress, and though nothing would ever make her beautiful in feature, or striking in figure, she had such a sweet, pleading, lovely expression of countenance that I could not think how any one could resist her. At last it was no longer a false alarm. The children cried out, not in vain. The six horses were clattering under the gateway, the carriage came in sight before the steps. Cecile dropped back in her chair as pale as death, murmuring: 'Tell me if he is there!'

Alas! 'he' was not there. I only saw M. de Solivet descend from the carriage and hand out my mother, my sister, and his two daughters. I could but embrace my poor sister-in-law, and assure her that I would bring her tidings of her husband, and then hurry away with Gaspard that I might meet my half-brother at the salon door. There he was, looking very happy, with a daughter in each hand, and they had lighted up into something like animation, which made Petronille especially show that she might some day be pretty. He embraced me, like the good-natured friendly brother he had always been, and expressed himself perfectly amazed at the growth and beauty of my little Marquis, as well he might be, for my mother and I both agreed that there was not such another child among all the King's pages.

I asked, as soon as I could, for M. d'Aubepine, and heard that he was attending the Prince, who would, of course, first have to dress, and then to present himself to the Queen-Regent, and kiss her hand, after which he would go to Madame de Longueville's reception of the King. It was almost a relief to hear that the Count was thus employed, and I sent my son to tell his aunt that she might be no longer in suspense.

I asked Solivet whether we might expect the young man on leaving the Louvre, and he only shrugged his shoulders and said: 'What know I?' It became plain to me that he would not discuss the matter before his daughters, now fourteen and fifteen, and we all had to sit down to an early supper, after which they were to be taken back to their convent. M. d'Aubepine appeared, and was quite cheerful, for she figured to herself once more that her husband was only detained by his duties and his value to his Prince, and was burning every moment to see his little ones. She asked questions about him, and became radiant when she heard of his courage at Lens, and the compliments that M. le Prince had paid to him.

After supper the little pensionnaires were to be taken back, and as some lady must escort them, I undertook the charge, finding with great delight that their father would accompany them likewise. I effaced myself as much as I could on the way, and let the father and daughters talk to one another; and they chattered freely about their tasks, and works, and playfellows, seeming very happy with him.

But on the way home was my opportunity, and I asked what my half-brother really thought of M. d'Aubepine.

'He is a fine young man,' he said.

'You have told me that before; but what hopes are there for his wife?'

'Poor little thing,' returned Solivet.

'Can he help loving her?' I said

'Alas! my sister, he has been in a bad school, and has before him an example—of courage, it is true, but not precisely of conjugal affection.'

'Is it true, then,' I asked, 'that the Princess of Conde is kept utterly in the background in spite of her mother-in-law, and that the Prince publishes his dislike to her?'

'Perfectly true,' said my brother. 'When a hero, adored by his officers, actually declares that the only thing he does not wish to see in France is his wife, what can you expect of them? Even some who really love their wives bade them remain at home, and will steal away to see them with a certain shame; and for Aubepine, he is only too proud to resemble the Prince in being married against his will to a little half-deformed child, who is to be avoided.'

I cried out at this, and demanded whether my little sister-in-law could possibly be thus described. He owned that she was incredibly improved, and begged my pardon and hers, saying that he was only repeating what Aubepine either believed or pretended to believe her to be.

'If I could only speak with him!' I said. 'For my husband's sake I used to have some influence with him. I would give the world to meet him before he sees the intendant and his wife. Could we contrive it?'

In a few moments we had settled it. Happily we were both in full dress, in case friends should have dropped in on us. Both of us had the entree at Madame de Longueville's, and it would be quite correct to pay her our compliments on the return of her brother.

I believe Solivet a little questioned whether one so headstrong had not better be left to himself, but he allowed that no one had ever done as much with Armand d'Aubepine as my husband and myself, and when he heard my urgent wish to forestall the intendant, whose wife was Cecile's old tyrant, Mademoiselle de Gringrimeau, he thought it worth the venture. He said I was a warlike Gildippe still, and that he would stand by me.

So the coachman received his orders; we fell in among the long line of carriages, and in due time made our way to the salon, where Madame le Duchesse de Longueville sat enthroned in all the glory of her fair hair and beautiful complexion, toying with her fan as she conversed with the Prince of Marsillac, the most favoured at that time of a whole troop of admirers and devoted slaves. She was not an intellectual woman herself, but she had beyond all others who I ever saw the power of leading captive the very ablest men.

The hero had not yet come from the palace, and having made our compliments, and received a gracious smile and nod, we stood aside, waiting and conversing with others, and in some anxiety lest the Prince should be detained at the Louvre. However, before long he came, and his keen eagle face, and the stars on his breast, flashed on us, as he returned the greetings of one group after another in his own peculiar manner, haughty, and yet not without a certain charm.

A troop of officers followed, mingling with the gay crowd of ladies and gentlemen, and among them Solivet pointed out the Count d'Aubepine. I should not otherwise have known him, so much was he altered in these six years, changing him from youth to manhood. His hair was much darker, he had a small pointed beard, and the childish contour of cheek and chin had passed away, and he was altogether developed, but there was something that did not reassure me. He seemed to have lost, with his boyhood, that individuality which we had once loved, and to have passed into an ordinary officer, like all the rest of the gay, dashing, handsome, but often hardened-looking men, who were enjoying their triumphant return into ladies' society.

Solivet had accosted him. I saw his eye glance anxiously round, then he seemed reassured, and came towards me with some eagerness, greeting me with some compliment, I know not what, on my appearance; but I cut this as short as I could be saying: 'Know you, Monsieur, why I am here? I am come to ask you to bestow a little half-hour on one who is longing to see you.'

'Madame, I am desolated to refuse you, but, you see, I am in attendance, and on duty; I am not the master!'

However, my brother observed that he would not be required for at least two hours, and his movements would be quite free until the party broke up. And after a little importunity, I actually carried him off, holding up his hands and declaring that he could not withstand Madame de Bellaise, so as to cast over his concession an air of gallantry without which I believe his vanity would never have yielded.

However, I had my hopes; I would not blame him when I had such an advantage over him as having him shut up with me in my coach, for we left Solivet to make his excuses, and as we told him, for a hostage, to come back when I released my prisoner. I trusted more to the effect of the sight of my sweet little Cecile than to any exhortation in my power; indeed, I thought I had better keep him in good humour by listening amiably to his explanation of the great favour that he was doing me in coming to see Madame, my mother, and how indispensable he was to M. le Prince.

He must have known what I was carrying him to see, but he did not choose to show that he did, and when he gave me his arm and I took him into the pansy salon, there sat my mother with my sister, two or three old friends who had come to congratulate her, and to see M. de Solivet, and Cecile, who had not been able to persuade herself to send her children to bed, though she knew not of my audacious enterprises.

I saw that he did not know her in the least, as he advanced to my mother, as the lady of the house, and in one moment I recollected how my grandfather had fallen in love with my grandmother without knowing she was his life. Cecile, crimson all over, with her children beside her, sprang forward, her heart telling her who he was. 'Ah, Monsieur, embrace your son,' she murmured. And little Armantine and Maurice, as they had been tutored, made their pretty reverences, and said, 'Welcome, my papa.'

He really was quite touched. There was something, too, in the surroundings which was sympathetic. He embraced them all, and evidently looked at his wife with amazement, sitting down at last beside her with his little boy upon his knee.

We drew to the farther end of the room that they might be unembarrassed. Annora was indignant that we did not leave them alone, but I thought he wanted a certain check upon him, and that it was good for him to be in the presence of persons who expected him to be delighted to see his wife and children.

I believe that that quarter of an hour was actual pain to Cecile from the very overflowing rush of felicity. To have her husband seated beside her, with his son upon his knee, had been the dream and prayer of her life for six years, and now that it was gratified the very intensity of her hopes and fears choked her, made her stammer and answer at random, when a woman without her depth of affection might have put out all kinds of arts to win and detain him.

After a time he put the child down, but still held his hand, came up to the rest of the company and mingled with it. I could have wished they had been younger and more fashionable, instead of a poor old Scottish cavalier and his wife, my mother's old contemporary Madame de Delincourt, and a couple of officers waiting for Solivet. Annora was the only young brilliant creature there, and she had much too low an opinion of M. d'Aubepine to have a word to say to him, and continued to converse in English with old Sir Andrew Macniven about the campaigns of the Marquis of Montrose, both of them hurling out barbarous names that were enough to drive civilized ears out of the room.

Our unwilling guest behaved with tolerably good grace, and presently made his excuse to my mother and me, promising immediately to send back Solivet to his friends. His wife went with him into the outer room, and when in a few minutes Armantine ran back to call me —

'Papa is gone, and mama is crying,' she said.

It was true, but they were tears of joy. Cecile threw herself on my bosom perfectly overwhelmed with happiness, poor little thing, declaring that she owed it all to me, and that though he could not remain now, he had promised that she should hear from him. He was enchanted with his children; indeed, how could he help it? And she would have kept me up all night, discussing every hair of his moustache, every tone in the few words he had spoken to her. When at last I parted from her I could not help being very glad. Was the victory indeed won, and would my Philippe's sister become a happy wife?

I trusted that now he had seen her he would be armed against Madame Croquelebois, who you will remember had been his grandmother's dame de compagnie, and a sort of governess to him. She had petted him as much as she had afterwards tyrannized over his poor little wife, and might still retain much influence over him, which she was sure to exert against me. But at any rate he could not doubt of his wife's adoration for him.

We waited in hope. We heard of the Prince in attendance on the Queen-Regent, and we knew his aide-de-camp could not be spared, and we went on expecting all the morning and all the evening, assuring Cecile that military duty was inexorable, all the time that we were boiling over with indignation.

My mother was quite as angry as we were, and from her age and position could be more effective. She met M. d'Aubepine one evening at the Louvre, and took him to task, demanding when his wife was to hear from him, and fairly putting him out of countenance in the presence of the Queen of England. She came home triumphant at what she had done, and raised our hopes again, but in fact, though it impelled him to action, there was now mortified vanity added to indifference and impatience of the yoke.

There was a letter the next day. Half an hour after receiving it I found Cecile sunk down on the floor of her apartment, upon which all her wardrobe was strewn about as if to be packed up. She fell into my arms weeping passionately, and declaring she must leave us. to leave us and set up her menage with her husband had always been her ambition, so it was plain that this was not what she meant; but for a long time she neither would nor could tell me, or moan out anything but a 'convent,' 'how could he?' and 'my children.'

At last she let me read the letter, and a cruel one it was, beginning 'Madame,' and giving her the choice of returning to Chateau d'Aubepine under the supervision of Madame Croquelebois, or of entering a convent, and sending her son to be bred up at the Chateau under a tutor and the intendant. She had quite long enough lived with Madame de Bellaise, and that young Englishman, her brother, who was said to be charming.

It was an absolute insult to us all, and as I saw at once was the work of Madame Croquelebois, accepted by the young Count as a convenient excuse for avoiding the ennui and expense of setting up a household with his wife, instead of living a gay bachelor life with his Prince. I did not even think it was his handwriting except the signature, an idea which gave the first ray of comfort to my poor sister-in-law. It was quite provoking to find that she had no spirit to resent, or even to blame; she only wept that any one should be so cruel, and, quite hopeless of being heard on her own defence, was ready to obey, and return under the power of her oppressor, if only she might keep her son. All the four years she had lived with us had not taught her self-assertion, and the more cruelly she was wounded, the meeker she became.

The Abbe said she was earning a blessing; but I felt, like Annora, much inclined to beat her, when she would persist in loving and admiring that miserable fellow through all, and calling him 'so noble.'

We did not take things by any means so quietly. We were the less sorry for my brother's absence that such an insinuation almost demanded a challenge, though in truth I doubt whether they would have dared to make it had he been at hand. Annora did wish she could take sword or pistols in hand and make him choke on his own words, and she was very angry that our brother de Solivet was much too cool and prudent to take Eustace's quarrel on himself.

Here, however, it was my mother who was most reasonable, and knew best how to act. She said that it was true that as this was my house, and the charge of M. d'Aubepine had been committed to me, I had every right to be offended; but as she was the eldest lady in the house it was suitable for her to act. She wrote a billet to him demanding a personal interview with him that he might explain the insinuations which concerned the honour of herself, her son, and her daughter.

I believe a duel would have been much more agreeable to him than such a meeting, but my mother so contrived it that he knew that he could not fail to meet her without its being known to the whole Court, and that he could not venture. So he came, and I never saw anything more admirably managed than the conference was on my mother's part, for she chose to have me present as mistress of the house. She had put on her richest black velvet suit, and looked a most imposing chatelaine, and though he came in trying to carry it off with military bravado and nonchalance, he was evidently ill at ease.

My mother then demanded of him, in her own name, her son's, and mine, what right or cause he had to make such accusations, as he had implied, respecting our house.

He laughed uneasily, and tried to make light of it, talking of reports, and inferences, and so on; but my mother, well assured that there was no such scandal, drove him up into a corner, and made him confess that he had heard nothing but from Madame Croquelebois. My mother then insisted on that lady being called for, sending her own sedan chair to bring her.

Now the Baronne de Ribaumont Walwyn was a veritable grande dame, and Madame Croquelebois, in spite of her sharp nose, and sharper tongue, was quite cowed by her, and absolutely driven to confess that she had not heard a word against Madame la Comtesse. All that she had gone upon was the fact of their residence in the same house, and that a servant of hers had heard from a servant of ours that M. le Baron gave her his hand to go in to dinner every day when there were no visitors.

It all became plain then. The intendant's wife, who had never forgiven me for taking her victim away from her, had suggested this hint as an excuse for withdrawing the Countess from me, without obliging the Count to keep house with her, and becoming the attentive husband, who seemed, to his perverted notions, a despicable being. Perhaps neither of them had expected the matter to be taken up so seriously, and an old country-bred Huguenot as Madame Croquelebois had originally been, thought that as we were at Court, gallantry was our natural atmosphere.

Having brought them to confession, we divided them. My mother talked to the intendante, and made her perceive what a wicked, cruel injustice and demoralization she was leading her beloved young Count into committing, injuring herself and his children, till the woman actually wept, and allowed that she had not thought of it; she wanted to gratify him, and she felt it hard and ungrateful that she should not watch over his wife and children as his grandmother had always intended.

On my side I had M. d'Aubepine, and at last I worked down to the Armand I had known at Nancy, not indeed the best of subjects, but still infinitely better than the conceited, reckless man who had appeared at first. The one thing that touched him was that I should think him disrespectful to me, and false to his friendship for my husband. He really had never thought his words would hurt me for a moment. He actually shed tears at the thought of my Philippe, and declared that nothing was farther from his intention than any imputation on any one belonging to me.

But bah! he was absolutely driven to find some excuse! How could he play the devoted husband to a little ugly imbecile like that, who would make him ridiculous every moment they appeared together? Yes, he knew I had done the best I could for her, but what was she after all? And her affection was worst of all. Everybody would made game of him.

There was no getting farther. The example of the Prince of Conde and the fear of ridicule had absolutely steeled his heart and blinded his eyes. He could not and would not endure the innocent wife who adored him.

Finally my mother, calling in Solivet, came to the following arrangement, since it was plain that we must part with our inmates. Cecile and her children were to be installed in the Hotel d'Aubepine, to which her husband did not object, since he would be either in attendance on the Prince, or with his regiment. This was better than sending her either to a convent or to the country, since she would still be within our reach, although to our great vexation we could not prevail so far as to hinder Madame Croquelebois from being installed as her duenna, the intendant himself returning to La Vendee.

To our surprise, Cecile did not seem so much dismayed at returning under the power of her tyrant as we had expected. It was doing what her husband wished, and living where she would have news of him, and perhaps sometimes see him.

That was all she seemed to think about, except that she would have her children still with her, and not be quite cut off from us.

And I took this consolation, that she was in better health and a woman of twenty-two could not be so easily oppressed as a sickly child of sixteen.

But we were very unhappy about it, and Annora almost frantic, above all at Cecile's meek submission. She was sure the poor thing would be dead in a month, and then we should be sorry.

CHAPTER XVIII. — TWELFTH NIGHT, OR WHAT YOU WILL.

My mother declared that M. d'Aubepine would fare the better if we left her alone and did not excite the jealousy of Madame Croquelebois, who would be quite capable of carrying her off into the country if she were interfered with.

Indeed it was not an easy or a pleasant thing to go about Paris just then, and we were obliged to stay at home. The town was in a restless state, mobs went about, hooting or singing political songs, or assembled in front of the Louvre to abuse the Cardinal, and any one who was supposed to belong to the Court party might at any time be mobbed. Annora and I much missed the explanations that our brother, Lord Walwyn, used to make to us; and the listening to his conversations with M. Darpent. The Duchess de Rambouillet and her family had wisely retired to their estates, so that there were no more meetings in the Salon Bleu; and after what my brother had said to me, I durst not make the slightest demonstration towards Clement Darpent, though I continued to give my weekly receptions to our poor hungry cavaliers, as I had promised Eustace that I would do. It was from one of them, Sir Andrew Macniven, a clever man who had been a law student in Scotland and at Leyden, that we came to some understanding of what was going on around us.

Under the great Cardinal de Richelieu, the Crown had taken more authority then ever, and raised taxes at its will. The Parliament was only permitted to register the edicts of the Crown, but not to refuse them, as it claimed to do. As nobody who was noble paid taxes the noblesse did not care, and there had hitherto seemed to be no redress. But at this moment, when the war taxes were weighing more heavily than ever, and the demand of a house-tax had irritated the people of Paris, there were a very large number of the nobility much incensed against Cardinal Mazarin, and very jealous of his favour with the Queen-Regent. What they would endure from a French nobleman like Richelieu they abhorred from a low-born foreigner such Mazarin was; and it seemed to the Parliament that this was the moment to make a stand, since they had the populace on their side, and likewise so many of the Court party. There was the Archbishop of Corinth, the Coadjutor to the Archbishop of Paris, who had been mortally offended by the way in which the Queen had treated him on the day of the barricades; there was the handsome, fair-haired Duke of Beaufort, a grandson of Henri IV., who used to be called 'Le roi des halles,' he was such a favourite with the market-women; there was the clever brilliant Prince de Marsillac (you know will his maxims, written after he had become Duke of Rochefoucauld). He could do anything with Madame de Longueville; and she was thought able to do anything with her brothers, the Prince of Code and Conti. Every one had been watching to see what side the Prince would take, but at this time he seemed inclined to the Crown, though it was not likely he could go on long without quarrelling with Mazarin. All this made the Frondeurs hope much from beginning to resist; but I remember Sir Andrew said that he did not believe that these nobles and princes cared in the least for relieving the people, but merely for overthrowing the Cardinal, and he could not find out that the Parliament had any definite scheme, or knew what they wished. In fact, Sir Andrew dreaded any movement. He had been so much disappointed, and so broken-hearted at the loss of friends and the ruin of the country, that his only thought was to leave all alone. And above all he so thought, when every letter from England told how the enemy were proceeding to hunt down his Sacred Majesty.

What a change it was when my son and I had to go into waiting at the Louvre! Before the Queen-Regent there was nothing but vituperation of the Parliament, but the Duke of Orleans hates the Cardinal quite as much as the Parisians did; and his daughter, Mademoiselle, wanted him to lead the Frondeuse, and chatted to me of her plan of leading the party, together with the Prince of Conde, whom she eagerly desired to marry if his poor wife could be divorced. I used to shake my head at her and say I knew she was too good at the bottom to desire anything so shocking, and she took it in good part. She was much better than she chose to seem.

Thus the eve of the Epiphany came, and there was a feast for the King and his little companions. Gaspard had the Bean, and the Queen crowned him and made him King of the night. King Louis himself had to bend the knee, which he did with the best grace in the world. (You must all have seen the little enamelled Bean-flower badge that your father received on that night.)

Every one went to see the children at their feast, where the little English lady Henrietta sat between her two royal cousins, looking like a rosebud, all ignorant, poor child, of the said disaster which was falling on her. Her mother was looking on, smiling in the midst of her cares to see the children's glee.

The Queen-Regent was in the highest spirits. We had never seen her dignity so relax into merriment as when she set the little ones to dance together after the supper was over; but she sent them to bed early, much earlier than her sons desired. We heard his real Majesty saying to Gaspard, 'M. le Marquis, since you are King of the Bean, command that we should be like all other revelers, and sit up till morning.'

My boy looked up to me, and read in my face that he must not presume.

'Ah! sire,' said he, 'though we are called kings, these ladies are the higher powers.'

It was applauded as a grand witticism, although Gaspard meant it in all simplicity, and had no notion of the meaning attributed to it. Nay, he thought all the praise was approval of him as a good boy inducing the King to be obedient.

After the children had gone to bed, including Mademoiselle's three little half-sisters, dull little girls of whom she spoke contemptuously but always treated very kindly, she led the way to the apartment where her father was sitting by a great fire, fretful with gout, and wanting the amusement which she tried to give him by describing the children's diversions. Some one came and whispered something to her, and in the tone of one who has an excellent joke to rehearse she went up to the Duke of Orleans, exclaiming —

'Monsieur! Here is news! We are all to start for St. Germain this very night!'

Monsieur made no answer, and immediately after bade her good night. She then went to her stepmother's room, and I remained with some of the other ladies, who were pretty well convinced that it was a true report, and that the Queen had been only waiting the arrival of the troops from the Low Countries to quit Paris and crush the resistance of the Parliament. What was to become of us we did not know, whether we were to stay or go; but as we heard no more, and Mademoiselle came out and went to bed, we followed her example.

Between three and four we were all awakened by a loud knocking at the door, and Mademoiselle's shrill voice calling out to her maids to open it. Through the anteroom, where the Comtess de Fiesque and I were sleeping, there came M. de Comminges. Mademoiselle, in her laced night-cap, rose on her pillows and asked—

'Are we going?'

'Yes, Mademoiselle,' was the reply. 'The King, the Queen, and Monsieur, are waiting for you in the court, and here is a letter from Monsieur.'

She put it aside, saying she did not want Monsieur's orders to make her obey those of the Queen, but he begged her to read it. She glanced at it, and then declared that she would be ready immediately. M. de Comminges departed, and then began the greatest bustle imaginable, everybody dressing at once in the greatest confusion, putting on each other's things by mistake, and Mademoiselle talking—talking through all.

They were afraid to leave her behind, she said, lest she should have headed a party. No doubt M. le Prince dreaded her influence, and so did the Queen. They had made her father issue his commands without warning lest she should disobey.

In fact she had the greatest desire to disobey, only she did not quite venture, and we her ladies had no notion what we were to do, whether to stay or go, while I was in great anxiety as to what they might have done with my boy.

Somehow or other we all found ourselves in the court of the Louvre, strongly lighted by flambeaux, and by the windows of the building. There stood a row of carriages; Mademoiselle called for hers, but it was not forthcoming, and M. de Comminges, bowing low, offered her his own; but another gentleman came up and handed her into the royal one, where already were the King and Queen, the two Princesses of Conde, the Prince of Conti, and a lady.

I heard Mademoiselle asserting her right to one of the best seats, and then declaring that she yielded 'as the young must give place to the old,' a little cut at the Princess Dowager of Conde. She bade M. de Fiesque follow with her carriage and properties, and we were left in the most wonderful confusion in that dark court, the carriages moving away one after another, the mounted servants carrying torches, and the guards trampling and clinking behind them; servants, gentlemen, and ladies running about wildly, some of the women crying and wringing their hands. Among these was Madame de Fiesque, who was of a timid nature, and was frightened out of her wits at the notion of having to follow, whither she did not even know, while I was equally wild, though I hope I did not make quite so much noise, about my son.

One of the gentlemen at last came and spoke to us, and told us that the King and Queen were gone to St. Germain. It had all been determined upon for some time past (as soon in fact as the Queen knew that the Prince of Conde would support her, and that the troops were near enough to be of use), and this night had been chosen because she could get off more easily in a time of revelry. Monsieur had known it all the evening, but had been afraid to tell his daughter because of 'her ideas,' which meant that he was by no means sure that she might choose to obey, unless she were taken by surprise, but might want to represent the House of Orleans at Paris. The Queen of England was not gone; and, as to M. le Marquis de Nidemerle—

That question was answered by a sound of bare, pattering feet, and a cry of 'Mamma, mamma!' and my little Marquis himself, with nothing on but his little white shirt and black velvet breeches, his long hair streaming behind him, came and threw himself on me, followed by two or three more little fellows in the same state of dishabille. 'Oh, mamma!' he cried, 'we thought they were all gone, and had left us to be murdered by the cruel Parliament; and then I saw you from the window in the court.' So there they all were, except one little Count from Burgundy, who slept serenely through the tumult.

By this time we could recollect that it was a January night, and that we had better retreat into the great hall, where the fire was not out. I had a great mind, since we were thus deserted, to return home with my son, but my poor Princess could not be left without a single attendant, or any clothes save what had been huddled on in haste, nor perhaps even a bed, for we knew that St. Germain was dismantled of furniture, and that no preparations had been made for fear of giving alarm.

M. de Fiesque declared that she should die if she tried to pass the streets of Paris, where we began to hear loud cries. The maids seemed to have all run away, and she implored me to go, with all that was most necessary, to Mademoiselle.

'You are English! You are a very Gildippe. You have been in the wars— you fear nothing,' said the poor woman. 'I implore you to go!'

And as I had my son with me, and it seemed to be a duty or even a charity that no one else would undertake, though it was not likely that any harm could come to us, I sent Gaspard to dress himself, with my faithful Nicolas, who had come to light. The gentlemen undertook to find us Mademoiselle's coach, and we hurried back to get together what we could for our mistress. I laugh now to think of M. de Fiesque and myself trying with our inexperienced hands to roll up a mattress and some bedding, and to find the linen and the toilet requisites, in which we had but small success, for the femmes de chamber kept everything, and had all either run away or slept too far off to hear us. We managed at last to fasten up the mattress with the other things in it, tied by a long scarf at each end, and dragging it to the top of the stairs we rolled it down each flight. At the second it upset at unfortunate lackey, who began to yell, firmly persuaded that it was a corpse, and that the Frondeurs had got in and were beginning a general slaughter.

How we recovered from the confusion I do not know, but Gaspard joined me at the top of the stairs, bringing with him a page of his own age, the little Chevalier de Mericour, whom he entreated me to take with us. All the other boys had relations close at hand; but this child's mother was dead, and his father and brothers with the army. Being really a cousin of Harry Merrycourt's, he had always seemed like a relation, and he was Gaspard's chief friend, so I was very willing to give him a seat in the carriage, which came from somewhere, and into which the mattress was squeezed by some means or other. Off we set, but no woman of any rank would accompany me, for they said I had the courage of an Amazon to attempt to make my way through the mob that was howling in the streets.

It certainly was somewhat terrible when we came out into the street thronged with people carrying lanterns and torches, and tried to make our way step by step. We had not gone far before a big man, a butcher I should think, held up a torch to the window, and seeing my son's long fair hair, shouted, 'The King! the King! Here is the Queen carrying the King and the Duke of Anjou!'

The whole mob seemed to surge round us, shrieking, screaming, and yelling; some trying to turn the horses, others insisting that we should alight. No one heard my assurances that we were no such personages, that this was Mademoiselle's carriage, and that the Queen was gone long ago; and, what was more fortunate, their ears did not catch young Mericour's denunciations of them as vile canaille. A market woman mounted on the step, and perceiving the mattress, screeched out, 'The Cardinal—they are carrying off the Cardinal rolled up in a mattress!'

Their fury was redoubled. I began to unite it to show them there was nothing, but we had drawn the knots too tight, and Gaspard's little sword would not of course cut, nay, the gleam of it only added to the general fury. I really think if the Cardinal had been there they would have torn him to pieces. They were trying to drag open the doors, and would have done so much sooner but for the crowds who were pushed against them and kept them shut. At last there seemed to be some one among them with a more authoritative tone. The pressure on the door lessened, and it was to my dismay torn open; but at that moment my son called out, 'M. Darpent! Oh, M. Darpent, come to my mother!' Immediately M. Clement Darpent, unarmed and in his usual dress, with only a little came in his hand, made his way forward. Before I saw him I heard his welcome voice calling, 'Madame de Bellaise here! I am coming, M. le Marquis! The Queen! Betise! I tell you it is a lady of my acquaintance.'

'The Cardinal! She is carrying off the Italian rolled up in a mattress! Down with the fox!' came another terrible outcry; but by this time M. Darpent had been hustled up to the door, and put himself between us and the throng. He could hear me now when I told him it was merely Mademoiselle's bedding which we were carrying out to her. He shouted out this intelligence, and it made a lull; but one horrid fellow in a fur cap sneered, 'We know better than that, Monsieur! Away with traitors! And those who would smuggle them away!'

'Oh! show it to them!' I cried; and then I saw a face that I had known in the hospital, and called him by name. 'Jean Marie, my good friend, have you your knife to cut these cords and show there is nothing inside?'

The man's honest face lighted up. 'Hein! The good tall lady who brought me bouillons! I warrant there is no harm in her, brothers! She's a good Frondeuse, and has nothing to do with foreign traitors.'

He ranged himself beside Clement Darpent, offering a big knife, wherewith in a moment the bands were cut and the mattress help up to view, with a few clothes inside.

I made my two defenders understand that they were Mademoiselle's garments, and when this was repeated there was a general shout: 'Vive la bonne dame! Vive Mademoiselle! Vive Monsieur! Vive la Fronde!'

Jean Marie, who had worked in a furniture shop, would have rolled up the bed in a trice much better than before, but M. Darpent observed that as we were not yet out of Paris is might bring us into trouble, and, inconvenient as it was, he advised us to keep it open till we were beyond the gates. He asked permission to accompany me to prevent any further annoyance, and Jean Marie, to the extreme disgust of the servants, mounted the box, to serve as an additional guard.

No one could be kinder than M. Darpent. He was very sad about this flight of the Court. He said he feared it was the beginning of a civil war, and that he had thought better of the blood royal and noblesse of France than to suppose they would assist a Spanish woman and an Italian priest to trample down and starve their fellow-countrymen in the name of a minor king. He expected that there would be a siege, for he was sure that the temper of the people was averse to yielding, and the bourgeois put their trust in the archers.

I asked if he thought there would be any danger, thinking that I would either join my mother and sister or endeavour to fetch them away; but he assured me that they would be safe. Was not the Queen of England left, as I assured him, and the Duchess of Longueville? M. le Prince would allow no harm to touch the place where lived the sister he so passionately loved. I might be secure that the Hotel de Nid de Merle was perfectly safe, and he would himself watch to see that they were not annoyed or terrified. He gave me the means of writing a billet to my mother from his little Advocate's portfolio, and he promised himself to convey it to her and assure her of our safety, a message which I thought would make him welcome even to her. He was most kind in every way, and when we came near the gate bethought him that the two little boys looked pale and hungry, as well they might. He stopped the carriage near a baker's shop, which was already open, and going in himself, returned with not only bread, but a jug and cup of milk. I think we never enjoyed anything so much; and in the meantime the excellent Jean Marie rolled up our mattress so close that, as Gaspard said, it could hardly have been supposed to contain in puppy dog.

They saw us safely through the barriers. M. Darpent gave his word for us, and out we went into the country while scarcely the dawn was yet seen. At a turn in the road we saw only the morning star hanging like a great lamp in the east, and I showed it to the little boys, and told them of the three kings led by the Star to the Cradle. I heard afterwards that the little Chevalier thought we saw the real Star in the East sent to guide us to St. Germain, forgetting that it was the wrong direction; but he had been very little taught, and this was the first he had ever heard of the Gospel, which was familiar to my boy. They both fell asleep presently on the cushions, and I think I did so likewise, for I was surprised to find myself at St. Germain in broad daylight. Everybody was gone to mass for the festival, and we crept in after them.

Mademoiselle was delighted to see me, and always believed we had made our passage so safely in consequence of the respect paid to her and her carriage. It was a strange day; no one did anything but run about and hear or tell news of how the people in Paris were taking the departure of the Court, and wonder when the troops would come up to begin the siege, or, what was more pressing, what was to be done for food and for bedding? We ate as we could. Eggs and fowls were brought in from the farms, but plates and dishes, knives and forks, were very scarce. Some of us were happy when we could roast an egg in the embers for ourselves, and then eat it when it was hard enough, and I thought how useful Annora would have been, who had done all sorts of household work during the troubles at home. But we were very merry over these devices.

The night was a greater difficulty. Most of the windows had no frames nor glass in them, and hardly any one had a bed. Mademoiselle slept in a long gallery, splendidly painted and gilt, but with the wind blowing at every crevice through the shutters, no curtains; only a few marble tables against the wall by way of furniture, and the mattress spread upon the floor for her and her youngest sister, who would not sleep unless she sang, and who woke continually.

I rolled up my two little boys in my great fur cloak, which I had happily brought with me, for no one seemed disposed to take any charge of poor little Mericour, and Nicolas fetches me the cushions from the carriage, so that they were tolerably comfortable.

As to us ladies and gentlemen, we rejoiced that at least faggots could be had. We made up a great fire, and sat round it, some playing at cards, other playing at games, telling stories, or reciting poetry, interspersed with the sillier pastime of love-making. Every one nodded off to sleep, but soon to wake again,—and, oh, how still we were, and how our bones ached after two such nights!

And the saddest and most provoking thing, at least to many of us, was the high spirits of the Queen-Regent.

To be sure, she had not been without a bed in an unglazed room all night, and had a few maids and a charge of clothes, but she had probably never been so much out of reach of state in her life, and she evidently found it most amusing. She did not seem to have an idea that it was a fearful thing to begin a civil war, but thought the astonishment and disappointment of the Parisians an excellent joke. Grave and stately as she was by nature, she seemed quite transformed, and laughed like a girl when no gold spoon could be found for her chocolate and she had to use a silver one. Yes, and she laughed still more at the ill-arranged limp curls and tumbled lace of us poor creatures who had sat up all night, and tried to dress one another, with one pocket-comb amongst us all!

All that day and all the text, however, parts of different people's equipages kept coming from Paris. Mademoiselle's were escorted by M. de Fiesque, who had been so civilly treated that Mademoiselle gave passports for the Queen's wagons to come through Paris; and it was considered to be a great joke that one of the bourgeois, examining a large box of new Spanish gloves, was reported to have been quite overcome by the perfume, and to have sneezed violently when he came to examine them.

We were in a strange state up there on the heights of St. Germain. Some of the Court had no hangings for their great draughty rooms, others had no clothes, and those who had clothes had no bedding. Very few of us had any money to supply our wants, and those who had soon lent it all to the more distressed. The Queen herself was obliged to borrow from the Princess Dowager, even to provide food, and the keeping up of separate tables was impossible. We all dined together, King and Queen, Monsieur, Madame, and all, and the first day there was nothing but a great pot au feu and the bouilli out of it; for the cooks had not arrived. Even the spoons and knives were so few that we had to wash them and use them in turn. However, it was all gaiety on those first days, the Queen was so merry that it was every one's cue to be the same; and as to the King and the Duke of Anjou, they were full of mischief; it was nothing but holiday to them to have no Court receptions.

At eight o'clock in the evening there came a deputation from Paris. They were kept waiting outside in the snow while the Queen considered whether to receive them; and she could hardly be persuaded to allow them to sleep under shelter at St. Germain, though on the road at that time of night they were in danger from brigands, traveling soldiers, and I know not what!

They were at last admitted to the ranger's lodgings, and had an interview with the Chancellor, who was harsh and peremptory, perhaps feeling himself avenged for his troubles and fright on the day of the barricades.

When I heard that the President Darpent was among the deputation I sent Nicolas to find out whether his son were there; and by and by I received a little billet, which excited much more attention than I wished. Some told me I was a Frondeuse, and M. le Baron de Lamont pretended to be consumed with jealousy. I had to explain publicly that it was only from my sister, and then they pretended not to believe me. It was in English, a tongue of which nobody knew a single word, except that scandal declared that the Duke of Buckingham had taught the Queen to say 'Ee lofe ou;' but it said only: 'We are quite well, and not alarmed, since we know you are safe. We had heard such strange rumors that my mother welcomed our friend as an angel of consolation.'

I translated this to all whom it concerned; but M. de Lamont annoyed me much with his curiosity and incredulity. However, when I found that the unfortunate deputies were permitted to spend the night in the guard-room I sent Nicolas to see whether he could be of any use to the Darpents. Truly it was a night when, as the English say, one would not turn out one's enemy's dog, and the road to Paris was far from safe; but the ranger's house was a wretched place for elderly men more used to comfort than even the noblesse, whose castles are often bare enough, and who are crowded and ill accommodated when in waiting at the palaces.

At that moment a bed was to ourselves a delightful luxury, which M. de Fiesque and I were to share, so Nicolas could not do much for poor old Darpent, whom he found wet through from having waited so long in the snow, melting as it fell; but he did lend him his own dry cloak, and got some hot drink for him. Clemet professed himself eternally grateful for this poor attention when in the morning I sent my son with another note in return to be sent to my mother and sister; and he promised to watch over them as his own life.

This was the last communication I had with my family for two months. The Queen had declared that her absence would be only 'a little expedition of a week;' but week after week passed on, and there we still were on the hill. The troops could not entirely surround Paris, but no such thing. I think we were, on the whole, more hungry than those whom we blockaded.

As each set of officials finished their time of waiting they retired, and nobody came to replace them, so our party became smaller from day to day, which was the less to be regretted as our Lent was Lent indeed. Nobody had any money, and provisions ran very short; everybody grumbled but the Queen and Cardinal, and Mademoiselle, who enjoyed the situation and laughed at everybody.

In the intervals of grumbling every one was making love. M. de Juvizy actually was presumptuous enough to make love to the Queen, or to boast that he did. Mademoiselle, I am sorry to say, was in love, or, more truly, in ambition with the Prince of Conde; M. de S. Maigrin was said to be in love with the Princess, M. de Chatillon with Mademoiselle de Guerchy, and so on.

Even I, who had always declared that it was a woman's own fault if she had a lover, did not escape. I had not my mother to shield me, and nobody had anything to do, so it was the universal fashion; and M. de Lamont thought proper to pursue me. I knew he was dissipated and good-for-nothing, and I showed the coldest indifference; but that only gave him the opportunity of talking of my cruelty, and he even persuaded Mademoiselle to assure me that he was in earnest.

'No doubt,' said I, 'he would like to meddle with the administration of Nid de Merle. I have no doubt he is in earnest about that!'

But there was no escape, as we lived, from being beset. We had all to attend the Queen to the Litanies at the chapel. She used to remain in her little orator praying long after they were finished, Mademoiselle with her, and, by her own account, generally asleep. I am ashamed to say how much chatter, and how many petits soins, went on among those waiting outside. I used to kneel, as I heard people say, like a grim statue over my chair, with my rosary hanging from my hands, for if I did but hear a rustle and turn my head, there stood M. de Lamont with a bonbonniere, or an offer to shield me from the draught, and I could hear a tittering behind me.

Yet there was enough to make us grave. In a fight with the Frondeurs for Charenton, M. de Chatillon, one of the handsomest and gayest of our cavaliers, was killed. He was the grandson of the Admiral de Coligny, and was said to have been converted to the Church by the miracle of the ducks returning regularly to the pond where the saint had bound them to come. I think he must have made up his mind beforehand. But it was a great shock to have that fine young man thus cut down the day after he had been laughing and dancing in our gallery. Yet all people seemed to think of, when everybody went to condole with his young widow in her bed, was that she had set herself off to the best advantage to captivate M. de Nemours!

And then came the great thunderbolt—the tidings of the death of the King of England! I knew it would almost kill Eustace; I thought of my poor godmother, Queen Henrietta, and there I was among people who did not really care in the least! It was to them merely a great piece of news, that enabled them to say, 'Yield an inch to the Parliament and see what it will come to.'

That kind, dignified, melancholy countenance as I last saw it was constantly before me. The babble of the people around seemed to me detestable. I answered at haphazard, and begged permission of Mademoiselle to keep my room for a day, as I thought I should be distracted if I could not get out of reach of M. de Lamont.

She gave permission, but she said it was an affectation of mine, for how could I care for a somber old prince whom I had not seen for ten years?

CHAPTER XIX. — INSIDE PARIS

Annora's narrative.

My sister has asked me to fill up the account of the days of the Fronde with what I saw within the city. She must permit me to do so in English, for I have taken care to forget my French; and if I write perilous stuff for French folk to read she need not translate it.

I will begin with that Twelfth-day morning when we were wakened by more noise and racket than even Paris could generally produce. There had been a little tumult about once a week for the last six months, so we could endure a great deal, but this was plainly a much larger one. Some of the servants who went out brought word that the Queen had carried off the King in order to be revenged on Paris, and that the people, in a rage, were breaking the carriages of her suite to pieces, plundering the wagons, and beating, if not killing, every one in them. We were of course mightily troubled for my sister, and being only two women we could not go out in quest of her, while each rumour we heard was more terrible than the last. Some even said that the Louvre had been asked and plundered; but old Sir Andrew Macniven, who had made his way through the mob like a brave old Scottish knight, brought us word that he could assure us that our own Queen was safe in her own apartments, and that there had been no attack on the palace.

Still he had himself seen carriages plundered and broken to pieces by the mob, and the gates were closely guarded. Seeing our distress, he was about to go with Abbe to the Louvre, to learn whether my sister and her son were there, when one of the servants came up to tell us that M. Clement Darpent requested to see my mother, having brought us tidings of Madame la Vicomtesse.

My poor mother never could endure the name of M. Darpent, because she did not like my brother's friendship with any one not noble, but she was as glad to see him then as if he had been a Montmorency or a Coucy.

I always like his manners, for they were even then more English than French. Though going through all due form, he always seemed to respect himself too much to let any one be supercilious with him; and however she might begin at a vast distance, she always ended by talking to him just as if he were, as she called it, our equal. As if he were not infinitely the superior of the hundreds of trumpery little apes of nobles who strutted about the galleries of the Louvre, with nothing to do but mayhap to carry the Queen's fan, or curl her poodle's tail!

I see I have been writing just as I felt in those fervent days of my youth, when the quick blood would throb at my heart and burn in my cheek at any slight to the real manhood and worth I saw in him, and preference for the poor cringing courtiers I despised. The thought of those old days has brought me back to the story as all then seemed to me—the high-spirited, hot-tempered maiden, who had missed all her small chances of even being mild and meek in the troubles at home, and to whom Paris was a grievous place of banishment, only tolerable by the aid of my dear brother and my poor Meg, when she was not too French and too Popish for me. But that was not her fault, poor thing.

My mother, however, was grateful enough to Clement Darpent for the nonce, when he told how he had seen Meg safe beyond the gates. Moreover, he assured us that so far from 8000 horse being ready to storm the city (I should like to have seen them! Who ever took a fortress with a charge of horse?) barely 200 had escorted their Majesties. The Coadjutor had shown M. Blancmesnil a note from the Queen telling him so, and summoning him to St. Germain.

It was likely, M. Darpent said, that the city would be besieged, but he did not foresee any peril for us, and he promised to watch over us, as he would over his own mother, and that he would give us continual intelligence so that we might provide for our safety. It was amusing to see how eagerly my mother accepted this offer, though she had almost forbidden him the house when my brother left us.

I am sure my mother was as uneasy as any of us when he did not appear on the morning after he had gone with his father on the deputation to St. Germain. However, he did come later on in the afternoon, bringing a note from Meg. He had not seen her, only Nicolas and little Gaspard, and he, like all the rest, was greatly incensed at the manner in which the magistrates had been treated. His father had, he said, caught a violent cold, and had been forced to go to bed at once. In fact it really was the poor old man's death-stroke, and he never quitted his chamber, hardly even his bed.

The Parliament, in a rage, put forth a decree, declaring the Cardinal an enemy to the State, and ordering him to leave the Court and kingdom on that very day, calling on all loyal subjects to fall on him, and forbidding any one to give him shelter.

We heard loud acclamations, which made us think something unusual was going on, and it was the publication of this precious edict. I wondered who they thought was going to attend to it when M. Darpent brought in a copy. And my mother began to cry and talk about Lord Strafford. I had to think of Eustace and bite my tongue to keep my patience at our noble 'thorough' Wentworth being likened to that base cringing Italian.

Clement Darpent said, however, that every one had passed it by acclamation, except Bernai, who was a mere cook, and gave fine dinners to such a set of low, loose creatures that he was called 'le cabaretier de la cour.' Moreover, they proceeded to give orders for levying 4000 horse and 10,000 foot. This really did mean civil war.

'I knew it,' said my mother, 'it is the next step after denouncing the King's minister. We shall see you next armed cap-a-pie, like our young advocates at home, all for the King's behalf, according to them.'

Of course she was thinking of Harry Merrycourt, but she was surprised by the answer.

'No, Madam, nothing shall induce me to bear arms against the King. So much have I learned from the two living persons who I esteem the most.'

'And they are?' asked my lady.

'My mother and monsieur votre fils,' he replied.

And I could not help crying out—

'Oh, sir, you are right. I know that Harry Merrycourt feels NOW that nothing can justify rebellion, and that he little knew whither he should be led.'

'And yet,' said he, clasping his hands together with intensity of fervour, 'when all is rotten to the core, venal, unjust, tyrannical, how endure without an endeavour at a remedy? Yet it may be that an imposing attitude will prevail! Self-defence without a blow.'

It seemed as if such war as they were likely to wage could do no one much damage, for they actually chose as their generalissimo that ridiculous little sickly being, the Prince de Conty, who had quarrelled with the Court about a cardinal's hat, and had run away from his mother's apron string at St. Germain to his sister's at Paris.

On recalling it, all was a mere farce together, and the people were always stringing together lampoons in rhyme, and singing them in the streets. One still rings in my head, about a dissolute impoverished Marquis d'Elbeuf, one of the house of Lorraine, whom the prospect of pay induced to offer his services to the Parliament.

'Le pauvre Monseigneur d'Elbeuf,
Qui n'avait aucun ressource,
Et qui ne mangeait que du boeuf.
Le pauvre Monseigneur d'Elbeuf,
A maintenant un habit neuf
Et quelques justes dans sa bourse.
Le pauvre Monseigneur d'Elbeuf,
Qui n'avait aucun ressource.'

There was more sense in taking the Duke of Bouillon, though he was not his brother, M. de Turenne. These young men were in high spirits. You will find no traces of their feelings in the memoirs of the time, for of course nothing of the kind would be allowed to pass the censors of the press. But there was a wonderful sense of liberty of speech and tongue during that siege. The younger gens de la robe, as they were called, who, like Clement Darpent, had read their Livy and Plutarch, were full of ideas of public virtue, and had meetings among themselves, where M. Darpent dwelt on what he had imbibed from my brother of English notions of duty to God, the King and the State. It may seem strange that a cavalier family like ourselves should have infused notions which were declared to smack of revolution, but the constitution we had loved and fought for was a very Utopia to these young French advocates. They, with the sanguine dreams of youth, hoped that the Fronde was the beginning of a better state of things, when all offices should be obtained by merit, never bought and sold, and many of them were inventions of the Court for the express purpose of sale. The great Cardinal had actually created forty offices for counselors merely in order to sell them and their reversions! The holders of these were universally laughed at, and not treated as on a level with the old hereditary office-bearers, who at least might think themselves of some use.

We smile sadly now to think of the grand aspirations, noble visions, and brave words of those young advocates, each of whom thought himself a very Epaminondas, or Gracchus, though M. Darpent, on looking back, had to confess that his most enthusiastic supporters were among the younger brothers, or those with less fortunate fathers, for whom the Paulette had never been paid, or who felt it very hard to raise. He himself brought sincere ardour for his own part, and was full of soaring hope and self-devotion, though I suspect his father would soon have silenced him if the poor man had been able to think of anything beyond his own sick-chamber.

The real absurdity, or rather the sadness, of it was, as we two saw, that the fine folk in whom the Parliament put its trust merely wanted to spite the Cardinal, and cared not a rush for the Parliament, unlike my Lord Essex, and our other Roundhead noblemen, who, right or wrong, were in honest earnest, and cared as much about the Bill of Rights and all the rest of their demands as Sir Harry Vane or General Cromwell himself, whereas these were traitors in heart to the cause they pretended to espouse. Even the Coadjutor, who was the prime mover of all, only wanted to be chief of a party.

One part of his comedy, which I should like to have seen, was the conducting the Duchesses of Longueville and Bouillon along the Greve to the Hotel de Ville to ask protection, though I do not know what for.

However, there they were, exquisitely dressed, with Madame de Longueville's beautiful hair daintily disheveled, on foot, and each with a child in her arms. Crowds followed them with shouts of ecstasy, and the Coadjutor further gratified the world by having a shower of pistoles thrown from the windows of the Hotel de Ville.

It was good sport to hear Sir Andrew Macniven discourse on the sight, declaring that the ladies looked next door to angels, and kenned it full well too, and that he marvelled what their gudemen would have said to see them make a raree show of themselves to all the loons in Paris!

The streets soon became as quiet as they ever were, and we could go about as usual, except when we had warning of any special cause for disturbance. We were anxious to know how poor little Madame d'Aubepine was getting on, and, to our surprise, we found her tolerably cheerful. In truth, she had really tamed the Croquelebois! As she said afterwards in her little pathetic tone, so truly French, when they both so truly loved Monsieur le Comte (wretch that he was) how could they differ? You see he was not present to cause jealousies, and when Madame Croquelebois found that Cecile never blamed him or murmured she began to be uneasy at his neglect and unkindness.

Though, of course, at that moment he was out of reach, being in the army that was blockading us. Not that we should ever have found out that we were blockaded, if we could have got any letters from any one, except for the scarcity of firewood. My mother wanted much to get to our own Queen, but the approaches to the Louvre were watched lest she should communicate with the Regent; and we were cut off from her till M. Darpent gave his word for us, and obtained for us a pass. And, oh! it was a sad sight to see the great courts and long galleries left all dreary and empty. It made me think of Whitehall and of Windsor, though we little knew that at that very time there was worse there than even desolation.

And when at last we reached our poor Queen's apartments, there was not a spark of fire in them. She was a guest there. She had no money, and all the wood had either been used up or pillaged; and there we found her, wrapped in a great fur cloak, sitting by the bed where was the little Lady Henrietta.

When my mother cried out with grief that the child should be ill, the poor Queen replied with that good-humoured laugh with which she met all the inconveniences that concerned herself alone: 'Oh, no, Madame, not ill, only cold! We cannot get any firewood, and so bed is the safest place for my little maid, who cares not if she can have her mother to play with her! Here is a new playfellow for thee, ma mie. Sweet Nan will sit by thee, and make thee sport, while I talk to her mother.'

So the child made the big four-post bed, all curtained round, into a fortress, and I besieged her there, till she screamed with glee, while the Queen took my mother's arm, and they paced the rooms together, sadly discussing the times and the utter lack of news from home, when the last tidings had been most alarming. Poor lady! I think it was a comfort to her, for she loved my mother; but we could not but grieve to see her in such a plight. As we went home we planned that we would carry a faggot in the carriage the next day, and that I would take it upstairs to her. And so I actually did, but the sentry insisted on knowing what I was carrying hidden in a cloak, and when he saw it, the honest man actually burst into tears that the daughter of Henri IV. should be in such straits. The Queen kissed me for it, and said I was like the good girl in Madame d'Aulnoy's tales, and she would fain be the benevolent fairy to reward me. And then the little Princess insisted that I was Capuchon Rouge, and that she was my Grandmother Wolf, and after making her great eyes at me, she ate me up with kisses over and over again! Ah! how happy children can be. It was strange to remember that this was the way King Charles's little daughter spent that 30th of January!

We had told M. Darpent of the condition in which we found the Queen, and he told the Coadjutor, who went himself to see her, and then stirred up the Parliament to send her regular supplies both of firing and provisions, so that she never suffered again in the same way.

Each day increased our anxiety for His Sacred Majesty. Lord Jermyn made his way into Paris, and came to consult with my mother, telling her that he had little doubt that the iniquitous deed had been consummated, and between them, by way of preparing the unhappy Queen, they made up a story that the King had been led out to execution, but had been rescued by the populace. I could not see that this would be of much use in softening the blow; in fact, I thought all these delicate false-hoods only made the suspense worse, but I was told that I was a mere downright English country lass, with no notion of the refinements such things required with persons of sensibility.

So I told them, if ever I were in trouble, all I asked of them was to let me know the worst at once. One great pleasure came to the Queen at this time in the arrival of the Duke of York, who made his way into Paris, and arriving in the midst of dinner, knelt before his mother. He knew no more of his father than we did, and the Queen's urgent entreaty, undertook to go to St. Germain with a letter from her, asking what Queen Anne had heard from England.

The siege was not so strait but that unsuspected persons could get in and out, but after all, the poor Queen's anxiety and suspense were such that Lord Jermyn was forced to disclose the truth to her before Sir Andrew came back with the letters. She stood like a statue, and could neither move nor speak till night, when the Duchess of Vendome came and caressed her until at last the tears broke forth, and she sobbed and wept piteously all night. The next day she retired into the Carmelite convent in the Faubourg St. Jaques, taking my mother with her. As, according to French fashion, I was not to be left to keep house myself, my mother invited Sir Francis and Lady Ommaney to come and take charge of me, and a very good thing it was, for we at least had food enough, and my dear good friends had very little.

We were all stunned by the dreadful news from England. It was very sad old Sir Francis, who had borne without complaint the loss of land, honours, and home, nay, who had stood by to see his only son die at Naseby, sitting like one crushed, and only able to mutter now and then: 'My Master, my good Master.' You might know an English exile in those days by the mourning scarf and sad countenance. I remember a poor wild cavalier whom my mother and Meg never liked to admit when Eustace was not at home, going down on his knees to Lady Ommaney for a bit of black silk, when he looked as if he was starving.

We could not, of course, have evening receptions for our poor hungry countrymen in the absence of my mother, and with such sorrow upon us all, but Lady Ommaney and I did contrive pies and pasties, and all sorts of food that could be sent as gifts without offence to the families we thought most straitened.

The poor of Paris itself were not so very ill-off, for there were continual distributions of money and flour to keep them in good humour, and there were songs about.

> 'Le bon tems que c'etait
> A Paris Durant la famine,

Tout le monde s'entrebaisait
A Paris Durant la famine,
La plus belle se contentait
D'un simple boisseau de farine.'

La plus belle was the Duchess of Longueville, who tried hard to persuade the people that she was one with them. Her second son had been born only a few days after her expedition to the Hotel de Ville, and she asked the City of Paris to stand godmother to him in the person of the provosts and echevins. Afterwards she had a great reception, which Clement Darpent attended, and he told us the next morning that it had been the most wonderful mixture of black gowns and cassocks, with blue scarfs and sword-knots, lawyers, ladies, warriors, and priests.

He continued to bring us tidings every day, and Sir Francis and Lady Ommaney really liked him, and said he was worthy to be an Englishman.

His father remained very ill, and day by day he told of the poor old man's pain and shortness of breath. Now Lady Ommaney had great skill in medicine, indeed there were those who said she had done the work of three surgeons in the war; and she had been of great service to my dear brother, Lord Walwyn, when he first came to Paris. She thought little or nothing of the French doctors, and waxed eloquent in describing to Clement Darpent how she would make a poultice of bran or of linseed. Now he had learned of my mother to read English easily, and to converse in it on all great matters of state and policy, but the household terms and idioms were still far beyond him, and dear good Lady Ommaney had never learned more French than enabled her to say 'Combien' when she made a purchase. Or if they had understood one another's tongue, I doubt me if any one could have learned the compounding of a poultice through a third person, and that a man!

So, while I was labouring to interpret, Lady Ommaney exclaimed, 'But why should I not come and show your mother?'

'Ah! if you would, Madame, that would verily be goodness,' returned Clement in his best English.

Well, I knew Eustace and Meg would have called me self-willed, when my mother had once made such a noise about our taking shelter from Broussel's mob at the Maison Darpent; but this was a mere visit of charity and necessity, for it was quite certain that the two good ladies could never have understood one another without me to interpret for them. Moreover, when Clement Darpent had rescued my sister from the mob, and was always watching to protect us, we surely owed him some return of gratitude, and it would have been mere bourgeois.

So I went with Lady Ommaney, and was refreshed by the sight of that calm face of Madame Darpent, which she always seemed to me to have borrowed from the angels, and which only grew the sweeter and more exalted the greater was her trouble, as if she imbibed more and more of heavenly grace in proportion to her needs.

We did our best, Lady Ommaney and I, to show and explain, but I do not think it was to much purpose. The materials were not like our English ones, and though mother and son were both full of thanks and gratitude, Madame Darpent was clearly not half convinced that what was good for an Englishman was good for a Frenchman, and even if she had been more fully persuaded, I do not think her husband would have endured any foreign treatment.

When we took leave she said, 'Permettez moi, ma chere demoiselle,' and would have kissed my hand, but I threw my arms round her neck embraced her, for there was something in her face that won my heart more than it had ever gone out to any woman I ever saw; and I saw by Lady Ommaney's whole face and gesture that she thought a great sorrow was coming on the good woman. I believe she was rather shocked, for she was a Huguenot by birth, and a Jansenist by conviction, and thus she did not approve of any strong signs of affection and emotion; but nevertheless she was touched and very kind and good, and she returned my embrace by giving me her sweet and solemn blessing.

And as he put me into the carriage, Clement, that foolish Clement, must needs thank me, with tears in his eyes, for my goodness to her.

'What do you mean, sir,' said I, 'by thanking me for what I delight in and value as a daughter?'

Whereupon I, equally foolish, knew what I had said, and felt my face and neck grow crimson all over, and what must he do, but kiss my hand in a rapture.

And all the way home I could hear old Lady Ommaney murmuring to herself, quite unconscious that she was speaking aloud, 'My stars! I hope I have not done wrong! What will my Lady Walwyn say? Not that he would be altogether a bad match for her after our notions. Her father was only a baron, and theirs is a good old family of the citizen sort, but then my Lady Walwyn is a Frenchwoman, and thinks all that is not noble the dirt under her feet.'

My heart gave a great bound, and then seemed to swell and take away my breath, so that I could not at first speak to stop those uttered thoughts, which made me presently feel as if I were prying into a letter, so as soon as I could get my voice I said, as well as I could, 'My Lady, I hear you.'

'Hear me! Bless me, was I talking to myself! I only was thinking that the poor old gentleman there is not long for this world. But maybe your mother would not call him a gentleman. Ha! What have they got written up there about the Cardinal?'

I read her the placard, and let her lead me away from the subject. I could not talk about it to any one, and how I longed for Eustace!

However, I believe terror was what most ailed the old gentleman (not that the French would call him so). He must always have been chicken-hearted, for he had changed his religion out of fear. His wife was all sincerity, but the dear good woman was religious for both of them!

And as time went on his alarms could not but increase. The Parliament really might have prevailed if it had any constancy, for all the provincial Parliaments were quite ready to take part with it, and moreover the Duke of Bouillon had brought over his brother, the Vicomte de Turenne, to refuse to lead his army against them, or to keep back the Spaniards. The Queen-Regent might really have been driven to dismiss the Cardinal and repeal the taxes if the city had held out a little longer, but in the midst the First President Mole was seized with patriotic scruples. He would not owe his success to the foreign enemies of his country, and the desertion of the army, and he led with him most of his compeers. I suppose he was right—I know Clement thought so—but the populace were sorely disappointed when negotiations were opened with the Queen and Court, and it became evident that the city was to submit without any again but some relaxation of the tax.

The deputies went and came, and were well mobbed everywhere. The Coadjutor and Duke of Beaufort barely restrained the populace from flying at the throat of the First President, who they fancied had been bribed to give them up. One wretch on the steps of the Palais de Justice threatened to kill the fine old man, who calmly replied, 'Well, friend, when I am dead I shall want nothing but six feet of earth.'

The man fell back, daunted by his quietness, and by the majesty of his appearance in his full scarlet robes. These alarms, the continual shouting in the streets, and the growing terror lest on the arrival of the Court all the prominent magistrates should be arrested and sent to the Bastille, infinitely aggravated President Darpent's disorder. We no longer saw his son every day, for he was wholly absorbed in watching by the sick-bed, and besides there was no further need, as he averred, of his watching over us. However, Sir Francis went daily to inquire at the house, and almost always saw Clement, who could by this time speak English enough to make himself quite intelligible, but who could only say that, in spite of constantly being let blood, the poor old man grew weaker and weaker; and on the very day the treaty was signed he was to receive the last rites of the Church.

.

CHAPTER XX. — CONDOLENCE

(By Margaret)

Our siege was over at last. I can hardly explain how or why, for there was no real settlement of the points at issue. I have since come to understand that the Queen and the Cardinal were alarmed lest the Vicomte de Turenne with his army should come to the assistance of his brother, the Duke of Bouillon, and thus leave the frontier open to the Spaniards; and that this very possibility also worked upon the First President Mole, who was too true a Frenchman not to prefer giving way to the Queen to bringing disunion into the army and admitting the invader. Most of the provincial Parliaments were of the same mind as that of Paris, and if all had united and stood firm the Court would have been reduced to great straits. It was well for us at St. Germain that they never guessed at our discomforts on our hill, and how impossible it would have been to hold out for a more complete victory.

I was glad enough to leave St. Germain the day after the terms had been agreed upon. The royal family did not yet move, but my term of waiting had long been expired; I burned to rejoin my mother and sister, and likewise to escape from the assiduities of M. de Lamont, who was becoming more insufferable than ever.

So I asked permission of the Queen to let my son resume his studies, and of Mademoiselle to leave her for the time. Both were gracious, though the Queen told me I was going into a wasp's nest; while, on the other hand, Mademoiselle congratulated me on returning to those dear Parisians, and said she should not be long behind me. I was too much afraid of being hindered not to set out immediately after having received my license, so as to take advantage of the escort of some of the deputies with whom I had a slight acquaintance. I also hoped to avoid M. de Lamont's leave-takings, but I was not fortunate enough to do this. The absurd man, learning that I was on the point of departure, came rushing headlong into the court where the carriages stood, having first disordered his hair and untied his scarf, so as to give himself a distracted appearance, and thus he threw himself on his knees between me and the coach door, declaring that I was killing him and breaking his heart by my cruelty.

I was very angry, and afraid of showing any excitement, lest it should give him any advantage, so I only drew up my head coldly and said:

'Let me pass, sir.' But that only made him throw himself on the ground as if he would kiss my robe, whereupon Gasppard, with his hand on his little sword, said: 'Why don't you give him a good kick, mama?' This made everybody laugh; and I said, still keeping my head stiff: 'We will go round to the other door, my son, since there is this obstruction in our way.'

This we did before he could follow us; and the last I saw of M. de Lamont as I quitted St. Germain, he was still kneeling in the court, in the attitude of an Orlando Furioso, reaching out his arms towards the departing carriage. I did not pity him, for I did not for a moment believe his passion a serious one, and I thought his wife would not be much happier than my poor little sister-in-law, about whom I was very anxious, and as to these extravagances, they were the ordinary custom of those who professed to be lovers. He was one of the equerries-in-waiting on the Duchess of Orleans, and thus happily could not follow; and I never rejoiced more than when Gaspard and I, with my two women, had turned our backs on St. Germain and began to descend through the scattered trees of the forest towards Paris.

No less than forty carriages came out to meet the deputies on their return, and our progress was very slow, but at last we found ourselves at our hotel, where we were entirely unexpected, and the porter was so much surprised that, instead of announcing us properly, he rushed into the courtyard, screaming out: 'Madame! Monsieur le Marquis!' The whole household came rushing down the steps pell-mell, so that it was plain at the first glance that my mother was not there. Annora was the first to throw herself into my arms, with a shriek and sob of joy, which gave me a pleasure I cannot describe when I contrasted this meeting with our former one, for now again I felt that we were wholly sisters.

Gaspard sprang to the Abbe's neck, and declared himself tired of his holidays, and quite ready to resume his studies. They would be much pleasanter than running after the King and Duke of Anjou, and bearing the blame of all their pranks. My mother, I heard, was at the Convent of St. Jaques with her poor bereaved Queen, and she had left my sister in the charge of Sir Francis and Lady Ommaney.

The old lady came to welcome me; Sir Francis was out gone to inquire for the President Darpent; and before I had been an hour in the house, I found how entirely different a world it was from that which I had left, and how changed were the interests that absorbed it. Of my poor little Cecile scarcely anything was known. Annora had only seen her once or twice, and even the poor English Queen was second in interest to the illness of M. Darpent, and the fatigues of his wife in nursing him. It seemed to me as if Lady Ommaney and my sister discussed, as if he had been their near relation, every symptom of him, who, in the eyes of all my recent companions, was nothing better than an old frondeur, a rebel richly deserving to be put to death.

If Lady Ommaney had understood French, I really believe she would have gone to help Madame Darpent, who had now been sitting up for several nights; and though her son was most dutiful, and shared her vigils, taking every imaginable care of his father, he could not relieve her materially. The old man died the morning after my return home, and Sir Francis, who had been to inquire, reported that the funeral was to take place the next night by Madame's desire, as she was resolved that it should not be made an occasion for the meeting of inveighing against the Government as the remote cause of his death.

The city was, in fact, in a very unquiet state; nevertheless, Queen Henrietta returned to her apartments at the Louvre, and my mother came back to us, though when she found me at home, she only remained for one night. The Queen wanted her, and it was not convenient, in the condition of things, to be carried about in a sedan chair. Moreover I had a visit from my sister-in-law; I was astonished at her venturing out, but though very thin, she looked radiant, for her husband had come into Paris in the train of the Princes, and had actually passed half an hour with her! I was less gratified when I found what he had come for. It was to desire his wife to come to me and inform me that it was the will and pleasure of the Prince of Conde that I should accept the addresses of the Baron de Lamont.

'Thank you, sister,' I said, smiling a little, for I knew it was of no use to scold her or argue with her, and I would have spoken of something else, but she held my hand and entreated:

'You will, then?'

'Oh! you have been charged to throw your influence into the scale,' I said, laughing; and the poor thing had to confess that he had said to her, with an air so noble, so amiable, that here was an opportunity of being of some real use to him if she would persuade Madame de Bellaise to marry M. de Lamont.

'To him!' I might well exclaim.

'Well, you see,' Cecile explained, 'M. le Prince said to him: 'The Bellaise is your sister-in-law, is she not? It is for you to overcome her ridiculous scruples and make her accept Lamont, who is desperately in love with her, and whose fortune needs to be repaired.''

'I see,' I replied; 'but I cannot carry my complaisance so far.'

'But,' faltered Cecile, 'he is very handsome and very distinguished —'

'Come, Cecile, you have done your duty. That is enough.'

But the poor little thing thought herself bound still to persuade me with the arguments put into her mouth, till I asked her whether she could wish me to forget her brother, or if in my place she would do such a thing as give a father like M. de Lamont to her children. Then she began to weep, and asked me to forgive her, ending in her simplicity with:

'The Prince would have been pleased with my husband, and perhaps he would borne me good will for it!'

'Ah! Cecile,' I said, embracing her; 'I would do much for you, but you must not ask me to do this.'

The next question was about a visit of condolence to be paid to Madame Darpent. We still kept the Ommaneys with us, on the pretext that the presence of a gentleman gave a sense of security in the condition of the city, but chiefly because we feared that they would be half-starved in their lodgings.

Sir Francis told us that Madame Darpent was, 'after your French fashion,' as he said, receiving visits of condolence in her bed, and, considering how good and obliging the young man had been, he supposed we should pay one. Annora's eyes shone, but to my surprise she said nothing, and I was quite ready to consent, since I too felt under such obligations to the younger Darpent that I could let no scruple about condescension stand in my way, and I was glad that my mother could not hear of it until after it was done.

Lady Ommaney, however, looked rather old and mysterious. She came to my room and told me that she thought I ought to know, though she had no opportunity of telling my mother, that she could not but believe that she had observed a growing inclination between Mistress Annora and the young Monsieur Darpent. I suppose my countenance showed a certain dismay, for she explained that it might be only an old woman's fancy; but knowing what were our French notions as to nobility and rank, and how we treated all honest gentry without titles like the dirt under our feet, she thought we ought to be warned. Though for her part, if the young gentleman were not a Papist and Frenchman, she did not see that Mistress Nan could do much better even if we were in England. Then she began giving me instances of barons' daughters marrying gentlemen learned in the law; and I listened with dismay, for I knew that these would serve to make my sister more determined, if it were really true that any such passion were dawning. I saw that to her English breeding it would not seem so unworthy as it would to us, but to my mother it would be shocking, and I could not tell how my brother would look on it. The only recommendation in my eyes would be the very contrary in his, namely, that she might be led to embrace our religion; but then I thought Clement Darpent so doubtful a Catholic that she would be more likely to lead him away. My confidence was chiefly in his bourgeois pride, which was not likely to suffer him to pay his addresses where they would be disdained by the family, and in his scrupulous good faith, which would certainly prevent his taking advantage of the absence of the maiden's mother and brother.

However, I knew my sister well enough to be aware that to contradict her was the surest mode of making her resolute, and I thought it wiser that there should be no appearance of neglect or ingratitude to rouse her on behalf of the Darpents. So I agreed with Lady Ommaney that we would seem to take no notice, but only be upon our guard. We did not propose Annora's accompanying us on our visit of condolence, but she was prepared when the carriage came round, and we made our way, falling into a long line of plain but well-appointed equipages of the ladies of the robe, who were all come on the same errand, and we were marshalled into the house, and up the stairs by lackeys in mourning.

At the top of the great staircase, receiving everybody, stood Clement Darpent, looking rather pale, and his advocate's black dress decorated with heavy weepers of crape. When he saw us his face lighted up, and he came down to the landing to meet us, an attention of course due to our rank; but it was scarcely the honour done to the family that made his voice so fervent in his exclamation, 'Ah! this is true goodness,' though it was only addressed to me, and of course it was my hand that he held as he conducted us upstairs, and to the great chamber where his mother sat up in her bed, not, as you may imagine, in the cloud of lace and cambric which had coquettishly shrouded the widowhood of poor little Madame de Chatillon. All was plain and severe, though scrupulously neat. There was not an ornament in the room, only a crucifix and a holy-water stoup by the side of the bed, and a priest standing by, of the grave and severe aspect which distinguished those connected with Port Royal aux Champs. Madame Darpent's face looked white and shrunken, but there was a beautiful peace and calmness on it, as if she dwelt in a region far above and beyond the trifling world around her, and only submitted, like one in a dream, to these outward formalities. I felt quite ashamed to disturb her with my dull commonplace compliment of condolence, and I do not think she in the least saw or knew who we were as her lips moved in the formula of thanks. Then Clement led us away in the stream to the buffet, where was the cake and wine of which it was etiquette for every one to partake, though we only drank out of clear glass, not out of silver, as when the mourners are noble. Monsieur Verdon and some familiars of the house, whether friends or relations I do not know, were attending to this, and there was a hum of conversation around; but there was no acquaintance of ours present, and nobody ventured to speak to us, except that Clement said: 'She will be gratified, when she has time to understand.' And then he asked whether I had heard anything of my brother.

As the streets were tolerably clear, I thought we had better drive at once to the Louvre, to see my poor god-mother Queen and my mother.

Certainly it was a contrast. Queen Henrietta had been in agonies of grief at first, and I believe no day passed without her weeping for her husband. Her eyes were red, and she looked ill; but she was quite as ready as ever to take interest in things around her; and she, as only English were present, made me come and sit on a stool at her feet and describe all the straits we had endured at St. Germain, laughing her clear ringing laugh at the notion of her solemn, punctilious Spanish sister-in-law living, as she said, en bergere in the middle of the winter, and especially amusing herself over her niece Mademoiselle's little fiction that her equipage had secured respect.

'That young Darpent is a useful and honest man,' she said. 'It is well if your beaux yeux have secured him as a protector in these times, my goddaughter.'

'It is for my brother's sake that he has been our friend,' I said stiffly, and my mother added that he had been engaged in our cause in the Ribaumont suit, as if that naturally bound him to our service, while the indignant colour flushed into Annora's cheek at thus dispensing with gratitude. However, we were soon interrupted, for now that the way into the city was opened, and the widowed Queen had left her first solitude, every one was coming to pay their respects to her; and the first we saw arrive was Mademoiselle, who had no sooner exchanged her compliments with her royal aunt, than, profiting by another arrival, she drew me into a window and began: 'But, my good Gildippe, this is serious. You have left a distracted lover, and he is moving heaven and earth to gain you. Have you considered? You would gain a position. He has great influence with M. le Prince, who can do anything here.'

'Ah! Mademoiselle! Your Royal Highness too!' was all I could say, but I could not silence her. M. de Lamont had interested the Prince of Conde in his cause, and Mademoiselle, with her insane idea of marrying the hero, in case the poor young Princess should die (and some people declared that she was in a decline), would have thought me a small sacrifice to please him. So I was beset on all sides. I think the man was really enough in love to affect to be distracted. Though far less good-looking in my early youth than my sister, I was so tall and blonde as to have a distinguished air, and my indifference piqued my admirer into a resolution to conquer me.

Mademoiselle harangued me on the absurdity of affecting to be a disconsolate widow, on the step in rank that I should obtain, and the antiquity of M. de Lamont's pedigree, also upon all the ladies of antiquity she could recollect who had married again; and when I called Artemisia and Cornelia to the front in my defence, she betrayed her secret, like poor Cecile, and declared that it was very obstinate and disobedient in me not to consent to do what would recommend HER to the Prince.

Next came M. d'Aubepine, poor young man, with the air of reckless dissipation that sat so ill on a face still so youthful, and a still more ridiculous affectation of worldly wisdom. He tried to argue me into it by assuring me that the Prince would henceforth be all-powerful in France, and that M. de Lamont was his protege, and that I was not consulting my own interest, those of my son, or of my family, by my refusal. When he found this ineffectual, he assured me peremptorily that it was the Prince's will, to which I replied, 'That may be, Monsieur, but it is not mine,' to which he replied that I was Mademoiselle, but that I should repent it. I said M. le Prince was not King of France, and I trusted that he never would be, so that I did not see why I should be bound to obey his will and pleasure. At which he looked so much as if I were uttering blasphemy that I could not help laughing. I really believe, poor fellow, that M. le Prince was more than a king to him, the god of his idolatry, and that all his faults might be traced to his blind worship and imitation.

I was not even exempt from the persuasions or commands of the great man himself, who was at that time dominating the councils of France, and who apparently could not endure that one poor woman should resist him. But he, being a Bourbon and a great captain to boot, set about the thing with a better grace than did the rest. It was in this manner. When peace, such as it was, was agreed upon, the Princes came in to Paris, and of course they came to pay their visit of ceremony to Queen Henrietta. It was when I happened to be present, and before leaving her apartment, the Prince came to me, and bending his curled head and eagle face, said, with a look and gesture clearly unaccustomed to opposition: 'Madame, I understand that you persist in cruelty to my friend, M. de Lamont. Permit me to beg of you to reconsider your decision. On the word of a Prince, you will not have reason to repent. He is under my protection.'

I thanked His Highness for his condescension, but I assured him that I had made up my mind not to marry again.

This made him frown, and his face, always harsh, and only redeemed from ugliness by the fire of his eyes, became almost frightful, so that it might have terrified a weak person into yielding; but of course all he could then do was to make a sign to M. de Lamont to approach, present him to me, and say, 'I have requested Madame to reconsider her decision,' with which he bowed and left us tete-a-tete in the throng.

Then I tried to cut short M. de Lamont's transports by telling him that he must not take the Prince's requesting as the same thing as my doing it. Moreover, I did what my mother said was brutal and unbecoming; I informed him that he was mistaken if he thought he should obtain any claim over my son's estate, for I had nothing but my husband's portion, and there were other guardians besides myself, who would not suffer a stranger to have any share in the administration. Therewith he vehemently exclaimed that I did him injustice, but I still believe that his intention was, if his Prince had remained all-powerful, to get the disposition of my son's property thrown into his hands. My brother Solivet was away with the army, Eustace in Holland, whence I longed to recall him.

Meantime, Sir Francis Ommaney had had become intimate with the Darpents, and so too had our good Abbe Bouchamp, who had assisted at the funeral ceremonies, and from whom the widow derived much consolation. From them we heard that she would fain have retired into the convent at Port Royal, only she would not leave her son. There were those who held that it was her duty not to let him stand between her and a vocation, especially as he was full grown, and already in the world; but she retained enough of her old training among the Huguenots to make her insist that since God had given her children, it was plain that He meant her to serve Him through her duty to them, and that if, through her desertion of him, Clement were tempted to any evil courses, she should never forgive herself. And our Abbe was the more inclined to encourage her in this resolve that he did not love the Jansenists, and had a mind sufficiently imbued with theology to understand their errors.

Certainly Clement showed no inclination to evil courses. In fact, he was so grave and studious that his mother cherished the hope of taking him with her to Port Royal to become one of the solitaries who transformed the desert into a garden. She said that with patience she should see him come to this, but in the meantime youth was sanguine, and he had not renounced the hope of transforming the world. I think she also foresaw that the unavowed love for Annora could scarcely lead to anything but disappointment, and she thought that, in the rebound, he would be willing to devote himself as one of those hermits.

He was certainly acting in a manner to astonish the world. He was not yet of sufficient age or standing to succeed to his father's chair as the President of one of the Chambers of the Parliament, but his promotion as one of the gens du roi (crown lawyers) had been secured by annual fees almost ever since he was born, and the robe of the Consellor who was promoted to the Presidency in the elder Darpent's room was awaiting him, when he declared his intention of accepting nothing that had been bought for him, but of continuing a simple advocate, and only obtaining what he could earn by his merits, not what was purchased. To this no doubt the feelings imbibed from my brother and sister had brought him. The younger men, and all the party who were still secret frondeurs, applauded him loudly, and he was quietly approved by the Chief President Mole who had still hopes that the domineering of the Prince of Conde and the unpopularity of Cardinal Mazarin would lead to changes in which ardent and self-devoted souls, like Clement's, could come to front and bring about improvements. The Coadjutor de Gondi, who was bent on making himself the head of a party, likewise displayed much admiration for one so disinterested, but I am afraid it was full of satire; and most people spoke of young Darpent as a fool, or else as a dangerous character.

And it might very possibly be that if he fell under suspicion, his solitude might not be that of Port Royal but of the Bastille. Yet I am not sure that his mother did not dread the patronage of the Coadjutor most of all.

CHAPTER XXI. — ST. MARGARET AND THE DRAGON

I was day after day worried and harassed by my suitor, so that I was very glad when, in the autumn, Madame de Rambouillet invited my sister and me to come and pass a few days with her, and see her vintage. We left my son under the care of the Abbe and of Sir Francis and Lady Ommaney, and set forth together in our coach with my women, and, as usual, mounted servants enough to guard us from any of the thieves or straggling soldiers who infested the roads.

For about a league all went well and quietly, but just at the cross-road leading to Chevreuse, a troop of horsemen sprang out upon us. There was a clashing of swords, a pistol-shot or two; I found myself torn from the arms in which my sister was trying to hold me fast, dragged out in spite of all our resistance, and carried into another carriage, at the door of which I was received by two strong arms; a handkerchief was thrown over my mouth to stop my screams, and though the inside of the coach was already darkened, my hands were tied and my eyes blinded as I was placed on the seat far in the corner; the door banged fast, and we drove swiftly away.

At first I was exhausted with my struggles, and in an agony of suffocation with the gag, which hindered me from getting my breath. I fancy I must have made some sound which showed my captors that unless they relieved me, I should perish in their hands. So the handkerchief was removed, and while I was panting, a voice said:

'It shall not be put on again, if Madame will give her word not to cry out.'

'It is of no use at present,' I gasped out, and they let me alone. I thought I knew that threats and entreaties could avail me little in the existing circumstances, and I thought it wiser to rally my forces for the struggle that no doubt was impending; so I sat as still as I could, and was rewarded by finding my hands unbound, when I tried to raise one to my face, and again the voice said:

'Believe us, Madame, you are with friends who would not hurt you for the universe.'

I made no answer. Perhaps it was in the same mood in which, when I was a child at home and was in a bad temper, I might be whipped and shut up in a dark room, but nothing would make me speak. Only now I said my prayers, and I am sure I never did so in those old days. We went on and on, and I think I must have dozed at last, for I actually thought myself wearied out with kicking, scratching, and screaming on the floor of the lumber-room at Walwyn, and that I heard the dear grandmother's voice saying:

'Eh! quoi! she is asleep; the sullen had stopped, and with the words, 'Pardon me, Madame,' I was lifted out, and set upon my feet; but my two hands were taken, and I was led along what seemed to be endless passages, until at length my hands were released, and the same voice said:

'Madame will be glad of a few moments to arrange her dress. She will find the bandage over her eyes easy to remove.'

Before, however, I could pull it away, my enemy had shut the door from the outside, and I heard the key turn in it. I looked about me; I was in a narrow paved chamber, with one small window very high up, through which the sunbeams came, chequered by a tall tree, so high that I knew it was late in the day, and that we must have driven far. There was the frame of a narrow bedstead in one corner, a straw chair, a crucifix, and an empty cell in a deserted convent; but there was a stone table projecting from the wall, on which had been placed a few toilette necessaries, and a pitcher of water stood on the floor.

I was glad to drink a long draught, and then, as I saw there was no exit, I could not but make myself more fit to be seen, for my hair had been pulled down and hung on my shoulders, and my face—ah! it had never looked anything like that, save on the one day when Eustace and I had the great battle, and our grand-mother punished us both by bread and water for a week.

After I had made myself look a little more like a respectable widow, I knelt down before the crucifix to implore that I might be defended, and not be wanting to my son or myself. I had scarcely done so, however, when the door was opened, and as I rose to my feet I beheld my brother-in-law, d'Aubepine.

'Armand, brother,' I cried joyfully, 'are you come to my rescue? Did you meet my sister?'

For I really thought she had sent him, and I readily placed my hand in his as he said: 'It depends only on yourself to be free.' Even then I did not take alarm, till I found myself in a little bare dilapidated chapel, but with the altar hastily decked, a priest before it in his stole, whom I knew for the Abbe de St. Leu, one of the dissipated young clergy about Court, a familiar of the

Conde clique, and, prepared to receive me, Monsieur de Lamont, in a satin suit, lace collar and cuffs, and deep lace round his boots.

I wrenched my hand from M. d'Aubepine, and would have gone back, but three or four of the soldiers came between me and the door. They were dragoons of the Conde regiment; I knew their uniform. Then I turned round and reproached d'Aubepine with his wicked treachery to the memory of the man he had once loved.

Alas! this moved him no longer. He swore fiercely that this should not be hurled at his head again, and throughout the scene, he was worse to me than even M. de Lamont, working himself into a rage in order to prevent himself from being either shamed or touched.

They acted by the will and consent of the Prince, they told me, and it was of no use to resist it. The Abbe, whom I hated most of all, for he had a loathsome face, took out a billet, and showed it to me. I clearly read in the large straggling characters — 'You are welcome to a corporal's party, if you can by no other means reduce the pride of the little droll. — L. DE B.'

'Your Prince should be ashamed of himself,' I said. 'I shall take care to publish his infamy as well as yours.'

The gentlemen laughed, the Abbe the loudest, and told me I was quite welcome; such victories were esteemed honourable.

'Yes,' I said, 'for a short time, among cowards and rogues.'

Armand howled at the word cowards.

'Cowards, yes,' I said, 'who must needs get a company of soldiers to overcome one woman.'

I saw a good long scratch on Lamont's face just then, and I flattered myself that it was due to Nan's nails. They all beset me, Lamont at my feet, pleading the force of his passion, entreating with all the exaggeration of the current language; the Abbe arguing about the splendid position I should secure for my son and myself, and the way I should be overthrown if I held out against the Prince; d'Aubepine raging and threatening. I had lost myself already, by my absence and goings on, the estate; the Prince had but to speak the word, and I should be in the Bastille.

'Let him,' I said.

'It is of no use to dally with her,' cried Armand. 'I will hold her while the rite is performed.'

I looked at him. I was quite as tall as he, and, I believe, quite as strong; at any rate he quailed, and called out:

'Have you any spirit, Lamont? Here, one of you fellows, come and help to hold her.'

'At your peril!' I said. 'Gentlemen, I am the widow of your brave officer, Captain de Bellaise, killed at Freibourg. Will you see this wrong done?'

'I command you, as your officer—forward!' he said; and though one wavered, the others stepped forward.

Then I saw there was only one thing to do. A big stone image stood near me. Before they could touch me I had fallen on my knees, and wound my arms so closely round it that they could not unloose them without absolute violence and injury. I knew that in such a position it was impossible even to go through the semblance of marrying me. I felt Armand's hand and the Abbe's try to untwist my arms and unclasp my hands, but they could not prevail against that grip with which I held, and I spoke not one word.

At last they drew back, and I heard them say one to the other: 'It is of no use. She must yield in time. Leave her.'

I heard them all clank out with their spurs, and lock the door, and then I looked up. There was no other way out of the little convent chapel, which looked as if it had been unused for years, except perhaps for an annual mass, but the altar had been dressed in preparation for the sacrilege that was intended. Then I turned to the figure to which I had clung, and I was encouraged by seeing that it bore the emblems of St. Margaret, my own patroness. I knew very well that my brother and sister would shake their heads, and say it was a superstitious fancy, if they called it by no harder name; but they did not understand our feelings towards the saints. Still it was not to St. Margaret I turned to help me, but to St. Margaret's Master and mine, when I prayed to be delivered from the mouth of the dragon, though I did trust that she was entreating for me.

I would not move away from her, I might need to clasp her at any moment; but I prayed fervently before the altar, where I knelt till I grew faint with weariness; and then I sat at her feet, and thought over all the possibilities of being rescued. If my sister were free I knew she would leave no stone unturned to deliver me, and that my rescue could be only a matter of time; but she might also have been seized, and if so—? Anyhow, I was absolutely determined that they should kill me before I consented to become the wife of M. de Lamont, or to give him any right over my son.

After a time the door was cautiously opened, and one of the dragoons came in, having taken off his boots and spurs that he might move more noiselessly.

'Madame,' he said, 'pardon me. I loved our brave captain; I know you. You sent me new linen in the hospital. Captain de Bellaise was a brave man.'

'And you will see no wrong done to his widow and child, my good friend?' I cried.

'Ah, Madame, you should command all of us. But we are under orders.'

'And that means doing me unmanly violence, unworthy of a brave soldier! You cannot help me?'

'If Madame would hear me! The gentlemen are at dinner. They may sit long over their wine to give them courage to encounter Madame again. My comrade, Benlot, is on duty. I might find a messenger to Madame's friends.'

Then he told me what I had little guessed, that we had been driven round and round, and were really only in the Faubourg St. Medand, in the Priory of the Benedictines, giving title and revenue to the Abbe St. Leu, which had contained no monks ever since the time of the Huguenots. He could go into Paris and return again before his turn to change guard was likely to come.

Should I send him, or should I thus only lose a protector? He so far reassured me that he said his comrades were, like himself, resolved not to proceed to extremities with the widow of their captain—above all in a chapel. They would take care not to exert all their strength, and if they could, without breach of discipline, they would defend me.

I decided. I knew not where my sister might be searching, or if she might not be likewise a prisoner; so I directed him first to the house of M. Darpent, who was more likely to know what to do than Sir Francis Ommaney. Besides, the Rue des Marmousets, where stood Maison Darpent, was not far off.

I heard a great clock strike four, five, six, seven, eight o'clock, and by and by there was a parley. M. de Lamont opened the door of the chapel, and as I shuddered and kept my arm on my patroness, he implored me to believe that no injury was intended to me—the queen of his thoughts, or some such nonsense—I might understand that by the presence of my brother-in-law. He only besought me not to hurt my precious health, but to leave the cold chapel for a room that had been prepared for me, and where I should find food.

'No,' I said; 'nothing should induce me to leave my protectress.'

At least, then, he conjured me to accept food and wine, if I took it where I was. I hastily considered the matter. There was nothing I dreaded so much as being drugged; and yet, on the other hand, the becoming faint for want of nourishment might be equally dangerous, and I had taken nothing that day except a cup of milk before we set out from home; and it was now a matter of time.

I told him, therefore, that I would accept nothing but a piece of bread and some pure water, if it were brought me where I was.

'Ah, Madame! you insult me by your distrust,' he cried.

'I have no reason to trust you,' I said, with a frigidity that I hoped would take from him all inclination for a nearer connection; but he only smote his forehead as if it had been a drum, and complained of my cruelty and obduracy. 'Surely I had been nurtured by tigresses,' he said, quoting the last pastoral comedy he had seen.

He sent M. d'Aubepine to conduct some servant with a tray of various meats and drinks; I took nothing but some bread and water, my brother-in-law trying to argue with me. This was a mistake on their part, for I was more angry with him than with his friend, in whom there was a certain element of extravagant passion, less contemptible than d'Aubepine's betrayal of Phillipe de Bellaise's widow merely out of blind obedience to his Prince. He assured me that resistance was utterly useless, that bets had passed at the Prince's court on the Englishwoman's being subdued by Lamont before mid-night, and the Prince himself had staked, I know not how much, against those who believed in my obstinacy. Therefore Armand d'Aubepine, who was flushed with wine, and not in the least able to perceive how contemptible he was, urged me to yield with the best grace I could, since there was no help for it. And so saying he suddenly pinioned both my arms with his own.

No help! Was there no help in Heaven above, or earth below? Was my dragoon on his way?

The doors opened. Again the Abbe opened his book.

'Brave dragoons!' I cried out; 'if there be not a man among you who will stir a hand to save me, bear witness that I, Margaret de Ribaumont, widow of Philippe de Bellaise, your own officer, protest against this shameful violence. Whatever is here done is null and void, and shall be made known to M. l'Abbe's superiors.'

There was a dead pause. Then Lamont whispered something to the priest, who began again. I felt Armand's held relaxing, and making a sudden struggle, I shook myself free with such force that he staggered back, while I bounded forward and snatched the book from the priest's hand, throwing it on the floor, and then, regaining once more the statue of St. Margaret, I stood grasping her with one arm with desperate energy, while I cried: 'A moi, soldiers of Freibourg!'

'Drag her away,' said d'Aubepine to the men.

'By your leave, my captain,' said their sergeant, 'except in time of war, it is not permitted to lay hands on any one in sanctuary. It is not within our discipline.'

D'Aubepine swore an oath that they would see what their Colonel said to their insubordination; but the sergeant replied, not without some malice:

'It falls within the province of the reverend Father.'

'I command you, then!' shrieked the Abbe, in a furry.

'Nay, Monsieur l'Abbe is not our officer,' said the sergeant, saluting with great politeness.

'Madame,' cried Lamont, 'will you cause these men to be put to death for disobedience to their officer?'

I scarcely believed him. And yet—

There was a sound at the outside.

'Make haste!' cried d'Aubepine. 'Here is the Prince come to see whether he has won his wager.'

CHAPTER XXII. — ST. MARGARET AND THE DRAGON

(By Annora)

A fine country to live in was la belle France, where a godly, modest, discreet, and well-living widow could be spirited away by main force from her sister and her servants, on the King's highway in broad daylight, and by soldiers wearing the King's own uniform! 'In the name of the Prince!' said they. Verily, I think it was in the name of the Prince of darkness. They tore poor Meg from me, though we both fought and struggled as hard as we could, in hopes of some one coming to our rescue. Luckily my gloves were off, and I think I gave a few tolerable scratches to somebody's face, in spite of his abominable cache-nez. If the servants had had a tenth part of the valour of our poor fellows who lie dead at Newburry and Alresford we could have brought her off; but these were but Frenchmen, and were overawed by those dragoons, or dragons, in their cuirasses.

When poor Meg was dragged out, I held her fast, and tumbled out with her; but even as we fell, she was rent from me, and I think I must have been half-stunned. At any rate, I found myself flung back into our own carriage, and the door shut upon me, while the horses were turned round, and we were made to gallop back by the road we had come.

Our women, screaming and crying like mad things, helped me up from the bottom of the carriage. I bade them hold their tongues and stop the horses. The one they could not do, the other they would not. So I was forced to open the door myself, and shout to the coachman to stop that instant. He would not at first, but happily I saw a pistol, which one of the wretches had dropped in the scuffle, and I threatened him with it. Then, when my voice could be heard, I ordered the two outriders to gallop after the coach in which my sister had been carried off, and see where she was taken, while we made as much speed as we could after them; but the cowardly rogues absolutely began to cry, and say that the leader of the party had turned the horses' heads, and declared that he would shoot any one dead who attempted to follow.

Luckily I was in a close-fitting black cloth suit, being still in mourning for our blessed martyr, and intending to make my toilette at Rambouillet. I bade one of the fellows who had dismounted to give me his cloak, and while they were still staring at me, I sprang into the saddle, arranged the cloak, and rode off in pursuit. I knew I could keep my seat even on a man's saddle, for cavaliers' daughters had had to do strange things, and it was thus that I was obliged to come away from my dear Berenger's side. But then I rode between my father and Eustace. Now, if I did not find out where my poor Margaret was gone, who was to deliver her?

The men had heart of grace enough to follow me, more of them, indeed, than I wanted, as of course it was better to go quietly than to have them clattering with me. I told them to keep a little in the rear, and I rode on, trying to see above the hedges the glancing of the helmets of the dragoons. Across some vineyards I once caught sight of something like a carriage and a troop of horse, quite in a different direction from what I expected, and presently, when I came to a cross-road, I saw by the marks in the mud and more that they must have turned that way. I must follow by such guidance as these supplied, and fortunately there had recently been rain, so that the wheel and hoof marks could be tracked. To my amazement they led through many turns and twists at last towards Paris; but to my dismay, when I came to the paved roads that surround the city, I lost all traces. I knew I was a remarkable figure when we were on the high roads, and so I kept back, making one of the servants inquire at a little cabaret on the road whether a carriage, attended by dragoons, had passed that way.

'Yes,' they brought me word. 'A close carriage, no doubt containing a state prisoner, had been escorted by dragoons on the way to the Bastille.'

The man brought me back the answer, weeping. I scolded the fellow well for thinking that these rogues SAYING Madame was at the Bastille made it so, and yet it echoed my own alarm. I had at least ascertained one point. She had not been transported to some solitary castle in the country, but must be near at hand.

I must now go home, and see what help was to be had; but as they would never let me pass the gates of Paris looking as I knew I must look, I was obliged to ride back and meet the carriage, which had bidden to follow us, and return to it in order to re-enter the city.

My mother was at St. Germain with our own Queen; who would be my resource? I thought I had better first go home and see what Sir Francis Ommaney's counsel would be, and whether he thought the English ambassador, Sir Richard Browne, could give any help, though, unfortunately, poor Meg was no longer an English subject. There was consternation enough when I came in with my terrible news, but at least there was common-sense, and not shrieking. Sir Francis recommended me at once to dress myself to go to St. Germain, while he would repair to the embassy, since Sir Richard was the most likely person to be able to advise him. We also thought of sending a courier to Solivet, who was with the army on the frontier; and I put on a dress fit to obtain admission at St. Germain. Lady Ommaney was scolding me into taking some food before starting, and crying, because she had a bad attack of rheumatism, and her husband would not let her go with us, when there was a knock, and one of the women ran in. 'News, news, Mademoiselle! News of Madame la Vicomtesse! But ah! she is in a sad plight.'

Down I ran headlong, and whom should I find but the dear and excellent Madame Darpent. She, who never left her home but for Church, had come to help us in our extremity. It seemed that Meg's dragoon (about whom she has told her own story) had disguised himself as soon as he came within Paris, and come in hot haste to M. Darpent, telling him how once my brave sister had repulsed the whole crew of villains, and how he had hurried away while the gentlemen (pretty gentlemen, indeed!) were drinking wine to get up their courage for another encounter, in which they were determined to succeeded since they were heavy bets at the Prince's camp that the pride of la grand Anglaise should be subdued before midnight. The dragoon had not ventured to come any farther than Maison Darpent, lest he should be missed and his comrades should not be able to conceal his absence but he assured M. Darpent that though they might appear to obey orders, they were resolved to give the lady every opportunity of resistance. Was she not the wife of the best captain they had ever had, and had she not knelt like one of the holy saints in a mystery play?

I was for setting forth at once with Sir Francis, sure that the iniquity could not proceed when it was made public. Of course we would have risked it, but we might not have been able to force our way in without authority, since the vile Abbe was on his own ground, and Madame Darpent told us her son had devised a better plan. He had gone to the Coadjutor, who in the dotage of his uncle, the Archbishop of Paris, exercised all his powers. As one of their monkish clergy, this same Abbe was not precisely under his jurisdiction, but the celebration of a marriage, and at such an hour, in a Priory Chapel, was an invasion of the privileges of the parish priest, and thus the Bishop of the See had every right to interfere. And this same Coadjutor was sure to have an especial delight in detecting a scandal, and overthrowing a plan of the Prince of Conde and the ruling party at Court, so that if he could be found there was little doubt of his assistance.

In order to lose no time, Clement Darpent had gone instantly in search of him, and his good mother had come at once in her sedan to see if I were returned, relieve our minds about my sister, and if my mother were within reach, prepare her to go in search of Margaret, since the Coadjutor, Bishop though he were, was still young, and not at all the sort of man who could be suffered to bring her home without some elder matron as her escort. Or if my mother were out of reach, Madame Darpent was prepared, as an act of charity and goodness, to go herself in quest of our poor Meg. The carriage had followed her to the door for the purpose as soon as it could be got ready, and to add to my exceeding gratitude, she was willing to take me with her. Sir Francis insisted on going to my mother. He said it was right, but we doubted whether it would do any good. We waited only for tidings which her son had promised to send, and they came at last in a small billet sent by one of his clerks. The Coadjutor had absolutely fired at the notion of such a hit to the opposite party, and was only getting together what were called the "First of Corinthians," namely, the corps who had belonged to him during the siege, and had obtained the nickname because he was titular Archbishop of Corinth.

Clement would not leave him a moment, lest he should be diverted from his purpose, but sent word to Madame Darpent that she, or whoever was to escort Madame de Bellaise, was to meet him at seven o'clock in the open space by the Barriere, showing a green light through the carriage window, when he would show a red one.

Oh! what might not had happened before we could get there! I thought I was used enough to suspense, I who had heard the rattle of the musketry in more than one battle, but I should have been wild had not that best of women held my hands and soothed me and helped me to say my prayers.

Hours seemed to go by as we sat in the dark with our lamp behind the green curtain over the window, but at last the trampling of horses was heard and the red light appeared. Presently Clement came to our door, and exchanged a few words, but he said he must return to the Coadjutor, who was in the best humour in the world.

The gates were closed, but the Coadjutor had no difficulty in passing them, and we followed in his train. It was a dark night, but mounted servants carried flambeaux, and we saw the light glance on the Corinthians who guarded us. At last we stopped. We could not see then, but I visited the place afterwards, and saw it was a tall brick house, with a high wall round a courtyard. Here the Coadjutor's carriage drew up, and entrance was demanded for "Monseigneur l'Archeveque de Corinthe, Coadjutor de Paris." It may be supposed that the dragoon who kept the door made no difficulty.

The carriage moved on, we drew up, and Clement, who had waited, handed us out saying: 'He tells me we are just in time. Be as silent as possible.'

We found the court lighted with torches, the Coadjutor's chaplain arranging his purple robe, as he walked on through the doors that were opened for him. Sir Francis led Madame Darpent, Clement gave me his had, as we followed closely and noiselessly.

The chapel had its great wax candles alight on the altar. We could see in, as we paused in the darkness of the antechapel, outside the screen, while the Coadjutor advanced the door. My Margaret knelt, clinging closely to a great stone image. The vile coward d'Aubepine was commanding—for we heard him—his soldiers to seize her. The Abbe stood finding the place in his book; Lamont was at a safe distance, however, trying to induce her to rise. The Coadjutor's clear voice was heard.

'Benedicite, Messieurs,' he said, and oh! the start they gave! 'What hole function am I interrupting, M. l'Abbe? The lady is in the attitude of a penitent, but I was not aware that it was one of the customs of your order to absolve thus in public.'

'Monseigneur,' said the Abbe, 'neither was I aware that Episcopal surveillance extended to religious houses.'

Margaret here broke in. She had risen to her feet, and looking at the Archbishop, with eyes beaming in her pale face, she cried: 'Oh! Monseigneur, you are come to save me! These wicked men are striving to marry me against my will.'

'To celebrate the marriage sacrament,' continued the Coadjutor, in his calm sneering tone; 'then M. l'Abbe, I suppose you have procured the necessary permission from the curate of the parish to perform the rite at this strange time and place? I am sorry, Messieurs, to break up so romantic a plan, savouring of the fine days of the quatre fils Aymon, but I must stand up for the claims of the diocese and the parish.'

M. de Lamont turned round to my sister, and made one of his lowest bows, such as no one but a French courtier CAN make (thank Heaven!).

'Madame,' he said, 'we are disconcerted, but I shall still put my trust in the truth that beauty ever pardons the efforts of love.'

'So it may be Monsieur,' returned Margaret, already fully herself, and looking as tall, white, and dignified among them as a goddess among apes, 'so it may be, where there is either beauty or love;' and she made him a most annihilating curtsey. Then turning to the Coadjutor she said: 'Monseigneur,

I cannot express my obligations to you;' and then as Clement stood behind him, she added: 'Ah, Monsieur, I knew I might reckon on you,' holding out her hand, English fashion. She did not see us, but M. d'Aubepine, who was slinking off the scene, like a beaten hound, as well he might, unaware that we were in the antechapel, caught his foot and spur in Madame Darpent's long trailing cloak, and came down at full length on the stone floor, being perhaps a little flustered with wine. He lay still for the first moment, and there was an outcry. One of the soldiers cried out to the other as Madame Darpent's black dress and white cap flashed into the light:

'It is the holy saint who has appeared to avenge the sacrilege! She has struck him dead.'

And behold the superstition affected even the licentious good-for-nothing Abbe. Down he dropped upon his knees, hiding his eyes, and sobbing out: 'Sancta Margarita, spare me, spare me! I vow thee a silver image. I vow to lead a changed life. I was drawn into it, holy Lady Saint. They showed me the Prince's letter.'

He got it all out in one breath, while some of them were lifting up d'Aubepine, and the Coadjutor was in convulsions of suppressed laughter, and catching hold of Clement's arm whispered: 'No, no, Monsieur, I entreat of you, do not undeceive him. Such a scene is worth anything! Madame, I entreat of you,' to Meg, who was stepping forward.

However, of course it could not last long, though as d'Aubepine almost instantly began to swear, as he recovered his senses, Madame Darpent unconsciously maintained the delusion, by saying solemnly in her voice, the gravest and deepest that I ever heard in a Frenchwoman: 'Add not another sin, sir, to those with which you have profaned this holy place.'

The Abbe thereupon took one look and broke into another tempest of entreaties and vows, which Madame Darpent by this time heard. 'M. l'Abbe,' she said, 'I pray you to be silent, I am no saint, but a friend, if Madame will allow me so to call myself, who has come to see her home. But Oh! Monsieur,' she added, with the wonderful dignity that surrounded her, 'forget not, I pray you, that what is invisible is the more real, and that the vows and resolution you have addressed to me in error are none the less registered in Heaven.'

Mocker as the Coadjutor habitually was, he stood impressed, and uttered no word to mar the effect, simply saying: 'Madame, we thank you for the lesson you have given us! And now, I think, these ladies will be glad to close this painful scene.'

Meg, who with Madame Darpent, had satisfied herself that the wretch d'Aubepine had not hurt himself anything like as much as he deserved, declared herself ready and thankful to go away. The Abbe and Lamont both entreated that she would take some refreshment before returning home, but she shuddered, and said she could taste nothing there, and holding tight by my arm, she moved away, though we paused while Madame Darpent was kneeling down and asking the Archbishop to bless her. He did so, and her spirit seemed to have touched his lighter and gayer one, and to have made him feel what he was, for he gave the benediction with real solemnity and unaffected reverence for the old lady.

He himself handed her into the carriage, and he must greatly have respected her, for though he whispered something to her son about the grand deliverance of the victim through St. Margaret and the Dragon (an irresistible pun on the dragoon), yet excellent story as could have been made of the free-thinking Abbe on his knees to the old Frondeur's widow, he never did make it public property. I believe that it is quite true, as my sister's clever friend Madame de Sevigne declares, that there was always more good in Cardinal de Retz, as he now is called, than was supposed.

Poor Meg had kept up gallantly through all her terrible struggle of many hours, but when we had her safely in the carriage in the dark, she sank back like one exhausted, and only held my hand and Madame Darpent's to her lips by turns. I wanted to ask whether she felt ill or hurt in any way, but after she had gently answered, 'Oh, no, only so thankful, so worn out,' Madame Darpent advised me not to agitate her by talking to her, but to let her rest. Only the kind, motherly woman wanted to know how long it was since she had eaten, and seeing the light of a little CABARET on the road, she stopped the carriage and sent her son to fetch some bread and a cup of wine.

For I should have said that M. Darpent had been obliged to return in the same carriage with us, since he could not accompany the Coadjutor on his way back. He wished to have gone outside, lest his presence should incommode our poor Meg; but it had begun to rain, and we could not consent. Nor was Meg like a Frenchwoman, to want to break out in fits the moment the strain was over.

He brought us out some galettes, as they call them, and each of us sisters had a draught of wine, which did us a great deal of good. Then we drove on in the dark as fast as we could, for the Coadjutor's carriage had passed us while we were halting, and we wanted to enter the gates at the same time with him.

I sat beside my sister, holding her hand, as it seemed to give her a sense of safety; Madame Darpent was on her other side, Clement opposite. We kept silence, for Madame Darpent declared that no questions ought to be asked of Madame de Bellaise till the next morning.

Presently we heard an unmistakable snoring from the old lady's corner, and soon after I felt my sister's fingers relax and drop mine, so that I knew she slept. Then I could not but begin to tell, in the quiet and stillness, how my dear brother would thank and bless him for what he had done for us.

I am an old woman now, but I have only to shut my eyes and it all comes back on me—the dark carriage, the raindrops against the window glancing in the light of the flambeaux, the crashing of the wheels, and the steady breathing of the sleepers, while we two softly talked on, and our hearts went out to one another, so that we knew our own feelings for one another.

I think it came of talking of Eustace and his not being able to keep back, that, though Eustace was in some sort the guiding star of his life, yet what he had done for us was not merely for my brother's sake, but for another much more unworthy, had he only known it.

Then he found he had betrayed himself, and asked my pardon, declaring that he had only meant to watch me at a distance (poor me), knowing well the vast gulf between our stations. What could I answer but that this was only French nonsense; that we knew better in England what a gentleman meant, and that I was sure that my brother would freely and joyfully give me to him, poor, broken, ruined cavalier exile as I was? And then we got hold of each other's hands, and he called me all sorts of pretty names in French and in English; and I felt myself the proudest and happiest maiden in France, or England to boot, for was not mine the very noblest, most upright and disinterested of hearts?

Only we agreed that it would be better to let no one at Paris know what was between us until my brother should return. We knew that he would be the most likely person to obtain my mother's consent, and he really stood in the place of a father to me; while if we disclosed it at once there was no knowing what my mother might not attempt in his absence, and his mother would never permit us to be in opposition to mine. She would not understand that, though I might not disobey my mother, it was quite impossible that my feelings and opinions should be guided by one of different religion, nation, and principles altogether.

However, we agreed to write to my brother in Holland as soon as we could find a safe conveyance, and when there were signs of waking on the part of our companions we unlocked the hands that had been clasping one another so tightly.

(Finished by Margaret.)

So you thought I was asleep, did you, Mistress Nan? I suppose after all these years you will not be ready to box my ears for having heard? It was no feigning; I really was so worn and wearied out that I lay back on the cushions they had arranged for me in a sort of assoupissement, only at first able to feel that I was safe, and that Annora was with me. She says that I dropped her hand. Well, perhaps I may have dozed for a moment, but it seems to me that I never lost the knowledge of the sound of the wheels, nor of the murmuring voices, though I could not stir, nor move hand nor foot, and though I heard it all, it was not till I was lying in bed the next morning that I recollected any part of it, and then it was more as if I had dreamt it than as a reality.

Moreover, Annora was hovering over me, looking perfectly innocent, and intent on making me rest, and feeding me upon possets, and burning to hear my story. Then came my mother from St. Germain, having received a courier who had been dispatched at dawn. She embraced me and wept over me, and yet — and yet I think there mingled with her feeling something of vexation and annoyance. If I were to be carried off at all by a man of rank and station, it would have been almost better if he had succeeded in marrying me than that the affair should be a mere matter of gossip. Certainly, that my rescue should be owing to one of the factious lawyers, and to that mischievous party leader the Coadjutor, was an unmixed grievance. After all my follies at Nid de Merle, I was quite sufficiently in ill odour with the Court to make it needful to be very careful. If I had only waited till morning, the Queen would have taken care to deliver me without my having given a triumph which the Frondeurs would not fail to make the most of.

'Where should I have been in the morning?' I said. 'Did she not know that the horrible wager related to midnight?'

She supposed any woman could take care of herself. At any rate I had contrived to offend everybody. The Prince was paramount at Court, and carried all before him. Mademoiselle, in her devotion to him, and the Queen-Regent would never forgive my trafficking with the Frondeurs. On the whole, my mother really thought that the best way to regain my favour or even toleration, would be to accept M. de Lamont with a good grace, since he was certainly distractedly in love with me, and if I fell into disgrace with the authorities, I might have my son and the administration of his property taken away from me in a still more distressing manner, whereas it would only depend on myself to rule M. de Lamont.

'I have only to say,' observed Annora, 'that if she were to do such a thing I should never speak to her again.'

Whereupon my mother severely reproved my sister, declaring that it was all her fault, and that she had gone beyond all bounds when left to herself, and would be a disgrace to the family.

Annora coloured furiously, and said she did not know what might be esteemed a disgrace in France, but she should certainly do nothing that would disgrace her English name. Then it flashed on me that what had passed in the carriage had been a reality, and I saw what she meant.

Of course, however, I did not betray my perception. Disputes between my mother and sister were what we all chiefly dreaded; it was so impossible to make them see anything from the same point of view, so I thought it best to turn the conversation back to my own affairs, by saying that I thought that to marry M. de Lamont would only make matters worse, and that no loss of favour or any other misfortune could be equal to that of being bound to such a husband as he had shown himself.

I had them all against me except my sister and my English friends, and my saintly guide, Father Vincent de Paul, who assured me that I was by no means bound to accept a man like that; and as for silencing scandal, it was much better to live it down. That devout widow, Madame de Miramion, had endured such an abduction as mine at hands of Bussy Rabutin, and had been rescued by her mother-in-law, who had raised the country-people. No one thought a bit the worse of her for it, and she was one of the foremost in her works of charity.

This gave me the comfort of knowing that I was right, and I knew besides that such a marriage would be a sore grief to my brother, so I resolved to hold out against all persuasions; but it was a wretched time that now began, for Lamont would not desist from persecuting me with his suit, and I had no remission from him either at Court or in my own house, for if I excluded him my mother admitted him. My mother dragged me to Court as a matter of form, but I was unwelcome there, and was plainly shown that it was so.

The Queen could not forgive me for being rescued by the Frondeurs; Mademoiselle was in the Prince's interest; the Prince was dominant, and all his satellites made it a point of honour that none of them should fail in carrying any point. Even Cecile d'Aubepine followed the stream. Her husband was very angry with her, and said I had put on grand airs, and made myself ridiculous; and the foolish little thing not only obeyed but believed him, though he neglected her as much as ever. I never dared to drive, scarcely ever to walk out, without escort enough to prevent any fresh attempt at abduction; and even my poor Gaspard was in disgrace, because he was not courtier enough to bear in silence taunts about his mother.

I had only one thing to look forward to, and that was the return of my brother. The new King of England had arrived, and we trusted that he would appear with him; but alas! no, he was detained on the King's business in Jersey, and could not come.

Meantime Annora kept her own counsel, and though she was my only supporter, except of course of Ommaneys, in my resistance, the want of confidence made a certain separation between us. I do not think she had any secret communication with Clement Darpent—they were too honourable for that—but she drew more to old Lady Ommaney than to me during this time.

Reports began to circulate that the Prince's insolence had gone too far, and that the Cardinal had been holding secret conferences with the Coadjutor, to see whether his help and that of Paris could be relied on for the overthrow of the Prince. I remember that Annora was in high spirits, and declared that now was the time for honest men if they only knew how to profit by it.

CHAPTER XXIII. — THE LION AND THE MOUSE

We were greatly amazed when late one January evening Cecile rushed into my room like one distracted, crying:

'The monsters, they have arrested him!'

We knew there was only on of the nobler sex in the eyes of my poor Cecile, and my first question was:

'What has he done?' expecting to hear that he had been fighting a duel, or committing some folly. My surprise was greater when I heard her answer:

'He was going to carry off the Cardinal's nieces.'

'He seems to have a turn for such exploits,' Annora said. 'Who wanted to marry them?'

'It was for no such thing!' Cecile said, with as much heat as she could show; 'it was to take them as hostages.'

'As hostages!'

'Oh, yes! Do not you know? For the Prince.'

Our astonishment was redoubled.

'Eh, quoi! Messieus les Prince de Conde and Conty, and the Duke of Longueville, are all arrested, coming from the council, by the treason of the Cardinal. They are sent off no one knows where, but my husband, you understand, was with M. de Boutteville and a hundred other brave officers in the garden of the Hotel de Conte when the news came. M. de Boutteville immediately proposed to gallop to Val de Grace and then seize on the Demoiselles Mazarin and Mancini as the best means of bringing the Cardinal to reason, and instantly it is done; but the cunning Cardinal had foreseen everything; the young ladies had been seized and carried off, I know not where,' and she burst into a flood of tears.

With some difficulty we elicited from her that she had learned the tidings from a sergeant who had been in attendance on the Count, and had fled when he was taken. At the same time horrible noises and shouts were heard all over the city.

'Treason! Treason! Down with the Cardinal! Beaufort is taken! The Coadjutor! Vengeance! Vengeance!'

Sir Francis hurried out to learn the truth, and then my mother in her fright cried out:

'Will no one come and protect us? Oh! where is M. Darpent?' while Annora called to me to take our cloaks and come up to the roof of the house to see what was going on. She was in high spirits, no doubt laughing within herself to see how every danger made my mother invoke M. Darpent, and finding in a tumult a sure means of meeting him, for she could trust to him to come and offer his protection.

I SAW that she heard his voice on the stairs before he actually made his appearance, telling my mother that he had hastened to assure her that we were in no danger. The rising was due to M. de Boutteville, who, being disappointed in his plan of seizing the Cardinal's nieces as hostages, had gone galloping up and down Paris with his sword drawn, shouting that the two darlings of the people, M. de Beaufort and the Coadjutor, had been seized. He wildly hoped that the uproar this was sure to excite would frighten the Queen-Regent into releasing the Princes as she had before released Broussel.

But the Coadjutor had come out with torches carried before him, and had discovered the name of the true prisoners, whose arrogance had so deeply offended the populace. He had summoned the Duke of Beaufort — the King of the Markets, as he was called — and he was riding about the streets with a splendid suite, whose gilded trappings glistened in the torchlight.

So deeply had the Prince's arrogance offended all Paris that the whole city passed from rage into a transport of joy, and the servants came and called us up to the top of the house to see the strange sight of the whole city illuminated. It was wonderful to behold, every street and all the gates marked out by bright lights in the windows, and in the open spaces and crossings of the street bonfires, with dark figures dancing wildly round them in perfect ecstasies of frantic delight; while guns were fired out, and the chorus of songs came up to us; horrid, savage, abusive songs, Sir Francis said they were, when he had plodded his way up to us on the roof, after having again reassured my mother, who had remained below trying to comfort the weeping Cecile.

Sir Francis said he had asked a tradesman with whom he dealt, ordinarily a very reasonable and respectable man, what good they expected from this arrest that it should cause such mad delirium of joy. The man was utterly at a loss to tell him anything but that the enemies of Paris were fallen. And then he began shouting and dancing as frantically as ever.

It was to his wife and me that the English knight told his adventures; Annora and M. Darpent had drawn apart on the opposite side of the paraget. If to Madame d'Aubepine this great stroke of policy meant nothing but that her husband was in prison, to my sister a popular disturbance signified chiefly a chance of meeting Clement Darpent; and Lady Ommaney and I exchanged glances and would not look that way. Nay, we stayed as long as we could bear the cold of that January night to give them a little more time. For, as I cannot too often remind you, my grand-daughters, we treated an English maiden, and especially one who had had so many experiences as my sister, very differently from a simple child fresh from her convent.

Nicolas at last came up with a message from Madame la Baronne to beg that we would come down. We found that the Intendante Corquelebois (erst Gringrimeau) had brought the children in a panic, lest the houses of the partisans of the Princes should be attacked. She had put on a cloak and hood, made them look as like children of the people as she could, and brought them on foot through the streets; and there stood the poor little things, trembling and crying, and very glad to find their mother and cling to her. She had never thought of this danger, and was shocked at herself for deserting them. And it was a vain alarm; for, as M. Darpent assured her, M. d'Aubepine was not conspicuous enough to have become a mark for public hatred.

She was a little affronted by the assurance, but we appeased her, and as the tumult was beginning to die away, M. Darpent took his leave, promising my mother to let her know of any measure taken on the morrow. He offered to protect Madame d'Aubepine and her children back to their own hotel, but we could not let the poor wife go back with her grief, nor the children turn out again on the winter's night. I was glad to see that she seemed now on perfectly good terms with herdame de compagnie, who showed herself really solicitous for her and her comfort, and did not seem displeased when I took her to my room. I found my poor little sister-in-law on the whole less unhappy than formerly. People do get accustomed to everything, and she had somehow come to believe that it was the proper and fashionable arrangement, and made her husband more distinguished, that he should imitate his Prince by living apart from her, and only occasionally issuing his commands to her. He had not treated her of late with open contempt, and he had once or twice take a little notice of his son, and all this encouraged her in her firm and quiet trust that in process of time, trouble, age, or illness would bring him back to her. Her eyes began to brighten as she wondered whether she could not obtain his liberty by falling at the Queen's feet with a petition, leading her children in her hands. 'They were so beautiful. The Queen must grant anything on the sight of her little chevalier!'

And then she had a thousand motherly anecdotes of the children's sweetness and cleverness to regale me with till she had talked herself tolerably happily to sleep.

We kept her with us, as there were reports the next day of arrests among the ladies of the Princes' party. The two Princesses of Conde were permitted to retire to Chantilly, but then the Dowager-Princess was known to be loyal, and the younger one was supposed to be a nonentity. Madame de Longueville was summoned to the Palace, but she chose instead to hide herself in a little house in the Faubourg St. Germain, whence she escaped to Normandy, her husband's Government, hoping to raise the people there to demand his release and that of her brothers.

The Prince's INTENDANT was taken, and there was an attempt to arrest the whole Bouillon family, but the Duke and his brother, M. de Turenne, were warned in time and escaped. As to the Duchess and her children, their adventures were so curious that I must pause to tell their story. A guard was sent to her house under arms to keep her there. There were four little boys, and their attendants, on seeing the guards, let them straight out through the midst of them, as if they were visitors, the servants saying: 'You must go away. Messieurs les petits Princes cannot play to-day. They are made prisoners.' They were taken to the house of Marshal de Guesbriant, where they were dressed as girls, and thus carried off to Bellechasse, whence they were sent to Blois.

There the little Chevalier of seven years old (Emmanuel Theodore was his name, and he is now a Cardinal) fell ill, and could not go on with his brothers when they were sent southwards, but was left with a lady named Flechine. By and by, when the Court came to Guienne, Madame de Flechine was afraid of being compromised if she was found to have a son of the Duke of Bouillon in the house. She recollected that there was in a very thick wood in the park a very thick bush, forming a bower or vault, concealed by thorns and briers. There she placed the little boy with his servant Defargues, giving them some bread, wine, water, a pie, a cushion, and an umbrella in case of rain, and she went out herself very night to meet Defargues and bring him fresh provisions. His Eminence has once told me all about it, and how dreadfully frightened he was a thunderstorm in the valet's absence, and when a glow-worm shone out afterwards the poor child thought it was lightning remaining on the ground, and screamed out to Defargues not to come in past it. He says Defargues was a most excellent and pious soul, and taught him more of his religion than ever he had known before. Afterwards Madame de Flechine moved them to a little tower in the park, where they found a book of the LIVES OF THE SAINTS, and Defargues taught his little master to make wicker baskets. They walked out on the summer nights, and enjoyed themselves very much.

As to poor Madame de Bouillon, her baby was born on that very day of the arrest. Her sister-in-law and her eldest daughter remained with her, and Madame Carnavalet; the captain of the guards had to watch over them all. He was of course a gentleman whom they already knew, and he lived with them as a guest. As soon as Madame de Bouillon had recovered, they began to play at a sort of hide-and-seek, daring him to find them in the hiding-places they devised, till at last he was not at all alarmed at missing them. Then M. de Boutteville and her daughter escaped through a cellar-window, and they would have got safely off, if the daughter had not caught the smallbox. Her mother, who was already on the way to Boxdeaux, came back to nurse her, and was taken by the bedside, and shut up in the Bastille.

The two Princesses were at Chantilly, and rumours reached us that the younger lady was about to attempt something for the deliverance of he husband, and thereupon M. d'Aubepine became frantic to join them, and to share in their councils. We tried to convince her that she could be of no use, but no—suppose they were going to raise their vassals, she could do the same by those of d'Aubepine, and she, who had hitherto been the most timid and helpless of beings, now rose into strong resolution and even daring. It was in vain that I represented to her that to raise one's vassals to make war on the King was rank rebellion. To her there was only one king— the husband who deserved so little from her. She had given him her whole devotion, soul and body, and was utterly incapable of seeing anything else. And Madame Croquelebois, being equally devoted to M. le Comte, was thus more in her confidence than we were. She told us at last with a thousand thanks that she had resolved on offering her services to the Princesses, and that she should send the children with Madame Croquelebois into Anjou; where she thought they would be safer than at Paris. We were sorry, but there was a determination now in our little Cecile that made her quite an altered woman. So she repaired to Montroud, where the younger Princess of Conde had retired, and was acting by the advice of M. Lenet, the Prince's chief confidant.

The next thing we heard of her was astonishing enough. The Princess, a delicate sickly woman, together with our little Countess, had left Montroud in the night with fifty horses. The Princess rode on a pillion behind M. de Coligny, Cecile in the same way, and the little Duke of Enghien was on a little saddle in front of Vialas, his equerry. On they went, day and night, avoiding towns and villages, and seldom halting except in the fields. Happily it was the month of May, or those two delicate beings never could have lived through it, but Cecile afterwards told us that she had never felt so well in her life.

Near the town of Saint Cere they met the Dukes of Bouillon and La Rochefoucauld, with eight hundred men, mostly gentlemen, who were ready to take up their cause. The Princess, hitherto so shy, gracefully and eagerly greeted and thanked them, and the little Duke made his little speech. 'Indeed I am not afraid of Mazarin any more, since I see you here with so may brave men. I only expect the liberty of my good papa through their valour and yours.'

There were great acclamations at this pretty little address, and then the boy rode with his mother through the eight squadrons in which the troop was drawn up, saluting the officers like a true little Prince, with his hat in his hand, while there were loud shouts of 'Vive le Roi! Vivent les Prince!' and such a yell of 'Down with Mazarin!' as made Cecile tremble.

She was expecting her own share in the matter all along, and presently she had the delight of seeing twenty more men coming with Croquelebois at their head, and by his side, on a little pony, her own little Maurice, the Chevalier d'Aubepine. Was not Cecile a proud woman then? I have a letter of hers which she says (poor dear thing!) that he was a perfect little Prince Charmant; and he really was a pretty little fellow, and very well trained and good, adoring her as she deserved.

I will go on with her story, though only at second hand, before I proceed with my own, which for a time took me from the scene of my friend's troubles. This is written for her grandchildren as much as my own and my sister's, and it is well they should know what a woman she truly was, and how love gave her strength in her weakness.

The Prince of Conde, whose history and whose troubles were only too like her own, already loved her extremely, and welcomed her little son as a companion to the Duke of Enghien. The Duke of Bouillon took them to his own fortress-town of Turenne, where they remained, while the little bourg of Brive la Gaillarde was taken from the royal troops by the Dukes. The regiment sent by the Cardinal to occupy the place was Prince Thomas of Savoy's gendarmes, and as of course they loved such generals as Turenne and Conde better than any one else, the loyalty of most of them gave way, and they joined the Princess's little army.

The Duke of Bouillon entertained his guests splendidly, though his poor Duchess was absent in the Bastille. The ladies had to dine every day in the great hall with all the officers, and it was a regular banquet, always beginning and ending with Conde's health. Great German goblets were served out to everybody, servants and all, and the Duke of Bouillon began by unsheathing his sword, and taking off his hat, while he vowed to die in the service of the Princes, and never to return his sword to the scabbard — in metaphor, I suppose — till it was over. Everybody shouted in unison, waved the sword, flourished the hat, and then drank, sometimes standing, sometimes on their knees. The two little boys, with their tiny swords, were delighted to do the same, though their mothers took care that there should be more water than wine in their great goblets.

I afterwards asked Cecile, who was wont to shudder at the very sight of a sword, how she endured all these naked weapons flourishing round her. 'Oh,' she said, 'did not I see my husband's liberty through them?'

The ladies were then escorted, partly on horseback, partly by boat, to Limeuil, and that same day their Dukes gained a victory over the royal troops, and captured all their baggage, treasure, and plate, so that Cecile actually heard the sounds of battle, and her husband might say, as the Prince did at Vincennes: 'A fine state of things that my wife should be leading armies while I am watering pinks.'

The wives had their pinks too, for the whole road to Bordeaux was scattered with flowers, and every one trooped out to bless the Princess and her son. As she entered the city the 400 vessels in the port fired all their guns three times over, and 30,000 men, escorting a splendid carriage, in which she went along at a foot's pace, came forth to welcome her. Her son was dressed in white taffety turned up with black and white feathers. He was held in a gentleman's arms at the window, and continually bowed, and held out his little hands to be kissed, saying that his father and grandfather had been quite right to love people who had such an affection for their house as these seemed to have. Maurice d'Aubepine, at the opposite window, was nodding away with a good-will at the people who were obliged to put up with him instead of the little Duke.

They came to a handsome house, which had been appointed for the Prince's gentleman, took great care of them, though the two Dukes remained outside with their little army. The next day the Princess, attended of course by Madame d'Aubepine, and a whole train of noblesse and influential people, went to the Parliament of Bordeaux with her petition for aid. She personally addressed each counsellor in the passage to the great hall, and represented to them the cruelty and ingratitude of Mazarin towards her husband, while her little son kissed and embraced and begged them for his father's liberty.

When all had assembled in the great chamber, and they had begun to deliberate, the Princess burst in on them, threw herself on her knees, and began a speech. When she broke off, choked by tears, her little son fell on his knees and exclaimed: 'Gentlemen, be instead of a father to me; Cardinal Mazarin has taken away mine!'

Then there was a general weeping, and the Parliament promised the Princess their protection. There was more hesitation about admitting the two Dukes, but at last it was done. There were the headquarters of the army that resisted the Crown. At least this was the principle on which the Duke of Bouillon acted. His family had from the first tried to maintain the privileges which the old feudal vassals attributed to themselves, and he was following up their traditions, as well as fighting for the deliverance of his wife from her captivity.

The Duke of Rochefoucauld was throughout more the lover of Madame de Longueville then anything else, and the Princess of Conde simply thought of obtaining her husband's release, and nothing else. She had no notions of State policy nor anything else of the kind, any more than had Madame d'Aubepine, who assisted daily at her little agitated court. They were the two gentlest, simplest, weakest conspirators who ever rebelled against the Crown, and it was all out of pure loyalty to the two husbands who had never shown a spark of affection, scarcely of courtesy, to either of them.

Well, the Queen herself and her son and all the Court came to reduce Bordeaux, Mademoiselle and all, for she had been for the time detached from the adoration of the Prince, by, of all things in the world, hopes given her of marrying her little cousin, the King, though he was only twelve and she was double that age. So Bordeaux was besieged, and held out against the royal troops for some days, being encouraged by the resolute demeanour of the Princess; but at last, when on the faubourgs had been taken, the Parliament, uneasy in conscience at resisting the Crown, decided on capitulating, and, to the bitter disappointment and indignation of the ladies, made no stipulations as to the liberty of the husband.

No attempt was made on the liberty of the lady herself, and she was ordered to depart to Chantilly. Though unwell, she had visited every counsellor in his own house, and done her utmost to prepare for the renewal of the resistance in case her husband was not released; and she was almost exhausted with fatigue when she went on board a vessel which was to take her to Larmont, whence she meant to go to Coutras, where she was to be permitted to stay for three days.

Many nobles and people of condition, and half the population of Bordeaux, came down to the port with her, uttering lamentations, benedictions on her and her boy, and curses on Mazarin.

While about to embark she met Marshal de la Meilleraye, who advised her to go and see the Queen at Bourg, and she accordingly put herself under his direction, Cecile of course accompanying her as her attendant. The Duke of Damville came to fetch them in a carriage, and after alighting at Marshal de la Meilleraye's quarters, kind messages of inquiry were sent them by the Court, even by the King and Queen. By every one indeed except Mademoiselle, who kept up her dislike.

My son, who was present, described all to me, and how his blood boiled at the scornful airs of Mademoiselle and the stiffness of the Queen. He said, however, that his aunt looked quite like a changed woman as she entered, leading Maurice in the rear of the other mother and son.

The poor Princess had been bled the day before, and had her arm in a scarf, and Mademoiselle actually tittered at the manner in which it was put on, when this devoted wife was presented to the Queen, leading her little son.

Falling on her knees before the Queen she made her a really touching speech, begging her to excuse the attempts of a lady who had the honour of being married to the first Prince of the blood, when she strove to break his fetters. 'You see us on our knees, Madame, to beg for the liberty of what is dearest to us. Grant it to the great actions the Monsieur mon mari has performed for the glory of your Majesty, and the life he has ventured so often in the service of the State, and do not refuse our tears and humble prayers.'

The Queen answered coldly enough. Cecile told me afterwards that it was like ice, dashing all her hopes, to see the stern, haughty dignity of Anne of Austria unmoved by the tender, tearful, imploring form of Claire Clemence de Breze, trembling all over with agitation, and worn down with all she had attempted. 'I am glad, cousin,' said the Queen, 'that you know your fault. You see you have taken a bed method of obtaining what you ask. Now your conduct is to be different, I will see whether I can give you what you desire.'

In spite of her fright and the Queen's chilly pride, Cecile, feeling that this was her only chance, fell almost on her face before the Queen, with Maurice by her side, and cried: 'Grace, grace, great Queen, for my husband.'

My little Marquis, as he told me, could not bear to see them thus alone, so he ran forward, and knelt on her other side, holding her hand. And he heard a horrid little laugh, something about a new edition and an imitation; but the Queen, who had forgotten all about her, asked who she was and what her husband was.

Then, when it was explained that the Count d'Aubepine had drawn his sword and tried to aid Boutteville, there was another smile. Perhaps it was that the contrast might mortify the poor Princess, but the Queen said:

'There! stand up, Madame la Comtesse! We will send orders that the Count shall be released. He has expiated his own zeal, and will know better another time.'

Can any one conceive our Cecile's joy? She rose up and embraced both the boys passionately, and Gaspard could not refrain from congratulating her with the words, scarcely complimentary: 'My aunt, is it not indeed the lion and the mouse? Now my uncle must love you, as my papa loved my mama.'

The Princess, always too sweet and gentle for envy, kissed and congratulated Madame d'Aubepine, and left her on retiring to Milly. Nor did Cecile quit the Court till she actually was the bearer of an order for the release of her husband.

CHAPTER XXIV. — FAMILY HONOUR

I have gone on with the d'Aubepine side of the story, but while these two devoted wives were making exertions at Bordeaux so foreign to their whole nature, which seemed changed for their husband's sake, I was far away at the time, even from my son.

It was in March that we received a letter from my brother, Lord Walwyn, bidding us adieu, being, when we received it, already on the high seas with the Marquis of Montrose, to strike another blow for the King. He said he could endure inaction no longer, and that his health had improved so much that he should not be a drag on the expedition. Moreover, it was highly necessary that the Marquis should be accompanied by gentlemen of rank, birth, and experience, who could be entrusted with commands, and when so many hung back it was the more needful for some to go. It was a great stroke to us, for besides that Sir Andrew Macniven went on reiterating that it was mere madness, and there was not a hope of success—the idea of Eustace going to face the winds of spring in the islands of Scotland was shocking enough.

'The hyperborean Orcades,' as the Abbe called them, made us think of nothing but frost and ice and savages, and we could not believe Sir Andrew when he told us that the Hebrides and all the west coast of Scotland were warmer than Paris in the winter.

After this we heard nothing—nothing but the terrible tidings that the Great Marquis, as the Cavaliers called him, had been defeated, taken by treachery, and executed by hanging—yes, by hanging at Edinburgh! His followers were said to be all dispersed and destroyed, and our hearts died within us; but Annora said she neither would nor could believe that all was over till she had more positive news, and put my mother in mind how many times before they had heard of the deaths of men who appeared alive and well immediately after. She declared that she daily expected to see Eustace walk into the room, and she looked round for him whenever the door was opened.

The door did open at last to let in tidings from the Hague, but not brought by Eustace. It was Mr. Probyn, one of the King's gentlemen, however, who told me he had been charged to put into my hands the following letter from His Majesty himself:—

'Madame—If you were still my subject I should command you, as you are ever my old playfellow. Meg, I entreat you to come without delay to a true subject and old playfellow of mine, who, having already sorely imperiled his neck and his health, and escaped, as they say, by the skin of his teeth, would fain follow me into the same jeopardy again did I not commit him to such safe warship as that of Madame de Bellaise. Probyn will tell you further. He also bears a letter that will secure you letters and passports from the Queen-Regent. When next you hear of me it will be with one of my crowns on my head.

CHARLES R.'

Therewith was a brief note from Eustace himself:—

'Sweet Meg—Be not terrified at what they tell you of me. I have been preserved by a miracle in the miserable destruction of our armament and

our noble leader. Would that my life could have gone for his! They take such a passing ailment as I have often before shaken off for more than it is worth, but I will write more from shipboard. Time presses at present. With my loving and dutiful greetings to my mother, and all love

to my sister, 'Thine,

'E. WALWYN AND RIBAUMONT.'

Mr. Probyn told us more, and very sad it was, though still we had cause for joy. When Montrose's little troop was defeated and broken up at the Pass of Invercharron my brother had fled with the Marquis, and had shared his wanderings in Ross-shire for some days; but, as might only too surely have been expected, the exposure brought back his former illness, and he was obliged to take shelter in the cabin of a poor old Scotchwoman. She— blessings be on her head!—was faithful and compassionate, and would not deliver him up to his enemies, and thus his sickness preserved him from being taken with his leader by the wretched Macleod of Assynt.

Just as he grew a little better her son, who was a pedlar, arrived at the hut. He too was a merciful man, and, moreover, was loyal in heart to the King, and had fought in Montrose's first rising; and he undertook to guide my brother safely across Scotland and obtain his passage in one of the vessels that traded between Leith and Amsterdam. Happily Eustace always had a tongue that could readily catch the trick of dialects, and this excellent pedlar guarded him like his own brother, and took care to help him through all pressing and perplexing circumstances. Providentially, it was the height of summer, and the days were at their longest and warmest, or I know not how he could have gone through it at all; but at last he safely reached Leith, passing through Edinburgh with a pack on his back the very day that the Marquis of Huntly was executed. He was safely embarked on board at Dutch lugger, making large engagement of payment, which were accepted when he was known to have estates in France as well as in England; and thus he landed at Amsterdam, and made his way to the Hague, where all was in full preparation for the King's expedition to Scotland on the invitation of the nation.

So undaunted was my dear brother's spirit that, though he was manifestly very ill from the effects of exposure and fatigue, and of a rough voyage in a wretched vessel, he insisted that he should recover in a few days, and would have embarked at once with the King had not absolute orders to the contrary, on his duty as a subject, been laid upon him. Mr. Probyn did not conceal from us that the learned Dutch physician, Doctor Dirkius, though his condition very serious, and that only great care could save his life.

Of course I made up my mind at once to set forth and travel as quickly as I could—the King had kindly secured my permission—and to take Tryphena with me, as she knew better than any one what to do for Eustace. Annora besought permission to accompany me, and, to my surprise, my mother consented, saying to me in confidence that she did not like leaving her in Lady Ommaney's care while she herself was with the Queen of England. Lady Ommaney was not of sufficient rank, and had ideas. In effect, I believe my mother had begun to have her suspicions about Clement Darpent, though separation a good thing, never guessing, as I did, that one part of Nan's eagerness to be with her brother was in order to confide in him, and to persuade him as she had never been able to do by letter. There remained my son to be disposed of, but I had full confidence in the Abbe, who had bred up his father so well, and my boy would, I knew, always look up to him and obey him, so that I could leave him in his care when not in waiting, and they were even to spend the summer together in a little expedition to Nid de Merle. I wanted to see my son love his country home as English gentlemen lover theirs; but I fear that can never be, since what forms affection is the habit of conferring benefits, and we are permitted to do so little for our peasants.

Thus, then, it was settled. I went to Mademoiselle, who was always good-natured where her vanity was not concerned, and who freely-granted me permission to absent myself. The Queen-Regent had been prepared by her nephew, and she made no difficulties, and thus my great traveling carriage came again into requisition; but as an escort was necessary, we asked

Sir Andrew Macniven to accompany us, knowing that he would be glad to be at the Hague in case it should be expedient to follow His English Majesty to Scotland. We sent a courier to find my brother Solivet at Amiens, that he might meet and come part of the way with us. As to M. de Lamont, I was no longer in dread of him, as he had gone off to join the troops which the Duke of Bouillon and Rochefoucauld were collecting to compel the deliverance of the Princes; but the whole time was a dangerous one, for disbanded soldiers and robbers might lurk anywhere, and we were obliged to take six outriders armed to the teeth, besides the servants upon the carriage, of all of whom Sir Andrew took the command, for he could speak French perfectly, having studied in his youth in the University of Leyden.

Thus we took leave of Paris and of my mother, many of our friends coming out with us the first stage as far as St. Denys, where we all dined together. I could have excused them, as I would fain have had my son all to myself, and no doubt my sister felt the same, for Clement Darpent had also come, for the Frondeurs, or those supposed to be Frondeurs, were at this time courted by both parties, by the friends of the Prince in order to gain their aid in his release, and by the Court in order to be strengthened against the Prince's supporters; and thus the lawyers were treated with a studied courtesy that for the time made it appear as if they were to be henceforth, as in England, received as gentlemen, and treated on terms more like equality; and thus Clement joined with those who escorted us, and had a few minutes, though very few, of conversation with my sister, in which he gave her a packet for my brother.

I was not obliged to be cautious about knowing anything now that I should be out of reach of my mother, and all was to be laid before my brother. I could say nothing on the road, for our women were in the coach with us. the posts were not to be so much relied on as they are at present, and we had to send relays of horses forward to await us at each stage in order to have no delay, and he, who had made the journey before, managed all this excellently for us.

At night we two sisters shared the same room, and then it was that I asked Nan to tell me what was in her heart.

'What is the use?' she said; 'you have become one of these proud French nobility who cannot see worth or manhood unless a man can count a lineage of a hundred ancestors, half-ape, half-tiger.'

However, the poor child was glad enough to tell me all, even though I argued with her that, deeply English as she was in faith and in habits and modes of thought, it would hardly result in happiness even if she did extort permission to wed one of a different nation and religion, on whom, moreover, she would be entirely dependent for companionship; since, though nothing could break the bonds of sisterly affection between her and me, all the rest of the persons of her own rank would throw her over, since even if M. Darpent could be ennobled, or would purchase an estate bringing a title, hers would still be esteemed a mesalliance, unworthy the daughter of Anselme de Ribaumont the Crusader, and of the 'Bravest of Knights,' who gained the chaplet of pearls before Calais.

'Crusader!' said Annora; 'I tell you that his is truly a holy war against oppression and wrong-doing. Look at your own poor peasants, Meg, and say if he, and those like him, are not doing their best to save this country from a tyranny as foul as ever was the Saracen grasp on the Holy Sepulchre!'

'He is very like to perish in it,' I said.

'Well,' said Nan, with a little shake in her voice, 'if they told those who perished in the Crusades that they died gloriously and their souls were safe, I am sure it may well be so with one who pleads the cause of the poor, and I despite of his own danger never drew his sword against his King.'

There was no denying, even if one was not in love, and a little tete montee besides, like my poor Nan, that there was nobility of heart in Clement Darpent, especially as he kept his hands clear of rebellion; and I would not enter into the question of their differing religions. I left that for Eustace. I was certain that Annora knew, even better than I did, that the diversity between our parents had not been for the happiness of their children. In my own mind I saw little chance for the lovers, for I thought it inevitable that the Court and the Princes would draw together again, and that whether Cardinal Mazarin were sacrificed or not, the Frondeurs of Paris would be overthrown, and that Darpent, whose disinterestedness displeased all parties alike, was very likely to be made the victim. Therefore, though I could not but hope that the numerous difficulties in the way might prevent her from being linked to his fate, and actually sharing his ruin.

She was not in my hands, and I had not to decide, so I let her talk freely to me, and certainly, when we were alone together, her tongue ran on nothing else. I found that she hoped that Eustace would invite her lover to the Hague, and let them be wedded there by one of the refugee English clergy, and then they would be ready to meet anything together; but that M. Darpent was withheld by filial scruples, which actuated him far more than any such considerations moved her, and that he also had such hopes for his Parliament that he could not throw himself out of the power of serving it at this critical time, a doubt which she appreciated, looking on him as equal to any hero in Plutarch's LIVES.

Our brother De Solivet met us, and conducted into Amiens, where he had secured charming rooms for us. He was very full of an excellent marriage that had been offered to him for one of his little daughters, so good that he was going to make the other take the veil in order that her sister's fortune might be adequate to the occasion; and he regretted my having left Paris, because he intended to have set me to discover which had the greatest inclination to the world and which the chief vocation for the cloister. Annora's Protestant eyes grew large and round with horror, and she exclaimed at last:

'So that is the way in which you French fathers deliberate how to make victims of your daughters?'

He made her a little bow, and said, with is superior fraternal air:

'You do not understand, my sister. The happiest will probably be she who leads the peaceful life of a nun.'

'That makes it worse,' cried Annora, 'if you are arranging a marriage in which you expect your child to be less happy than if she were a nun.'

'I said not so, sister,' returned Solivet, with much patience and good-humour. 'I simply meant what you, as a Huguenot, cannot perceive, that a simple life dedicated to Heaven is often happier than one exposed to the storms and vicissitudes of the world.'

'Certainly you take good care it should prove so, when you make marriages such as that of the d'Aubepines,' said Nan.

Solivet shrugged his shoulders by way of answer, and warned my afterwards to take good care of our sister, or she would do something that would shock us all. To which I answered that the family honour was safe in the hand of so high-minded a maiden as our Annora, and he replied:

'Then there is, as I averred, no truth in the absurd report that she was encouraging the presumptuous advances of that factious rogue and Frondeur, young Darpent, whom our brother had the folly to introduce into the family.'

I did not answer, and perhaps he saw my blushes, for he added:

'If I thought so for a moment, she may be assured that his muddy bourgeois blood should at once be shed to preserve the purity of the family with which I have the honour to be connected.'

He was terribly in earnest, he, a Colonel in His Majesty's service, a father of a family, a staid and prudent man, and more than forty years old! I durst say no more but that I though Eustace was the natural protector and head of the Ribaumont family.

'A boy, my dear sister; a mere hot-headed boy, and full of unsettled fancies besides. In matters like this it is for me to think for the family. My mother depends on me, and my sister may be assured that I shall do so.'

I wondered whether my mother had given him a hint, and I also considered whether to put Annora upon her guard; but there was already quite enough mutual dislike between her and our half-brother, and I thought it better not to influence it. Solivet escorted us as far as his military duties permitted, which was almost to Calais, where we embarked for the Meuse, and there, when our passports had been examined and our baggage searched, in how different a world we found ourselves! It was like passing from a half-cultivated, poverty-stricken heath into a garden, tilled to the utmost, every field beautifully kept, and the great haycocks standing up tall in the fields, with the hay-makers round them in their curious caps, while the sails of boats and barges glided along between the trees in the canals that traversed them unseen; and as to the villages, they were like toys, their very walks bright with coloured tiles, and the fronts of the houses shining like the face of a newly-washed child. Indeed, as we found, the maids do stand in front of them every morning and splash them from eaves to foundation with buckets of water; while as to the gardens, and with palings painted of fanciful colours. All along the rivers and canals there were little painted houses, with gay pavilions and balconies with fanciful carved railings overhanging the water, and stages of flower-pot arranged in them. Sometimes a stout Dutch vrow with full, white, spotless sleeves, many-coloured substantial petticoats, gold buckles in her shoes, and a great white cap with a kind of gold band round her head, sat knitting there; or sometimes a Dutchman in trunk hose was fishing there. We saw them all, for we had entered a barge or trekschuyt, towed by horses on the bank, a great flat-bottomed thing, that perfectly held our carriage. Thus we were to go by the canals to the Hague, and no words can describe the strange silence and tranquillity of our motion along still waters.

My sister and her nurse, who had so often cried out against both the noisiness and the dirtiness of poor France, might well be satisfied now. They said they had never seen anything approaching to it in England. It was more like being shut up in a china closet than anything else, and it seemed as if the people were all dumb or dead, as we passed through those silent villages, while the great windmills along the banks kept waving their huge arms in silence, till Annora declared she felt she must presently scream, or ride a tilt with them like Don Quixote.

And all the time, as we came nearer and nearer, our hearts sank more and more, as we wondered in what state we should find our dear brother, and whether we should find him at all.

CHAPTER XXV. — THE HAGUE

At last we passed a distant steeple and large castle, which we were told belonged to Ryswyk, the castle of the Prince of Orange; then we went along through long rows of trees, and suddenly emerging from them we beheld a vast plain, a great wood, and a city crowned with towers and windmills.

Sir Andrew had been there before, and after showing our passports, and paying our fare to the boatman, who received it in a leathern bag, he left the servants to manage the landing of the carriage at the wharf, and took us through the streets, which were as scrupulously clean and well-washed, pavement and all, as if they had been the flags of an English kitchen, and as silent, he said, as a Sunday morning in Edinburgh. Even the children looked like little models of Dutchmen and Dutchwomen, and were just as solid, sober, and silent; and when Sir Andrew, who could speak Dutch, asked a little boy our way to the street whence my brother had dated his letter, the child gave his directions with the grave solemnity of a judge.

At last we made out way to the Mynheer Fronk's house, where we had been told we should find my Lord Walwyn's lodgings. It was a very tall house, with a cradle for a stork's nest at the top, and one of the birds standing on a single long thin leg on the ridge of the very high roof. There were open stalls for cheese on either side of the door, and a staircase leading up between. Sir Andrew made it known to a Dutchman, in a broad hat, that we were Lord Walwyn's sisters come to see him, and he thereupon called a stout maid, in a snowy round cap and kerchief, who in the first place looked at our shoes, then produced a brush and a cloth, and, going down on her knees, proceeded to wipe them and clean them. Sir Andrew submitted, as one quite accustomed to the process, and told us we might think ourselves fortunate that she did not actually insist on carrying us all upstairs, as some Dutch maids would do with visitors, rather than permit the purity of their stairs and passages to be soiled.

He extracted, meantime, from the Dutchman, that the Englishman had been very ill with violent bleedings at the lungs, but was somewhat better; and thus we were in some degree prepared, when we had mounted up many, many stairs, to find our Eustace sitting in his cloak, though it was a warm summer day, with his feet up on a wooden chair in front of him, and looking white, wasted, weak, as I had never seen him.

He started to his feet as the door opened and he beheld us, and would have sprung forward, but he was obliged to drop back into his chair again, and only hold out his arms.

'My sisters, my sisters!' he said; 'I had thought never to have seen you again!'

'And you would have sailed again for Scotland!' said Annora.

'I should have been strong in the face of the enemy,' he replied, but faintly.

There was much to be done for him. The room was a very poor and bare one, rigidly clean, of course, but with hardly and furniture in it but a bed, table, and two chairs, and the mistress or her maid ruthlessly scoured it every morning, without regard to the damp that the poor patient must inhale.

It appeared that since his expedition to Scotland the estate in Dorset had been seized, so that Harry Merrycourt could send him no more remittances, and, as the question about the Ribaumont property in Picardy was by no means decided, he had been reduced to sad straits. His Dutch hostess was not courteous, and complained very much that all the English cavaliers in exile professed to have rich kindred who would make up for everything, but she could not see that anything came of it. However, she did give him house-room, and, though grumbling, had provided him with many comforts and good fare, such as he was sure could not be purchased out of the very small sum he could give her by the week.

'And how provided?' he said. 'Ah! Nan, can you forgive me? I have had to pledge the last pearl of the chaplet, but I knew that Meg would redeem it.'

He had indeed suffered much, and we were eager to do our utmost for his recovery. We found the house crowded with people, and redolent of cheese. This small, chilly garret chamber was by no means proper for a man in his state of health, nor was there room for us in the house. So, leaving Nan with him, I went forth with Sir Andrew to seek for fresh lodgings. I need not tell how we tramped about the streets, and asked at many doors, before we could find any abode that would receive us. There were indeed lodgings left vacant by the gentlemen who had attended the King to Scotland, but perforce, so many scores had been left unpaid that there was great reluctance to receive any cavalier family, and the more high-sounding the name, the less trust there was in it. Nothing but paying down a month beforehand sufficed to obtain accommodation for us in a house belonging to a portly widow, and even there Nan and I would have to eat with the family (and so would my brother if he were well enough), and only two bedrooms and one sitting-room could be allotted to us. However, these were large and airy; the hangings, beds, and linen spotless; the floors and tables shining like mirrors; the windows clean, sunny, and bright; so we were content, and had our mails deposited there at once, though we could not attempt to move my brother so late in the day.

Indeed, I found him so entirely spent and exhausted by his conversation with Annora, that I would not let him say any more that night, but left him to the charge of Tryphena, who would not hear of leaving him, and was very angry with Mistress Nan, who, she said, in her English speech, would talk a horse's head off when once she began. In the morning Sir Andrew escorted us to the lodgings, where we found my brother already dressed, by the help of Nicolas, and looking forward to the change cheerfully. I have given Sir Andrew my purse, begging him, with his knowledge of Dutch, to discharge the reckoning for me, after which he was to go to find a chair, a coach, or anything that could be had to convey my brother in, for indeed he was hardly fit to walk downstairs.

Presently the Scottish knight knocked at the door, and desired to speak with me. 'What does this mean, Madame?' he said, looking much amused. 'My Lord here has friends. The good vrow declares that all his charges have been amply paid by one who bade her see that he wanted for nothing, and often sent dainty fare for him.'

'Was no name given?'

'None; and the vrow declares herself sworn to secrecy; but I observed that by a lapsus linguoe she implied that the sustenance came from a female hand. Have you any suspicions that my lord has a secret admirer?'

I could only say that I believed that many impoverished cavaliers had met with great and secret kindness from the nobility of Holland; that the King of England, as he knew, had interested himself about my brother, and as we all had been, so to say, brought up in intimacy with the royal family, I did not think it impossible that the Princess of Orange might have interested herself about him, though she might not wish to have it known, for fear of exciting expectations in others. Of course all the time I had other suspicions, but I could not communicate them, though they were increased when Sir Andrew went with Eustace's pledge to redeem the pearl; but he came back in wrath and despair, telling me that a rascally Dutch merchant had smelt it out, and had offered a huge price for it, which the goldsmith had not withstood, despairing of its ransom.

Eustace did not ask who the merchant was, but I saw the hot blood mounting in his pale cheek. Happily Annora was not present, so inconvenient questions were avoided. He was worn out with the being carried in a chair and then mounting the stairs, even with the aid of Sir Andrew's arm.

Tryphena, however, had a nourishing posset for him, and we laid him on a day-bed which had been made ready for him, where he smiled at us, said, 'This is comfort,' and dropped asleep while I sat by him. There I stayed, watching him, while Nan, whose nature never was to sit still, went forth, attended by Sir Andrew and Nicolas, to obtain some needments. If she had known the language, and if it had been fitting for a young demoiselle of her birth, she might have gone alone; these were the safest streets, and the most free from riot or violence of any kind that I ever inhabited.

While she was gone, Eustace awoke, and presently began talking to me, and asking me about all that had passed, and about which we had not dared to write. Nan, he said, had told him her story, and he was horrified at the peril I had incurred. I replied that was all past, and was as nothing compared with the consequences, of which my sister had no doubt informed him. 'Yes,' he said, 'I did not think it of Darpent.' I said I supposed that the young man could not help the original presumption of loving Annora, and that I could bear testimony that they had been surprised into confessing it to one another. He sighed, and said: 'True. I had thought that the barrier between the robe and the sword was so fixed in a French mind that I should as soon have expected Nicolas to aspire to Mademoiselle de Ribaumont's hand as Clement Darpent.'

'But in her own eyes she is not Mademoiselle de Ribaumont so much as Mistress Annora Ribmont,' I said; 'and thus she treated him in a manner to encourage his audacity.'

'Even so,' said Eustace, 'and Annora is no mere child, not one of your jeunes filles, who may be disposed of at one's will. She is a woman grown, and has been bred in the midst of civil wars. She had refused Harry Merrycourt before we left home, and she knows how to frighten away all the suitors our mother would find for her. Darpent is deeply worthy. We should esteem and honour him as a gentleman in England; and were he there, and were our Church as once it was, he would be a devout and thankful member of it. Margaret, we must persuade my mother to consent.'

I could not help rejoicing; and then he added: 'The King has been well received, and is about to be crowned in Scotland. It may well be that our way home may be opened. In that case, Meg, you, my joint-heiresses, would have something to inherit, and before going to Scotland I had drawn up a will giving you and your Gaspard the French claims, and Annora the English estates. I know the division is not equal; but Gaspard can never be

English, and Annora can never be French; and may make nearly as much of an Englishman of Darpent as our grandfather was.'

'Nay, nay, Eustace,' I said; 'the names of Walwyn and Ribaumont must not be lost.'

'She may make Darpent deserve a fresh creation, then,' he answered, smiling sadly. 'It will be best to wait a little, as I have told her, to see how matters turn out at home.'

I asserted with all my heart, and told him what our brother Solivet had said.

'Yes,' he said; 'Solivet and our mother will brook the matter much better if she is to live in England, the barbarous land that they can forget. And if I do not live, I will leave them each a letter that they cannot quite disregard.'

I said I was glad he had not consented to Annora's notion of bringing Darpent to Holland, since Solivet might lie in wait for him, and besides, it would not be treating our mother rightly.

'No,' said Eustace; 'if I am ever strong enough again I must return to Paris, and endeavour to overcome their opposition.' And he spoke with a weary sigh, though I augured that he would soon improve under our care, and that of Tryphena, who had always been better for him than any doctor. Then I could not help reproaching him a little with having ventured himself in that terrible climate and hopeless cause.

'As to the climate, that was not so much amiss,' said Eustace. 'Western Scotland is better and more wholesome than these Dutch marshes. The sea-gull fares better than the frog.'

'But the cause,' I said. 'Why did you not wait to go with the King?'

'There were reasons, Meg,' he said. 'The King was hounding—yes, hounding out the Marquis to lead the forlorn hope. Heaven forgive me for my disloyalty in thinking he wished to be quit of one so distasteful to the Covenanters who have invited him.'

And when I broke forth in indignation, Eustace lowered his voice, and said sadly that the King was changed in many points from the Prince of Wales, and that listening to policy was not good for him. Then I asked why, if the King hounded, as he called it, the Marquis, on this unhappy expedition, should Eustace have share in it?

'It was enough to anger any honest man,' said Eustace, 'to see the flower of all the cavaliers thus risked without a man of rank or weight to back him, with mere adventurers and remnants of Goring's fellows, and

Irishmen that could only do him damage with the Scots. I, with neither wife nor child, might well be the one to share the venture.'

'Forgetting your sisters,' said I. 'Ah, Eustace, was there no other cause to make you restless?'

'You push me hard, Meg. Yes, to you I will say it, that there was a face among the ladies here which I could not look on calmly, and I knew it was best for her and for myself that I should be away.'

'Is she there still?' I asked.

'I know not. Her husband had taken her to his country-house last time I heard, and very few know that I am not gone with the King. It was but at the last moment that he forbade me. It is better so.'

I thought of what his hostess had told me, but I decided for the present to keep my own counsel.

We thought it right to pay our respects to the Princess of Orange, but she was keeping very little state. Her husband, the Stadholder, was on bad terms with the States, and had just failed in a great attack on Amsterdam; and both he and she were indisposed. The Princess Royal replied therefore to our request for admittance, that she could not refuse to see such old friends of her family as the ladies of Ribaumont, but that we must excuse her for giving us a private reception.

Accordingly we were conducted through numerous courts, up a broad staircase of shining polished wood, through a large room, to a cabinet hung with pictures, among which her martyered father held the foremost place. She was a thin woman, with a nose already too large for her face, inherited no doubt from her grandfather, the Grand Monarque, and her manner had not the lively grace of her mother's, but seemed as if it had been chilled and made formal by her being so early transported to Holland. She was taken thither at ten years old, and was not yet nineteen; and though I had once or twice played with her before my marriage, she could not be expected to remember me. So the interview was very stiff at first, in spite of her kind inquiries for my brother, whom she said the King loved and valued greatly. I wondered whether it could have been she who had provided for his needs, and threw out a hint to see if so it were, but she evidently did not understand me, and our visit soon ended.

Our way of life at the Hague was soon formed. Eustace was our first thought and care, and we did whatever we thought best for his health. I would fain have taken him back to Paris with us, but autumn was setting in, and he was not in a state to be moved, being only able to walk from one room to the other, and I could hardly hope that he would gain strength before the winter set in, since a sea voyage would be necessary, as we could not pass through the Spanish Netherlands that lay between us and France. Besides, while the King was in Scotland, he always entertained the hope of a summons to England. Other exiles were waiting in the same manner as ourselves, and from time to time we saw something of them. The gentlemen would come and sit with my brother, and tell him of the news, and we exchanged visits with the ladies, whom Annora recognised at the room where an English minister held their service; but they were a much graver and quieter set of exiles than those we had known at Paris. They could hardly be poorer than those; indeed, many were less strained, but they did not carry off their poverty in the same gay and lively manner, and if they had only torn lace and soiled threadbare garments, they shut themselves up from all eyes, instead of ruffling gaily as if their rags were tokens of honour.

Besides, more than one event occurred to sadden that banished company. The tidings came of the death of the young Lady Elisabeth, who had pine away in the hands of her keepers, and died a week after her arrival at Carisbrooke, where her father had been so long a prisoner, her cheek resting her open Bible.

Annora, who had known her as a grave, sweet, thoughtful child, grieved much for her, broken-hearted as she seemed to have been for her father; and the Princess of Orange, knowing that Nan had seen the poor young lady more lately than herself, sent for her to converse and tell of the pretty childish ways of that 'rosebud born in snow,' as an English poet prettily termed the young captive.

Ere long the poor Princess was in even more grievous trouble. Her husband, the young Prince of Orange, died of smallpox, whereupon she fell into such transports of grief that there was the greatest anxiety respecting her, not only from compassion, but because she was the staunch supporter of her exiled family to the best of her ability.

Eight days later, on her own nineteenth birthday, her son was born; and in such gloom, that it was a marvel that mother or babe survived, for the entire rooms were hung with black, and even the cradle of the child was covered completely with black velvet, so that the poor little puny infant seemed as if he were being put into a coffin. We saw the doleful chamber ourselves, for Eustace sent us to pay our respects, and Queen Henrietta honoured me with commands to write her a report of her widowed daughter and first grandson.

For we were still at the Hague, Eustace gradually regaining strength, and the bleedings had almost entirely ceased; but the physician who attended him, the best I think whom I have even known, and whose regimen did him more good than any other he had adopted, charged me, as I valued his life, not to attempt a journey with him till after the winter should be over, and summer entirely set in. If the effusion of blood could be prevented he might even yet recover and live to old age, but if it recurred again Dr. Dirkius would not answer for his life for an hour; nor must he do aught that would give him a rheum or renew his cough.

After all, we were very peaceful and happy in those rooms at the Hague, though Eustace was very anxious about the King, Annora's heart was at Paris, and I yearned after my son, from whom I had never thought to be so long parted; but we kept our cares to ourselves, and were cheerful with one another. We bought or borrowed books, and read them together, we learned to make Holland lace, studied Dutch cookery, and Annora, by Eustace's wish, took lessons on the lute and spinnet, her education in those matters having been untimely cut short. By the way, she had a real taste for music, and the finding that her performance and her singing amused and refreshed him gave her further zeal to continue the study and conquer the difficulties, though she would otherwise have said she was too old to go to school.

Then the frost set in, and all the canals and sluggish streams were sheets of ice, to which the market people skated, flying along upon the ice like birds. We kept my brother's room as warm as it was in our power to do, and made him lie in bed till the house was thoroughly heated, and he did not suffer much or become materially worse in the winter, but he was urgent upon us to go out and see the curious sights and share the diversions as far as was possible for us. Most of the Dutch ladies skated beautifully, and the younger ones performed dances on the ice with their cavaliers, but all was done more quietly than usual on account of the mourning, the Prince of Orange being not yet buried, and his child frail and sickly. The Baptism did not take place till January, and then we were especially invited to be present. Though of course my brother could not go, Annora and I did so. The poor child had three sets of States-General for his godfathers, his godmothers being his grandmother, the elder Princess of Orange, and his great aunt, Queen Elisabeth of Bohemia. The Duke of York, who had lately arrived, was asked to carry the little Prince to church, but he shuddered at the notion of touching a baby, as much as did his sister a the idea of trusting her precious child with him, so the infant was placed in the arms of one of his young aunts, Mademoiselle Albertine of Nassau.

I saw no more than a roll of ermine, and did not understand much of the long sermon with which the Dutch minister precluded the ceremony, and which was as alien to my sister's ideas of a christening as it was to mine. Many other English ladies were mingled with the Dutch ones in the long rows that lined the aisle, and I confess that my eyes wandered a good deal, guessing which were my countrywomen. Nearly opposite to me was one of the sweetest faces I have ever seen, the complexion quite pearly white, the hair of pale gold, in shining little rings over the brow, which was wonderfully pure, though with an almost childish overtone. There was peace on the soft dark eyes and delicately-moulded lips and the fair, oval, though somewhat thin cheeks. It was a perfect refreshment to see that countenance, and it reminded me of two most incongruous and dissimilar ones—namely, the angelic face of the Dutchess de Longueville when I had first seen her in her innocent, untainted girlhood, and of the expression on the worn old countenance of Madame Darpent.

I was venturing a glance now and then to delight myself without disconcerting that gentle lady, when I felt Annora's hand on my arm, squeezing so hard, poor maid, that her fingers left a purple mark there, and though she did not speak, I beheld, as it were, darts and arrows in the gleam of her eyes. And then it was that I saw on the black velvet dress worn by the lady a part of a necklace of large pearls—the pearls of Ribaumont—though I should not have known them again, or perhaps would Nan, save for the wearer.

'Flaunting them in our very faces,' muttered poor Nan; and if eyes could have slain, hers would have killed the poor Vrow van Hunker on the spot. As it was, the dark eyes met her fierce glance and sunk beneath it, while such a painful crimson suffused the fair cheeks that I longed to fly to the rescue, and to give at least a look of assurance that I acquitted her of all blame, and did not share my sister's indignation. But there was no uplifting of the eyelids again till the ceremony was ended, and we all had to take our places again in one of the thirty state coaches in which the company had come to the christening.

I saw Madame van Hunker led out by a solid, wooden-faced old Dutchman, who looked more like her father than her husband; and I told Annora that I was sure she had worn the pearls only because he compelled her.

'Belike,' said my sister. 'She hath no more will of her own than a hank of flax! That men can waste their hearts on such moppets as that!'

But though we did not at all agree on the impression Madame van Hunker had made on us, we were of one mind to say nothing of it to Eustace.

Another person laid her hand on Annora's arm as she was about to enter our carriage. 'Mistress Ribmont!' she exclaimed; 'I knew not that you were present in this land of our exile.'

I looked and saw a lady, as fantastically dressed as the mourning would permit, and with a keen clever face, and Nan curtsied, saying: 'My Lady Marchioness of Newcastle! let me present to you my sister, Madame la Vicomtesse de Bellaise.'

She curtsied and asked in return for Lord Walwyn, declaring that her lord would come and see him, and that we must come to visit her. 'We are living poorly enough, but my lord's good daughter Jane Doth her best for us and hath of late sent us a supply; so we are making merry while it lasts, and shall have some sleighing on ice-hills to-morrow, after the fashion of the country. Do you come, my good lad is cruelly moped in yonder black-hung place, with his widowed sister and her mother-in-law, and I would fain give him a little sport with young folk.'

Lady Newcastle's speech was cut short by her lord, who came to insist on her getting into the coach, which was delaying for her, and on the way home Nan began to tell me of her droll pretensions, which were like an awkward imitation of the best days of the Hotel Rambouillet.

She also told me about the noble-hearted Lady Jane Cavendish, the daughter of the Marquis's first marriage—how she held out a house of her father against the rebels, and acted like a brave captain, until the place was stormed, and she and her sister were made prisoners. The Roundhead captain did not treat them with over-ceremony, but such was the Lady Jane's generous nature that when the Royalists came to her relief, and he was made captive in his turn, she saved his life by her intercession.

She had since remained in England, living in a small lodge near the ruins of her father's house at Bolsover, to obtain what she could for his maintenance abroad, and to collect together such remnants of the better times as she might, such as the family portraits, and the hangings of the hall. I longed to see this very worthy and noble lady, but she was out of our reach, being better employed in England. Nan gave a little sigh to England, but not such a sigh as she would once have heaved.

And we agreed on the way home to say nothing to my brother of our meeting with poor Millicent.

My Lord Marquis of Newcastle showed his esteem for my brother by coming to see him that very day, so soon as he could escape from the banquet held in honour of the christening, which, like all that was done by the Dutch, was serious and grim enough, though it could not be said to be sober.

He declared that he had been ignorant that Lord Walwyn was at the Hague, or he should have waited on him immediately after arriving there, 'since nothing,' said the Marquis, 'does me good like the sight of an honest cavalier.' I am sure Eustace might have said the same; and they sat talking together long and earnestly about how it fared with the King in Scotland, and how he had been made to take the Covenant, which, as they said, was in very truth a dissembling which must do him grievous ill, spiritually, however it might serve temporally. My Lord repeated his lady's invitation to a dinner, which was to be followed up by sleighing on hills formed of ice. Annora, who always loved rapid motion as an exhilaration of spirits, brightened at the notion, and Eustace was anxious that it should be accepted, and thus we found ourselves pledged to enter into the diversions of the place.

CHAPTER XXVI. — HUNDERSLUST

So to my Lord Marquis of Newcastle's dinner we went, and found ourselves regaled with more of good cheer than poor cavaliers could usually offer. There was not only a good sirloin of beer, but a goose, and many choice wild-fowl from the fens of the country. There was plum porridge too, which I had not seen since I left England at my marriage. Every one was so much charmed at the sight that I thought I ought to be so too, but I confess that it was too much for me, and that I had to own that it is true that the English are gross feeders. The Duke of York was there, looking brighter and more manly than I had yet seen him, enlivened perhaps by my Lady Newcastle, who talked to him, without ceasing, on all sorts of subjects. She would not permit the gentlemen to sit after dinner, because she would have us all out to enjoy her sport on the ice-hills, which were slopes made with boards, first covered with snow, and then with water poured over them till they were perfectly smooth and like glass. I cannot say that I liked the notion of rushing down them, but it seemed to fill Annora with ecstasy, and my lady provided her with a sleigh and a cavalier, before herself instructing the Duke of York in the guidance of her own sledge upon another ice-hill.

My Lord Marquis did me the honour to walk with me and converse on my brother. There was a paved terrace beneath a high wall which was swept clear of snow and strewn with sand and ashes, so that those who had no turn for the ice-hills could promenade there and gaze upon the sport. When his other duties as a host called him away, his lordship said, with a smile, that he would make acquainted with each other two of his own countrywomen, both alike disguised under foreign names, and therewith he presented Madame van Hunker to me. Being on the same side of the table we had not previously seen one another, nor indeed would she have known me by sight, since I had left England before her arrival at Court.

She knew my name instantly, and the crimson colour rushed into those fair cheeks as she made a very low reverence, and murmured some faltering civility.

We were left together, for all the other guest near us were Hollanders, whose language I could not speak, and who despised French too much to learn it. So, as we paced along, I endeavoured to say something trivial of the Prince's christening and the like, which might begin the conversation; and I was too sorry for her to speak with the frigidity with which my sister thought she ought to be treated. Then gradually she took courage to reply, and I found that she had come in attendance on her stepdaughter Cornelia, who was extremely devoted to these sleighing parties. The other daughter, Veronica, was at home, indisposed, having, as well as her father, caught a feverish cold on a late expedition into the country, and Madame would fain have given up the party, as she thought Cornelia likewise to be unwell, but her father would not hear of his favourite Keetje being disappointed. I gather that the Yung-vrow Cornelia had all the true Dutch obstinacy of nature. By and by she ventured timidly, trying to make her voice sound as if she were only fulfilling an ordinary call of politeness, to hope that my Lord Walwyn was in better health. I told her a little of his condition, and she replied with a few soft half-utterance; but before we had gone far in our conversation there was a sudden commotion among the sleighing party — an accident, as we supposed — and we both hurried forward in anxiety for our charges. My sister was well, I was at once reassured by seeing her gray and ermine hood, which I knew well, for it was Mademoiselle van Hunker who lay insensible. It was not from a fall, but the cold had perhaps struck her, they said, for after her second descent she had complained of giddiness, and had almost immediately swooned away. She was lying on the sledge, quite unconscious, and no one seemed to know what to do. Her stepmother and I came to her; I raised her head and put essences to her nose, and Madame van Hunker took off her gloves and rubbed her hands, while my Lady Newcastle, hurrying up, bade them carry her into the house, and revive her by the fire; but Madame van Hunker insisted and implored that she should not be taken indoors, but carried home at once, showing a passion and vehemence quite unlike one so gentle, and which our good host and hostess withstood till she hinted that she feared it might be more than a swoon, since her father and sister were already indisposed. Then, indeed, all were ready enough to stand aloof; a coach was procured, I know not how, and poor Cornelia was lifted into it, still unconscious, or only moaning a little. I could not let the poor young stepmother go with her alone, and no one else would make the offer, the dread of contagion keeping all at a distance, after what had passed. At first I think Madame van Hunker hardly perceived who was with her, but as I spoke a word or two in English, as we tried to accommodate the inanimate form between us, she looked up and said: 'Ah! I should not have let you come, Madame! I do everything wrong. I pray you to leave me!' Then, as I of course refused, she added: 'Ah, you know not—' and then whispered in my ear, though the poor senseless girl would scarce have caught the sound, the dreadful word 'smallpox.' I could answer at once that I had had it—long, long ago, in my childish days, when my grandmother nursed me and both my brothers through it, and she breathed freely, I asked her why she apprehended it, and she told me that some weeks ago her husband had taken the whole party down to his pleasure-house in the country, to superintend some arrangement in his garden, which he wished to make before the frost set in.

He and his daughter Veronica had been ailing for some days, but it was only on that very morning that tidings had come to the Hague that the smallpox had, on the very day of their visit, declared itself in the family of the gardener who kept the house, and that two of his children were since dead. Poor Millicent had always had a feeble will, which yielded against her judgment and wishes. She had not had the malady herself, 'But oh! my child,' she said, 'my little Emilia!' And when I found that the child had not been on the expedition to Hunderslust, and had not seen her father or sister since they had been sickening, I ventured to promise that I would take her home, and the young mother clasped my hand in fervent gratitude.

But we were not prepared for the scene that met us when we drove into the porte cochere. The place seemed deserted, not a servant was to be seen but one old wrinkled hag, who hobbled up to the door saying something in Dutch that made Madame van Hunker clasp her hands and exclaim: 'All fled! Oh, what shall we do?'

At that moment, however, Dr. Dirkius appeared at the door. He spoke French, and he explained that he had been sent for about an hour ago, and no sooner had he detected smallpox than Mynheer's valet had fled from his master's room and spread the panic throughout the household, so that every servant, except one scullion and this old woman, had deserted it. The Dutch have more good qualities than the French, their opposites, are inclined to believe, but they have also a headstrong selfishness that seems almost beyond reach. Nor perhaps had poor Mynheer van Hunker been a master who would win much affection.

I know not what we should have done if Dr. Dirkius had not helped me to carry Cornelia to her chamber. The good man had also locked the little Emilia into her room, intending, after having taken the first measures for the care of his patients, to take or send her to the ladies at Lord Newcastle's, warning them not to return. Madame van Hunker looked deadly pale, but she was a true wife, and said nothing should induce her to forsake her husband and his daughters; besides, it must be too late for her to take precautions. Dirkius looked her all over in her pure delicate beauty, muttering what I think was: 'Pity! pity!' and then agreed that so it was. As we stood by the bed where we had laid Cornelia, we could hear at one end old Hunker's voice shouting—almost howling—for his vrow; and likewise the poor little Emilia thumping wildly against the door, and screaming for her mother to let her out. Millicent's face worked, but she said: 'She must not touch me! She had best not see me! Madame, God sent in you an angle of mercy. Take her; I must go to my husband!'

And at a renewed shout she ran down the corridor to hide her tears. The doctor and I looked at one another. I asked if a nurse was coming. Perchance, he said; he must go and find some old woman, and old Trudje must suffice meantime. There would as yet be no risk in my taking the child away, if I held her fast, and made her breathe essences all through the house.

It was a strange capture, and a dreadful terror for the poor little girl. By his advice I sprinkled strong essences all over the poor little girl's head, snatched her up in my arms, and before she had breath to scream hurried down stairs with her. She was about three years old, and it was not till I was almost at the outer door that she began to kick and struggle. My mind was made up to return as soon as she was safe. It was impossible to leave that poor woman to deal alone with three such cases, and I knew what my brother would feel about it. And all fell out better than I could have hoped, for under the porte cochere was the coach in which we had come to Lady Newcastle's. My sister, learning that I had gone home with Madame van Hunker, had driven thither to fetch me, and Nicolas was vainly trying to find some one to tell me that she was waiting. I carried the child, now sobbing and calling for her mother, to the carriage, and explained the state of affairs as well as I could while trying to hush her. Annora was quick to understand, and not slow to approve. 'The brutes!' she said. 'Have they abandoned them? Yes, Meg, you are safe, and you cannot help staying. Give me the poor child! I will do my best for her. O yes! I will take care of Eustace, and I'll send you your clothes. I wish it was any one else, but he will be glad. So adieu, and take care of yourself! Come, little one, do not be afraid. We are going to see a kind gentleman.'

But as poor little Emilia knew no English, this must have failed to console her, and they drove away amid her sobs and cries, while I returned to my strange task. I was not altogether cut off from home, for my faithful Nicolas, though uncertain whether he had been secured from the contagion, declared that where his mistress went he went. Tryphena would have come too, but like a true old nurse she had no confidence in Mistress Nan's care of my brother, or of the child, and it was far better as it was, for the old women whom the doctor found for us were good for nothing but to drink and to sleep; whereas Nicolas, like a true French laquais, had infinite resources in time of need. He was poor Madame's only assistant in the terrible nursing of her husband; he made the most excellent tisanes and bouillons for the patients, and kept us nurses constantly supported with good meats and wines, without which we never could have gone through the fatigue; he was always at hand, and seemed to sleep, if he slept at all, with one ear and one eye open during that terrible fifteen days during which neither Madame van Hunker, he, nor I, ever took off our clothes. Moreover, he managed our communication with my family. Every day in early morning he carried a billet from me which he placed in a pan of vinegar at their door; and, at his whistle, Annora looked out and threw down a billet for me, which, to my joy and comfort, generally told me that my brother was no worse, and that the little maid was quite well, and a great amusement to him. He was the only one who could speak any Dutch, so that he had been able to do more with her than the others at her first arrival; and though she very soon picked up English enough to understand everything, and to make herself understood in a droll, broken baby tongue, she continued to be devoted to him. She was a pretty, fair child of three years old, with enough of Dutch serenity and gravity not to be troublesome after the first shock was over, and she beguiled many of his weary hours of confinement by the games in which he joined her. He sent out to by for her a jointed baby, which Annora dressed for her, and, as she wrote, my lord was as much interested about the Lady Belphoebe's robes (for so had he named her) as was Emilia, and he was her most devoted knight, daily contriving fresh feasts and pageants for her ladyship. Nan declared that she was sometimes quite jealous of Belphoebe and her little mistress; but, on the whole, I think she enjoyed the months when she had Eustace practically to herself.

For we were separated for months. Poor Cornelia's illness was very short, the chill taken at the sleighing party had been fatal to her at the beginning of the complaint, and she expired on the third day, with hardly any interval of consciousness.

Her sister, Veronica, was my chief charge. I had to keep her constantly rolled in red cloth in a dark room, while the fever ran very high, and she suffered much. I think she was too ill to feel greatly the discomfort of being tended by a person who could not speak her language, and indeed necessity enabled me to understand a tongue so much like English, which indeed she could herself readily speak when her brain began to clear. This, however, was not for full a fortnight, and in the meantime Mynheer van Hunker was growing worse and worse, and he died on the sixteenth day of his illness. His wife had watched over him day and night with unspeakable tenderness and devotion, though I fear he never showed her much gratitude in return; he had been too much used to think of woman as mere housewifely slaves.

She had called me in to help in her terror at the last symptoms of approaching death, and I heard him mutter to her: 'Thou hast come to be a tolerable housewife. I have taken care thou dost not lavish all on beggarly stranger.'

At least so the words came back on me afterwards; but we were absorbed in our attendance on him in his extremity, and when death had come at last I had to lead her away drooping and utterly spent. Alas! it was not exhaustion alone, she had imbibed the dreadful disease, and for another three weeks she hung between life and death. Her stepdaughter left her bed, and was sent away to the country-house to recover, under the care of the steward's wife, before Millicent could open her eyes or lift her head from her pillow; but she did at last begin to revive, and it was in those days of slow convalescence that she and I became very dear to one another.

We could talk together of home, as she loved to call England, and of her little daughter, of whom Annora sent me daily reports, which drew out the mother's smiles. She could not be broken-hearted for Mynheer van Hunker, nor did she profess so to be, but she said he had been kind to her—much kinder since she had really tried to please him; and that, she said—and then broke off—was after he—your brother—my lord—And she went no further, but I knew well afterwards what that chance meeting had done for her—that meeting which, with such men as I had too often seen at Paris, might have been fatal for ever to her peace of mind and purity of conscience by renewing vain regrets, not to be indulged without a stain. Nay, it had instead given her a new impulse, set her in the way of peace, and helped her to turn with new effort to the path of duty that was left to her. And she had grown far happier therein. Her husband had been kinder to her after she ceased to vex him by a piteous submission and demonstrative resignation; his child had been given to brighten her with hope; and that she had gained his daughter's affection I had found by Veronica's conversation about her, and her tears when permitted to see her—or rather to enter her dark chamber for a few moments before going to Hunkerslust, the name of the country-house near Delf. Those days of darkness, when the fever had spent itself, and the strength was slowly returning, were indeed a time when hearts could flow into one another; and certainly I had never found any friend who so perfectly and entirely suited me as that sweet Millicent. There was perhaps a lack of strength of resolute will; she had not the robust temper of my high-spirited Annora, but, on the other hand, she was not a mere blindly patient Grisel, like my poor sister-in-law, Cecily d'Aubepine, but could think and resolve for herself, and hold staunchly to her duty when she saw it, whatever it might cost her; nor did terror make her hide anything, and thus she had won old Hunker's trust, and he had even permitted her to attend the service of exiled English ministers at the Hague.

One of them came to see her two or three times—once when she seemed to be at the point of death, and twice afterwards, reading prayers with her, to her great comfort. He spoke of her as an angel of goodness, spending all the means allowed her by her husband among her poor exiled countrymen and women. And as she used no concealment, and only took what was supplied to her for her own 'menus plaisirs,' her husband might grumble, but did not forbid. I knew now that my brother had loved in her something more than the lovely face.

And oh for that beauty! I felt as though I were trying to guard a treasure for him as I used every means I had heard of to save it from disfigurement, not permitting one ray of daylight to penetrate into the room, and attempting whatever could prevent the marks from remaining. And here Millicent's habits of patience and self-command came to her aid, and Dr. Dirkius said he had never had a better or a gentler sick person to deal with.

Alas! it was all in vain. Millicent's beauty had been of that delicate fragile description to which smallpox is the most fatal enemy, with its tendency not only to thicken the complexion, but to destroy the refined form of the features. We were prepared for the dreadful redness at first, and when Millicent first beheld herself in the glass she contrived to laugh, while she wondered what her little Emilia would say to her changed appearance, and also adding that she wondered how it fared with her step-mother, a more important question, she tried to say, than for herself, for the young lady was betrothed to a rich merchant's son, and would be married as soon as the days of mourning were over. However, as Veronica had never been reckoned a beauty, and les beaux yeux de sa cassette had been avowedly the attraction, we hoped that however it might be, there would not be much difference in her lot.

We were to joint her at Hunkerslust to rid ourselves of infection, while the house was purified from it. Before we went, Annora daily brought little Emilia before the window that her mother might see the little creature, who looked so grown and so full of health as to rejoice our hearts. My brother and sister seemed to have made the little maid much more animated than suited a Dutch child, for she skipped, frolicked, and held up her wooden baby, making joyous gestures in a way that astonished the solemn streets of Graavehage, as the inhabitants call it. She was to come to us at Hunkerslust so soon as the purification was complete; and then I was to go back to my brother and sister, for as the spring advanced it was needful that we should return to France, to our mother and my son.

It was April by the time Madame van Hunker was fit to move, and the great coach came to the door to carry us out the three or four miles into the country. I shall never forget the charm of leaving the pest-house I had inhabited so long, and driving through the avenues, all budding with fresh young foliage, and past gardens glowing with the gayest of flowers, the canals making shining mirrors for tree, windmill, bridge, and house, the broad smooth roads, and Milicent, holding one of my hands, lay back on the cushions, deeply shrouded in her widow's veil, unwilling to speak, but glad of the delight I could not help feeling.

We arrived at the house, and entered between the row of limes clipped in arches. Never did I behold such a coup d'oeil as the garden presented, with its paved and tiled paths between little beds of the most gorgeous hyacinths and tulips, their colours assorted to perfection, and all in full bloom. I could not restrain a childish cry of wonder and absolute joy at the first glance; it was such a surprise, and yet I recollected the next moment that there was something very sad in the display, for it was in going to superintend this very garden that poor Mymheer van Hunker had caught his death, and here were these his flowers blooming away gaily in the sun unseen by him who had cared for them so much.

Veronica had come to meet us, and she and her step-mother wept in each other's arms at the sight and the remembrances it excited; but their grief was calm, and it appeared that Veronica had had a visit from her betrothed and his mother, and had no reason to be dissatisfied with their demeanour. Indeed, the young lady's portion must be so much augmented by her sister's death that it was like to compensate for the seams in her cheeks.

No matter of business had yet come before the widow, but it was intimated to her that the notary, Magister Wyk, would do himself the honour of coming to her at Hunkerslust so soon as she felt herself strong enough to receive him, and to hear the provisions of the will.

Accordingly he came, the whole man impregnated with pungent perfumes and with a pouncet-box in his hand, so that it almost made one sneeze to approach him. He was by no means solicitous of any near neighbourhood to either of the ladies, but was evidently glad to keep the whole length of the hall-table between them and himself, at least so I heard, for of course I did not thrust myself into the matter, but I learned afterwards that Mynheer van Hunker had left a very large amount of money and lands, which were divided between his daughters, subject to a very handsome jointure to his wife, who was to possess both the houses at the Hague and at Hunkerslust for her life, but would forfeit both these and her income should she marry any one save a native of the States of Holland. Her jewels, however, were her own, and the portion she had received from her father, Sir James Wardour.

As she said to me afterwards, her husband hated all foreigners, and she held him as having behaved with great kindness and liberality to her; but, she added with a smile, as she turned bravely towards a mirror behind her, he need not have laid her under the restriction, for such things were all over for her. And happily he had not forbidden her to do as she pleased with her wealth.

That very evening she began to arrange for packets of dollars from unknown hands to find themselves in the lodgings of the poorest cavaliers; and for weekly payments to be made at the ordinaries that they might give their English frequenters substantial meals at a nominal cost. She became quite merry over her little plots; but there was a weight as of lead on my heart when I thought of my brother, and that her freedom had only begun on such terms. Nay, I knew not for what to hope or wish!

Permission had been given for Emilia to return to her mother, and as Veronica had some purchases to make in the city, she undertook to drive in in the coach, and bring out her little sister. I should have availed myself of the opportunity of going back with her but that Millicent would have had to spend the day alone, and I could see that, though her mother's heart hungered for the little one, yet she dreaded the child's seeing her altered face. She said she hoped Veronica might not return till twilight or dusk, so that Emilia might recognize her by her voice and her kisses before seeing her face.

She had been bidden to be out in the air, and she and I had walked down the avenue in search of some cukoo-flowers and king-cups that grew by the canal below. She loved them, she said, because they grew at home by the banks of the Thames, and she was going to dress some beaupots to make her chamber gay for Emilia. The gardens might be her own, but she stood in too much awe of the gardener to touch a tulip or a flower-de-luce, scarce even a lily of the valley; but when I taxed her with it, she smiled and said she should ever love the English wild-flowers best.

So we were walking back under the shade of the budding lime-tress when a coach came rolling behind us. The horses were not the fat dappled grays of the establishment, but brown ones, and Millicent, apprehending a visit from some of her late husband's kindred, and unwilling to be seen before they reached the house, drew behind a tree, hoping to be out of sight.

She had, however, been descried. The carriage stopped. There was a joyful cry in good English of 'Mother! mother! mother!' and the little maiden flew headlong into her arms, while at the same moment my dear brother, looking indeed thin, but most noble, most handsome, embraced me. He explained in a few words that Mademoiselle van Hunker was dining with her future mother-in-law, and that she had permitted him to have the honour of giving up his charge to Madame.

Millicent looked up at him with the eyes that could not but be sweet, and began to utter her thanks, while he smiled and said that the pleasure to him and Annora had been so great that the obligation was theirs.

The little girl, now holding her hand, was peering up curiously under her hood, and broke upon their stiffness and formality by a sudden outcry:

'No! no! mother is not ugly like Vronikje. She shall not be ugly. She is Emilia's own dear pretty mother, and nobody shall say no.'

No doubt the little one felt the inward attraction of child to mother, that something which so infinitely surpasses mere complexion, and as she had been warned of the change, and had seen it in her sister, she was really agreeable surprised, and above all felt that she had her mother again.

Millicent clasped her to her bosom in a transport of joy, while Eustace exclaimed:

'The little maid is right; most deeply right. That which truly matters can never be taken away.'

Then Millicent raised her eyes to him and said, with quivering lip: 'I had so greatly dreaded this moment. I owe it to you, my lord, that she has come to me thus.'

Before he could answer Emilia had seen the golden flowers in her mother's hand, and with a childish shriek of ecstasy had claimed them, while Millicent said:

'I had culled them for thee, sweetheart.'

'I'll give some to my lord!' cried the child. 'My lord loves king-cups.'

'Yes,' said Eustace, taking the flowers and kissing the child, but with his eyes on her mother's all the time; 'I have loved king-cups ever since on May day when there was a boat going down the river to Richmond.'

Her eyes fell, and that strange trembling came round her mouth. For, as I learned afterwards from my sister, it was then that they had danced in Richmond Park, and he had made a crown of king-cups and set it on her flaxen hair, and then and there it was that love had first begun between those two, whom ten years had so strangely changed. But Eustace said no more, except to tell me that he had come to ask if I could be ready to return to Paris the second day ensuing, as Sir Edward Hyde was going, and had a pass by which we could all together go through the Spanish Netherlands without taking ship. If Madame van Hunker could spare me on such sudden notice he would like to take me back with him at once.

There was no reason for delay. Millicent had her child, and was really quite will again; and I had very little preparation to make, having with me as little clothing as possible. She took Eustace to the tiled fireplace in the parlour, and served him with manchet-cake and wine, but prayed him to pardon her absence while she went to aid me. I think neither wished for a tete-a-tete. They had understood one another over the king-cups, and it was no time to go farther. I need not tell of the embraces and tears between us in my chamber. They were but natural, after the time we had spent together, but at the end Millicent whispered:

'You will tell him all, Margaret! He is too noble, but his generous soul must feel no bondage towards one who has nothing—not even a face or a purse for him.'

'Only a heart,' I said. But she shook her head in reproof, and I felt that I had done wrong to speak on the matter.

After a brief time we took leave with full and stately formality. I think both she and I were on our guard against giving way before my brother, who had that grave self-restrained countenance which only Englishmen seem able to maintain. He was thin, and there was a certain transparency of skin about his cheeks and hands; but to my mind he looked better than when he left us at Paris, and I could not but trust that the hope which had returned to him would be an absolute cure for all his ill-health. I saw it in his eyes.

We seated ourselves in the carriage, and I dreaded to break the silence at first, but we had not long turned into the high road from the avenue when hoofs came behind us, and a servant from Hunkerslust rode up to the window, handing in a packet which he said had been left behind.

I sat for a few minutes without opening it, and deemed it was my Book of Hours, for it was wrapped in a kerchief of my own; but when I unfolded that, behold I saw a small sandal-wood casket, and turning the key, I beheld these few words—'Praying my Lord Walwyn to permit restitution to be made.—M. van H.' And beneath lay the pearls of Ribaumont.

'No! no! no, I cannot!' cried my brother, rising to lean from the window and beckon back the messenger; but I pulled him by the skirts, telling him it was too late, and whatever he might think fit to do, he must not wound the lady's feelings by casting them back upon her in this sudden manner, almost as if he were flinging them at her head. He sat down again, but reiterated that he could not accept them.

I told him that her jewels were wholly her own, subject to no restrition, but this only made him ask me with some displeasure whether I had been privy to this matter; the which I could wholly deny, since not a word had passed between us, save on the schemes for sending aid to the distressed families.

'I thought not,' he returned; and then he began to show me, what needed little proof, how absolutely inexpedient it was for his honour or for hers, that he should accept anything from her, and how much more fitting it was that they should be absolutely out of reach of all intercourse with one another during her year of mourning, or until he could fitly address her.

'No,' he said; 'the pearls must remain hers unless she can come with them; or if not, as is most like, we shall be the last of the Ribaumonts—and she may do as she will with them.'

'You have no doubts, Eustace?' I cried. 'You care not for her wealth, and as to her face, a year will make it as fair and sweet as ever.'

'As sweet in my eyes, assuredly!' he said. But he went on to say that her very haste in this matter was a token that she meant to have no more to do with him, and that no one could wish her to give up her wealth and prosperity to accept a poor broken cavalier, health and wealth alike gone.

I would have argued cheeringly, but he made me understand that his own Dorset estates, which Harry Merrycourt had redeemed for him before, had been absolutely forfeited by his share in Montrose's expedition. The Commonwealth had in a manner condoned what had been done in the service of King Charles, but it regarded as treason the espousing the cause of his son; and it was possible that the charge on the Wardour estates might be refused to Millicent should she unite herself with one who was esteemed a rebel.

My mother's jointure had been charged on the Ribaumont estate, and if Eustace failed to gain the suit which had been lingering on so long, there would hardly be enough rents to pay this to her, leaving almost nothing for him. Nor, indeed, was it in my power to do much for their assistance, since my situation was not what it would have been if my dear husband had lived to become Marquis de Nidemerle. And we were neither of us young enough to think that even the most constant love could make it fit to drag Millicent into beggary. Yet still I could see that Eustace did not give up hope. The more I began to despond, the more cheerful he became. Was not the King in Scotland, and when he entered England as he would certainly do next summer, would not all good Cavaliers—yes, and all the Parliament men who had had enough of the domineering of General Cromwell—rise on his behalf? My brother was holding himself in readiness to obey the first summons to his standard, and when he was restored, all would be easy, and he could offer himself to Millicent worthily.

Moreover, my mother had written something about a way that had opened for accommodating the suit respecting the property in Picardy, and Eustace trusted the report all the more because our brother Solivet had also written to urge his recall, in order to confer with his antagonist, the Comte de Poligny, respecting it. So that, as the dear brother impressed on me, he had every reason for hoping that in a very different guise; and his hopes raised mine, so that I let them peep through the letter with which I returned the jewels to Millicent.

CHAPTER XXVII. — THE EXPEDIENT

(Annora's Narrative)

And what was this expedient of their? Now, Madame Meg, I forewarn you that what I write here will be a horror and bad example to all your well-brought-up French grandchildren, demoiselles bien elevees, so that I advise you to re-write it in your own fashion, and show me up as a shocking, willful, headstrong, bad daughter, deserving of the worst fate of the bad princesses in Madame d'Aulnoy's fairly tales. Nay, I am not sure that Mademoiselle de Nidemerle might not think I had actually incurred a piteous lot. But chacun a son gout.

Well, this same expedient was this. M. de Poligny, who claimed the best half of the Picardy estates in right of a grant from Henry III. when in the power of the League, had made acquaintance with our half-brother, Solivet, who had presented him to our mother, and he had offered, with the greatest generosity possible—said my mother—to waive his claims and put a stop to the suit (he knew it could not hold for a moment), provided she would give her fair daughter to his son, the Chevalier de Poligny, with the reversion of the Ribaumont property, after my brother, on whom, vulture that he was, he had fixed his eyes, as a man in failing health. My mother and her eldest son were absolutely enraptured, and they expected Eustace to be equally delighted with this escape from all difficulties. They were closeted with him for two hours the morning after our return, while Meg was left to enjoy herself with her son, and to converse with M. d'Aubepine. That poor little thing's Elysium had come to an end as soon as the Princes were released from prison. No sooner did her husband find that his idol, the Prince on Conde, showed neither gratitude nor moderate civility to the faithful wife who had fought so hard for him, than his ape must needs follow in his track and cast off Cecile—though, of course, she still held that his duty kept him in attendance on the Prince, and that he would return to her.

I do not know whether they were afraid of me, for not a word did any of them say of the results of their conferences, only I was informed that we were to have a reception in the evening, and a new white taffeta dress, with all my mother's best jewels, was put out for me, and my mother herself came to preside at my toilette and arrange my curls. I did not suspect mischief even then, for I thought it was all in honour of Solivet's poor little Petronille, whom he had succeeded in marrying to a fat of Duke. What a transformation it was from the meek little silent persionnaire without a word to say for herself, into a gay butterfly, with a lovelock on her shoulder, a coquettish twist of her neck, and all the language of the fan, as well as of tongue, ready learned! I do not think her father was quite happy about her manners, but then it served him right, and he had got a dukedom for his grandchildren by shutting up his other poor daughter in a convent.

By and by I saw my brother bowing with extra politeness, and then Solivet found me out, and did himself the honour to present to me Monsieur le Comte de Poligny, who, in his turn, presented M. le Chevalier. The Count was a rather good-looking Frenchman, with the air of having seen the world; the Chevalier was a slight little whipper-snapper of a lad in the uniform of the dragoons, and looking more as if he were fastened to his sword and spurs than they to him. I think the father was rather embarrassed not to find me a little prim demoiselle, but a woman capable of talking about politics like other people; and while I rejoiced that the Cardinal had been put to flight by the Prince, I told them that no good would come of it, unless some one would pluck up a spirit and care more for his fellow-creatures than for his own intrigues.

Solivet looked comically dismayed to hear such independent sentiments coming out of my mouth; I know now that he was extremely afraid that M. de Poligny would be terrified out of is bargain. If I had only guessed at his purpose, and that such an effect might be produced, I would almost have gone the length of praising Mr. Hampden and Sir Thomas Fairfax to complete the work; instead of which I stupidly bethought me of Eustace's warning not to do anything that might damage Margaret and her son, and I restrained myself.

The matter was only deferred till the next morning, when I was summoned to my mother's chamber, where she sat up in bed, with her best Flanders-lace nightcap and ruffles on, her coral rosary blessed by the Pope, her snuff-box with the Queen's portrait, and her big fan that had belonged to Queen Marie de Medicis, so that I knew something serious was in hand; and, besides, my brothers Solivet and Walwyn sat on chairs by the head of her bed. Margaret was not there.

'My daughter,' said my mother, when I had saluted her, and she had signed to me to be seated, 'M. le Comte de Poligny has done you the honour to demand your hand for his son, the Chevalier; and I have accepted his proposals, since by this means the proces will be terminated respecting the estates in Picardy, and he will come to a favourable accommodation with your brother, very important in the present circumstances.'

I suppose she and Solivet expected me to submit myself to my fate like a good little French girl. What I did was to turn round and exclaim: 'Eustace, you have not sold me for this?'

He held out his hand, and said: 'No, sister. I have told my mother and brother that my consent depends solely on you.'

Then I felt safe, even when Solivet said:

'Nor does any well-brought-up daughter speak of her wishes when her parents have decided for her.'

'You are not my parent, sir,' I cried; 'you have no authority over me! Nor am I what you call a well-brought-up girl—that is, a poor creature without a will!'

'It is as I always said,' exclaimed my mother. 'She will be a scandal.'

But I need not describe the whole conversation, even if I could remember more than the opening. I believe I behaved very ill, and was in danger of injuring my own cause by my violence; my mother cried, and said I should be a disgrace to the family, and Solivet looked fierce, handled the hilt of his sword, and observed that he should know how to prevent that; and then Eustace took my hands, and said he would speak with me alone, and my mother declared that he would encourage me in my folly and undutifulness; while Solivet added: 'Remember we are in earnest. This is no child's play!'

A horrible dread had come over me that Eustace was in league with them; for he always imperatively cut me short if I dared to say I was already promised. I would hardly speak to him when at last he brought me to his own rooms and shut the door; and when he called me his poor Nan, I pushed him away, and said I wanted none of his pity, I could not have thought it of him.

'You do not think it now,' he said; and as I looked up into his clear eyes I was ashamed of myself, and could only murmur, what could I think when I saw him sitting there aiding in their cruel manoeuvres,—all for your own sake, too?

'I only sat there because I hoped to help you,' he said; and then he bade me remember that they had disclosed nothing of these intentions of theirs in the letters which spoke of an accommodation. If they had done so, he might have left me in Holland with some of the English ladies so as to be out of reach; but the scheme had only been propounded to him on the previous morning. I asked why he had not refused it at once, and he pointed out that it was not for him to disclose my secret attachment, even had it been expedient so to do. All that he had been able to do was to declare that the whole must depend on my free consent. 'And,' he said, with a smile, 'methought thereby I had done enough for our Nan, who has no weak will unless by violence she over-strain it.'

I felt rebuked as well as reassured and strengthened, and he again assured me that I was safe so long as he lived from being pressed into any marriage contract displeasing to me.

'But I am promised to M. Darpent,' was my cry. 'Why did you hinder me from saying so?'

'Have you not lived long enough in France to know that it would go for nothing, or only make matters worse?' he said. 'Solivet would not heed your promise more than the win that blows, except that he might visit it upon Darpent.'

'You promised to persuade my mother,' I said. 'She at least knows how things go in England. Besides, she brought him here constantly. Whenever she was frightened there was a cry for Darpent.'

Eustace, however, thought my mother ought to know that my word was given; and we told her in private the full truth, with the full approbation of my mother, the head of the family, and he reminded her that at home such a marriage would be by no means unsuitable. Poor mother! she was very angry with us both. She had become so entirely imbued with her native French notions that she considered the word of a demoiselle utterly worthless, and not to be considered. As to my having encouraged Avocat Darpent, une creature comme ca, she would as soon have expected to be told that I had encouraged her valet La Pierre! She was chiefly enraged with me, but her great desire was that I should not be mad enough, as she said, to let it be known that I had done anything so outrageous as to pass my word to any young man, above all to one of inferior birth. It would destroy my reputation for ever, and ruin all the chance of my marriage.

Above all, she desired that it should be concealed from Solivet. She was a prudent woman, that poor mother of mine, and she was afraid of her son's chastising what she called presumption, and thus embroiling himself with the Parliament people. I said that Solivet had no right over me, and that I had not desire to tell him, though I had felt that she was my mother and ought to be warned that I never would be given to any man save Clement Darpent; and Eustace said that though he regretted the putting himself in opposition to my mother, he should consider it as a sin to endeavour to make me marry one man, while I loved another to whom I was plighted. But he said that there was no need to press the affair, and that he would put a stop to Darpent's frequenting the house, since it only grieved my mother and might bring him into danger. He would, as my mother wished, keep out attachment as a secret, and would at present take no steps if I were unmolested.

In private Eustace showed me that this was all he could do, and counseled me to put forward no plea, but to persist in my simple refusal, lest I should involve Clement Darpent in danger. Had not Solivet ground his teeth and said order should be taken if he could believe his sister capable of any unworthy attachment? 'And remember,' said Eustace, 'Darpent is not in good odour with either party, and there is such a place as the Bastille.'

I asked almost in despair if he saw any end to it, or any hope, to which he said there always was hope. If our King succeeded in regaining his crown we could go home, and we both believed that Clement would gladly join us there and become one of us. For the present, Eustace said, I must be patient. Nobody could hinder him from seeing Darpent, and he could make him understand how it all was, and how he must accept the ungrateful rebuffs that he had received from my mother.

No one can tell what that dear brother was to me then. He replied in my name and his own to M. de Poligny, who was altogether at a loss to understand that any reasonable brother should attend to the views of a young girl, when such a satisfactory parti as his son was offered, even though the boy was at least six years younger than I was; and as my mother and Solivet did not fail to set before me, there was no danger of his turning out like that wretch d'Aubepine, as he was a gentle, well-conducted, dull boy, whom I could govern with a silken thread if I only took the trouble to let him adore me. I thanked them, and said that was not exactly my idea of wedded life; and they groaned at my folly.

However, it turned out that M. de Poligny really wished his little Chevalier to finish his education before being married, and had only hastened his proposals because he wished to prevent the suit from coming up to be pleaded, and so it was agreed that the matter should stand over till this precious suitor of mine should have mastered his accidence and grown a little hair on his lip. I believe my mother had such a wholesome dread of me, especially when backed by my own true English brother, that she was glad to defer the tug of war. And as the proces was thus again deferred, I think she hoped that my brother would have no excuse for intercourse with the Darpents. She had entirely broken off with them and had moreover made poor old Sir Francis and Lady Ommaney leave the Hotel de Nidemerle, all in politeness as they told us, but as the house was not her own, I should have found it very hard to forgive their expulsion had I been Margaret.

As for me, my mother now watched over me like any other lady of her nation. She resorted far less to Queen Henrietta than formerly, and always took me with her whenever she went, putting an end now, in my twenty-fourth year, to the freedom I had enjoyed all my life. She did not much like leaving me alone with Eustace, and if it had not been for going to church on Sunday, I should never have gone out with him. He was not strong enough now to go to prayers daily at Sir Richard Browne's chapel, but he never failed that summer to take me thither on a Sunday, though he held that it would be dishonourable to let this be a way for any other meetings.

My mother had become devout, as the French say. She wore only black, went much more to church, always leaving me in the charge of Madame Croquelebois, whom she borrowed from the d'Aubepines for the purpose, and she set all she could in train for the conversion of my brother and myself. There was the Abbe Walter Montagu, Lord Mandeville's brother, and one or two others, who had despaired of our Church and joined hers, and she was always inviting them and setting them to argue with us. Indeed, she declared that one chief reason of her desiring this wedding for me was that it would bring me within the fold of the true Church. They told us that our delusion, as they called our Church, was dead; that the Presbyterians and Fifth Monarchy men and all their rabble had stifled the last remnant of life that had been left in her; that the Episcopacy, even if we scouted the Nag's Head fable, was perishing away, and that England was like Holland or the Palatinate. But Eustace smiled gravely at them, and asked whether the Church had been dead when the Roman Emperors, or the heretic Arians, persecuted her, and said that he knew that, even if he never should see it, she would revive brighter and purer than ever—as indeed it has been given to us to behold. That dear brother, he was so unlike the Calvinists, and held so much in common with the French Church, that the priests always thought they were converting him; but he stood all the firmer for knowing what was truly Catholic. Of course it was no wonder that as Walter Montagu, like all my Lord Mandeville's sons, had been bred a Puritan, he should have been amazed to perceive that the Roman Catholics were not all that they had been painted, and should find rest in the truths that had been hidden from him; but with us it was quite otherwise, having ever known the best alike of ours and of theirs. The same thing was going on at the Louvre.

Queen Henrietta was bent on converting her son, the Duke of Gloucester. He was a dear good lad of twelve years old, who had just been permitted to join her. I think the pleasantest times I had at all in those days were with him. He clung to us because I had known and loved his sweet sister, the Lady Elisabeth, who had been his companion in his imprisonment, and though he seldom spoke of her it was easy to see that the living with her had left a strong mark on his whole character.

I knew that Eustace had seen the Darpents and made Clement understand that I was faithful, and that he was to believe nothing that he heard of me, except through my brother himself. That helped me to some patience; and I believe poor Clement was so much amazed that his addresses should be tolerated by M. le Baron de Ribaumont that he was quite ready to endure any suspense.

There were most tremendous disturbances going on all the time out of door. Wonderful stories came to us of a fearful uproar in the Parliament between the Prince and the Coadjutor de Gondi, when the Duke of Rochefoucauld got the Coadjutor between two folding-doors, let down the iron bar of them on his neck, and was as nearly as possible the death of him. Then there was a plot for murdering the Prince of Conde in the streets, said to be go up by the Queen-Regent herself, after consulting one of her priests, who told her that she might regard the Prince as an enemy of the State, and that she might lawfully rid herself of him by private means when a public execution was inexpedient. A fine religion that! as I told my mother when M. d'Aubepine came in foaming at the mouth about it; though Eustace would have persuaded me that it was not just to measure a whole Church by one priest. The Prince fortified his house, and lived like a man in a state of siege for some time, and then went off to Chantilly, take d'Aubepine with him — and every one said a new Fronde was beginning, for the Queen-Regent was furious with the Princes, and determined to have Cardinal Mazarin back, and the Prince was equally resolved to keep him out, while as to the Parliament, I had no patience with it; it went on shilly-shallying between the two, and had no substance to do anything by hang on to some selfish Court party.

There were a few who understood their real interests, like the old Premier-President Mathieu Mole, and these hoped that by standing between the two parties they might get the only right thing done, namely, to convoke the States-General, which is what really answers to our own English Parliament. People could do things then in Paris they never dream of now; and Clement Darpent worked hard, getting up meetings among the younger counsellors and advocates, and some of the magistrates, where they made speeches about constitutional liberty, and talked about Ciecero, who was always Clement's favourite hero. My brother went to hear him sometimes, and said he had a great gift of eloquence, but that he was embarked on a very dangerous course. Moreover, M. Darpent had been chosen as a deputy of the Town Council at the Hotel de Ville. This council consisted of the mayor and echevins, as they called them, who were something like our aldermen, all the parish priests, deputies from the trades, and from all the sixteen quarters of the city, and more besides. They had the management of the affairs of the city in their hands, and Clement Darpent, owning a house, and being respected by the respectable citizens of his department of St. Antoine, was chosen to represent it. Thus he felt himself of use, which always rejoiced him. As to me, I only saw him once that whole autumn, and then I met him by accident as I was walking with Eustace and Margaret in the Cours de la Reine. [footnote: the Champs-Elysees]

We were in high spirits, for our own King had marched into England while Cromwell was beating the covenanting rogues in Scotland, and Eustace was walking and riding out every day to persuade himself that he was in perfect health and fit to join his standard. That dear brother had promised that if he went to England I should come with him, and be left with old Mrs. Merrycourt, Harry's mother, till Clement could come for me. Then Eustace, with his own lands again, could marry his Millicent, and throw over the Dutchman's hoards, and thus we were full to the brim of joyous plans, and were walking out in the long avenue discussing them most gladly together, when, to add to our delight, Clement met us in his sober lawyer's suit, which became him so well, coming home from a consultation.

The Queen-Regent had promised to convoke the States-General, and he explained to us both how all would come right there. The bourgeois element from all the Parliaments of the provinces would be strong enough to make a beginning towards controlling the noblesse, divided as it was, and at feud with the Crown. Some of the clergy at least would be on their side, and if the noblesse would bear part of the burthens of the State, and it could be established that taxes should not be imposed without the consent of the people, and that offices should not be sold, all would be well for the country. Meg herself took fire, and began to hope that a new state of things would begin in which she might do some good to those unfortunate peasants of her son's who weighed so heavily on her tender heart. Eustace told him he would be another Simon de Montfort, only not a rebel. No; he was determined to succeed by moral force, and so was his whole party (at least he thought so). They, by their steady loyalty, would teach the young King and his mother how to choose between them and the two selfish factions who were ready to fight with the King himself, provided it was also against a Conde or a Mazarin.

It looked very beautiful indeed. I was roused from my selfish ill-humour, felt what my Clement was worth, and went heart and soul into the matter, and we all four were just as happy over these hopes as if we had not seen how things had turned out at home, and that no one, either Kings or Parliaments, or nobility either, know where to stop; but that if you do not get an absolute tyrant, you run the risk of a Long Parliament, a ruling army, a 30th of January, and a Lord Protector. But we were all young and hopeful still, and that straight walk in the Cours de la Reine was a paradise to some of us, if a fool's paradise. For look you! in these great States-General, who but Clement Darpent the eloquent would make speeches, and win honours that would give him a right to rewards for higher than the hand of a poor exiled maiden, if I were still an exile? Though he declared that I had been his inspiration, and helped to brace him for the struggle, and far more truly, that my dear brother had shown him what a nobleman, bred under English law, could be, when neither ground down by the Crown, nor forced to do nothing but trample on his vassals.

And Meg began to hope for her Gaspard. She told how the young King was fond of him, and really seemed fired by some emulation at finding that a boy so much younger than himself knew more than he did. Our boy was reading Virgil and Plutarch's lives. He told the stories to the young King, who delighted to listen, though the Duke of Anjou thought everything dull except cards, tennis, and gossip. The King was even beginning to read to himself. 'And,' said Clement, when he heard it, 'let him be fired with the example of Agis or Clomenes, and what may he not do for France?' Oh, yes! we were very happy, though we talked of hardly anything but politics. It was the last happy day we were to have for a good while to come.

CHAPTER XXVIII. — THE BOEUF GRAS

(Annora's Narrative)

I said it was a fool's paradise, and it did not last long. The Queen-Regent had a convenient fashion of making nothing of her promises. She did not think base burghers and lawyers human creatures towards whom honour was necessary, and she naturally expected the States-General to act our Long Parliament over again.

It seems that Kings of France come of age at fourteen; and on the day that young Louis was thirteen he was declared to be major, and his mother ceased to be Regent, though she managed everything just as much as if she had still written Anne R. at the end of all the State papers. The advantage to the Court was that no promises or engagements made in his minority were considered to be binding. And so the whole matter of the States-General went to the wall.

There was a magnificent ceremony at the Parliament House, the old hall of the Augustins. The little King held a bed of justice, upon a couch under a purple velvet canopy, with all his grandees round him. I would not go to see it, I thought it a wicked shame to set up a poor boy to break all the solemn pledges made in his name, and I knew it was the downfall of Clement's hopes; but Meg went in her Princess's suite, and I had her account of it, the King looking very handsome with his long fair hair, and bowing right and left, with such a dignity and grace that no one saw what a little bit of a fellow he really was. Poor child! the best thing they could have taught him would have been to worshipping and loving no one but himself. Of course Meg saw nothing so plainly as how beautiful her little Marquis looked among the attendant young nobles, and I must own that he was a very fine fellow, and wonderfully little spoiled considering the sort of folk with whom he lived. On that ceremonial day there came doleful tidings to us. Worcester had been the scene of a massacre rather than a fight, and my brother was in despair and misery at not having been there — as if his single arm could have retrieved the day! — thinking shame of himself for resting at home while sword and block were busy with our friends, and no one knew where the King was. I know not whether it were the daunting of his hopes or the first beginning of the winter cold; but from that time he began to decline from the strength he had gained while I had him to myself in Holland, free from all pressing cares.

However, he still rode out in attendance on the Duke of Gloucester, who always preferred him to any other of the gentlemen who waited on the Queen. One evening in October he stayed out so late that we had begun to be anxious at his being thus exposed to the air after sunset, when he came up to our salon in high spirits, telling us that he had been returning with the Duke from a ride on the Amiens Road when they saw some altercation going on at the barriers between the guard and a gentleman on horseback, shabby and travel-stained, whom they seemed unwilling to admit. For the Parisians, who always worship success and trample on misfortune, had, since the disaster at Worcester, shown themselves weary of receiving so many unlucky cavaliers, and were sometimes scantly civil. The stranger, as he saw the others come up, called out: 'Ha, Walwyn, is it you? You'll give your word for me that the Chevalier Stuart is an honest fellow of your acquaintance, though somewhat out at elbows, like other poor beggars.'

And then Eustace saw that it was the King, sun-burnt, thin, and ill-clad, grown from a lad to a man, but with his black eyes glittering gaily through all, as no one's ever did glitter save King Charles's. He gave his word, and passed him through without divulging who he was, since it would not have been well to have had all the streets turn out to gaze on him in his present trim, having ridden on just as he crossed from Brigthelmstone. The two brothers did not know one another, not having met since Prince Henry was a mere infant of four or five years old; and Eustace said he found the little fellow drawing himself up, and riding somewhat in advance, in some princely amazement that so shabby a stranger should join his company so familiarly and without any check from his companion.

The King began to ask for his mother, and then, at a sign and hint from Eustace, called out:

'What! Harry, hast not a word for thy poor battered elder brother?'

And the boy's face, as he turned, was a sight to see, as Eustace told us.

He had left Queen Henrietta embracing her son in tears of joy for his safe return, and very thankful we were, though it did but take out first reception at the Louvre to see that though the King was as good-humoured, gracious, and merry as ever, he was not changed for the better by all he had gone through. He had left the boy behind him, and now seemed like a much older man, who only laughed and got what amusement he could out of a world where he believed in nothing noble nor good, and looked forward to nothing.

The old ladies said he had grown like his grandfather, Henri IV., and when this was repeated Eustace shook his head, and told Meg that he feared it was in one way true enough, and Meg, who always hoped, bade us remember how many years the Grand Monarque had to dally away before he became the preserver and peace-maker of France.

However, even Meg, who had always let the King be like an old playfellow with her, was obliged to draw back now, and keep him at the most formal distance. I never had any trouble with him. I do not think he liked me; indeed I once heard of his saying that I always looked like a wild cat that had got into the salon by mistake, and was always longing to scratch and fly. He would be quite willing to set me to defend a castle, but for the rest—-

It was not he whom I wished to scratch—at least as long as he let me alone—but M. de Poligny, who took to paying me the most assiduous court wherever I went, for his little schoolboy of a son, till I was almost beside myself with fear that Clement Darpent might believe some false report about me.

And then spring was coming on, and Eustace as yet made no sign of going to Holland. He only told me to be patient, and patience was becoming absolutely intolerable to my temper. Meantime, we heard that the First President, Mathieu de Mole, who had some time before been nominated Keeper of the Seals, but had never excised the functions of the office, had nominated M. Darpent to be his principal secretary at Paris, remaining there and undertaking his correspondence when he was with the Court. Clement had been recommended for this office by his brother-in-law, one of the Gneffiers du Roi, who was always trying to mediate between the parties. Mole was thoroughly upright and disinterested, and he had begged Clement to undertake the work as the one honest man whom he could trust, and Clement had such an esteem for him that he felt bound to do anything he could to assist him, in his true loyalty.

'I shall tell the King the truth,' said the good old man, 'and take the consequences.'

And his being in office gave another hope for better counsels and the States-General.

So Lady Ommaney told me, but I was anxious and dissatisfied. I had like Clement better when he had refused to purchase an office, and stood aloof from all the suite of the Court. She soothed me as best she could, and, nodding her head a little, evidently was hatching as scheme.

Now the children had a great desire to see the procession in the Mid-Lent week. It is after what we call Mothering Sunday — when the prettiest little boy they can find in Paris rides through the streets on the largest white ox. Now the lodgings whither Sir Francis and Lady Ommaney had betaken themselves, when my mother had, so to speak, turned them out, had a balcony with an excellent view all along the quais, and thither the dear old lady invited Meg, Madame d'Aubepine, and me, to bring Gaspard, with Maurice and Armantine; and I saw by her face that the bouef gras was not all that there was for me to see.

We went early in the day, when the streets were still not overmuch crowded, and we climbed up, up to the fifth story, where the good old lady contrived to make the single room her means could afford look as dainty as her bower at home, though she swept it with her own delicate white hands. There was an engraving of the blessed Martyr over the chimmey-piece, the same that is in the Eikon Basilike, with the ray of light coming down into his eye, the heavenly crown awaiting him, the world spurned at his feet, and the weighted palm-tree with Crescit sub pondere virtus. And Sir Francis's good old battle-sword and pistols hung under it. It made me feel quite at home, and we tried to make the children enter into the meaning of the point. At least Meg did, and I think she succeeded with her son, who had a good deal of the true Ribaumont in him, and whom they could not spoil even by all the misrule that went on at Court whenever the Queen was out of sight. He stood thoughtful by the picture while the little d'Aubepines were dancing in and out of the balcony, shrieking about every figure they saw passing in the road below.

Sir Francis, after receiving us, had gone out, as he said, to see what was going on, but I think he removed himself in order to leave us more at our ease. By and by there was a knock at the door, and who should come in but M. Darpent, leading a little boy of five or six years old, his nephew, he said, whom Lady Ommaney had permitted to bring to see the sight.

I heard afterwards that it was pretty to see the different ways of the children, and how Maurice d'Aubepine drew himself up, put on his hat, laid his hand on his ridiculous little sword, and insisted that the little Clement Verdon should stand behind him and his sister, where he could see nothing, while Gaspard de Nidermerle, with an emphatic 'Moi, je suis getilhomme,' put the stranger before himself and looked over his head, as he could easily do, being two or three years older.

Well, I lost my chance; I never saw the great ox wreathed with flowers, nor the little boy on his back, nor all the butchers with their cleavers round him, nor the procession of the trades, the fishwomen, dames des halles, as they called them, all in their white caps and short petticoats, singing a ballad in honour of the Duke of Beaufort, the faggot-carriers with sticks, the carpenters with tools, all yelling out songs in execration of Cardinal Mazarin, who had actually entered France with an army, and vituperating with equal virulence the Big Beard, as they called the President Mole.

They told me the sight had been wonderful, but what was that to me when Clement Darpent stood before me? He looked then and worn, and almost doubtful how to address me; but Lady Ommaney said, in her hearty way:

'Come, come, young folks, you have enough to say to one another. Sit down there and leave the ox to the children and us old folks in our second childhood. You believe and old woman now, M. Darpent?'

'You never distrusted me?' I demanded.

He said he had never distrusted my heart, but that he had heard at all hands of the arrangement with M. de Poligny, whose lawyer had actually stopped proceedings on that account. My brother had indeed assured him that he did not mean to consent; and he ought, he allowed, to have rested satisfied with that assurance, but—He faltered a little, which made me angry. The truth was that some cruel person had spoken to him as if my dear Eustace and his protection would soon be removed; and while Solivet was at hand, Eustace, in his caution, he refrained from such intercourse with Clement as could excite suspicion. Besides, he was a good deal away at St. Germain with the Duke. All this I did not understand. I was vexed with Clement for having seemed to doubt us, and I did not refrain from showing my annoyance that he should have accepted any kind of office in the rotten French State. It seemed to me a fall from his dignity. On this he told me that it was not purchased, and it was serving under a true and loyal man, whom he felt bound to support. If any one could steer between the Prince and the Cardinal, and bring some guarantee for the people out of the confusion, it was the Keeper of the Seals, the head of the only party who cared more for the good of the country than their private malice and hatred.

'And,' he said diffidently, 'if under M. Mole's patronage, the steps could be gained without loss of honour or principle, you remember that there is a noblesse de la robe, which might remove some of Madame de Ribaumont's objections, though I do not presume to compare it with the blood of the Crusaders.'

I am ashamed to say that I answered, 'I should think not!' and then I am afraid I reproached him for bartering the glorious independence that had once rendered him far more than noble, for the mere tinsel show of rank that all alike thought despicable. How I hate myself when I recall that I told him that if he had done so for my sake he had made a mistake; and as for loyalty rallying round the French Crown, I believed in no such thing; they were all alike, and cared for nothing but their ambitions and their hatreds.

Before anything had been said to soften these words — while he was still standing grave and stiff, like one struck by a blow — in came the others from the window. Meg, in fact, could not keep Cecile d'Aubepine back any longer from hindering such shocking impropriety as out tete-a-tete. We overheard her saving her little girl from corruption by a frightful French fib that the gentleman in black was Mademoiselle de Ribaumont's English priest.

I am sure out parting need have excited no suspicions. We were cold and grave and ceremonious as Queen Anne of Austria herself, and poor Lady Ommaney looked from one to the other of us in perplexity.

I went home between wrath and shame. I knew I had insulted Clement, and I was really mortified and angry that he should have accepted this French promotion instead of fleeing with us, and embracing our religion. I hated all the French politics together a great deal too much to have any comprehension of the patriotism that made him desire to support the only honest and loyal party, hopeless as it was. I could not tell Meg about our quarrel; I was glad Eustace was away at the English's ambassador's. I felt as if one Frenchman was as good, or as bad, as another, and I was more gracious to M. de Poligny than ever I had been before that evening.

My mother had a reception in honour of its being Mid-Lent week. Solivet was there, and, for a wonder, both the d'Aubepines, for the Count had come home suddenly with message from the Prince of Conde to the Duke of Orleans.

CHAPTER XXIX. — MADAME'S OPPORTUNITY

(Annora's Narrative)

The Prince of Conde and Cardinal Mazarin were in arms against one another. The Queen and her son were devoted to Mazarin. The loyal folk in Paris held to the King, and were fain to swallow the Cardinal because Conde was in open rebellion. Monsieur was trying to hold the balance with the help of the Parliament, but was too great an ass to do any such thing. The mob was against everybody, chiefly against the Cardinal, and the brutal ruffians of the Prince's following lurked about, bullying every one who gave them umbrage, with some hope of terrifying the Parliament magistrates into siding with them.

It was therefore no great surprise to Eustace and Sir Francis Ommaney the next evening, when they were coming back on foot from the Louvre, to hear a scuffle in one of the side streets.

They saw in a moment half of dozen fellows with cudgels falling on a figure in black, who vainly struggled to defend himself with a little thin walking rapier. Their English blood was up in a moment two masked figures and hearing them egging on their bravoes with 'Hola, there! At him! Teach him to look at a lady of rank.'

The little rapier had been broken. A heavy blow had made the victim's arm fall, he had been tripped up, and the rascals were still belabouring him, when Eustace and Sir Francis sprang in among them, crying, 'Hold, cowardly rascals!' striking to the right and left, though with the flat of their swords, of which they were perfect masters, for even in their wrath they remembered that these rogues were only tools. And no doubt they were not recognized in the twilight, for one of the masked gentlemen exclaimed:

'Stop, sir! this is not a matter for gentlemen. This is the way we punish the insolence of fellows whose muddy blood would taint the swords of a noble.'

At the same moment Eustace saw that the victim, who had begun to raise himself, was actually Clement Darpent. He knew, too, the voice from the mask, and, in hot wrath, exclaimed:

'Solivet, you make me regret that you are my brother, and that I cannot punish such a cowardly outrage.'

'But I am no brother of yours!' cried d'Aubepine, flying at him. 'Thus I treat all who dare term me coward.'

Eustace, far taller and more expert in fence, as well as with strength of arm that all his ill-health had not destroyed, parried the thrust so as to strike the sword out of d'Aubepine's hand, and then said:

'Go home, Monsieur. Thank your relationship to my sister that I punish you no further, and learn that to use other men's arms to strike the defenceless is a stain upon nobility.'

And as the wretched little Count slunk away he added

'Solivet, I had though better things of you.'

To which Solivet responded, with the pretension derived from his few years of seniority:

'Bah! brother, you do not understand, half a foreigner as you are. This was the only way left to me to protect my sister from the insults your English folly had brought on her.'

Eustace made no answer. He could not speak, for the exertion and shock had been too much for him. His mouth was filled with blood. They were all about him in an instant then, Solivet and Darpent both in horror, each feeling that he might in a manner have been the cause of that bleeding, which might in a moment be fatal. Eustace himself knew best what to do, and sat down on the step leaning against Sir Francis, so as not to add to the danger.

The fray had been undisturbed. In that delectable city people held aloof from such things instead of stopping them, but a doctor suddenly appeared on the scene, 'attracted like a vulture,' as Sir Francis said; and they had some ado to prevent him from unbuttoning Eustace's doublet to search for a wound before they could make him understand what had really happened. They obtained a fiacre, and Eustace was placed in it. In this condition they brought him home and put him to bed, telling us poor women only that he had interfered in a street fray and over-exerted himself. It was shock enough for us to find all the improvements of a whole year overthrown, as he lay white and still, not daring to speak.

They had agreed on the way home to keep us in ignorance, or at least to let us think that the attack had been made by strangers, simply because of his connection with the Big Beard. Meg's Nicolas was first to tell us that it was M. Darpent whom they had rescued, and that he had called at the porter's lodge on his way home to inquire for M. le Baron, bruised all over, and evidently seriously hurt. And while still trying to disbelieve this, another report arrived through the maidservants that M. de Solivet and d'Aubepine had soundly cudgeled M. Darpent, and that M. le Baron and M. d'Aubepine had fought a duel on the spot, in which my brother had been wounded.

Meg was nearly as frantic as I was. We could not speak to Eustace, and Solivet and d'Aubepine, finding themselves known, had both hurried away at peep of day, for it was a serious thing to have nearly killed a man in office; but Meg desired that if Sir Francis called to inquire for my brother we should see him, and she also sent Nicolas to inquire for M. Darpent, who, we heard, was confined to his bed with a broken arm.

Poor Clement! such was his reward for the interview where I had used him so ill, and been so unjust to him. For, as we came to understand, it really was all that wretched little Cecile's fault. She would do anything to please that husband of hers, and she communicated to him that she understood the secret of my resistance to the Poligny match, and had been infinitely shocked at my behaviour at Lady Ommaney's.

The cowardly fellow had hated Clement ever since the baffling of the attempt on Margaret. So he told Solivet, and they united in this attack, with a half a dozen of their bravoes, got together for the occasion! We heard the truth of the affair from Sir Francis, and it was well for Solivet that he was out of my reach!

> As for my mother, she thought it only an overflow of zeal for the honour of the family, and held it to be my fault that her dear son had been driven to such measures. Nothing was bad enough for the Ommaneys! Nothing would restore my reputation but marrying the little Chevalier at Easter. And in the midst, just as Eustace was a little better, and there was no excuse for refusing to obey the drag of her chains, Margaret was summoned away to attend on her absurd Princess, who was going to Orleans, by way of keeping the Cardinal's forces out of her father's city.
>
> Margaret had kept things straight. I do not know how it was, but peace always went away with her; and my mother did things she never attempted when the real lady of the house was at home. And yet I might thank my own hasty folly for much of what befell.

Eustace was much better, sitting up in his night-gown by the fire, and ready, as I thought, to talk over everything, and redress my wrongs, or at least comfort the wretchedness that had grown upon me daily since that miserable quarrel with Clement. I poured it all out, and even was mad enough to say it was his fault for delaying so long the journey to the Hague. Clement, who had been well-nigh ready to join us and be a good Protestant, was going back to the old delusions, and taking office under the Government; and even if the bravoes had not killed him, he would be spoilt for any honest Englishwoman; and I might as well take that miserable little schoolboy, which I supposed was all my brother wished. Then the estate would be safe enough.

Eustace could only assure me that the delay was as grievous to him as to me. indeed, as I could see in a more reasonable mood, he had been unable to get from Ribaumont the moneys needful for the journey, the steward not venturing to send them while the roads were so unsafe; but when he begged me to have patience, it seemed to sting my headstrong temper, and I broke out in some such words as these: 'Patience! Patience! I am sick of it. Thanks to your patience, I have lost Clement. They have all but murdered him! and for yourself, you had better take care Millicent van Hunker does not think that such patience is only too easy when she has neither wealth nor beauty left!'

'Hush, Annora,' he answered, with authority and severity in his tone, but not half what I deserved; 'there is great excuse for you, but I cannot permit such things to be said.'

Here Tryphena came in and scolded me for making him talk; I saw how flushed he was, and became somewhat frightened. They sent me away, and oh! how long it was ere I was allowed to see him again! For in the morning, after a night of repenting and grieving over my heat, and longing to apologise for having reproached him for the delay which was as grievous to him as to me, the first thing I heard was that M. le Baron was much worse; he had had a night of fever; there was more bleeding, and much difficulty of breathing. My mother was with him, and I was on no account to be admitted.

And when I came out of my room, there sat Madame Croquelebois, who had been sent for from the Hotel d'Aubepine to keep guard over me, day and night; for she was lodged in that cabinet of my sister's into which my room opened, and my door on the other side was locked. It was an insult, for which the excuse was my interview with Clement. It made me hot and indignant enough, but there was yet a further purpose in it.

The next thing was to send for a certain Frere Allonville, a man who had been a doctor before he was converted and became a Dominican friar, and who still practiced, and was aid to do cures by miracle. I know this, that it would have been a miracle if his treatment had cured my brother, for the first thing he did was to bleed him, the very thing that Dr. Dirkius had always told us was the sure way to kill him, when he was losing so much blood already. Then the friar turned out Tryphena, on the plea that he must have a nurse who understood his language. As if poor Tryphena, after living thirteen years in France, could not understand the tongue quite enough for any purpose, and as if she did not know better how to take care of Eustace than any one else! But of course the language was not the real reason that she was shut out, and kept under guard, as it were, just as much as I was, while a Sister of Charity was brought in to act as my brother's nurse, under my mother, who, look you, never had been nurse at all, and always fainted at any critical moment.

Assuredly I knew why they were thus isolating my brother from all of us. I heard steps go upstairs, not only of the Dominican quack doctor, but of the Abbe Montagu, who had been previously sent to convert us. The good old Bonchamp, who had a conscience, was away at St. Germain with Gaspard de Nidemerle, and I—I had no one to appeal to when I knew they were harassing the very life out of my dearest, dearest brother, by trying to make him false to the Church and the faith he had fought for. I could do nothing—I was a prisoner; all by my own fault too; for they would have had no such opportunity had I not been so unguarded towards my brother. When I did meet my mother it chafed me beyond all bearing to see her devout air of resignation and piety. Her dear son was, alas! in the utmost danger, but his dispositions were good, and she trusted to see him in the bosom of the true Church, and that would be a consolation, even if he were not raised up by a miracle, which would convince even me. Poor woman, I believe she really did expect that his conversion would be followed by a miraculous recovery. I told her she was killing him—and well! I don't know what I said, but I think I frightened her, for she sent Mr. Walter Montague to see what he could do with me.

I told him I wondered he was not ashamed of such a conversion, supposing he made it, which I was sure he would not, as long as my brother retained his senses.

To which he answered that Heaven was merciful, and that so long as one was in communion with the true Church there was power to be redeemed in the next world, if not in this.

'A sorry way of squeezing into Heaven,' I said; and then he began arguing, as he had done a hundred times before, on the blessing and rest he had found in the Church, after renouncing his errors. And no wonder, for it is well known that my Lord Mandeville brought up his family to be mere Puritans. However, I said: 'Look you here, Mr. Montagu; if my brother, Lord Walwyn, gave himself to you of deliberate mind, with full health and faculties, you might think him a gain indeed. Or if you like it better, he would have a claim to the promises of your Church; but if you merely take advantage of the weakness of a man at the point of death to make him seem a traitor to his whole life, why, then, I should say you trusted, more than I do, to what you call Divine promises.'

He told me—as they always do—that I knew nothing about it, and that he should pray for me. But I had some trust that his English blood would be guilty of no foul play. I was much more afraid of the Dominican; only one good thing was that the man was not a priest. So went by Good Friday and Easter Eve. They would not let me go to church for fear I should speak to any one. Madame Croquelebois and my mother's old smirking tire-woman, Bellote, took turns to mount guard over me. I heard worse and worse accounts of my dear brother's bodily state, but I had one comfort. One of the servants secretly handed Tryphena this little note addressed to me, in feeble straggling characters:—

'Do what they may to me my will does not consent. Pray for me. If word were taken to the K. E. W. and R.'

It was some comfort that I should have that to prove what my brother was to the last. I made me able to weep and pray—pray as I had never prayed before—all that night and that strange sad Easter morning, when all the bells were ringing, and the people flocking to the churches, and I sat cut off from them all in my chamber, watching, watching in dread of sounds that might tell me that my dearest and only brother, my one hope, was taken from me, body and soul, and by my fault, in great part.

Oh! what a day it was, as time went on. Madame Croquelebois went to high mass, and Bellote remained in charge. I was, you understand, a prisoner at large. Provided some one was attending me, I went into any room in the house save the only one where I cared to be. And I was sitting in the salon, with my Bible and Prayer-book before me—not reading, I fear me, but at any rate attesting my religion, when there came up a message that Son Altesse Royale, the Duke of Gloucester, requested to be admitted to see Mademoiselle de Ribaumont.

Nobody made any question about admitting a Royal Highness, so up he came, the dear boy, with his bright hazel eyes like his father's, and his dark shining curls on his neck. He had missed me at the ambassador's chapel, and being sure, from my absence, that my brother must be very ill indeed, he had come himself to inquire. He could as yet speak little French, and not understanding what they told him at the door, he had begged to see me.

It did not take long to tell him all, for Bellote did not understand English; I showed him the note, and he stood considering. He was not like his brothers, he had not lived in vain all those years with his sister Elisabeth in captivity, for there was a grave manliness about him though he was only thirteen. He said: 'do you think Lord Walwyn would see me? I am used to be with a sick person.'

Eagerly I sent up word. I knew my mother would never refuse entrance to royal blood; nor did she. She sent word that the Duke would do her son only too much honour by thus troubling himself. I did not miss the chance of marshalling him upstairs, and gaining one sight of my brother—oh! so sadly wasted in these few days, his cheeks flushed, his breath labouring, his eyes worn and sleepless, as he lay, raised high on his pillow. He looked up with pleasure into the Duke's face. My mother was making speeches and ceremonies; but after bowing in reply, the Duke, holding Eustace's hand, leant over him and said; 'Can I do anything for you? Shall I send for a chaplain?'

Eustace's eye brightened, and he answered in a voice so faint that the Prince only heard by bending over him:

'An order from the King for some one to remain—Then I need not be ever watching—'

'I shall wait till he comes,' said the Prince and Eustace gave SUCH a look of thankfulness, and pressed the hand that had been laid in his.

The Duke, with politeness, asked permission of my mother to write a billet to his brother, with a report of Lord Walwyn, at the writing-table in the room. He wrote two—one to the King, another to the chaplain, D. Hargood, bidding him obtain orders from King Charles to remain with Lord Walwyn; and he despatched them by the gentleman who had followed him, asking permission of my mother to remain a little while with my lord.

Poor mother! she could not refuse, and she did, after all, love her son enough to be relieved, as an air of rest and confidence stole over his features, as the princely boy sat down by him, begging that he might spare some one fatigue while he was there. She sent me away, but would not go herself; and I heard afterwards that the Duke sat very still, seldom speaking. Once Eustace asked him if he had his Book of Common Prayer, for his own had been put out of his reach.

'This is my sister's,' said the Duke, taking out a little worn velvet book. 'Shall I read you her favourite Psalm?'

He read in a low gentle voice, trained by his ministry to his sweet sister. He read the Easter Epistle and Gospel too; and at last Eustace, relaxing the weary watch and guard of those dreadful days, dropped into a calm sleep.

If a miracle of recovery could be said to have been wrought, surely it was by Duke Henry of Gloucester.

Long and patiently the boy say there; for, as it turned out, the King was in the Cours de la Reine playing at bowls, and it was long before he could be found, and when Dr. Hargood brought it at last the Prince had actually watched his friend for four hours. He might well say he had been trained in waiting! And he himself gave the bouillon, when Eustace awoke without the red flush, and with softer breathing!

The King had actually done more than the Duke had asked; for he had not only given orders that the chaplain should come, and, if desired, remain with Lord Walwyn, but he had also sent the Queen's physician, the most skilful man at hand, to oust the Dominican. We heard that he had sworn that it was as bad as being in a Scotch conventicler to have cowls and hoods creeping about your bed before you were dead, and that Harry had routed them like a very St. George.

CHAPTER XXX. — THE NEW MAID OF ORLEANS

(Margaret's Narrative)

I was summoned to the Luxembourg Palace on the Tuesday in Holy Week, the 25th of March. My dear brother was then apparently much better, and gaining ground after the attack of hemorrhage caused by his exertions to save M. Darpent from the violence of his assailants.

He did not appear to need me, since he could not venture to talk more than a few words at a time; and, besides, my year's absence had left me in such arrears of waiting that I could not ask for leave of absence without weighty grounds. My mother was greatly displeased with me for not having cut short the interview between Darpent and Annora, although it seemed to have served her purpose by embroiling them effectually; but she could not overlook so great an impropriety; and I confess that I was not sorry to avoid her continual entreaties to me to give up all intercourse alike with the Darpents and Ommneys, and all our English friends. I had satisfied myself that M. Darpent was in no danger, and I was willing to let the matter blow over, since Lady Ommaney, though imprudent, had only done a good-natured thing from the English point of view.

I found my Princess in great excitement. Cardinal Mazarin had rejoined the King and Queen, and they were at the head of one army, the Prince of Conde was at the head of another. The Parliament view both Cardinal and Prince as rebels, and had set a price upon the Cardinal's head. On the whole, the Prince was the less hated of the two, yet there were scruples on being in direct opposition to the King. The Cardinal de Retz was trying to stir the Duke of Orleans to take what was really his proper place as the young King's uncle, and at the head of the Parliament, to mediate between the parties, stop the civil war, convoke the States-General, and redress grievances. But to move Monsieur was a mere impossibility; he liked to hear of his own power, but whenever anything was to be done that alarmed him, he always was bled, or took physic, so as to have an excuse for not interfering.

And now the royal army was approaching Orleans, and Monsieur could not brook that the city, his own appanage, should be taken from him. Yet not only was he unwilling to risk himself, but the Coadjutor and he were alike of opinion that he ought not to leave Paris and the Parliament. So he had made up his mind to send is daughter, who was only too much charmed to be going anywhere or doing anything exciting, especially if it could be made to turn to the advantage of the Prince of Conde, whom she still dreamt of marrying.

I found her in a state of great importance and delight, exclaiming: 'My dear Gildippe, I could not do without you! We shall be in your element. His Royal Highness and M. le Cardinal de Retz have both been breaking my head with instructions, but I remember none of them! I trust to my native wit on the occasion.'

We all got into our carriages, a long train of them, at the Luxembourg, with Monsieur looking from the window and waving his farewell to his daughter, and the people called down benedictions on her, though I hardly know what benefit they expected from her enterprise. We had only two officers, six guards, and six Swiss to escort us; but Mademoiselle was always popular, and we were quite safe.

We slept at Chartres, and there met the Duke of Beaufort, who rode by the carriage-window; and by and by, at Etampes, we found 500 light horse of Monsieur's regiment, who all saluted. Mademoiselle was in ecstasies; she insisted on leaving her carriage, and riding at their head, with all the ladies who could sit on horseback; and thus we came to Toury, where were the Duke de Nemours and others of the Prince's party.

My heart was heavy, I hardly knew why, with fore-bodings about what might be passing at home, or I should have enjoyed the comedy of Mademoiselle's extreme delight in her own importance, and the councils of war held before her, while the Dukes flattered her to the top of her bent, laughed in their sleeve, and went their own way. She made us all get up at break of day to throw ourselves into Orleans, and we actually set out, but we had to move at a foot's pace, because M. de Beaufort had, by accident or design, forgotten to command the escort to be in attendance.

By and by a message was brought by some gentlemen, who told Mademoiselle that the citizens of Orleans had closed their gates and were resolved to admit nobody; that the Keeper of the Seals was on the farther side, demanding entrance for the royal troops; and they were afraid of the disorderly behaviour of any soldiers. They were in a strait between the King and their Duke's daughter, and they proposed to her to go to some neighbouring house and pretend illness until the royal forces should have passed by, when they would gladly admit her.

Mademoiselle was not at all charmed by this proposal, and she answered with spirit: 'I shall go straight to Orleans. If they shut the gates I shall not be discouraged. Perseverance will gain the day. If I enter the town my presence will restore the courage of all who are well affected to His Royal Highness. When persons of my rank expose themselves, the people are terribly animated, and they will not yield to people of small resolution.'

So into the carriage she got, taking me with her, and laughing at all who showed any alarm. Message upon message met us, supplicating her not to come on, as she would not be admitted; but her head only went higher and higher, all the more when she heard that the Keeper of the Seals was actually at the gates, demanding entrance in the name of the King.

About eleven o'clock we reached the Porte Banniere, and found it closed and barricaded. The guards were called on to open to Mademoiselle d'Orleans Montpensier, the daughter of their lord; but all in vain, though she had not a soldier with her, and promised not to bring in either of the Dukes of Nemours or Beaufort.

We waited three hours. Mademoiselle became tired of sitting in the carriage, and we went to a little inn, where we had something to eat, and, to our great amusement, the poor, perplexed Governor of the town sent her some sweetmeats, by way, I suppose, of showing his helpless good-will. We then began to walk about the suburbs, and I though of the Battle of the Herrings and the Maid of Orleans, and wondered which was the gate by which she entered. One of the gentlemen immediately complimented Mademoiselle on being a second Maid of Orleans, and pointed out the gate, called Le Port de Salut, as connected with the rescue of the place. We saw the Marquis d'Allins looking out at the window of the guardroom, and Mademoiselle made signs to him to bring her the keys, and let her in, but he replied by his gestures that he could not. The situation was a very strange one. Mademoiselle, with her little suite of ladies, parading along the edge of the moat, vainly trying to obtain admission, while the women, children, and idlers of Orleans were peeping over the ramparts at us, shouting:

'Vive le Roi! Vivent les Princes! Point de Mazarin!' and Mademoiselle was calling back: 'Go to the town hall, call the magistrates, and fetch the keys!' Nobody stirred, and at last we came to another gate, when the guard presented arms, and again Mademoiselle called to the captain to open. With a low bow and a shrug, he replied: 'I have no keys.'

'Break it down, then,' she cried. 'You owe more obedience to your master's daughter than to the magistrates.'

He bowed.

The scene became more and more absurd; Mademoiselle began to threaten the poor man with arrest.

He bowed.

He should be degraded.

He bowed.

He should be drummed out of the service.

He bowed.

He should be shot.

He bowed.

We were choking with laughter, and trying to persuade her that threats were unworthy; but she said that kindness had no effect, and that she must now use threats, and that she knew she should succeed, for an astrologer had told her that everything she did between this Wednesday and Friday should prosper—she had the prediction in her pocket. By this time we had coasted along the moat till we came to the Loire, where a whole swarm of boatmen, honest fellows in red caps and striped shirts, came up, shouting, 'Vive Monsieur!' 'Vive Mademoiselle!' and declaring that it was a shame to lock her out of her fathers own town.

She asked them to row her to the water-gate of La Faux, but they answered that there was an old wooden door close by which they could more easily break down. She gave them money and bade them do so, and to encourage them climbed up a steep mound of earth close by all over bushes and briars, while poor Madame de Breaute stood shrieking below, and I scrambled after.

The door was nearly burst in, but it was on the other side of the moat. The water was very low, so two boats were dragged up to serve as a bridge, but they were so much below the top of the ditch that a ladder was put down into one, up which Mademoiselle dauntlessly mounted, unheeding that one step was broken, and I came after her. This was our escalade of Orleans.

She ordered her guards to return to the place where the carriages had been left, that she might show how fearless she was. The boatmen managed at last to cut out two boards from the lower part of the door. There were two great iron bars above them, but the hole was just big enough to squeeze through, and Mademoiselle was dragged between the splinters by M. de Grammont and a footman. As soon as her head appeared inside the gate the drums beat, there were loud vivats, a wooden arm-chair was brought, and Mademoiselle was hoisted on the men's shoulders in it and carried along the street; but she soon had enough of this, caused herself to be set down, and we all joined her, very dirty, rather frightened, and very merry. Drums beat before us, and we arrived at the Hotel de Ville, where the police bows and the embarrassed faces of the Governor and the magistrates were a sight worth seeing.

However, Mademoiselle took the command, and they all made their excuses and applied themselves to entertaining her and her suit, as carriages were not admitted, for we were in a manner besieged by the Keeper of the Seals; and in the early morning, at seven o'clock, Mademoiselle had to rise and go through the streets encouraging the magistrates to keep him out.

She was a sort of queen at Orleans, and we formed a little Court. I really think this was the happiest time in her life, while she had a correspondence with the Prince of Conde on the one hand, and her father on the other; and assisted at councils of war outside the gates, as she kept her promise, and admitted none of the leaders of the belligerent parties into the city.

They were stormy councils. At one of these the Duke of Beaufort and Nemours had a dispute, drew their swords, and were going to attack one another, when Mademoiselle, by entreaties and commands, forced them to lay down their arms.

All this time I had no news from my family. We were in a strange condition. Here was I following Mademoiselle, who represented her father and the neutral party, but was really devoted to the Prince; my son was in attendance on the King, whom we were keeping out of his own city; my mother, brother, and sister were in Paris, which held for the Parliament. My half-brother, Solivet, had repaired to M. de Turenne's army, which was fighting for the King, and my brother-in-law, d'Aubepine, was on the staff of the Prince.

There was scarcely any family that was not divided and broken up in the same way, and it was hard to say why there was all this war and misery, except that there was irreconcilable hatred between the Prince and the Cardinal, and the Queen was determined to cling to the latter.

I knew nothing of what was passing at home till a day or two after Easter Sunday, when one of the gentlemen of the household of the Duke of Orleans, who had come with letters for Mademoiselle, seemed surprised to see me, and on my pressing him for intelligence, he told me that my dear brother was at the point of death. He was quite sure of it, for he had spoken with M. de Poligny, who told him that M. de Ribaumont was daily visited by the Abbe Montagu, was in the best possible dispositions, and would receive the last sacraments of our Church.

I knew not what to believe. All I was sure of was that I must be wanted, and that it would break my heart not to see my dearest brother again. Mademoiselle was a kind mistress, and she consented to my leaving her, and there was no danger in ladies traveling, though a good deal of difficulty in getting horses.

At last, however, I found myself at my own door, and in one moment satisfied myself that my brother was living, and better. My mother was in the salon, in conversation with M. de Poligny, who had the good judgment to withdraw.

'Ah! my dear,' she said, 'we have had frightful scenes! I had almost gained my dear son's soul, but alas! it might have been at the cost of his life, and I could not but be weak enough to rejoice when your sister's obstinacy snatched him from me. After all one is a mother! and the good Abbe says a pure life and invincible ignorance will merit acceptance! Besides, the Duke of Gloucester did him the honour to sit an hour by him every day.'

I asked for my sister, and heard that she was with him. For, though my mother said poor Annora's ungovernable impetuosity had done him so much harm, nay, nearly killed him, he was now never so tranquil as when she was in his sight, and the English physician, who had been sent by the King himself, declared that his life still depended on his being kept free from all agitation.

'Otherwise,' said my mother, 'I could bring about the marriage with the little Chevalier. Annora has renounced her disobedient folly, and would make no more resistance; but M. de Poligny, of course, cannot proceed further till your brother is in condition to settle the property on her.'

I asked in wonder whether my sister had consented, but my mother seemed to think that the break with Darpent had settled that matter for ever.

And when I saw my poor Annora, she was altered indeed. The bright colour had left her cheeks, her eyes looked dim and colourless, her voice had lost its fresh defiant ring; she was gentle, submissive, listless, as if all she cared for in life had gone from her except the power of watching Eustace.

He looked less ill than I had dreaded to see him. I think he felt at rest after the struggle he had undergone to preserve the faith he really loved. He had never relaxed his guard for a single moment till the Duke of Gloucester had come, fearing that if he ceased his vigilance, that might be done which we felt to be mercy, but which he could not submit to. He always had a calmly resolute will, and he knew now that he must avoid all agitation until he was able to bear it; so he would not ask any questions. He only showed me that he was glad of my return, pointed to Nan, saying: 'She has been sorely tried, take care of her,' and asked me if I could find out how it fared with Darpent.

It was too late to do anything that evening, and I went to mass as early as I could in the morning, that the streets might be quiet; and when I rose from my knees I was accosted by a Sister of Charity who told me that there was terrible need at the Hotel Dieu. Men were continually brought in, shockingly injured in the street frays that were constantly taking place, and by the violences of the band of robbers and bravoes with whom the Duke of Orleans surrounded his carriage, and there was exceedingly little help and nursing for them, owing to the absence of the Queen, and of so many of the great ladies who sometimes lavished provisions, comforts, and attendance on the patients.

I had three hours to spare before any one would be up, so I went home, got together all the old linen and provisions I could muster, told my sister where I was going, and caused my chairmen to carry me to the hospital. The streets were perfectly quiet then, only the bakers' boys running about with their ells of bread, the water-carriers and the faggot-men astir, and round the churches a few women hurrying to their prayers, looking about as if half dreading a tumult.

Poor people! I had never seen the hospital so full, or in so sad a condition. The Sisters and the priests of St. Lazare were doing their utmost, and with them a very few ladies. I had staid long enough to fear that I must be needed at home when I saw another lady coming to take my place, and recognized Madame Darpent. We met with more eagerness than the good old devout dame usually allowed herself to show, for each accepted the appearance of the other as a token of the improvement of out patients at home. She said her son was nearly well in health, but that his arm was still unserviceable, having been cruelly twisted by the miscreants who had attacked him; and when I told her that my brother was likewise recovering, she exclaimed:

'Ah! Madame, I dare not ask it; but if Madame la Vicomtesse could kindly leave word of the good news as she passes our house, it would be a true charity to my poor son. We have heard sad accounts of the illness of M. de Ribaumont. The servants at the Hotel de Nidemerle confirmed them, and my son, knowing that M. le Baron was hurt in his behalf, has been devoured with misery. If Madame could let him know at once it would spare him four or five hours of distress, ere I can leave these poor creatures.'

'Perhaps he would like to see me,' I said; and the old lady was ready to embrace me. She would not have dared to ask it; but I knew how glad Eustace would be to have a personal account of him.

It was still early, and I met with no obstruction. My message was taken in to ask whether M. Darpent would see me, and he came down himself to lead me upstairs, looking very pale and worn, and giving me his left hand, as in a broken voice he made polite speeches on the honour I had done him.

'At least, Madame,' he said, trembling, so that he was obliged to lean on the chair he was setting for me, 'let me hear that you are come to tell me no bad news.'

I assured him of the contrary, and made him sit down, while I told him of my brother's improvement, and anxiety respecting himself.

'I may tell him that you are a convalescent, and able to employ yourself in deep studies,' I said, glancing at a big black book open on the table beside the arm-chair where he had been sitting.

'It is St. Augustine,' he said. 'I have been profiting by my leisure. I have almost come to the conclusion that there is nothing to be done for this unhappy France of ours but to pray for her. I had some hopes of the young King; but did Madame hear what he did when our deputies presented their petition to the States-General? He simply tore the paper, and said: 'Retire, Messieur.' He deems despotism his right and duty, and will crush all resistance. Men, like the Garde des Sceaux, have done their best, but we have no strength without the nobility, who simply use us as tools to gratify their animosity against one another.'

'Only too true!' I said. 'There is not even permission given to us nobles to do good among our own peasants.'

'There is permission for nothing but to be vicious sycophants,' cried he bitterly. 'At least save for the soldier, who thinks only of the enemies of France. Ah! my mother is right! All we can do to keep our hands unstained is to retire from the world, and pray, study, and toil like the recluses of Port Royal.'

'Are you thinking of becoming one of them?' I exclaimed.

'I know not. Not while aught remains to be done for my country. Even that seems closed to me,' he answered sadly. 'I am unfortunate man, Madame,' he added; 'I have convictions, and I cannot crush them as I see others, better than I, can do—by appealing to simple authority and custom.'

'They kept you from your Counsellor's seat, I know,' said I.—'And made every one, except M. le Premier President, mistrust me for a conceited fellow. Well, and now they must keep me from casting in my lot with the recluses who labour and pray at Port Royal aux Champs, unless I can satisfy myself on scruples that perhaps my Huguenot breeding, perhaps my conversations with M. votre frere, have awakened in me. And — and — though I have the leisure, I know my head and heart are far from being cool enough to decide on points of theology,' he added, covering his face for a moment with his hand.

'You a recluse of Port Royal! I cannot believe in it,' I said. 'Tell me, Monsieur, is your motive despair? For I know what your hopes have been.'

'Ah, Madame, then you also know what their overthrown has been, though you can never know what it has cost me. Those eyes, as clear-sighted as they are beautiful, saw only too plainly the folly of expecting anything in the service I was ready to adopt, and scorned my hopes of thus satisfying her family. I deserved it. May she find happiness in the connection she has accepted.'

'Stay, sir,' I said. 'What has she accepted? What have you heard?'

He answered with a paler look and strange smile that his clerk had been desired by M. de Poligny's notary to let him see the parchments of the Ribaumont estate, preparatory to drawing up the contract of marriage, to be ready to be signed in a week's time.'

'Ah, sir,' I said, 'you are a lawyer, and should know how to trust to such evidence. The contract is impossible without my brother, who is too ill to hear of it, and my sister has uttered no word of consent, nor will she, even though she should remain unmarried for life.'

'Will she forgive me?' he exclaimed, as though ready to throw himself at my feet.

I told him that he must find out for himself, and he returned that I was an angel from heaven. On the whole I felt more like a weak and talkative woman, a traitress to my mother; but then, as I looked at him, there was such depth of wounded affection, such worth and superiority to all the men I was in the habit of seeing, that it was impossible not to feel that if Annora had any right to choose at all she had chosen worthily.

But I thought of my mother, and would not commit myself further, and I rose to leave him; I had, however, waited too long. The mob were surging along the streets, as they always did when the magistrates came home from the Parliament, howling, bellowing, and yelling round the unpopular ones.

'Death to the Big Beard!' was the cry, by which they meant good old Mathieu Mole, who had incurred their hatred for his loyalty, and then they halted opposite to the Maison Darpent to shout: 'Death to the Big Beard and his jackal!'

'Do not fear, Madame, it will soon be over,' said Darpent. 'It is a little amusement in which they daily indulge. The torrent will soon pass by, and then I will do myself the honour of escorting you home.'

I thought I was much safer than he, and would have forbidden him, but he smiled, and said I must not deny him the pleasure of walking as far as the door of the Hotel de Nidemerle.

'But why do they thus assail you and the Garde des Sceaux?' I asked.

'Because so few in this unfortunate country can distinguish between persons and causes,' he said. 'Hatred to Mazarin and to the Queen as his supporter is the only motive that sways them. If he can only be kept out they are willing to throw themselves under the feet of the Prince that he may trample them to dust. Once, as you know, we hoped that there was public spirit enough in the noblesse and clergy, led by the Coadjutor, to join with us in procuring the assembling of the States-General, and thus constitutionally have taken the old safeguards of the people. They deceived us, and only made use of us for their own ends. The Duke of Orleans, who might have stood by us, is a broken reed, and now, in the furious clash of parties, we stand by, waiting till the conqueror shall complete our destruction and oppression, and in the meantime holding to the only duty that is clear to us — of loyalty to the King, let that involve what it may.'

'And because it involves the Cardinal you are vituperated,' I said. 'The Court ought to reward your faithfulness.'

'So I thought once, but it is more likely to reward our resistance in its own fashion if its triumph be once secured,' he answered. 'Ah, Madame, are visions of hope for one's country mere madness?'

And certainly I felt that even when peace was made between him and my sister, as it certainly soon would be, the future looked very black before them, unless he were too obscure for the royal thunderbolts to reach.

However, the mob had passed by, to shriek round the Hotel de Ville.

Food and wine were dealt out to them by those who used them as their tools, and they were in a frightful state of demoralization, but the way was clear for the present, and Clement Darpent would not be denied walking by my chair, though he could hardly have guarded me, but he took me through some by-streets, which avoided the haunts of the mob; and though he came no further than our door, the few words I ventured to bring home reassured Eustace, and made Annora look like another being.

CHAPTER XXXI. — PORTE ST. ANTOINE

(Margaret's Narrative)

When I try to look back on the time that followed, all is confusion. I cannot unravel the threat of events clearly in my own mind, and can only describe a few scenes that detach themselves, as it were, from a background of reports, true and false, of alarms, of messages to and fro, and a horrible mob surging backwards and forwards, so that when Mademoiselle returned to Paris and recalled me, I could only pass backwards and forwards between the Louvre and the Hotel de Nidemerle after the servants had carefully reconnoitred to see that the streets were safe, and this although I belonged to the Orleans' establishment, which was in favour with the mob. Their white scarves were as much respected as the tawny colours of Conde, which every one else wore who wished to be secured from insult.

I longed the more to be at home because my very dear brother, now convalescent, was preparing everything for his journey to the Hague. He had an interview with M. de Poligny, and convinced him that it was hopeless to endeavour to gain Annora's consent to the match with his son, and perhaps the good gentleman was not sorry to withdraw with honour; and thus the suit waited till the Parliament should be at leisure to attend to private affairs.

My mother was greatly disappointed, above all when my brother, in his gentle but authoritative manner, requested her to withdraw her opposition to my sister's marriage with Darpent, explaining that the had consented, as knowing what his father's feeling would have been towards so good a man. She wept, and said that it certainly would not have been so bad in England, but under the nose of all her friends — bah! and she was sure that Solivet would kill the fellow rather than see canaille admitted into the family. However, if the wedding took place at the Hague, where no one would hear of it, and Annora chose to come back and live en bourgeoise, and not injure the establishment of the Marquis de Nidemerle, she would not withhold her blessing. So Annora was to go with Eustace, who indeed had not intended to leave her behind him, never being sure what coercion might be put on her.

In the meantime it was not possible for any peaceful person, especially one in my brother's state of health, to leave Paris. The city was between two armies, if not three. On the one side was that of the Princes, on the other that of M. le Marechal de Turenne, with the Court in its rear, and at one time the Duke of Lorraine advanced, and though he took no one's part, he felled the roads with horrible marauders trained in the Thirty Year's War. The two armies of Conde and Turenne skirmished in the suburbs, and it may be imagined what contradictory reports were always tearing us to pieces. Meantime Paris was strong enough to keep out either army, and that was the one thing that the municipality and the Paliarment were resolved to do. They let single officers of the Prince's army, himself, the Duke of Beaufort, Nemours, the Court d'Aubepine, and the rest, come in and out, but they were absolutely determined not to be garrisoned by forces in direct rebellion to the King. They would not stand a siege on their behalf, endure their military license, and then the horrors of an assault. The Duke of Orleans professed to be of the same mind, but he was a mere nonentity, and merely acted as a drag on his daughter, who was altogether devoted to the Prince of Conde. Cardinal de Retz vainly tried to persuade him to take the manly part of mediation, that would have been possible to him, at the head of the magistracy and municipality of Paris.

The Prince—Heaven forgive him—and the Duke of Beaufort hoped to terrify the magistracy into subservience by raising the populace against them. Foolish people! as if their magistrates were not guarding them from horrible miseries. In fact, however, the mobs who raved up and down the streets, yelling round the Hotel de Ville, hunting the magistrates like a pack of wolves, shouting and dancing round Monsieur's carriage, or Beaufort's horse—these wretches were not the peaceable work-people, but bandits, ruffians, disbanded soldiers, criminals, excited by distributions of wine and money in the cabarets that they might terrify all who upheld law and order. If the hotels of the nobles and magistrates had not been constructed like little fortresses, no doubt these wretches would have carried their violence further. It seems to me, when I look back at that time, that even in the Louvre or the Luxembourg, one's ears were never free from the sound of howls and yells, more or less distant.

Clement Darpent, who had been separated from his work by his injury, and had not resumed it, so far as I could learn, was doing his best as a deputy at the Hotel de Ville to work on those whom he could influence to stand firm to their purpose of not admitting the King's enemies, but, on the other hand, of not opening their gates to the royal arm itself till the summons to the States-General should be actually issued, and the right of Parliament to refuse registration acknowledged. His friends among the younger advocates and the better educated of the bourgeois had rallier round him, and in the general anarchy made it their business to protect the persons whom the mob placed in danger. My mother, in these days of terror, had recurred to her former reliance on him, and admitted him once more. I heard there had been no formal reconciliation with Annora, but they had met as if nothing had happened; and it was an understood thing that he should follow her to the Hague so soon as there should be an interval of peace; but he had a deep affection for his country and his city, and could not hear of quitting them, even for Annora's sake, in this crisis of fate, while he had still some vision of being of use, and at any rate could often save lives. Whenever any part of the mob was composed of real poor, who had experienced his mother's charities, he could deal with them; and when they were the mere savage bandits of the partisans, he and his friends scrupled not to use force. For instance, this I saw myself. The Duke of Orleans had summoned the Prevot des Marchands and two of the echevins to the Luxembourg, to consult about supplies. The mob followed them all the way down the street, reviling them as men sold to Mazarin, and insisting that they should open the gates to the Prince. When they were admitted the wretches stood outside yelling at them like wolves waiting for their prey. I could not help appealing to Mademoiselle's kindness of heart, and asking if they could not be sheltered in the palace, till the canaille grew tired of waiting. She shrugged her shoulders, and called them miserable Mazarinites, but I think she would have permitted them to remain within if her father had not actually conducted them out, saying, 'I will not have them fallen upon IN HERE,' which was like throwing them to the beasts. We ladies were full of anxiety, and all hurried up to the roof to see their fate.

Like hungry hounds the mob hunted and pelted these respectable magistrates down the Rue de Conde, their robes getting torn as they fled and stumbled along, and the officers, standing on the steps of the hotel of M. le Prince, among whom, alas! was d'Aubepine. Waved their yellow scarves, laughed at the terror and flight of the unhappy magistrates, and hounded on the mob with 'Ha! There! At him! Well thrown!'

Suddenly a darker line appeared, advancing in order; there was a moment's flash of rapiers, a loud trumpet call of 'Back, ye cowards!' The row of men, mostly in black hats, with white collars, opened, took in among them the bleeding, staggering, cruelly-handled fugitives, and with a firm front turned back the vile pursuers. I could distinguish Clement Darpent's figure as he stood in front, and I could catch a tone of his voice, though I could not made out his words, as he reproached the populace for endeavouring to murder their best friends. I felt that my sister's choice had been a grand one, but my heart sank as I heard the sneer behind me: 'Hein! The conceited lawyers are ruffling it finely. They shall pay for it!'

There was a really terrible fight on the steps of the Parliament House, when the mob forced the door of the great chamber, and twenty-five people were killed; but Darpent and his little party helped out a great many more of the counsellors, and the town-guard coming up, the mob was driven off. That evening I saw the Cardinal de Retz. He was in bad odour with Monsieur and Mademoiselle, because he was strongly against the Prince, and would fain have stirred the Duke of Orleans to interfere effectively at the head of the Parliament and city of Paris; but a man of his rank could not but appear at times at the Duke's palace, and on this fine May evening, when all had gone out after supper into the alleys of the garden of the Luxembourg, he found me out. How young, keen, and lively he still looked in spite of his scarlet! How far from one's notions of an Eminence!

'That was a grand exploit of our legal friend, Madame,' he said; 'but I am afraid he will burn his fingers. One is not honest with impunity unless one can blindly hang on to a party. Some friend should warn him to get out of the way when the crash comes, and a victim has to be sacrificed as a peace-offering. Too obscure, did Madame say? Ah! that is the very reason! He has secured no protector. He has opposed the Court and the Prince alike, and the magistrates themselves regard him as a dangerous man, with those notions a lui about venality, and his power and individuality, and therefore is factious, and when the Court demands a Frondeur there will be no one except perhaps old Mole to cry out in his defence, and Mole is himself too much overpowered. Some friend should give him a hint to take care of himself.'

I told my brother as soon as I could, and he ardently wished to take Darpent away with him when it should be possible to quit Paris; but at that moment Clement and his young lawyers still nourished some wild hope that the Parliament, holding the balance between the parties, might yet undeceive the young King and save the country.

The climax came at last on the second of July. M. le Prince was outside the walls, with the Portes St. Antoine, St. Honore, and St. Denis behind him. M. de Turenne was pressing him very hard, endeavouring to cut him off from taking up a position on the other side of the army, at the confluence of the Seine and the Marne. The Prince had entreated permission to pass his baggage through the city, but the magistrates were resolved not to permit this, not knowing what would come after. Some entrenchments had been thrown up round the Porte St. Antoine when the Lorrainers had threatened us, and here the Prince took up his position outside the walls. There, as you remember, the three streets of Charenton, St. Antoine, and Charonne all meet in one great open space, which the Prince occupied, heaping up his baggage behind him, and barricading the three streets—M. de Nemours guarded one, Vallon and Tavannes the other two. The Prince, with the Duke of la Rochefoucauld and fifty more brave gentlemen, waited ready to carry succour wherever it should be needed. Within, the Bastille frowned over all.

We were waiting in the utmost anxiety. A message came to Mademoiselle, at the Louvre, from the Prince, entreating her not to abandon him, or he would be crushed between the royal forces and the walls of Paris. Monsieur had, for a week, professed to be ill, but, on driving through the streets, lined with anxious people, and coming to the Luxembourg, we found him on the steps.

'I thought you were in bed,' said his daughter.

'I am not ill enough to be there,' he answered; 'but I am not well enough to go out.'

Mademoiselle entreated him, in her vehement way, either to mount his horse and go to help M. le Prince, or at least to go to bed and act the invalid for very shame; but he stood irresolute, whistling, and tapping on the window, too anxious to undress, and too timid to go out. Annora would have been ready to beat him. I think his daughter longed to do so. She tried frightening him.

'Unless you have a treaty from the Court in your pocket I cannot think how you can be so quiet. Pray, have you undertaken to sacrifice M. le Prince to Cardinal Mazarin?'

He whistled on without answering, but she persevered, with alternate taunts and threats, till at last she extracted from him a letter to the magistrates at the Hotel de Ville, telling them that she would inform them of his intentions. Off, then, we went again, having with us Madame de Nemours, who was in an agony about her husband, and presently we were at the Hotel de Ville, where we were received by the Prevot des Marchands, the echevins, and Marshal de l'Hopital, Governor of Paris—all in the most intense anxiety. She was brought into to great hall, but she would not sit down—giving her father's letter, and then desiring that the town-guard should take up arms in all the quarters. This was already done. Then they were to send the Prince 2000 men, and to put 400 men under her orders in the Place Royale. To all this they agreed; but when she asked them to give the Prince's troops a passage through the city, they demurred, lest they should bring on themselves the horrors of war.

Again she commanded, she insisted, she raved, telling them that if they let the Prince's army be destroyed those of M. de Turenne would assuredly come in and sack the city for its rebellion.

Marshal l'Hopital said that but for Mademoiselle's friends, the royal army would never have come thither at all, and Madame de Nemours began to dispute with him, but Mademoiselle interfered, saying: 'Recollect, while you are discussing useless questions the Prince is in the utmost danger;' and, as we heard the cries of the people and beyond them the sharp rattle of musketry, she threatened them with appealing to the people.

She was really dignified in her strong determination, and she prevailed. Evil as the whole conduct of the Prince had been, no doubt the magistrates felt that it would be a frightful reproach to let the flower of the gentlemen of France be massacred at their gates. So again we went off towards the Port St. Antoine, hearing the firing and the shouts louder every minute, at the entrance of Rue St. Antoine we met M. Guitaut on horse-back, supported by another man, bare-headed, all unbuttoned, and pale as death. 'Shalt thou die?' screamed out Mademoiselle, as we passed the poor man, and he shook his head, though he had a great musket ball in his body. Next came M. de Vallon, carried in a chair, but not too much hurt to call out: 'Alas, my good mistress, we are all lost.'

'No, no,' she answered; 'I have orders to open a retreat.'

'You give me life,' he said.

More and more wounded, some riding, some on foot, some carried on ladders, boards, doors, mattresses. I saw an open door. It was that of Gneffier Verdon, Clement's brother-in-law, and Darpent was assisting to carry in a wounded man whose blood flowed so fast that it made a stream along the pavement before the door. Mademoiselle insisted on knowing who it was, and there was only too much time, for, in spite of our impatience and the deadly need, we could only move at a foot's pace through the ghastly procession we were meeting. The answer came back—'It is the Count d'Aubepine. He would bleed to death before he could be carried home, so M. Darpent has had him carried into his sister's house.'

My heart was sick for poor Cecile. 'My brother-in-law!' I said. 'Oh, Mademoiselle, I entreat of you to let me go to his aid.'

'Your amiable brother-in-law, who wanted to have you enlevee! No, no, my dear, you cannot be uneasy about him. The Generalissime of Paris cannot spare her Gildippe.'

So I was carried on, consoling myself with the thought that Madame Verdon, who was as kind as her mother, would take care of him. When we came near the gate Mademoiselle sent orders by M. de Rohan to the captain of the gate to let her people in and out, and, at the same time, sent a message to the Prince, while she went into the nearest house, that of M. de Croix, close to the Bastille.

Scarcely were we in its salon when in came the Prince. He was in a terrible state, and dropped into a chair out of breath before he could speak. His face was all over dust, his hair tangled, his collar and shirt bloody, his cuirass dinted all over with blows, and he held his bloody sword in his hand, having lost the scabbard.

'You see a man in despair,' he gasped out. 'I have lost all my friends. Nemours, de la Rochefoucauld, Clinchamp, d'Aubepine, are mortally wounded;' and, throwing down his sword, he began tearing his hair with his hands, and moving his feet up and down in an agony of grief.

It was impossible not to feel for him at such a moment, and Mademoiselle came kindly up to him, took his hand, and was able to assure him that things were better than he thought, and that M. de Clinchamp was only two doors off, and in no danger.

He composed himself a little, thanked her passionately, swallowed down some wine, begged her to remain at hand, then rushed off again to endeavour to save his friends, now that the retreat was opened to them. Indeed, we heard that M. de Turenne said it seemed to him that he did not meet one but twelve Princes of Conde in that battle, for it seemed as if he were everywhere at once.

We could only see into the street from the house where we were, and having received some civil messages from the Governor of the Bastille, Mademoiselle decided on going thither. The Governor turned out the guard to salute Mademoiselle, and at her request conducted us up stone stair after stone stair in the massive walls and towers. Now and then we walked along a gallery, with narrow doors opening into it here and there; and then we squeezed up a spiral stone stair, never made for ladies, and lighted by narrow loopholes. In spite of all the present anxiety I could not help shuddering at that place of terror, and wondering who might be pining within those heavy doors. At last we came out on the battlements, a broad walk on the top of the great square tower, with cannon looking through the embrasures, and piles of balls behind them, gunners waiting beside each. It was extremely hot, but we could not think of that. And what a sight it was in the full glare of the summer sun! Mademoiselle had a spy-glass, but even without one we could see a great deal, when we were not too much dazzled. There was the open space beneath us, with the moat and ditch between, crowded with baggage, and artillery near the walls, with gentlemen on foot and horseback, their shorn plumes and soiled looks telling of the deadly strife—messengers rushing up every moment with tidings, and carrying orders from the group which contained the Prince, and wounded men being carried or helped out at the openings of the three chief suburban streets, whose irregular high-roofed houses and trees, the gray walls and cloisters of the abbey, hid the actual fight, only the curls of smoke were rising continually; and now and then we saw the flash of the firearms, while the noise was indescribable — of shots, shrieks, cries to come on, and yells of pain. My brother told me afterwards that in all the battles put together he had seen in England he did not think he had heard half the noise that came to him in that one afternoon on the top of the Hotel de Nidemerle. The Cavaliers gave a view halloo, and cried, 'God save the King!' the Ironsides sang a Psalm, and then they set their teeth and fought in silence, and hardly any one cried out when he was hurt — while here the shots were lost in the cries, and oh! how terrible with rage and piteous with pain they were!

Beyond the houses and gardens, where lie the heights of Charonne, were to be seen, moving about like ants, a number of troops on foot and on horseback, and with colours among them. Mademoiselle distinguished carriages among them. 'The King is there, no doubt,' she said; and as I exclaimed, 'Ah! yes, and my son,' she handed me the glass, by which I could make out what looked very like the royal carriages; but the King was on horseback, and so was my dear boy, almost wild with the fancy that his mother was besieged, and scarcely withheld from galloping down by assurances that no lady was in the slightest danger.

Below, in the hollow, towards where Bagnolet rose white among the fields and vineyards, the main body of Turenne's troops were drawn up in their regiments, looking firm and steady, in dark lines, flashing now and then in that scorching July sunshine, their colours flying, and their plumes waving. A very large proportion of them were cavalry, and the generals were plainly to be made out by the staff which surrounded each, and their gestures of command.

We presently saw that the generals were dividing their horse, sending one portion towards Pincourt, the other towards Neuilly. Mademoiselle, who really had the eye of a general, instantly divided that they were going to advance along the water-side, so as to cut off the retreat of the Prince's forces by interposing between thefaubourg and the moat, and thus preventing them from availing themselves of the retreat through Paris. M. le Prince was, as we could perceive, on the belfry of the Abbey of St. Antoine, but there he could not see as we could, and Mademoiselle instantly dispatched a page to warm him, and at the same time she gave orders to the artillerymen to fire on the advancing troops as soon as they came within range. This was the most terrible part to me of all. We were no longer looking on to save life, but firing on the loyal and on the army where my son was. Suppose the brave boy had broken away and ridden on! I was foolish enough to feel as if they were aiming at his heart when the fire and smoke burst from the mouths of those old brass guns, and the massive tower seemed to rock under our feet, and the roar was in our ears, and Madame de Fiesque and the other ladies screamed in chorus, and when the smoke rolled away from before our eyes we could see that the foremost ranks were broken, that all had halted, and that dead and wounded were being picked up.

In very truth that prompt decision of Mademoiselle's saved the Prince's army. Turenne could not send on his troops in the face of the fire of the Bastille, and, for aught he knew, of the resistance of all his army through the Porte St. Antoine without the loss of one wounded man or a single gun. Mademoiselle, having seen the effect of her cannon, came down again to provide for wine and food being sent to the exhausted soldiers, who had been fighting all day in such scorching heat that we heard that at the first moment of respite, M. le Prince hurried into an orchard, took off every fragment of clothing, and rolled about on the grass under the trees to cool himself after the intolerable heat.

Just as I emerged from the court of the Bastille, some one touched me, and said, 'Pardon me, Madame,' and, looking round, I saw M. Darpent, with his hat in his hand. 'Madame,' he entreated, 'is it possible to you to come to poor M. d'Aubepine? I have fetched her to her husband, but there will be piteous work when his wound is visited, and she will need all the support that can be given to her. My mother and sister are doing all in their power, but they have many other patients on their hands.'

I hurried to my Princess, and with some difficulty obtained a hearing. She called up M. Darpent, and made him tell her the names of all the five sufferers that he and his sister had taken into the Verdon house, and how they were wounded, for Conde's followers being almost all noble, she knew who every one was. Two were only slightly wounded, but two were evidently dying, and as none of their friends were within reach, Madame Darpent and her daughter were forced to devote themselves to these, though fortunately they had not been brought in till her son had piloted M. d'Aubepine through the crowded streets — poor little Cecile! who had hardly ever set foot on the pavement before. Her Count was in a terrible state, his right leg having been torn off by a cannon-ball below the knee, and he would have bled to death long before reaching home had not Clement Darpent observed his condition and taken him into the house, where Madame had enough of the hereditary surgical skill acquired in the civil wars to check the bleeding, and put a temporary dressing on the wounds until a doctor could be obtained; for, alas! they were only too busy on that dreadful day.

Mademoiselle consented to part with me when she had heard all, suddenly observing, however, as she looked at Darpent: 'But, Monsieur, are you not the great Frondeur with ideas of your own? Did not this same d'Aubepine beat you soundly? Hein! How is it that you are taking him in —? Your enemy, is he not?'

'So please your Royal Highness, we know no enemies in wounded men,' replied Darpent, bowing.

Her attention was called off, and she said no more, as Clement and I hastened away as fast as we could through a by-street to avoid the march of the troops of Conde, who were choking the Rue St. Antoine, going, however, in good order. He told me on the way that M. d'Aubepine had shown great courage and calmness after the first shock, and after a few questions had hung on his arm through the streets, not uttering a word, though he felt her trembling all over, and she had instantly assumed the whole care of her husband with all the instinct of affection. But as he and his mother felt certain that amputation would be necessary, he had come to fetch me to take care of her.

Fortunately for us, we had not to cross the Rue St. Antoine to enter the Maison Verdon, but Clement opened a small door into the court with a private key, presently knocking at a door and leading me in. Armand d'Aubepine had been the first patient admitted, so his was the chief guest-chamber — a vast room, at the other end of which was a great bed, beside which stood my poor Cecile, seeing nothing but her husband, looking up for a moment between hope and terror in case it should be the surgeon, but scarcely taking in that it was I till I put my arms round her and kissed her; and then she put her finger to her lips, cherishing a hope that because the poor sufferer had closed his eyes and lay still in exhaustion, he might sleep. There he lay, all tinge of colour gone from his countenance, and his damp, dark hair lying about his face, and with my arm round her waist stood watching till he opened his eyes with a start and moan of pain, and cried, as his eye fell on me: 'Madame! Ah! Is Bellaise safe?' Then, recollecting himself: 'Ah no! I forgot! But is he safe — the Prince?'

I told him that the Prince and his army were saved, feeling infinitely touched that his first word should have been of my Philippe, whom he seemed to have forgotten; but indeed it was not so. His next cry was: 'Oh! Madame, Madame, would that this were Freiburg! Would that I could die as Philippe die! Oh! help me!'

Cecile threw herself forward, exclaiming, in broken words, that he must not say so; he would not die.

'You, too,' he said, 'you, too—the best wife in the world—whom I have misused—Ah! that I could begin all over again!'

'You will—you will, my most dear!' she cried. 'Oh! the wound will cure.'

And, strange mixture that he was, he moaned that he should only be a poor maimed wretch.

Darpent now brought in a priest, fresh from giving the last Sacraments to the two mortally-wounded men. The wife looked at him in terror, but both he and Clement gently assured her that he was not come for that purpose to M. la Comte, but to set his mind at rest by giving him absolution before the dressing of the wound. Of course it was a precaution lest he should sink under the operation; and as we led her from the bedside, Clement bade me not let her return as yet.

But that little fragile creature was more entirely the soul of Love than any other being I have known. She did, indeed, when we had her in Madame Verdon's little oratory hard by, kneel before the crucifix and pray with me, but her ear caught, before mine, the departing steps of the priest, and the entering ones of the surgeon. She rose up, simply did not listen to my persuasions, but walked in with quiet dignity. Madame Darpent was there, and would have entreated her to retire, but she said: 'This is a wife's place.' And as she took his hands she met a look in his eyes which I verily believe more than compensated to her for all the years of weary pining in neglect. The doctor would have ordered her off, but she only said: 'I shall not cry, I shall no faint.' And they let her keep his hand, though Clement had to hold him. I waited, setting our hostess free to attend to one of her dying charges, from whom she could ill be spared.

And Cecile kept her word, though it was a terrible time, for there was no endurance in poor Armand's shallow nature, and his cries and struggles were piteous. He could dare, but not suffer, and had not both she and Clement been resolute and tranquil, the doctor owned that he could not have succeeded.

'But Madame la Comtesse is a true heroin,' he said, when our patient was laid down finally, tranquil and exhausted, to be watched over through the night.

The time that followed was altogether the happiest of all my poor sister-in-law's married life. Her husband could hardly bear to lose sight of her for a moment, or to take anything from any hand save hers. If Madame Darpent had not absolutely taken the command of both she would never have had any rest, for she never seemed sensible of fatigue; indeed, to sit with his hand in hers really refreshed her more than sleep. When she looked forward to his recovery, her only regret was at her own wickedness in the joy that WOULD spring up when she thought of her poor cripple being wholly dependent on her, and never wanting to leave her again. I had been obliged to leave her after the first night, but I spent much of every day in trying to help her, and she was always in a tearful state of blissful hope, as she would whisper to me his promises for the future and his affectionate words — the fretful ones, of which she had her full share, were all forgotten, except by Clement Darpent, who shrugged his shoulders at them, and thought when he had a wife —

Poor Armand, would he have been able, even as a maimed man, to keep his word? We never knew, for, after seeming for a fortnight to be on the way to recovery, he took a turn for the worse, and after a few days of suffering, which he bore much better than the first, there came that cessation of pain which the doctors declared to mean that death was beginning its work. He was much changed by these weeks of illness. He seemed to have passed out of that foolish worldly dream that had enchanted him all his poor young life; he was scarcely twenty-seven, and to have ceased from that idol-worship of the Prince which had led him to sacrifice on that shrine the wife whom he had only just learned to love and prize. 'Ah! sister,' he said to me, 'I see now what Philippe would have made me.'

He asked my pardon most touchingly for his share in trying to abduct me, and Clement Darpent's also for the attack on him, though, as he said, Darpent had long before shown his forgiveness. His little children were brought to him, making large eyes with fright at his deathlike looks, and clinging to their mother, too much terrified to cry when he kissed them, blessed them, and bade Maurice consider his mother, and obey her above all things, and to regard me as next to her.

'Ah! if I had had such a loving mother I should never have become so brutally selfish,' he said; and, indeed, the sight of her sweet, tender, patient face seemed to make him grieve for all the sins of his dissipated life. His confessor declared that he was in the most pious disposition of penitence. And thus, one summer evening, with his wife, Madame Darpent, and myself watching and praying round him, Armand d'Aubepine passed away from the temptations that beset a French noble.

I took my poor Cecile home sinking into a severe illness, which I thought for many days would be her death. All her old terror of Madame Croquelebois returned, and for many nights and days Madame Darpent or I had to be constantly with her, though we had outside troubles enough of our own. Those two sick-rooms seem to swallow up my recollection.

CHAPTER XXXII. — ESCAPE

(Annora's Narrative)

There was indeed a good deal passing beyond those rooms where Margaret was so absorbed in her d'Aubepines that I sometimes thought she forgot her own kindred in them. Poor things! they were in sad case, though how Cecile could break her heart over a fellow who had used her so vilely, I could never understand. He repented, they said. So much the better for him; but a pretty life he would have led her if he had recovered. Why, what is there for a French noble to do but to fight, dance attendance on the King, and be dissipated? There is no House of Lords, no Quarter-Sessions, no way of being useful; and if he tried to improve his peasantry he is a dangerous man, and they send him a lettre de cachet. He has leave to do nothing but oppress the poor wretches, and that he is fairly obliged to do, so heavy are his expenses at Court. The King may pension him, but the pension is all wrung out of the poor in another shape! Heaven knows our English nobles are far from what they might be, but they have not the stumbling-blocks in their way that the French have under their old King, who was a little lad then, and might have been led to better things if his mother had had less pride and more good sense.

Gaspard de Nidemerle does the best he can. He is a really good man, I do believe, but he has been chiefly with the army, or on his own estate. And he can effect little good, hampered as he is on all sides.

In those days, Clement Darpent was sad enough at heart, but he did not quite despair of his country, though things were getting worse and worse. Mademoiselle had saved the Prince and his crew, besotted as she was upon them; and finely they requited Paris, which had sheltered them. All the more decent folk among them were lying wounded in different houses, and scarcely any of their chiefs were left afoot but the Duke of Beaufort, with his handsome face and his fine curls of flaxen hair, looking like a king, but good for nothing but to be a king of ruffians.

What does the Prince do but go to the Hotel de Ville with the Duke of Orleans and Beaufort, at six o'clock in the evening of the 4th of July, under pretence of thanking the magistrates and deputies of letting him in. Then he demanded of them to proclaim that the King was a prisoner in Mazarin's hands, and to throw themselves into the war. They would do no such thing, nor let themselves be intimidated, whereupon the Prince went out on the steps, and shouted to his rabble rout, where there were plenty of soldiers in disguise, who had been drinking ever since noon: 'These gentlemen will do nothing for us,' he cried. 'Do what you like with them.'

And then, like a coward, he got into a carriage with Monsieur and drove off, while M. de Beaufort, in a mercer's shop, acted general to the mob, who filled the whole place. It was a regular storm. Flags with 'Arret d'Union' were displayed, shots fired, the soldiers got into the houses and aimed in at the windows, logs of wood smeared with fat were set fire to before the doors so as to burn them down.

Clement, who was a depute for his arrondissement, had, while this was going on, been getting together the younger and stronger men with the guard, to make a barricade of benches, tables, and chairs; and they defended this for a long time, but ammunition failed them, and the barricade began to give way amid the shouts of the mob. The poor old men crouching in the halls were confessing to the cures, expecting death every moment; but, happily, even that long July evening had an end; darkness came down on them, and there were no lights. The mob went tumbling about, at a greater loss than the deputies and magistrates, who did at least know the way. Clement, with a poor old gouty echevin on his arm, struggled out, he knew not how, into one of the passages, where a fellow rushed at them, crying, 'Down with the Mazarins!' but Clement knew by his voice that he was no soldier or bandit, but a foolish artisan, and at haphazard said: 'Come, come, my good lad, none of this nonsense. This gentleman will give you a crown if you will help him out.'

The man obeyed directly, muttering that he only did as others did; and when they had got out into the street, Clement, finding himself not far from the place where the lights and voices showed him that some one was in command, managed to get to the mercer's shop with the poor old echevin, where he found M. de Beaufort, with his hair shining in the lamplight, his yellow scarf, and his long white feather, hanging over the features that were meant to be like an angel's. When Clement, in aftertimes, read the Puritan poet Milton's PARADISE LOST, he said he was sure that some of the faces of the fallen spirits in Pandemonium had that look of ruined beauty that he saw in the King of the Markets on that night.

Some of the town councilors who had got out sooner had gone to entreat the Duke of Orleans to stop the massacre, but he would Do nothing but whistle, and refer them to his nephew De Beaufort. They were standing there, poor men, and he tapping his lip with his cane, stroking down his moustache, and listening to them with a sneer as they entreated him not to let their fellows perish. And then among them stood up Clement, with his old echevin by his side. He was resolved, he said, and began 'Son of Henri IV., will you see the people perish whom he loved from the bottom of his heart? Yes, Monsieur, you inherit the charm by which he drew hearts after him, and was a true king of men! Will you misuse that attraction to make them fly at one another's throats? In the name of the great Henri and his love for his people, I appeal to you to call off yonder assassins.'

He had so far prevailed that Beaufort muttered something about not knowing things had gone so far, and assured the magistrates round him of his protection. He even went to the door and told some of his prime tools of agitation that it was enough, and that they might give the signal of recall; but whether things had gone too far, or whether he was not sincere, the tumult did not quiet down till midnight. After all, the rogues had the worst of it, for two hundred bodies of theirs were picked up, and only three magistrates and twenty-five deputies, though a good many more were hurt.

Clement saw his old echevin safe home, left word at our house that he was unhurt, but did not come in; and at Maison Verdon, no one had even guessed what danger he was in, for all the attention of the household was spent on the wounded men, one of whom died that night.

Things got worse and worse. Eustace was very anxious to leave Paris before the summer was over, lest bad weather should make him unable to travel. The year he had put between himself and Millicent had more than run out; and besides, as he said to me, he would not expose himself again to undergo what he had endured in his former illness, since he could have no confidence that my mother, and even Margaret, might not be driven to a persecution, which, if his senses should fail him, might apparently succeed. 'Nor,' said he, 'can I leave you unprotected here, my sister.'

We lingered, partly from the difficulty of getting horses, and the terrible insecurity of the roads, partly from the desire to get Clement to attend to Cardinal de Retz's warning and escape with us. There was no difficulty on his mother's account. She was longing to enter Port Royal, and only delayed to keep house for him, with many doubts whether she were not worldly in so doing; but he still felt his voice and presence here in the Hotel de Ville a protest, and he could not give up the hope of being of use to his country.

Meantime, M. de Nemours recovered from his wound only to be killed in a duel by M. de Beaufort, his brother-in-law; the Prince of Conde's rage at his defeat threw him into a malignant fever; the Duke of Orleans was in despair at the death of his only son, a babe of five years old; the Fronde was falling to pieces, and in the breathing time, Eustace obtained a pass from our own King, and wrote to Solivet, who was with the royal army outside, to get him another for himself and me—explaining that he was bound by his promise to Madame van Hunker, and that his health was in such a state that my care was needful to him.

Solivet answered the letter, sending the passport, but urging on him to remain at Paris, which would soon be at peace, since Mazarin was leaving the Court, and a general amnesty was to be proclaimed if the gates of Paris were opened to the King without the Cardinal.

But there were to be exceptions to this amnesty, and Solivet wrote at the same time to my mother. I have not the letter, and cannot copy it, but what he said was to urge her not to permit my brother to drag me away to Holland, for when he was gone all might still be arranged as she wished. As to 'ce coquina de Darpent,' as Solivet kindly called him, he had made himself a marked man, whom it was dangerous to leave at large, and his name was down for Vincennes or the Bastille, if nothing worse, so that there need be no more trouble about him. So said my half-brother, and he had no doubt made himself certain of the fact, in which he somewhat prematurely exulted.

My poor dear mother! I may seem to have spoken unkindly and undutifully about her in the course of these recollections. She was too French, and I too English, ever to understand one another, but in these last days that we were together she compensated for all that was past. She could not see a good and brave young life consigned to perpetual imprisonment only for being more upright than his neighbours; she did remember the gratitude she owed even to a creature comme ca, and I even believe she could not coolly see her daughter's heart broken. She had not even Margaret to prompt or persuade her, but she showed the letter at once to Eustace, and bade him warn his friend. Oh, mother, I am thankful that you made me love you at last!

Eustace drove first to the office, and got his passes countersigned by the magistracy for himself and me and our servant, showing a laquais whose height and complexion fairly agreed with those of Clement Darpent. There was no time to be lost. In the dusk of an August evening my brother was carried to the corner of the Rue St. Antoine in my mother's sedan. He could not walk so far, and he did not wish to attract observation, and he reached the house on foot, cloaked, and with his hat slouched. He found that Clement had received a note, as he believed from the Coadjutor, who always knew everything, giving the like warning that he would be excluded from the amnesty. His hopes of serving his country were over, and he felt it so bitterly, and so grieved for it, that he scarcely thought at first of his personal safety. It was well we had thought for him.

Eustace had brought a suit of our livery under his cloak, and he and poor Madame cut Clement's hair as short as if he had been a Roundhead. She had kept plenty of money in the house ever since she had feared for her son, and this they put in a belt round his waist. Altogether, he came out not at all unlike the laquais Jacques Pierrot, whom he was to personate. Eustace said the old lady took leave of her son with her stern Jansenist composure, which my tender-hearted Clement could not imitate. Eustace rejoined the chairmen and came back through the dark streets, while Clement walked at some distance, and contrived to slip in after him. My mother had in the meantime gone to the Hotel d'Aubepine and fetched poor Meg.

Cecile had just taken the turn, as they say, and it was thought she would live, but Meg could scarcely be spared from her, and seemed at first hardly to understand that our long-talked-of departure was suddenly coming to pass. It was well that she had so much to occupy her, for there was no one save her son, whom she loved like that brother of ours, and she would not, or could not, realise that she was seeing him for the last time.

It was a hot August night, and we worked and packed all through it, making Eustace lie down and rest, though sleep was impossible, and he said he wanted to see Meg and his mother as long as he could. As to Clement, we were afraid of the servants noticing him, so Eustace had locked him up in his own room, but he slept as little as any of us, and when his breakfast was brought him, he had never touched his supper. Certainly mine was the saddest bridegroom who ever stole away to be married; but I could forgive him. Did I not know what it was to be an exile, with one's heart torn for one's country's disgrace?

The difficulty was to get rid of the real Jacques Pierrot, but he gave us a little assistance in that way by coming crying to M. le Baron, to ask permission to take leave of his mother in the Faubourg St. Denis. This was readily granted to him, with strong insistence that he should be back by eleven o'clock, whereas we intended to start as soon as the gates were opened, namely, at six. Eustace had some time before purchased four mules and a carriage. He was not fit to ride in bad weather, and for me to have made a journey on horseback would have attracted too much attention, but the times were too uncertain for us to trust to posting, and mules, though slower than horses, would go on longer without resting, and were less likely to be seized by any army. I would take no maid-servant, as she would only have added to our dangers.

We ate our hearts till seven, when we succeeded in getting the mules to the door, and haste softened the parting for the moment. Indeed, Eustace and Meg had said much to each other in the course of the night. We had both knelt to ask my mother's forgiveness for having so often crossed her, and she finally wept and fainted, so that Meg was wholly occupied in attending to her.

Clement stood by the carriage, looking his part so well that my first impression was 'that stupid Jacques has come back after all.' Our anxiety now was to be entirely out of reach before the fellow came back, and hard was it to brook the long delay at the Porte St. Denis ere the officials deigned to look at us and our passes. However, my brother had gone through too many gates no to know that silver and an air of indifference will smooth the way, so we came through at last without our valet having been especially scanned.

Beyond the gates the sight was sad enough, the houses in the suburbs with broken windows and doors as though pillaged, the gardens devastated, the trees cut down, and the fields, which ought to have been ripening to harvest, trampled or mown for forage, all looking as if a hostile invader had been there, and yet it was the sons of the country that had done this, while swarms of starving people pursued us begging. Alas! had we not seen such a sight at home? We knew what it must be to Clement, but as he sat by the driver we durst not say a word of comfort to him.

At our intended resting-place for the night—I forget the name of it—we found every house full of soldiers of the royal army, and but for our passes I do not know what we should have done. Before every door there were dragoons drinking and singing round the tables, and some were dancing with the girls of the village. Some of them shouted at us when they saw we were coming from Paris, and called us runaway rebels; but Eustace showed his pass, told them what it was, for they could not read, and desired their officer to be fetched. He came out of the priest's house, and was very civil. He said Colonel de Solivet had desired that all assistance should be given to us, but that we had not been expected so soon. He really did not know where to quarter the lady or the mules, and he advised us to go on another league, while he dispatched an orderly with the intelligence to the colonel. There was nothing else to be done, though my brother, after his sleepless night, was becoming much exhausted, in spite of the wine we gave him, while as to the mules, they had an opinion of their own, poor things, as to going on again, and after all sorts of fiendish noises from the coachman, and furious lashings with his whip, the dragoons pricked them with their swords, and at last they rushed on at a gallop that I thought would have shaken Eustace to death.

However, before we had gone very far Solivet rode out to meet us. It was another cause of anxiety, although it was dusk, and he had expected us to have slept at St. Denis and to have arrived the next day, and he asked, what could have made us start so early, just as if we had been criminals fleeing from justice; but he took us to the chateau where he was quartered, and, though they were much crowded there, the family tried to make us comfortable. The master of the house gave up his own bed to my brother, and I shared that of his mother. 'Jacques' in his character of valet, was to attend on his master, and sleep on the floor; and this gave the only opportunity of exchanging any conversation freely, but even this had to be done with the utmost caution, for the suite of rooms opened into each other, and Solivet, who was very anxious about Eustace, came in and out to see after him, little guessing how much this added to the inward fever of anxiety which banished all sleep from his eyes.

The kind people thought him looking so ill the next morning that they wanted to bleed him, and keep us there for a few days, but this was not to be thought of, as indeed Eustace declared, when I felt some alarm, that he could not be better till he was out of French territory.

So we pushed on, and Solivet rode beside the window all day, making our course far safer and easier in one way, but greatly adding in others to the distressful vigilance that coloured Eustace's thin cheeks and gleamed in his eyes, and made his fingers twitch at his sword whenever there was an unexpected halt, or any one overtook us. He conveyed us quite beyond the army, and brought us as far as Beuvais, where he made himself our host at the Lion Rouge, and gave us an excellent supper, which I could hardly swallow when I thought of his barbarous intentions towards Clement, who had to wait on us all the time, standing behind my chair and handing dishes.

I believe Solivet really meant to be a good brother; but his words were hard to endure, when he lectured us each apart, with all the authority of a senior—told me that Eustace was dying, and that every mile he traveled was hastening his end, laughing to scorn that one hope which buoyed me up, the Dirkius could do more for him than any one else, and almost commanding me to take him home again to Paris while it was possible.

And he equally harassed Eustace the next morning with representations of the folly of taking me away to Holland, and breaking off the advantageous Poligny match, to gratify my headstrong opposition and desire for a mesalliance, which would now happily be impossible, the fellow having ruined himself.

The fellow entered at that moment with M. le Baron's coat and boots, and Eustace could hardly repress a smile. We could not but rejoice when Solivet took leave of us at the carriage door, very affectionate, but shrugging his shoulders at our madness, and leaving a corporal and his party to guard us to the frontier. They prolonged the sense of constraint, and forced us to be very guarded with poor Clement, but otherwise they were very useful. The inhabitants fancied us by turns great princes or great criminals, or both, being escorted out of the country. Once we were taken for the Queen escaping with the Cardinal, another time for the Prince of Conde eloping with Mademoiselle; but any way of soldiers secured for us plenty of civility, and the best food and lodgings to be had. They pricked on our mules with a good-will, and when one of them fell lame they scoured the neighbourhood to find another, for which Eustace endeavoured to pay the just price, but I am afraid it went into the corporal's pocket, and Clement never so nearly betrayed himself as when he refused to share with the escort the reckoning of which they stripped the landlord. Integrity in a Parisian valet was all too suspicious! However, to us they behaved very well; and, if all we heard were true, their presence may have saved us from being robbed, if not murdered, long before we reached the frontier.

CHAPTER XXXIII. — BRIDAL PEARLS

When once over the border, and our passports duly examined, we breathed freely, and at our first resting-place Clement took out a suit of my brother's clothes and appeared once more as a gentleman, except for his short hair. He was able, whenever French would serve, to take the management of our journey.

We finished it as before in a canal boat, and the rest of mind and body, and the sense of approaching Millicent, certainly did Eustace good; the hectic fever lessened, and though he slept little at night, he had much good slumber by day, lying on cloaks on deck as we quietly glided along the water, between the fields full of corn, with harvest beginning, and the tall cocks of hay in the large fields, all plenty and high cultivation, and peaceful industry, in contrast with the places we had left devastated by civil war, and the famished population.

The comparison made Clement groan; and yet that canal journey had a pensive joy about it, as we sat beside our sleeping brother and conversed freely and fearlessly, as we had never been able to do for ten minutes together in all the long years that we had loved one another. There was something very sweet in the knowing that, exile as he was, he and I must be all the world to one another. And so indeed it has been. After our stormy beginning, our life has been well-nigh like our voyage on that smooth Dutch stream.

However, the sorrows were not yet over, although at that time we trusted that there would be healing for my dear brother in the very air of the Hague. We landed on a fine August evening, and were at once recognized by some of the English gentlemen who had little to do but to loiter about the quays and see the barges come in. It rejoiced my heart to hear my brother called Lord Walwyn again, instead of by his French title. Yet therewith, it was a shock to see how changed they thought him since he had left them a year before; but they vied with one another in helping us, and we were soon housed in good lodgings. I knew what Eustace most wished to learn, and asked, with as good an air of indifference as I could assume, whether Vrow van Hunker were in the town. 'Vrow van Hunker, the Providence of the Cavaliers?' asked one. 'No; she is at her country-house, where she hath taken in there or four poor starving ladies and parsons with their families.'

When I heard how she was using old Van Hunker's wealth — in providing for our poor loyal folk, and especially for the clergy, pensioning some, hospitably receiving others in her own house, and seeking employment for others — I had to repent of all the scorn with which I had looked on Millicent Wardour as a poor fickle creature, and now I had to own that my brother's love had been as nearly worthy of him as any creature could be.

Eustace would not, however, go to visit her until he had seen Dr. Dirkius, to whom he repaired early the next day, having caused a hackney coach to be ordered against his return, and bestowed Clement on an English friend who could speak French well. For Eustace held that it would be more fitting, in the sight of the world, for me to go with him to visit Madame van Hunker.

The carriage was at the door when he came back from the physician's. There never was anything to find fault with in his looks, and on this day, with his light brown hair and beard freshly-trimmed and shinning, his clear skin with the red colour in his cheek, and his bright eyes, in their hollow caves, there was something so transparent and sublimated in his aspect, that I thought that he looked more like a spirit than a bridegroom. He was gave and silent by the way, and there was something about him that withheld me from asking what Dirkius had said to him.

Thus we reached the entrance of the great double avenue, along which, as we presently saw, two English clergymen were walking together in conversation, and we saw a little farther on some children at play.

'This is well,' said Eustace, as he looked out. 'I thank God for this! It will be all the better for her that such a good work is begun.'

'Nay,' said I, 'but what will the poor things do when she loses old Hunkers's gold?'

'Sister,' said Eustace, 'I have left this too long, but I thought you understood that I am never like to wed my poor Millicent.'

'Dirkius?' I said.

'Dirkius does but confirm what I have known ever since the spring, and so have you too, Nan, that it would be a miracle should I be here after this winter.'

I had known it by my inner conviction, and heard him say the like often before; it was only a fancied outward hope that had been sustaining me, and I could obey when he bade me look cheerfully on Millicent, and remember the joy it was to him to see her at all, and, above all, employed in such tasks as would bring comfort to her.

The great Dutch house seemed full of English. Gentlewomen were sitting in the tapestried hall, spinning or working with their needle. We had been known to one or two of them in former times, and while they greeted us word was taken to Madame van Hunker that we were there, and a servant brought us word to ask us to come to her in her own parlour. There, up a few shallow steps, in a quiet, cool, wainscoted room, adorned with Eastern porcelain on shelves, we found her with her little daughter at her knee.

She met us at the door with a few faltering words, excusing herself for having given us the trouble to come to her.

'Best so, Millicent,' said Eustace, and as he spoke she lifted her eyes to his face and I saw a look of consternation pass over her features at sight of his wasted looks; but I only saw it for a moment, for he put an arm round her, and kissed her brow, as she hid her face against him.

The child, not contented with my embrace, ran and pulled his coat, crying, 'My lord, my lord, I can speak English now;' and he stooped to kiss her, while her mother turned to me with swimming eyes of mute inquiry, as of one who saw her long-cherished hope fulfilled only for her sorrow. She was less altered than had been feared. That smooth delicacy of her skin was indeed lost which had made her a distinguished beauty; but she still had a pair of eyes that made her far from insignificant, and there was an innocence, candour, and pleading sweetness in her countenance that—together, perhaps, with my pity—made even me, who had hitherto never liked her, lover her heartily.

I heard little or nothing of what they said to one another, being employed in keeping the child from them. She prattled freely in English, and was pleased to show me her baby-house, a marvel of Dutch neatness of handiwork, like that one which Madame van Hunker brought you, my daughter Peggy, when you were a little one. The doll we had given her had, however, the place of honour. Her sister, little Emilia told me, was married a month ago, and she was proceeding to make the little Dutch puppets in her baby-house enact the wedding, one being dressed in a black gown and stiff ruff, like a Genevan minister, when she caught a tone that made her cry out that mother was weeping, and stump across the floor in her stout little shoes to comfort her, before I could hinder her.

My brother and her mother set her down between them, and I had nought to do but to put in order the baby-house, till a great bell clanged through the house, which was the signal for dinner. Madame van Hunker was calmer by that time, and let Eustace hand her down, and place her at the head of the table, where she had around her no less than four families and two widows of our poor exiled Cavaliers and clergy. We had not found ourselves in so English a world for years past.

The hostess sat as one in a dream, doing her part like one moved by wires, and eating scarce anything, while Eustace showed all his usual courtliness of manner and grace. After dinner, he rested on a couch, as was his wont, before going back, and Millicent drew me into her chamber and wept on my neck, as she made me tell her all she had not been able to learn from him.

He had been very tender with her, and tried to persuade her that it was all for the best, and that there was happiness for them in the having no one between them now. She, poor woman, would fain, as I saw, have thrown aside all her houses and wealth to be his, and to tend him, were it merely for a few weeks, and she felt as if her love was strong enough to be his cure; but he had spoken of the cruel selfishness of giving away her power of aiding all these our fellow-countrymen in order that they two might come together for what he knew would be so brief a time. Yet he had not taken all hope from her, for he had talked of their reconsidering the matter if he were in better health after the winter, and, meantime, they could see each other often.

Poor thing! I believe she expected the miracle that might make him yet recover, and so she bore up, while Eustace was verily happy—having lived, as it were, nearly into spiritual love, and left behind that which had been earthly and corporeal, and thus he was content to rest. He had strained himself very hard to accomplish the journey, bring Clement and me into safety, and see Millicent again, and when the effort ceased, we fully saw, for the first time, how great it had been, and how far he was gone on that other journey. I do not think he crossed the threshold of our lodging half a dozen times after our arrival; but Millicent came into her town-house, and was with him every day. She had fitted the great dining chamber of that town-house as a chapel for our English service, and my brother went thither on two Sundays, on the second of which he saw M. Darpent received into our English Protestant Church. Clement had long inclined that way, having never forgotten the Huguenot training of his childhood, and the studies he had made, when his mother impelled him towards Port Royal, having resulted in farther doubts and yearning towards what Eustace had told him of our doctrine. Conversation with the learned Dr. Elson, one of our exiled divines, had completed the work, though he made his profession with pain and grief, feeling it a full severance from his country and his mother.

And the last time my dear brother left the house was to give me to his friend. He was anxious that I should be Clement's wife before he left me, and there was no fear that we should starve, for, through trustworthy merchants, a small amount of the Darpent money had been transmitted to him before the State laid hands on his property as that of a fugitive. He might have bought himself a share in one of the great trading houses, or have—which tempted him most—gone out to the plantations in the new countries of Java or America; but Eustace prayed him to pledge himself to nothing until he should hear from Harry Merrycourt, to whom my brother had sent a letter before quitting Paris.

We would have had a quiet wedding, but Eustace was resolved, as he said, that all the world should know that it was not done in a corner, and Madame van Hunker WOULD give the wedding feast, and came to dress me for my bridal. You know the dress: the white brocade with hyacinth flowers interwoven in the tissue—and when she had curled my hair after her fancy, she kissed me and clasped round my neck the pearls of Ribaumont. I told her I would wear them then to please her and Eustace, and, in truth, I knew in my heart that I was the last true Ribaumont bride that ever would wear them. We were wedded in the chapel in Madame van Hunker's house; and the Princess-Royal was there, and the Duke of York, and my Lord and Lady of Newcastle, and I know not who besides—only remembering that they all knew how to treat Clement as a man of distinction, who had, like them, given up all for conscience sake, and he, in his plain lawyer's suit, with his fine, clear-cut face and grave eyes, looked, even in spite of his close-cropped head, as veritable a gentleman as any of them. The festivities ended the dinner, that being as much as my brother was able for. We went quietly back to our lodgings in Millicent's coach, and Eustace went to rest on his bed, till she should have bidden farewell to her guests and could come and sup with us; but he and Clement forbade me to take off my finery, for it tickled their eyes.

And thus, when tidings came to the door that a gentlemen from England desired to see my Lord Walwyn, Harry Merrycourt, after all these years of seeing nothing but sad-coloured Puritan dames, came in upon this magnificent being in silvered brocade.

He said he thought he had stumbled on the Princess-Royal at least, and it was a descent to hear it was only plain Mistress Darpent! Harry had a good wife of his own by that time, who suited him far better than I should have done. Indeed, I believe he had only thought of wedding me to relieve my family from me. And when he saw how unlike M. Darpent was to all he had ever thought or believed of Frenchmen, and heard how well he spoke English, and how he had borne himself at Paris, he quite forgave me, and only thought how he could serve Eustace, the man whom he had always loved beyond all others.

He was practicing law in London still, but he had had time to repent of having been on the wrong side when he saw what it had come to, and had the Protector at the head of affairs. He said, however, that negotiations for peace with France were like to begin, and that Mr. Secretary Milton was casting about for one learned in French law to assist in drawing the papers, so that he had little doubt that Mr. Darpent would be readily taken into one of the public officers in London.

Moreover, he said that the Walwyn property had been sequestered, but no one had yet purchased it, and he thought that for a fair sum, it might be redeemed for the family.

When Eustace and Millicent found that I would not hear of keeping the pearls, declaring that such things were not fit for a poor exiled lawyer's wife, Millicent said they had always felt like hot lead on her neck. To compound the matter, Eustace persuaded her to have the chaplet valued by a Dutch jeweller, and to ask Margaret and Solivet, the guardians of the young Marquis de Nidemerle, to purchase them for him.

To Margaret was left whatever of the property M. Poligny would spare, and if Gaspard should have sons, one would bear the title of Ribaumont, though the name would be extinct. So it was fitting that the pearls should return to that family, and the fair value, as we hoped, sufficed, in Harry Merrycourt's hands, to redeem, in my husband's name, the inheritance my brother had always destined for me.

This was the last worldly care that occupied our believed brother. He said his work was done, and he was very peaceful and at rest. His strength failed very fast after Harry Merrycourt came. Indeed, I think he had for months lived almost more by force of strong will than anything else, and now he said he had come to his rest. He passed away one month after my wedding, on the 16th of October 1652, very peacefully, and the last look he gave any one here was for Millicent. There was a last eager, brighter look, but that was for nothing here.

The physicians said he died of the old wound in the lungs received at Naseby, so that he gave his life as much for the cause as my father and Berenger had done, though he had had far, far more to suffer in his nine years of banishment.

We left him in a green churchyard by the waterside, and Millicent saying through her tears that he had taught her to find comfort in her married life, and that he had calmed her and left her peace and blessing now in the work before her. And then we sailed with sore hearts for England, which was England still to me, though sadly changed from what I had once known it. We had come to think that there was no hope of the right cause ever prevailing, and that all that could be done was to save our own conscience, and do our best to serve God and man. 'The foundations are cast down, and what hath the righteous done?'

We were met by Harry Merrycourt, who had obtained the employment for Clement that he had hoped for. It was well, for, when Walwyn was repurchased, all our money had been sunk in it, and enough borrowed to consume the rents for some years to come, and thus we had to live very frugally in a little house in Westminster; but as for that, I was far happier marketing in the morning with my basket on my arm, cooking my husband's supper, making his shirts, and by and by nursing my babe, than ever I had been in all the stiff state and splendour of poor Margaret's fine salons. Camlet suits me better than brocade, and a basket of fresh eggs better than a gold-enamelled snuff-box. While, though I did long to see the old home again, I knew it would be bare of those who had made it dear, and, besides, it would be as well that M. Darpent should rub off as much as might be of his French breeding before showing him among the Thistlewoods and Merrycourts, and all the rest of our country-folk. Moreover, after the stir of Paris he might have found himself dull, and he had the opportunity of studying English law; ay, and I saw him yearly winning more and more trust and confidence among those who had to do with him, and forming friendships with Mr. John Evelyn and other good men.

So, when better times came round, and we had our King and Court back, on the very day of my Harry's birth, M. Darpent was recommended to my Lord Clarendon as too useful a secretary to be parted with, and therewith the great folk remembered that I came of an old Cavalier family. Indeed Queen Henrietta had promised my mother and sister to seek me out, though may be she would never have recollected it. After all it was the Duke of Gloucester who actually came and found me, riding up to our door with only one gentleman, and he no other than good old Sir Francis Ommaney.

Prince Henry was a fine youth, far handsomer and more like his blessed father than his brothers, and with as bright a wit and as winning and gracious as the King. He reproached me for not having come to see his mother, and asked merrily if I had turned Roundhead as well Frondeuse. I told him I had a good excuse, and showed him my three children, the youngest not yet a month old, and the other two staring open-mouthed to see a Prince so like other gentlemen.

Whereupon he asked if the little one was yet christened, and did him the honour to offer to be his godfather; and he noted that little Eustace promised to be like his uncle, and spake, with tears in his eyes, of the blessing my brother had been to him in his earlier stay at Paris, and how the remembrance of that example had helped him through the days when he had to undergo the same persuasions to forsake his father's Church.

So whereas the two first christenings had been done privately, as among those under persecution, Master Harry was baptized in state and splendour in St. Margaret's Church in full and open day, with all the neighbours gaping to see the Duke come forth, leading Mistress Darpent by the hand.

Thus I had to turn out my fine gowns (grown all too tight for me) and betake me to the Queen, who had become a little old woman, but was as gay and kind as ever, and told me much about my mother and sister. The King himself came and spoke to me, and said he supposed I wished to have the old title revived; but I told him, with all thanks, that I liked my husband better by his own name than by that which I had rather leave sacred to my brother; whereat he laughed, and said he must make a low bow to me, as being the first person he had met who had nothing to ask from him.

That was all I saw of the Court. Before many weeks had passed the cruel smallpox had carried off the young Duke of Gloucester in his twentieth year, taking him, mayhap, from the evil to come, in his bright youth and innocence, for had he lived, and kept himself unsoiled even to these days, he might have been sorely tempted to break that last promise made when he sat on his father's knee.

Soon after Madame van Hunker came to England. There was Wardour property, which had descended to her, and she was glad to have a good cause for bringing her daughter Emilia to England. My children all knew and loved the fair and saint-like lady full of alms-deeds, and with the calm face that always was ready with comfort and soothing. The very sight of it would rest the fretful, hasty spirit; and I was thankful indeed that when Emilia married, her mother still abode near to us — I felt her like my guardian spirit.

My husband kept his post till my Lord Clarendon went out and the Cabal came in, and then, not liking those he had to work with, he gave up his office, and we retired into the country, while our children were still young enough to grow up in the love to Walwyn that I had always felt.

CHAPTER XXXIV. — ANNORA'S HOME

It seemed as if I had scarcely time to understand what was the meaning of my party with my beloved brother and sister. My poor Cecile was still so ill that I could hardly attend to anything else, and when I returned in the morning I found that, missing me, she had fallen into another crisis, and that all the danger was renewed.

However, the poor frail creature lived, little as she cared to do so, except to pray for the soul of the husband to whom her whole being had been given, ever since they had wedded her to him as a mere child. It was well that I had her to attend to, or my home would have seemed very desolate to me, empty as it now was of my brother and sister, and with my mother spending her time between her Queen and her favourite convent. Happily for me there was no longer required to be in waiting, but was free to finish his education. Indeed, I believe the Queen had found out that Gaspard had put into King Louis's head certain strange ideas about sovereigns and subjects, so that she was glad to keep him at a distance. Queen Henrietta bade me take care what I was doing. Thus Cardinal Mazarin being absent, and the events of former years not brought to mind, it was possible to obtain permission to retire for a time to our estates. Indeed I fancy it was meant to disgrace two such Frondeuses as we were supposed to have been.

Cecile recovered something like health in the country, but she would not hear of doing anything save entering a convent. She longed to be constantly praying for her husband, and she felt herself utterly incapable of coping with the world, or educating her son. She took her little girl with her to be a pensionnaire at the Visitation, and entrusted her boy to me, to be brought up with mine. They have indeed always been like brothers, and to me the tenderest and most dutiful of sons. Maurice d'Aubepine never ceased to love his own mother, but as a sort of saint in a shrine, and he used to say that when he went to see her he always felt more as if he had been worshipping than making a visit.

I had learned a little prudence by my former disasters among the peasantry at Nid de Merle, and we did contrive to make them somewhat happier and more prosperous without giving umbrage to our neighbours. They learned to love M. le Marquis with passionate devotion, and he has loved them in his turn with equal affection. I delight to hear the shouts of ecstasy with which they receive him when he is seen riding through the narrow lanes of the Bocage on a visit to his mother and his home.

The King has always treated him with distinguished politeness, but without seeming desirous to retain him about Court, so that, as you know, he has always had employment either in the army or in governments, gaining ample honour, but without enjoying personal favour or intercourse with the King, who, it may be, trusts his loyalty, without brooking his plain speaking.

I saw my sister once again. When she had at last settled in the old chateau, and after my son and nephew had made their first campaign at the siege of Lille, we had to join in the progress of the Court to Dunkirk and Lille to see the King's new fortifications. A strange progress it was to me, for Mademoiselle was by this time infatuated by her unfortunate passion for the Duke of Lauzun, and never ceased confiding to me her admiration and her despair whenever there was a shower of rain on his perruque. However, when the Duchess of Orleans crossed to England I obtained permission to go with my son to visit our relations, since it was then the object to draw together as close as possible the links between the countries.

It was a joyous visit, though it was a shock to me to see the grand old castle of the Walwyn replaced by a square Dutch-looking brick house of many windows, only recently built, and where I remembered noble woods and grand trees to see only copse-wood and fields. But who could regret anything when I saw my dear sister, a glad, proud, happy wife and mother, a still young, active, and merry matron, dazzlingly fair as ever, among her growing sons and pretty daughters, and indeed far more handsome than when she sat in the salons of Paris, weary and almost fierce, in her half-tamed, wild-cat days, whereas now her step was about the house and garden everywhere, as the notable housewife and good mother.

And her husband—Mr. Darpent, as every one called him, with true English pronunciation—it amused us to see how much of an Englishman he had become, though Harry Merrycourt told us the squires had began by calling him Frenchy, and sneering at his lack of taste and skill in their sports; but they came to him whenever they had a knotty point to disentangle in law or justice, they turned to him at Quarter-Sessions for help; and though they laughed at the plans of farming, gardening, and planting he had brought from Holland, or had learned from Mr. Evelyn of Says Court, still, when they saw that his trees grew, his crops prospered, and his sheep fetched a good price at market, some of them began to declare he was only too clever, and one or two of the more enlightened actually came privately to ask his advice.

It was pleasant to see him in his library, among books he had picked up, one by one, at stalls in London, where he read and wrote and taught his sons, never long without the door being opened by Nan to see whether his fire needed a fresh log, or whether his ink-stand were full, or to announce that the pigs were in the garden, and turn out all his pupils in pursuit! Interrupt as she would, she never seemed to come amiss to him.

He was glad to talk over all the affairs of our country with us. In his office in London he had of course been abreast with facts, but he was keenly interested in all the details of the Prince's return to favour, of the Cardinal's death, of the King's assumption of the entire management of State affairs, and of the manner in which the last hopes of the Parliament of Paris had been extinguished. France was—as he allowed to my eager son—beginning to advance rapidly on the road of glory, it might be of universal empire. He agreed to it, but, said he, with a curious perverse smile: 'For all that, M. le Marquis, I remain thankful that my wife's inheritance is on this side of the Channel, and though I myself may be but an exile and a fugitive, I rejoice that my sons and their children after them will not grow up where there is brilliancy and grandeur without, but beneath them corruption and a people's misery!'